MW01093807

The Christmas Token

Hardman Holidays Book 2
A Sweet Historical Western Romance

By
USA Today Bestselling Author
SHANNA HATFIELD

The Christmas Token
Copyright © 2013
by Shanna Hatfield

ISBN-13: 978-1493763221
ISBN-10: 1493763229

*To the humble, the kind,
the forgiving, and the grateful...*

Books by Shanna Hatfield

FICTION

CONTEMPORARY

Blown Into Romance
Love at the 20-Yard Line
Learnin' the Ropes
QR Code Killer
Rose
Saving Mistletoe
Taste of Tara

Rodeo Romance
The Christmas Cowboy
Wrestlin' Christmas
Capturing Christmas
Barreling Through Christmas
Chasing Christmas

Grass Valley Cowboys
The Cowboy's Christmas Plan
The Cowboy's Spring Romance
The Cowboy's Summer Love
The Cowboy's Autumn Fall
The Cowboy's New Heart
The Cowboy's Last Goodbye

Silverton Sweethearts
The Coffee Girl
The Christmas Crusade
Untangling Christmas

Women of Tenacity
A Prelude
Heart of Clay
Country Boy vs. City Girl
Not His Type

HISTORICAL

Hardman Holidays
The Christmas Bargain
The Christmas Token
The Christmas Calamity
The Christmas Vow
The Christmas Quandary
The Christmas Confection

Pendleton Petticoats
Dacey
Aundy
Caterina
Ilsa
Marnie
Lacy
Bertie
Millie
Dally

Baker City Brides
Tad's Treasure
Crumpets and Cowpies
Thimbles and Thistles
Corsets and Cuffs
Bobbins and Boots

Hearts of the War
Garden of Her Heart
Home of Her Heart

Chapter One

Eastern Oregon, 1895

With a lightly perfumed handkerchief held to her nose, Genevieve Eloise Granger shot a disdainful look at the filthy man sitting to her left, blocking both her view out the stage window and any hope she had of drawing a breath of fresh air.

"Deplorable, disgusting boor," she muttered, wondering if a shortage of water or sense had resulted in her seatmate's pungent condition.

A turn of her head to the right revealed a cowboy seated inappropriately close to her side, gazing at her with a lecherous grin.

She shrank back against the stiff seat, trying to make room between the two males intent on making her trip into the wilds of Oregon even more miserable.

After spending three days on a sooty, malodorous train, she disembarked in Heppner only to endure the last twenty miles of her journey crowded into a stagecoach with a bunch of ill-mannered men.

When she voiced her disapproval of the insufficient space inside the stage, the driver had the unmitigated gall to suggest she make do with the seating available, ride on top, or walk to Hardman.

As soon as she arrived at her brother's home in the pathetically backward little town, she planned to pen a letter to the stage company voicing her complaints to someone with the authority to make changes in their passenger accommodations.

Grateful the October day wasn't exceedingly warm, Genevieve, known to family and friends as Ginny, flapped the handkerchief, stirring the air in front of her face, praying they would soon reach their destination.

The cowboy sitting next to her rubbed his arm against her side and blew his breath across her neck. She glowered at him as she picked up her reticule and smacked him across the chest with it.

"Sir, I do not know what sort of lady you think I am, but I assure you I will not put up with your shenanigans!"

"No shenanigans, ma'am." The cowboy grinned broadly as he winked and placed his hand on her knee, squeezing it with an intimacy he had no right to pursue.

"You brute! I've given you ample warning," Ginny exclaimed, reaching up and pulling the pin from her hat before stabbing it into the hand of the cowboy.

Yelping in pain, he jerked his hand back and sucked on the spot of skin between his thumb and forefinger where she'd buried the pin.

"Please keep your extremities, looks, vile thoughts, and smile to yourself for the remainder of our expedition." Ginny poked the pin back in her hat and leveled the man with a cold glare as he slid over, giving her a few inches of space. "If you should fail to do so, I'll find a spot guaranteed to be more painful than your hand to jab my pin next time."

She looked up to see all eyes on her as she returned the handkerchief to her face, drawing a shallow breath. When the three men sitting across from her began laughing and slapping their legs, she fought back the urge to lecture them on their raucous behavior.

"I'm so wholly pleased to know I've provided you gentlemen, a term I use loosely you can be certain, with entertainment to take your minds off the fact we've been stuffed into this detestable conveyance like cattle in a train car." Her traveling companions were bright enough to recognize the hint of sarcasm in her voice. "Rest assured, however, any further abuse of propriety will not be taken lightly. Should any of you so much as even think of doing anything untoward, I promise it will not be to your benefit."

"Sure, honey. Whatever ya say," the smelly beast beside her stated, shifting his bulk closer to the window and further away from her remarkably sharp hatpin, and even sharper tongue. "I don't rightly know what all ya said, but we'll leave ya be. I ain't got a hankerin' to explain to the missus why some riled up woman run my hand through with her hatpin."

"Very well." Ginny nodded triumphantly to her traveling companions. The men sat quietly for the remainder of the trip.

As the stage rocked to a stop in Hardman, Ginny tugged her gloves down on her hands, stuffed her hanky into her reticule and prepared to be the first to exit.

Fearful of what she might do next, the men leaped out and grabbed their belongings, giving the driver a brief warning of the violent woman inside while moving hastily down the street.

Trying to disembark with a semblance of decorum proved more challenging than Ginny could manage with her limbs stiff from the long trip across the country and her cramped position on the stage.

Stepping on the ruffle of her skirt as she placed her dainty foot out the door, she tripped and fell in an undignified heap on her knees in the mud at the bottom of the stage step.

"Well, missy, if ya'd just held yer horses a minute, I would've given ya a hand," the driver said, trying to hide his laugh at the haughty woman's current disheveled state.

He looked down at her from where he stood on the top of the stage.

"Perhaps if you'd been able to move your rotund girth down here faster, the necessity of exiting the stage unassisted wouldn't have arisen," Ginny said, pulling herself from the mud to her feet and shaking her hands to dislodge the clumps clinging to her gloved fingers.

"Is that right?" the driver asked, grim-faced as he held one of her bags in his hands.

"That is correct." Annoyed at the bumpkin who sold too many seats on the stage, leaving her uncomfortable the entire trip, she also noted his obvious lack of concern that she be treated like a lady. "Only a buffoon would oversell the stage like that, drive at such a breakneck speed, and then offer such little regard for the wellbeing of his passengers."

Fisting her hands at her hips, she gave him a cool glare, waiting for his apology.

"In that case, I reckon my rotund girth, as ya put it, doesn't feel like carefully moving yer bags down there, so here ya go."

Ginny gasped as the driver threw the bag in his hands at her, hitting her in the chest and knocking her into the mud, square on her backside.

"Well! I never..." she huffed as he tossed the rest of her bags on the boardwalk behind her. Climbing down, he set her trunk next to her bags, shook his head and left her sitting with mud oozing through her skirt as he walked off in the direction of the saloon.

Struggling to gain her feet, she was near tears when a gloved hand reached down and pulled her upright.

Raising her gaze to that of her rescuer, she sucked in a gulp of air as she recognized the face of the boy who'd captured her heart ten years ago in the handsome man smiling at her.

Bearing little trace of her childhood playmate and youthful love, this man with the warm hazel eyes and charming smile looked strong, confident, and sure of himself.

"If it isn't Miss Granger." Blake Stratton smirked at the tiny blonde standing before him, dripping mud from the feather on her fashionable hat to the toes of her expensive shoes. "Just in off the stage, are we?"

"Oh, I, um... you see..." Ginny lost the ability to think upon seeing Blake. His slight British accent coupled with his inviting grin caused any manner of distressing thoughts to flit through her head, the most predominant being her desire for his kiss.

"Luke expects you?" Blake asked as he took the bag from her muddy hands and picked up two others, leaving the rest sitting on the boardwalk. Motioning to a redheaded boy down the street, the lad returned his wave then ran his direction.

"Percy, would you keep an eye on Miss Granger's things until Luke can retrieve them?" Blake asked, fishing in his pocket for a coin and handing it to the boy.

"Thanks, Mr. Stratton. You can count on me to keep an eye on her stuff. Is she Mr. Luke's sister?" the boy asked, looking at the stranger like some great novelty that fell off the stage.

"That she is, Percy." Blake patted the boy on the back then offered his arm to Ginny.

Starting to grasp his arm, Ginny pulled back at the last second, realizing she would soil his shirt with mud dripping from her head to her feet.

"Thank you, Mr. Stratton, but I do believe I best keep my hands to myself." Finally finding her tongue, she observed Blake's strong shoulders and muscular arms as he hefted her bags. He waited for her to precede him down the boardwalk toward the end of town where her brother and sister-in-law lived.

"So Luke and Filly knew you'd be on the stage today?" Blake tried not to laugh as the mud-drenched feather on Ginny's hat drooped pitifully near her eye. He wanted to yank the ridiculous bit of millinery from her head and see if her hair remained as wild and curly as it had been the last time he'd seen it ten years ago — the day she left town and took his heart right along with her.

"Not exactly," Ginny admitted as they walked past the bank her brother owned. She gazed in the window, but couldn't see through the bars covering the outside well enough to tell if he was inside or not.

"Then what, exactly, does that mean?" Blake asked, wondering why Ginny suddenly returned to Hardman. She hadn't set foot in the town since her parents moved back to New York a decade earlier. Dora and Greg Granger visited Luke with some regularity, but Ginny never accompanied them.

"It means I may have failed to follow the proper protocol required when one goes visiting socially. There wasn't sufficient time to inform them of my impending visit," Ginny said as they walked past the newspaper office. Despite the distraction Blake provided, she noticed the town didn't seem much different than it had the day she left.

"Do your parents know you're here?" Blake asked, beginning to think Ginny hadn't changed at all, or at least hadn't grown up since he'd last set eyes on her lovely face.

"At this particular time, they believe I'm visiting a friend in Boston for a few days. I shall certainly advise them of my current whereabouts once I have the opportunity to refresh my appearance and partake in a moment of rest." Ginny stopped and stared at the imposing Granger House, located on the edge of town at the end of the boardwalk.

Recalling how much she liked the house when her parents built it, she admired the colorful flowers blooming along the front porch and the tasteful arrangement of fall leaves and pinecones set in a large basket by the front door. Cattle grazed in the pasture behind the house and she could see Luke's beloved horses in the corral by the barn.

"The place looks well-kept," Ginny said, suddenly fearful of marching up the steps and introducing herself to the woman Luke married almost two years ago.

Gone on a tour of Europe when he wed, she managed to find some reason not to come with her parents when they visited the previous summer. She made plans to visit friends when Luke and Filly traveled to New York.

Curiosity about her sister-in-law was getting the best of her as she stood gazing up at her childhood home. Ginny wondered if the woman appeared as beautiful in person as she looked in the photograph her mother had on display in their front parlor.

"Luke and Filly have truly made it into a home," Blake said, nudging Ginny with one of her bags as she started down the front walk, forcing her to take a step into the grass.

Glaring at him over her shoulder, she huffed in irritation. "What are you doing?"

"I'm attempting to direct you to the kitchen door so you don't track that muddy mess all through Filly's house. There's no need to make extra work for her needlessly." Blake stepped off the front walk and motioned Ginny toward the door on the side of the house.

Swallowing back the rebuke that began working its way out her lips, Ginny nodded her head and followed Blake. He seemed quite familiar with both Luke and Filly, but then she supposed in the small town, everyone knew everyone else's business.

They were almost up the back steps when a large, furry beast ran around the corner of the wraparound porch and knocked into Ginny's knees, throwing her off balance.

Falling backward, she felt Blake's hand on her rump as he reached out to steady her from his position several steps below.

"Down, Bart! Stay down!" Blake commanded the dog. The animal dropped to his hindquarters on the top step and sat looking at them with a big doggy grin.

"This is Luke's dog, Bart. He's a good fellow, just too friendly sometimes." Blake rushed up the steps and offered Ginny his hand as she glared at the dog.

"My stars!" Ginny studied the animal. He didn't appear to be of any particular breed and certainly didn't exhibit the finest manners.

"He'll grow on you." Blake raised his hand and tapped on the back door.

"I somehow doubt it." Ginny stood slightly behind him, mortified at meeting her brother's wife in such an unkempt state. "Perhaps no one is home..." Ginny suggested as the door swung open and a beautiful woman with bright green eyes and gorgeous mahogany hair greeted them with a friendly smile.

"Hello, Blake. What brings you by today? We weren't expecting you to start on the project until next week," Filly Granger said, wiping her hands on her apron and motioning for Blake to step inside the kitchen. Noticing the mud-covered woman behind him, she tried not to laugh at the bedraggled spectacle dripping mud on her clean kitchen floor.

"You poor thing, come in, come in." Filly motioned the girl into the kitchen. "I'm Filly Granger. Welcome to Hardman and Granger House."

"Actually, Filly, she's quite familiar with both the town and your home," Blake said, setting down the bags and taking a step toward the door.

Filly looked at him in confusion, waiting for an explanation.

Tipping his head at Ginny, he gave her a look that said she had better speak up and do it quickly.

"Filly, it's my pleasure to finally meet you, although I do apologize for my less than suitable appearance. That ghastly stage driver should be drawn and quartered for his abhorrent attitude toward his passengers. It is completely unacceptable and I plan to take up the matter with his superiors posthaste," Ginny said, flicking the soggy feather dangling near her eye away from her cheek.

"I'm so sorry, but I'm still uncertain as to who you are." Filly gazed from Ginny to Blake.

"I'm Genevieve Granger, Luke's sister." She tipped her head politely toward Filly. Her parents' praise of Luke's bride didn't do the woman justice. She was tall, graceful, lovely, and gracious. Everything Ginny had long ago decided she would never be.

"Don't let her mislead you into thinking she can put on airs here in your home," Blake said, grinning at Ginny. "You'll find soon enough that Luke calls her Ginny Lou, just to ruffle her bloomers, and despite her ladylike comportment, she has a foul temper and a wicked tongue."

Filly stifled a laugh at the look Ginny shot Blake. He grinned at them both then, with a word of farewell, made his way out the door.

"That... man is thoroughly vexing and entirely incorrigible," Ginny said, barely resisting the urge to stamp her foot. She had often wondered what she would do, how she would feel, if she saw Blake again. The unsettled fluttering in her stomach wasn't what she expected, neither was her longing to wrap her arms around his strong form and rest against his chest.

Giving herself a mental shake to clear her thoughts, she looked at Filly and smiled. "I do apologize for the mess I'm about to make all over the house, but may I please have a bath and can you please have Luke fetch my trunk and the rest of my bags?" Ginny asked imploringly as she removed her ruined hat and dropped it on the floor next to her.

"My gracious, of course, Ginny," Filly said, hurrying to help the girl remove her mud-coated attire.

Blake Stratton stood outside Granger House for a moment, trying to regain his equilibrium. The world as he knew it whirled off center the moment he watched Ginny Granger fall in the mud when the stage driver tossed a bag at her.

He laughed at the sight she made with that bedraggled hat and mud dripping down her finely made traveling suit. It was hard to believe she'd finally returned to Hardman.

When they were in their teens, he'd made foolish plans to marry her someday. Based on their past, he assumed Luke would have mentioned expecting her for a visit if he'd been privy to her plans.

Apparently, her impetuous, headstrong tendencies weren't curtailed through the years, although she'd obviously perfected her manners and pretentious behavior.

Small in stature, she'd always been a little spitfire, one he'd hoped to make his own when she'd reached maturity. Unfortunately, her parents moved to New York before that happened.

Waiting as the family prepared to board the stage on Christmas Day, Blake remembered tugging Ginny behind the blacksmith's shop and stealing a kiss then pressing a small gift he'd labored many hours to create into her hand.

She'd promised to love him forever, but he never heard from her again. The numerous letters he wrote to her arrived in a box one summer afternoon, all unopened.

Gathering what was left of his broken heart and pride, he moved on with his life, even if he'd not fallen in love again.

They were both so young then, just seventeen and fifteen, they had no business making any promises, much less expecting one another to keep them.

Walking back toward town, Blake wondered what brought Ginny to Hardman. He knew, through Luke, she was yet unmarried. According to her brother, Ginny had no interest in matters as mundane as domestic bliss. She preferred to spend her time traveling, taking up causes, and campaigning for what she perceived to be right.

Picturing her big blue eyes gazing up at him with mud speckling her cheeks, Blake felt a chuckle work its way up his chest and out his mouth as he opened the door to the Hardman Bank.

"Hi, Blake. What tickled your funny bone today?" Luke Granger asked as he stood from his desk and stuck out a hand to his friend.

"Your sister, actually," Blake said, grinning as a confused Luke stared at him. "She arrived on the afternoon stage in a flurry of mud and a wealth of insults aimed at the driver."

Snatching his hat off the coat rack behind him, Luke walked toward the door with Blake beside him. "Ginny? Ginny's here? Well, I'll be... did she say anything to you about why she came?"

"Not a word. As would be expected, she brought a trunk and several bags with her. I gave Percy a coin to keep watch over her things until you can collect them."

"Thank you so much." Luke pumped Blake's hand again. "I'll see if George at the mercantile will let me borrow his wagon for a moment. Otherwise, I'll run home and hitch my buggy."

"I can ask George. I'm heading that direction anyway," Blake offered, part of him anxious to see what

Ginny looked like devoid of the mud covering her from head to toe.

The smart thing for him to do would be to ignore her very existence, the way she'd ignored him when she left Hardman all those years ago. Where she was concerned, though, Blake knew his common sense often failed him.

"I appreciate the offer, Blake, but I'll take care of it. I'm sure you have better things to do than escort my mouthy sister around town," Luke said with a grin, knowing Ginny had a multitude of opinions and wasn't afraid of expressing them.

"All right. I'll see you at church Sunday." Blake nodded at Luke as he continued down the street to the livery where he'd left his horse while he took care of some business around town.

"You're welcome to join us after services for lunch, if you'd like," Luke offered, as he opened the mercantile door.

"Thanks, I'll take you up on that offer." Blake wondered how he'd make it until Sunday before seeing Ginny.

Considering the fact he hadn't seen her in almost ten years, he supposed a couple of days wouldn't make much difference.

Chapter Two

"I can't believe you ran away from home, Ginny Lou. Are you ever going to grow up?" Luke asked as they sat at the cozy table in the kitchen eating the delicious dinner Filly prepared.

Luke turned his icy blue eyes to Ginny, pinning her with his gaze while his wife kicked his shin beneath the table. Ignoring the kick and look of reprimand sent his direction, he continued to press his sister for details.

"How irresponsible are you? Running off across the country alone, letting Mother and Dad think you were in Boston." Luke set down his fork and continued his tirade. "Anything could have happened to you. What if someone tried to abduct you or... or..."

"Luke," Filly said softly, placing a gentle hand on his arm, calming his agitated state. She didn't think Ginny needed to undergo an inquisition when she was tired from her travels. Anyone could see the girl looked weary.

"Dear brother of mine, I realize I should have been more forthcoming with my plans, but there is no need for you to carry on so. I'm not only fine, but perfectly able to care for myself and defend myself if need be," Ginny said, thinking of the grabby cowboy who'd think twice before he fingered a woman's knee again. "I did intend to go to Boston to visit a friend but my plans changed at the last moment and I decided to come see you and finally meet Filly."

"What changed your plans?" Luke asked, still not willing to let the subject of her unexpected arrival go until he unearthed the reason behind it. Ginny could have met Filly any number of times in the past two years and had conveniently presented excuses for either not traveling to Hardman or not being home when he and Filly visited New York. He didn't believe for one minute she came to Hardman solely to meet his wife and play the part of the adoring sibling.

Knowing his spoiled sister as well as he did, Luke had no doubt there was some underlying reason for her trip across the country. He wouldn't let the matter drop until he found out exactly what.

"Fate."

Caught in the midst of taking a drink of water to cool his heating temper, Luke snorted water out his nose at Ginny's comment. Spluttering, he coughed a few times before he could speak again.

"Look, Ginny Lou, cut the pretense and tell me plainly what you're doing here. I mean it," Luke warned, glaring at his sibling.

"I've asked you a million times to not call me Ginny Lou." Annoyed by the nickname, she realized her brother did know her well. Too well, apparently. "It makes it sound as though I should be barefoot and brainless, feeding chickens or churning butter, or some such thing."

"So you view farm women as unintelligent and beneath you?" Filly asked, feeling her temper start to rise since she grew up on a farm and several of her friends were farm wives.

In that moment, Ginny realized she tread on very thin ice. Her brother was already skeptical about her motives for visiting unannounced while Filly had been nothing but kind and gracious to her. She didn't want to get on the woman's bad side.

Curbing both her irritation and blunt words, she turned big blue eyes, suddenly moist with emotion, to her sister-in-law.

"My sincere apologies, Filly. I did not intend for my comment to offend. I merely meant that the name is undignified and makes me feel like a country bumpkin. That is precisely why my pesky brother insists on using it," Ginny said, trying to work up a few tears to further her cause.

While Filly's face softened and she reached out to pat her hand, Luke shook his head and leaned back in his chair.

"Enough, Ginny. I won't have your theatrics in my home. You couldn't care less if your comment offended anyone, so don't pretend otherwise. Furthermore, you meant every word you said and I know you're trying really hard to work up a few tears to garner Filly's sympathy. Now, I'll ask one final time… What you are doing here? If I don't receive a satisfactory answer, you'll find your prim and proper bustle on tomorrow's stage heading back to New York."

Ginny stuck out her bottom lip in a pout and glared at Luke. "Must you always be so beastly to me? I'm your only sibling, Luke. You'd think you'd care for me, a little. If Mother were here…"

"If Mother was here I'd say exactly the same thing and this time she might even agree with me. In case you haven't noticed, Mother isn't quite like she used to be." Luke cast a glance at Filly, giving her a wink that Ginny couldn't see.

The change in Dora Granger occurred through Filly's kindness to her despite the harsh way she treated the girl upon first meeting her.

"Fine. You win." Ginny sat straight in the chair and plucked nervously at her napkin. Her pout and tears disappeared instantly. "The reason I came here…"

"Ran away," Luke supplied.

"Came to stay with you." Defiantly, Ginny lifted her chin, "is due to extenuating circumstances that are beyond my ability at this particular time to control."

"And these circumstances would be?" Luke asked, fast losing patience with his sister.

"Well, you see, when I was touring Europe, I met a man. An American. He was also on tour with friends and we happened to run into each other numerous times. He escorted me to a ball or two and then he somehow latched onto the mistaken idea that I was interested in a future with him. Something that involved a permanent attachment." She spoke quickly as though the words spewed out from some well deep inside her. "He resides in New York and has made an absolute pest of himself. He won't leave me alone, Luke. Everywhere I go, he's there and he's been telling people we're engaged. I can't abide the man. He positively makes my skin crawl."

"You poor dear," Filly said, gently patting Ginny's hand and offering her a compassionate smile.

"His name, Ginny. What is the man's name?" Luke asked impatiently.

"Nigel Pickford," Ginny whispered, refusing to look at Luke as she glued her gaze to her half-eaten meal.

"Pickford? Not the son of ol' Morton Pickford?"

At Ginny's nod, Luke raked his hand through his hair and let out a sigh.

"You've landed in it this time, for sure, haven't you, Ginny?"

"I don't understand, Luke. Who are the Pickfords?" Filly asked, looking from Ginny's distraught features to the lines furrowing Luke's forehead, a telltale sign of his concern.

"One of the wealthiest families in New York, tied to just about every aspect of business you could think of from politics to shipping and transportation." Luke studied Ginny. She truly did appear to be upset. "What do Mother and Dad say about all this?"

"At first, Mother was thrilled Nigel wanted to court me, but eventually she agreed with Father that the man is absolutely unbalanced. Not only that, but he isn't what I have in mind for a husband, should I ever lose my sense and decide to wed. He's pale and thin and… ghastly."

"And who, dear sister, do you have in mind for a suitable husband?" Luke asked with a hint of censure in his tone. "What are your top requirements for filling that lofty and unenviable position?"

Ginny's thoughts flew of their own accord to Blake Stratton. Now there was a man of both physical beauty and an honorable heart. She recalled the way his brown hair peeked from beneath the brim of his hat, his hazel eyes twinkled with mirth mingled with surprise, and his white-toothed grin made her smile at him in return. His shoulders were broad, his arms strong, and his voice kind.

Wondering what happened to the gentle boy who had promised to love her forever, she was beside herself when he never wrote her a single letter. She wrote him dozens but never received a reply. After six months, she finally gave up hope of ever hearing from him and avoided returning to Hardman so she'd never have to lay eyes upon him.

Although, after seeing him today, she was glad she'd made the impetuous trip to Oregon for no reason other than to see Blake's smile once again.

"I don't have any man in particular in mind. I just know Nigel is not the one for me," she said, looking first at Filly then at Luke.

"Fair enough. Now, enlighten us as to why your trip to Boston turned out to be one to visit us here instead,"

Luke prompted. "And no falderal about how you were dying to see me and meet Filly."

"I arrived at the train station and happened to see Nigel. It was obvious he was looking for me. The thought of him following me to Boston made my stomach churn, so I charmed my way to the front of the line, bought a one-way ticket for Hardman and here I am," Ginny glanced at Luke. "I realize I should not have assumed you'd be pleased to see me, or at the very least offer me refuge in my little storm, but I'm begging you, Luke. Please don't send me back to New York. Not yet. I need some time to figure out what I'm going to do about my future."

Luke stood and walked around the table and pulled Ginny to her feet, kissing the top of her head and enfolding her into a warm hug.

"You're welcome to stay as long as you like, but just be mindful that I won't put up with any stories, exaggerations, or excuses." Luke returned to his seat next to Filly. "I'll expect you to earn your keep. There aren't servants here to see to your every whim. We just have Mrs. Kellogg who comes a few times a week to help Filly with the housework. You'll have responsibilities to assist in maintaining order in our home, and you'll be respectful to our friends and us. Understood?"

"Perfectly," Ginny said, hoping Luke really didn't expect her to work around the house. Although Filly seemed to take great pleasure in keeping house and cooking, Ginny had no experience in the domestic arts and no inclination to learn.

"Perhaps before we send you back to New York, you'll learn something useful you can apply toward corralling that future husband you mentioned," Luke teased, returning his attention to his meal, ignoring Ginny's frustrated sigh and the smile Filly hid behind her napkin.

With Ginny in town, he had no doubt life at Granger House was about to become quite lively.

"That was one of the best meals I've eaten in a very long time," Blake said, looking to the end of the dining room table where Filly sat blushing at his compliment. "I don't know when I've eaten pork so tender it just fell apart at the touch of my fork. And this pie, Filly, it is truly beyond delicious."

"Doesn't it seem a complete shame Luke gets to enjoy food like this on a daily basis?" asked Chauncy Dodd, pastor of the Hardman Christian Church. He took another bite of his apple pie, topped with freshly whipped cream.

As Luke's oldest and closest friend, Chauncy felt it his duty to torment the man whenever the opportunity arose.

"What is a shame," Abby Dodd teased, reaching over to pat her husband's stomach, "is that unlike you, Luke doesn't gain an ounce from all of Filly's wonderful food. He exhibits some control over himself, instead of eating like a gluttonous beast whenever he sits at the table."

"Did you all hear that? Oh, wife, how you cut me to the quick," Chauncy said, taking Abby's hand in his and kissing her fingers.

"Kiss mine hand, Daddy. Kiss mine," little Erin chirped from her high chair, placed between Filly and Abby. Almost two years old, Erin had a strong vocabulary and an endearing smile along with a head full of dark curls and beautiful blue eyes.

"Here's one for you, sweetness," Chauncy said, blowing his daughter a kiss. Waving her plump little fist in the air, Erin knew the routine well, catching something she couldn't see and slapping her hand to her cheek.

"Aunt Fiwwy kiss mine, too." Erin turned her charming smile to Filly. Although the Dodd and Granger families weren't related by blood, Erin knew Filly and Luke as her doting aunt and uncle.

Filly picked up the tiny hand, playfully nibbling the fingers, making Erin giggle gleefully.

"Isn't it about time you had one of those?" Chauncy asked Luke, tipping his head toward Erin. Filly took the toddler out of her high chair and settled the sweet little girl across her lap.

The rich mahogany curls of his hostess bent over the head of dark brown ringlets made such a picture of pure love and adoration, it stirred something in Blake's chest. Something he'd long ago buried and declared forgotten. Glancing across the table, he felt Ginny's eyes lingering on him and saw a look pass across her features that resembled regret.

All eyes suddenly turned to Luke as he choked on a bite of pie and began coughing violently.

Abby shook her head at Chauncy, giving him a dressing down with her look without saying a word.

At Luke's continued coughing, Ginny leaned over and whacked her brother's back a few times.

"Please stop, Ginny Lou," Luke said, taking a sip of water, once his coughing subsided. "You'll dislodge something vital whomping at me like that."

"Just trying to help, big brother." Ginny smiled sweetly, although hitting Luke had been quite satisfactory. The man had turned into a tyrant since she'd last seen him.

Her beloved brother no longer doted on her or gave her his undivided attention. Instead, his attention was focused, and quite rightly, on his lovely wife.

That first night, after the debacle at dinner and his extracting the truth out of her, she was ready to retire to her room for a good night's rest. Starting up the stairs to her old room, Luke grabbed her arm and ushered her down the hall to the bedroom that belonged to the cook when her parents lived at Granger House.

Tremendously insulted that he expected her to stay downstairs, he quietly told her the two bedrooms downstairs were for guests and she could either stay there or find her way to the boarding house.

He'd even made her get out of bed at an unreasonable hour so she could help Filly with breakfast.

When she grumbled about that, he threatened to send her out to gather the eggs from the small henhouse by the barn. Speechless at the very notion of sticking her hand into a nest already occupied by a chicken, Ginny clamped her lips together and set the breakfast table without a further word of complaint.

This morning, instead of letting her sleep in, he bellowed down the hall for her to hurry up since it was their Sunday to help set things up at church before services.

Tired from her recent travels and continuing efforts at keeping her wayward tongue from getting her into more trouble with her brother, since she was temporarily at his mercy, she liked the idea of an afternoon nap.

Biting her cheek to keep a yawn from escaping, she listened to the good-natured teasing going on around the table. She wondered when Blake became such good friends with Luke and Chauncy, they all seemed quite familiar with one another. They did play together as boys, but she didn't think they were close friends back then since Blake was a few years younger than the other two.

"How long will you be staying, Ginny?" Abby asked as she helped Filly begin gathering dirty dishes to return to the kitchen.

"I'm not yet certain. I considered staying through the holidays, since Mother and Dad are planning to spend

Christmas here, but Luke may decide to send me home before then." Ginny smiled at Abby. For a big gangly oaf, as her mother so often described Chauncy Dodd, he married a very pretty woman who appeared to have manners, refinement, and an aura of elegance about her.

"I hope you'll be here for a while," Blake heard himself say then wondered what possessed him to voice his thoughts. He had no intention of getting involved with Ginny Granger again. As spoiled and ornery as she was when he knew her, she seemed to have gotten worse with age. The woman sitting at the dining room table was arrogant, headstrong, and opinionated.

All through the morning church service, he'd forced himself not to notice the streaks of gold in her blond hair or the wayward curls escaping the pile on top of her head as they danced enticingly along her delicate neck. Sitting in the row behind her, he inhaled her sweet fragrance every time she moved. So distracted by her presence, he almost missed Chauncy's call to stand for the closing hymn.

Now, seated across the table from her, he realized some part of him was still interested in Ginny Granger. Some stupid, obviously idiotic part of him that didn't realize the danger involved in caring for the smart-mouthed woman.

She'd leave his heart in an even more destitute condition than she had as a young girl because it would be broken by a grown woman. A decidedly beautiful, lusciously curved woman who could no doubt cause him more pain and torment than he ever wanted to endure.

Turning his attention to the banter going on between Luke and Chauncy, he did his best to ignore the way Ginny's big blue eyes kept glancing at him, how her dark lashes fanned against her porcelain cheeks, and her pink lips slipped into a becoming pout.

Feeling the temperature in the room suddenly rise, Blake fought the urge to tug at his shirt collar. Instead, he placed his napkin beside his plate and arose, drawing all the attention his direction.

"Sincere thanks to you, Filly, for this lovely meal. You've outdone yourself once again, and I appreciate the invitation to join you for one of your delectable feasts." Blake lifted Filly's hand in his and kissed the back of it with a gallant flair.

"Mine, Unca Bake. Kiss mine, too," Erin said, leaning against his leg, holding up her chubby fist.

Blake squatted down, so he was closer to eye level with the child. Pressing his lips to the tiny hand with a noisy smack, he tickled the little imp beneath her chin, eliciting a giggle.

"Tank you." Erin held her hand against her chest while her other clung to Abby's skirt.

"Leaving so soon, Blake?" Luke asked, getting to his feet and shaking his hand. "No need to rush off."

"I really must be on my way, but I do thank you for your hospitality and the comfort of spending a lovely afternoon at Granger House with such pleasant company," Blake said, his British accent increasing in direct proportion to the unsettled feelings Ginny evoked just by looking at him.

Blake tipped his head her direction as he stepped away from the table. "Miss Granger, nice to see you again."

"You as well, Mr. Stratton." Ginny frowned at Luke as he gave her a gentle shove in Blake's direction.

"Be a good sister and walk Blake to the door, Ginny Lou. Please." Luke grinned at her with a knowing look in his eye. "You look like you need a breath of fresh air."

Biting her tongue to keep from telling him what she thought of his behavior, she tossed her head and stomped after Blake. She found him at the hall tree in the front entry, taking his hat off a hook.

"You don't need to see me out. I can find my way," Blake said, both glad and dismayed to have a moment alone with Ginny. She was even more beautiful than he remembered.

"For some reason, Luke is sure you'll get lost between the front door and the road, so I'm to accompany you down the walk." Blake's fingers briefly touched her back as he held the door and followed her outside. She attempted to ignore the thrill that raced through her.

Out of the corner of her eye, she watched him settle his hat on his head as they strolled down the front walk. Her fingers itched to run through his thick hair and may have done just that if Bart hadn't run around the house and into her skirts, nearly toppling her to the grass.

Blake's quick reflexes kept her on her feet, although his arms wrapped around her waist and held her against his chest.

Ginny could have kissed the mutt on his furry head for the result of his actions. In no hurry to leave the wonderful warmth of Blake's arms, she let him hold her a moment before stepping away.

"That beast is the most ill-behaved lunkhead I've ever encountered." She glared at the dog while silently singing his praises. "Must you be so ornery?"

"Don't begrudge Bart a little fun." Blake hunkered down and rubbed his hands over the back of the dog. Bart immediately rolled on his side while Blake gave his belly a good scratching. "You're a fine dog, aren't you, old boy?"

Bart yipped happily, got to his feet, and lapped at Blake's face, making him chuckle. Rubbing the dog's ears one last time, Blake stood and continued down the walk. Ginny kept in step with him, wishing she'd followed her impulse to bury her fingers in Blake's hair.

She'd never done that as a girl and she had no idea where such an errant idea came from now. It must be the vital masculinity so readily apparent in Blake causing her to think such unacceptable thoughts. Despite his cultured speech and accent, a rugged element clung to him, piquing her interest and leaving her thoroughly intrigued.

"I didn't see your parents at church. Are they well?" Ginny asked, groping for a safe topic of conversation. One that wouldn't make her think of Blake's strong arms or muscled chest or how badly she wanted one of his kisses.

"They are indeed well, at least at the writing of their last letter." At Ginny's confused look, he continued. "They returned to England six years ago."

"Oh. I had no idea. I'm sorry, Blake. I'm sure you miss them terribly." She remembered how close Blake had always been with his parents. "Do you see them at all?"

"We try to get together at least once a year. I spent the holidays with them two years ago, they were here to visit in the early summer, and I'm planning a trip to see them in the spring." Blake stopped next to his horse where it stood tied to a post near the fence around the front yard. "Although I miss them, I'm happy for them to return to their lives near London. Father missed it more than he ever let on."

"Do you still live at the farm?" Ginny remembered many meals she'd eaten at the humble Stratton home. Lacking servants and the air of pretentiousness that clung to Granger House, Ginny remembered feeling the love shared among the Stratton family. When she was with Blake, it encompassed her, too.

Not for the first time, she wished things had ended differently with the handsome man.

"Yes. I rent most of the ground to a neighbor to farm, but I've still got a few cattle, and Dad's horses, and my workshop there." He adjusted the cinch on his saddle for something to do with his hands. If he didn't keep them occupied, he was afraid they might reach out and pull Ginny to his chest again. The feel of her leaning against him a moment ago scrambled what few wits he had left in her presence.

"Workshop?"

"I'm a carpenter, Ginny. You knew I loved to work with wood. It's what I always wanted to do." He turned to look at her, wondering if she'd listened to any of his dreams and plans when they were younger. Working with wood was the only thing that stirred an unquenchable passion in him, other than her. "I went to Portland and spent two years studying with a master carpenter before coming back here and opening my own business."

"I'm happy for you." Memories of how much Blake loved working with wood, how talented he was at it, filled her thoughts.

The little lump of smooth wood in her pocket was a constant reminder of both his talent and the love she'd left behind when her parents carted her off to New York. She wondered if her infatuation with Blake had anything to do with her parents moving when they did. Her mother had such great aspirations of Ginny marrying well and a poor boy who planned to be a humble carpenter didn't fit in Dora's plans at all. Especially not when Ginny was only fifteen and had her whole life ahead of her.

Wondering what might have happened if her parents had stayed in Hardman, Ginny changed the direction of her thoughts before she grew maudlin.

"Me, too." Grateful his parents encouraged him to follow his dreams and made it possible for him to go to Portland, he never took the sacrifices they made for him for granted. "It's a good, honest life."

Ginny studied the toes of her shoes peeking out from the hem of her dress instead of listening to the voice in her head telling her to reach up and trace her finger over the familiar mole on Blake's cheek. He'd always hated it, but she thought it somehow kept him from looking too perfect.

"Ginny?"

"Yes?"

"Did you ever miss it here, in all those years you were gone?" Blake asked. *Did you miss me?*

"I did, Blake. There were some things, people, I missed so much my heart ached just thinking about them." Curious, she contemplated why Blake would ask such a question. He was the one who broke his promise to keep in touch. He was the one who broke her heart.

"I see," Blake said, not really seeing anything. He hoped he was one of the people she'd missed, but knew it wasn't likely. If she'd missed him that much, she would have written him at least one letter. "I better go. I've got things to do at home."

"Certainly." She took a step away from the warmth and wonderful masculine scent of Blake. Spending the last several years surrounded by the soft, spoiled boys in her crowd, she found Blake beyond appealing and entirely fascinating.

"Enjoy your afternoon, Ginny," he said, mounting his horse. Starting to turn away, he stopped, reaching down and rubbing his fingers across her smooth cheek. "For what it's worth, I'm glad you're home."

Before she could utter a reply, he turned, urging his horse down the street.

Chapter Three

As she sat at the breakfast table, yawning over a cup of tepid tea, Ginny couldn't fathom how Filly and Luke could both be so wide-awake and chipper at such a detestable hour of the morning.

Taking pity on her, Luke merely raised an eyebrow her direction when she slumped in her chair at the table wearing an old dress with her hair falling around her in a wild tangle. Even after eating breakfast, she still felt half-awake and unable to function. She barely acknowledged Luke's departure to work or the sound of Filly beginning to wash laundry.

Contemplating the amount of effort it would take to wander back to bed versus resting her head on the table for a while, Ginny stifled a yawn when a knock sounded at the kitchen door.

"Ginny, would you mind answering that please?" Filly called from the room off the kitchen where she was doing laundry.

Muttering to herself about ill-mannered people who didn't know better than calling so early in the day, she yanked open the door to see Blake standing on the step, wearing a broad grin as one hand patted Bart on the head.

"Miss Granger," Blake said, amused by her disheveled state, as well as the shock widening her big blue eyes. Not only was her dress sadly in need of an acquaintance with a hot iron, she'd missed a couple buttonholes, resulting in the front of her gown looking like a drunk fastened it together. Combined with her untamed, blond curls flying every direction, she appeared more like a child playing dress up rather than a woman grown.

"My stars!" Ginny's hands flew to her unruly hair as Blake stepped inside, carrying a large toolbox. "Blake, er... Mr. Stratton. What are you doing here so early in the day?"

"Is that Blake, Ginny?" Filly stuck her head out of the laundry room.

"As a matter of fact, it is." Ginny wanted to throw something at Filly's smirking face. Her sister-in-law knew Blake was coming and never said a word about it during breakfast.

"I'll be right there," Filly called. She entered the kitchen wiping wet hands on her apron. "Good morning, Blake. You're right on time. Can I make you a cup of coffee? Maybe offer you a leftover muffin?"

"I've had my breakfast, but I do thank you for the offer. Maybe you'll save that muffin for later this morning, if I need a break from my work." Blake smiled at Filly although his eyes remained firmly fixed on Ginny.

Following the direction of his gaze, Filly swallowed back a grin. "Blake is going to do some work in the corner bedroom upstairs. The last storm we had knocked a limb through the window and the rain all but ruined part of the wall and floor."

"The brown room?" Ginny realized she hadn't even looked around upstairs to see if Filly and Luke had redecorated any of the bedrooms.

"Yes, that's the one. I'm afraid the beautiful woodwork beneath the window is beyond repair. Luke and I were in Portland for a few days when it happened and Mrs. Kellogg, bless her heart, didn't realize anything was amiss since we keep the extra bedrooms closed most of the time."

"That's unfortunate," Ginny said, wishing someone had mentioned Blake's impending arrival. She had a sneaking suspicion Luke instructed Filly to feign innocence in the matter.

"Shall I show you the room?" Filly asked, turning to Blake.

Nodding his head, he followed Filly, tugging mischievously on one of Ginny's errant curls as he walked by whispering, "You might want to have another go at getting dressed this morning."

Ginny's gaze dropped to the front of her gown and she felt hot embarrassment fill her cheeks. Waiting until she heard Filly and Blake's footsteps on the stairs, she ran down the hall to her room and dug through her clothes, finding one of her favorite dresses.

"That man is such a... a... oh!" Mad beyond words, she hurriedly changed clothes, put on her shoes and worked a brush through her hair. Piling it on top of her head, she jabbed in enough hairpins to keep it somewhat contained.

Studying her image in the mirror above the dressing table, she eyed herself critically. Deciding she looked fit to be seen, she harbored no small sense of irritation toward her sister-in-law for not giving her fair warning that Blake would be knocking on the door before she made herself presentable for the day.

Luke probably planned for her to be embarrassed all along, knowing she'd drag herself to the table with her hair uncombed and whatever dress she happened to find with her eyes half shut. Her brother wasn't nearly as funny as he thought himself to be.

With all thoughts of a nap thoroughly chased from her head, Ginny instead found herself trying to think of some reason to go upstairs and watch Blake work.

Returning to the kitchen, she tied one of Filly's voluminous aprons around her waist and stood looking at the orderly kitchen, wondering what she could do to be useful.

It didn't take long for her to observe Luke's wife worked every bit as hard as he did. In the time it took Ginny to make herself a cup of tea, Filly could have a cake batter mixed, baking in the oven, or the dishes washed and dried. Twice, the woman had even gone out in the evening to help Luke feed the livestock.

Accustomed to a leisurely pace with no expectations of actually accomplishing anything, Ginny felt useless around Filly. As much as it rankled, she couldn't bring herself to resent her sister-in-law. The woman was kind, gracious, big-hearted, and a lot of fun. On top of that, Luke clearly adored her and Ginny was beginning to as well.

"Oh, there you are." Filly breezed into the kitchen, her apron damp from finishing the washing. "Would you like to help me make some cookies?"

"Certainly." Ginny had no idea where to start. Filly gave her direction as she creamed butter and sugar then added the eggs, baking powder, salt, and flour.

"Then we just roll it out like this." Filly rolled the cookie dough on the floured surface of the counter. "Would you like to cut out the cookies?"

"Yes, please." Ginny picked up the glass Filly indicated and cut perfect circles in the sweet dough. She used to sit in the kitchen and watch their cook make cookies. The woman often allowed her to cut out the dough, at least until Dora discovered her in the kitchen and shooed her off to practice playing the piano or work on her embroidery skills. Blake's mother also tried to teach her some useful skills, to no avail.

"Now, just sprinkle a little sugar on top." Filly hid a smile as Ginny laboriously spread sugar on the tops of the cookies.

Sliding the baking sheets filled with cookies into the oven, Filly quickly washed the dishes then began preparations for lunch.

"What are you making now?" Ginny watched as Filly peeled potatoes and carrots.

"Beef stew." Filly removed the lid from the meat she'd started simmering earlier that morning. "Luke's quite partial to it."

"Why do you cook the meat before you add the rest?" Ginny questioned as Filly added chunks of potatoes and sliced carrots to the stew pot.

Filly offered her sister-in-law a kind smile. "The meat takes longer to cook and become tender. If we put the vegetables in as long as the meat, they'd be mushy by the time the stew was finished. This way both the meat and the vegetables come out just right."

Ginny nodded her head, realizing for perhaps the first time in her life she had a marginal interest in the process used to create the delicious meals she'd always taken for granted.

Taking a tray out of a cupboard, Filly poured hot coffee into a small pot, added cups, napkins and a plate of the warm sugar cookies then handed it to Ginny.

"I'm sure Blake could use a break. Would you take that up to him?" Filly tipped her head toward the hallway and back stairs.

"Don't you think… maybe you should…" Ginny sighed, out of excuses as she removed her apron. Straightening her shoulders, she carried the tray down the hall and up the back stairs.

Taking a deep breath, she walked into the corner bedroom and set the tray down on a dresser. Glancing around, she noted the room looked much like it did the last time she'd seen it a decade ago.

She'd always thought the room dark and masculine with its wood paneling halfway up the wall, dark walnut furniture, and dark-colored linens.

A cream quilt with brown leaves stitched across the top in an interesting pattern now covered the bed, adding light and warmth to the dark space. Both windows lacked any coverings, allowing the sunshine to dapple across the bed and part of the floor.

Observing Blake, she realized he must not have heard her come in as she stood watching him pry a board away from the wall. His shirt stretched across his shoulders and arms, outlining the strength clearly evident there, while his well-fitting work pants highlighted the muscles in his thighs as he worked a piece of wood loose.

When he bent over to pick up the board, a little gasp escaped her lips at the sight before her. Blake's gaze collided with hers when he looked over his shoulder to catch her studying him.

Almost dropping the pry bar on his foot at the vision she created, Blake took a moment to absorb her beauty.

While he preferred seeing her hair down and wild, he admitted the blond curls piled on her head were both feminine and becoming, especially when a few had already worked their way free, flowing softly around her face.

The peach and cream confection she wore accented her womanly figure while infusing her cheeks with a touch of color. He assumed the tight-waisted gown was probably the latest fashion.

Watching as her hands nervously twisted around each other, she stood soundlessly staring at him. It would be an easy thing to become lost in those vibrant blue eyes.

Feeling a tug in his heart pulling him toward her, he fought to resist it.

"Filly thought you could use a break," Ginny finally spoke, breaking the silence that fell between the two of them, dropping the gaze Blake had held captive.

"That's kind of her." Blake wiped his hands along the sides of his pants and accepted the cup of coffee Ginny held out to him. Drinking the rich brew, Blake helped himself to a cookie, still warm from the oven. "It's always a pleasure to do work for your brother and his wife."

"Why is that?" Distracted by the movement of Blake's sculpted lips, Ginny thought they were such perfect lips, especially on such a handsome man.

"Because no one else makes coffee as good as Filly and they rarely give me freshly baked cookies for a snack." Blake grinned as he took another cookie. Noticing a second cup on the tray, he motioned for Ginny to pour herself some coffee.

Jittery enough without the coffee, Ginny poured half a cup just for something to do with her hands. The way her palms moistened and thoughts addled in Blake's presence, she thought it a small miracle she didn't drop her cup on the floor.

"What are you working on today?" Blake asked, leaning against the dresser as he contentedly munched his third cookie.

"I helped Filly make the cookies," she blurted. Searching for something meaningful she had planned to do before the day was through, unable to come up with a single thing.

He raised an eyebrow her direction. "You helped make the cookies?"

"I watched while Filly mixed the dough then I cut them out. Doesn't that count for something?" Ginny asked, flustered. Blake knew she couldn't boil water without scorching the pan.

"They are the most perfectly round cookies I've eaten for a long, long time." His wink made a blush fill her hot cheeks. She wondered if he referred to the cookies she'd helped his mother make so many years ago.

"That's kind of her." Blake wiped his hands along the sides of his pants and accepted the cup of coffee Ginny held out to him. Drinking the rich brew, Blake helped himself to a cookie, still warm from the oven. "It's always a pleasure to do work for your brother and his wife."

"Why is that?" Distracted by the movement of Blake's sculpted lips, Ginny thought they were such perfect lips, especially on such a handsome man.

"Because no one else makes coffee as good as Filly and they rarely give me freshly baked cookies for a snack." Blake grinned as he took another cookie. Noticing a second cup on the tray, he motioned for Ginny to pour herself some coffee.

Jittery enough without the coffee, Ginny poured half a cup just for something to do with her hands. The way her palms moistened and thoughts addled in Blake's presence, she thought it a small miracle she didn't drop her cup on the floor.

"What are you working on today?" Blake asked, leaning against the dresser as he contentedly munched his third cookie.

"I helped Filly make the cookies," she blurted. Searching for something meaningful she had planned to do before the day was through, unable to come up with a single thing.

He raised an eyebrow her direction. "You helped make the cookies?"

"I watched while Filly mixed the dough then I cut them out. Doesn't that count for something?" Ginny asked, flustered. Blake knew she couldn't boil water without scorching the pan.

"They are the most perfectly round cookies I've eaten for a long, long time." His wink made a blush fill her hot cheeks. She wondered if he referred to the cookies she'd helped his mother make so many years ago.

Looking for any distraction, she set her cup back on the tray then walked over to the wall where Blake worked. It appeared several of the boards, both in the paneling and floor, had warped from the exposure to the rain.

"Will this be hard to repair?" Ginny ran her hand over one of the boards Blake already removed. Wincing, she felt a splinter slide into her palm.

Before she could pull it out, Blake stood beside her, taking her hand in his.

"Hurt?" Carefully, he picked at it with his long, tapered fingers.

"A little," Ginny admitted, thinking she might faint from the feel of Blake's hand holding hers, his heat permeating her side, his breath blowing across her skin as he bent over the splinter. Quickly taking his knife from his pocket, he removed the splinter then pressed moist lips to the spot, making her stomach flutter. The sensation created by his lips against her skin was enough to make her lightheaded.

"Better?" he asked, releasing her hand and stepping back across the room, gulping his coffee and setting the cup on the tray.

"Yes. Thank you." Rattled, she picked up the tray and started to leave the room. Blake's hand stopped her escape.

"I appreciate the coffee and cookies, Ginny. Thank you for bringing them up to me." He forced himself to let go of her arm, to step away from the woman who twisted his heart in knots and his thoughts into a jumbled mess. What was he thinking, kissing her palm? His lips still tingled from the contact.

He really wanted to haul her into his arms and kiss her until the only thing she could do was cling to him, whispering his name. Since that wasn't going to happen, he took another step back.

"You're welcome." She practically ran down the stairs to the kitchen, startling Filly as she slammed the tray on the counter.

"Whatever is the matter?" Filly noticed the bright flush on Ginny's cheeks and the narrowed glare the girl leveled on her.

"Don't be coy, Filly. You sent me up there on purpose. I'm sure Luke informed you Blake used to be my beau. From now on, if you want him to have a break with refreshments, you'll have to deliver it to him." Angry, Ginny crossed her arms and glared at Filly. "I don't know what you and that thick-headed brother of mine think you are doing, but I beg of you to stop. I have no plans to ever become the property of a man, any man, and especially not that man, so please just stop."

"I'm sorry, Ginny." Filly walked over to hug the much shorter and smaller girl. "You and Blake both seemed so happy to see each other, Luke just thought that maybe…"

"There are no maybes where Blake Stratton is concerned. Please, Filly, I can't…" Ginny stopped as tears clogged her throat. "Please just leave it alone. Some things once done can't be undone."

Filly nodded her head without saying anything further.

Ginny took a deep breath and looked around the kitchen, inhaling the scent of the beefy stew as well as bread baking.

"If you wouldn't mind, I'd like to run a letter to Mother over to the post office. I could walk home with Luke on my way back." Desperate to escape the confines of the house and the proximity of Blake, she searched for any excuse to leave. Her hand still tingled from his touch and she desperately wanted to feel his lips on her skin again.

"That would be fine, Ginny." Filly smiled at her encouragingly. "Would you mind stopping by the mercantile and picking up some sugar on your way back? I'm out and with your brother's sweet tooth that will never do."

"I'd be happy to." She disappeared to her room and returned with a fashionable hat and jacket in place. Tugging on a pair of gloves, she kissed Filly's cheek, picked up the market basket, and breezed out the door.

Bart was nowhere to be seen, so Ginny hurried down the walk, sighing in relief at not encountering the furry beast. Luke said the dog was used to being able to play with him and Filly and didn't want to leave her out of the fun. He assured Ginny once she and Bart became accustomed to each other, she'd enjoy the canine.

She didn't know if that would ever happen, but she did appreciate his efforts at pushing her into Blake's arms Sunday. Then again, being close to Blake was dangerous to her mental wellbeing and she'd do well to take a wide berth around him from now on.

In no hurry as she ran errands, Ginny wandered through town, looking in windows and admiring the display in Abby Dodd's dress shop window. Abby waved for her to come in.

Quickly sticking her head inside, she thanked Abby and told her she'd come back on a day when she had more time. In no mood to think about clothes or fashions, visions of Blake bent over working on the wood paneling filled her head.

Hastening her step toward the bank, she walked inside in time to see Luke shrug into his coat.

"May I help you, miss?" A handsome young man greeted her as she stood near the door, waiting for her brother to turn around.

"No, thank you. I'm here to collect Mr. Granger for lunch." Ginny gave her brother a saucy smile as he turned and grinned.

"Ginny, you've not yet met my assistant, Arlan Guthry. He keeps me in line and the accounts straight. I couldn't run the business without him. Arlan, this is my sister, Genevieve Granger, although we all call her Ginny." Luke smiled at the mannerly gentleman who took his sister's hand in his. His assistant was about to fall under her spell.

"My pleasure to make your acquaintance, ma'am," Arlan said sincerely, stunned by the petite beauty standing before him.

"Thank you, Mr. Guthry. The pleasure is mine." Flirtatiously, she smiled at the younger man. "I'm sure we'll meet again since I'll be staying in town for a while."

"I look forward to it." Arlan watched her leave on Luke's arm.

"Can you tone down your charm a bit, Ginny Lou?" Luke admonished as they walked toward Granger House. "Arlan isn't one of your empty-headed, deep-pocketed ninnies. He's a good man and a friend, and I won't have you trifling with him."

She set her feet and refused to take another step with her overbearing brother. Ginny crossed her arms in front of her chest and glared at her older sibling. "I don't trifle with anyone, Luke Granger, and well you know it. I am, after all, well past the age of being declared an old maid and have moved right into spinsterhood. If I was a trifling sort of woman, I'd have a string of broken-hearted chaps in my wake and a ring on my finger."

"According to Dad, you don't want to get married, thinking it an institution for the insane or weak-minded. As far as that string of broken-hearted men left in your wake, you've done more than your fair share, my darling sister." Luke took Ginny's elbow and propelled her down the boardwalk toward home. "Blake was the first and apparently poor Nigel Pickford is the latest."

"How dare you bring up Blake or Nigel? You know Mother was beside herself when she thought I might actually marry Blake someday. Besides, he obviously didn't feel the same way about me as I felt about him. In any case, we were both so young, how could we have possibly known what we felt was real? It was a childish infatuation."

"Really?" Luke tried not to lose his patience with his sister. He knew leaving Blake had been traumatic for her and he wondered if she'd ever again allow herself to love anyone.

"Really, you... you... barbaric cavedweller. In case you haven't noticed, women are capable of carrying on a fulfilling life without marrying or having children. Furthermore, cease in your efforts to throw Blake and I together. I mean it. Be nice or I'll leave and not tell you, or anyone else, where I'm going."

"Now, Ginny Lou, just calm down." Luke stopped outside the kitchen door. With perfect clarity, he recalled why he hadn't minded being on the opposite side of the country from his sister. She was every bit as mule-headed and opinionated as him. Maybe even more so. "I'm sorry I brought up Nigel. I know he must be awful for you to run off and not even tell the folks where you were going. By the way, I received a telegram from them today."

"What did they say?" Ginny asked as they went in the kitchen door and removed their outerwear.

"To tell you if you ever disappear like that again, I have permission to beat you into submission."

Ginny shook her head at Luke, knowing he was teasing.

"Hello, wife!" Luke swept Filly into a hug and kissed her on the lips on his way through the kitchen to wash his hands in the bathroom.

Somewhat appalled by the blatant displays of affection between Luke and Filly, Ginny secretly wished she'd someday know that kind of love.

"Here's your sugar." Ginny set the basket on the counter and washed her hands at the kitchen sink. "May I help with anything?"

"Can you slice the bread?" Filly asked as she ladled stew into bowls and set them on the table.

"Even I can manage that much," Ginny said, her good humor restored after her discussion with Luke.

"Thank you." After filling glasses with milk, Filly set butter and jam on the table, then finished the final layer of frosting on a chocolate cake.

Ginny set the bread on the table and looked around, counting four place settings. Blake must still be working upstairs.

Holding back the groan of despair that threatened to erupt from her throat, she gave her brother a harsh look as he returned to the kitchen, Blake following behind him.

"Blake's doing a great job up there." Luke motioned the carpenter to the table. Blake held out Ginny's chair and waited while Luke held Filly's before taking a seat, exhibiting the fine manners his parents taught him.

"I hate to see the wood ruined. It's such beautiful walnut." Blake bowed his head as Luke offered thanks for the meal.

"Can you salvage any of it?" Luke asked, passing the bread to Blake and smiling at his wife for preparing one of his favorite meals.

"It would be small pieces, if any." Blake buttered his bread and slathered it with berry jam.

"If you can use it for something, take it." Luke nodded his approval at Filly as he took a bite of tender beef.

"I'll pay you for what I can use." Blake savored the rich stew and warm bread, as well as the company. Ginny sat next to him and her light, floral fragrance teased his nose above the appetizing scents of the meal.

"Nonsense." Luke stared at Blake. "I'd have to haul it off or find something to do with it, so you're doing me a favor by taking it."

Blake nodded his head in acceptance and continued eating his meal. Filly asked if he'd heard from his parents lately. When he nodded his head, she inquired about an addition they recently added to their home in the English countryside.

Ginny sat entranced, listening to Blake's voice and his descriptions of the landscape around his parents' country home.

Growing up, rumors abounded about the Stratton family. One of the most prevalent was that Blake's parents, Robert and Sarah, were disgraced royalty, disowned and run out of the country for some heinous deed.

Spending many hours in their company, Ginny couldn't picture either of them doing anything unlawful, cruel, or evil. They both were always so compassionate and kind. Blake's mother was loving, witty and domestic — the epitome of what Ginny wished her mother would be when she was a young girl. Robert Stratton was terrible at farming, but he had a wonderful way with horses. When Ginny moved from Hardman, he had built up quite a reputation for training and breeding only the best.

"I wish we could see their home someday." Wistful, Filly smiled at Luke.

"My family would welcome you with open arms." Blake grinned at Filly then Luke. "If you ever want to go for a visit, just let me know. They'd love to see a friendly face or two from here."

"That's a kind offer." Luke thought it would be fun to take Filly on an extended trip. "Maybe in the spring."

"Did you visit any villages when you were in England, Ginny?" Filly asked, looking at her with interest.

"No. I spent all my time in London," Ginny said. In fact, she spent most of her time trying to evade Nigel and his ardent pursuit of her hand in marriage.

"No doubt you became well versed with the offerings at the theater, the best dress shops, and perhaps a confectionery or two," Blake teased, knowing Ginny well.

"Perhaps," she said, annoyed he would know exactly how she spent her time in the city.

Luke asked Blake questions about his carpentry business then the conversation moved to a project Chauncy asked him to complete for the Christmas season. Ginny only half listened, turning her attention instead to the fact that it didn't sound like Blake had a lot of work lined up, other than new pews at the church.

Deciding she'd make it her mission to drum up business for Blake, her mind began whirling with possibilities.

Chapter Four

Blake whistled as he walked through town, looking in store windows and waving at friends. He started to stroll past the mercantile when Percy Bruner ran out the door and caught his attention.

"Mr. Stratton, my ma wants to talk to you. Can you come in for a minute?" Percy asked with a gap-toothed smile.

"Of course, young man." Blake ruffled Percy's tousled red hair and grinned at the boy's bright freckles, untucked shirt, and dirt-covered knees. Almost eight, Percy was quite a handful for his parents to manage, even if he was a hard worker.

Stepping into the store, the scents of leather and gunpowder mixed with cinnamon and dill, creating an interesting aroma in the fall air. Pumpkins sat in a large barrel by the door. Blake recalled seeing Filly cart one home the previous afternoon from where he worked on the frame of the upstairs bedroom window.

Ginny had been conspicuously absent from the house the past two days and he wondered if pressing his lips to her palm had unsettled her as much as it had him.

He knew it was nothing short of foolish to entertain any thoughts of the woman, but he couldn't quite force the vision of her in that peach-colored gown from his mind.

The only thing that chased it away was picturing her dripping mud, standing in the street looking like a half-drowned kitten. That image always made him laugh and the thought of it forced a broad smile to break out across his face.

Raising a hand to Aleta Bruner to let her know he'd wait while she helped the customer at the counter, he wandered over to look through their selection of work gloves. He'd worn a hole through the fingers of his and needed a new pair. Trying on a few, he made his selection and stepped up to the counter.

"You look pleased about something, Blake," Aleta said, ringing up his gloves and handing them back to him.

"It's such a pretty autumn day, how could you help but smile?" Blake stuffed the gloves in his pocket. "Percy said you wanted to speak to me about something. What can I do for you and George?"

"We heard you were looking for some additional work and we've been meaning to get in touch with you anyway to have you build more shelves in our storeroom. Would you be interested?" Aleta asked.

"I'd be happy to build your shelves and can get to it in a week or two." Aleta's words caused him to experience a sudden prick of concern. "Where did you hear I need additional work? With the holidays coming, I usually end up with so many projects, I stay up a lot of nights to get them all done by Christmas Eve."

"Oh," Aleta said in surprise. "Well, she said… I just thought… if you don't have time to do the shelves, they can wait until January."

"I'll build your shelves for you as soon as possible, but who is she? Who implied I needed work?"

"It might have been… or perhaps it was…" Aleta stammered, her face blushing red.

"Let me guess." Blake's jaw tightened in irritation. "It wouldn't have been Ginny Granger, by chance?"

Aleta nodded her head, suddenly finding a speck of dust on the counter in need of immediate attention as she picked up a rag and vigorously rubbed at the surface.

"I thought so." Blake clenched his hand into a fist. He was one of the most peaceable men in town, but that woman knew how to provoke him more than anyone else ever had. He could only imagine what she'd said to his neighbors and friends. How could she possibly think he needed more work? "You don't happen to know if she mentioned my need for work to anyone else, do you?"

"Actually, Mrs. Ferguson from the boarding house mentioned something about it this afternoon when she came in for some soap and Mrs. Camden inquired if I knew more detail about your sudden need for work when she purchased thread this afternoon." Aleta shook her head. "Oh, and Mrs. Daily from the newspaper office said her husband was printing some flyers to put up around town."

"Thank you, Mrs. Bruner." Blake tipped his hat then ran out the door and down the street to the newspaper office.

"Mr. Daily," Blake called as he opened the door, hoping his voice carried over the running press. "Mr. Daily?"

"Hello, Blake. How does life find you on this glorious day?" Ed Daily asked as he wiped his ink-stained hands on his apron and stretched one out to Blake.

"Concerned, mostly," Blake muttered, shaking Ed's hand.

"Sorry, I didn't catch that!" the man shouted.

"Did Ginny Granger order some flyers for my business?" Blake fought the urge to punch something. He couldn't recall the last time he'd been this angry.

"Yes, she did. Got them right here." Ed dug through stacks of papers on a desk. He retrieved a pile neatly tied with twine. "She also said she wanted to purchase an ad for next week's paper."

"Never mind the ad." Fury built from Blake's toes to his head. "If she comes in asking for anything to be printed or advertised in regard to me or my business, would you please check with me first or completely disregard it altogether? She seems to have taken it upon herself to act on my behalf unbeknownst to me."

"You don't say." Ed offered Blake a mischievous grin. "Then you aren't just a stone's throw away from 'destitution and despair' as she put it?"

"What?" Blake yelled, his voice echoing through the building as the press stopped running. "That woman is an infernal…"

Taking a deep breath, Blake asked how much he owed for the flyers, paid the bill, and stalked out the door.

Infuriated, he read one of the flyers, his anger changing from bubbling to a full-fledged boil. How dare that meddlesome woman? Spreading rumors around town, as if his family hadn't always had plenty following their every move.

He couldn't imagine what inspired Ginny to tell folks he needed work. In fact, Blake had plenty of work to keep him busy. When he wasn't working on projects for the good people of Hardman, he crafted unique chairs and side tables that were quite popular at a furniture store in Portland as well as several locations in England. He shipped the finished pieces to his parents who then managed his overseas sales.

Blake absolutely didn't need more work, and he was a long way from destitute. What no one knew, especially the gossiping busybodies in town, was that his father held titles.

The Earl of Roxbury brought his wife and son to America when Blake was quite young. Outcast from the family by his brother, Reginald, who was desperate to claim all the family lands and titles for his own, he refused to acknowledge Blake or his mother as part of the family.

The entire situation began when Blake's parents, Robert and Sarah, fell in love. She worked as a maid at the family estate. When Robert confessed his feelings, Sarah tried to convince him he couldn't marry her, but marry her he did, upsetting his parents and brother. When Blake was born three years later, Robert decided he didn't want to raise his child around the hostile environment created by his power-hungry brother and disapproving father. They never forgave him for marrying beneath him, so he brought his little family to America for the opportunity to start fresh.

Six years ago, they received a letter from Robert's ailing father asking for their return home when Reginald died in a hunting accident.

Called back to England, Robert planned to pay one last visit to the old man. His father passed away during their visit, leaving everything to Robert and Sarah. Assuming his titular responsibilities as Earl, Robert invited Blake to return to England. Anytime he wished, Blake knew he could join his parents at their estate outside London and take his rightful title of viscount.

He preferred, however, living a quiet, simple life in America. He'd grown up there and planned to die in Hardman, on the land his father worked so hard to keep during the years when they had nothing except each other.

Walking toward Granger House, Blake wondered what Miss Ginny Granger would say if she knew he had more money than all the Granger family together, not to mention ties to royalty.

He bet even her mother couldn't turn up her snobbish nose at that.

Not even noticing Bart as the dog ran out to greet him, Blake absently patted his head and stormed down the back walk.

Rapping briskly on the kitchen door, he wasn't surprised to see Filly open it with a friendly smile.

"Did you forget something, Blake? You just left a little while ago." She motioned him into the kitchen.

"No, I didn't." He held onto his anger with both hands, refusing to take any of it out on Filly. She was kindness itself and had no ability to control her impetuous, impertinent sister-in-law. "Would Ginny, by chance, be around?"

"She's supposed to be dusting the books in the library, but she's most likely curled up with one in front of the fire." Filly tilted her head toward the hall. "Go right ahead."

"Thank you." After nodding politely, Blake marched down the hall. His boot steps proclaimed his anger every bit as much as the tension in his shoulders and the set of his jaw.

Stepping into the library, he looked around at the walls filled with shelves of books and interesting objects, masculine leather-covered furniture, and a fire popping merrily in the fireplace.

Ginny sat just as Filly predicted, curled into a chair with her feet under her, an open book on her lap and a loose strand of silky golden hair wrapped around her finger. Slightly parted, her pink lips moved as though she read quietly to herself. Her discarded dust rag sat on a corner of Luke's desk, apparently long forgotten by her casual and comfortable pose in the chair.

Transfixed by the picture she made, he shoved down any tender feelings for the beguiling woman and let his indignation have full reign.

"Well, isn't this just a picture of domesticity, little Miss Busybody?" Blake sneered as he walked farther into the room.

"Oh!" Ginny said, startled at his voice near her chair. The book fell to the floor and before Ginny could retrieve it, Blake grabbed it, looking at the title.

"Love poems, is it?"

Ginny blushed to be caught reading such drivel, but with thoughts of Blake consuming her, the slim volume of heartfelt prose captured her interest.

"What are you doing, Blake? Why are you here?" she asked, trying to untangle her legs from her skirt so she could get to her feet.

"Let's just see what you were reading, shall we?" Blake opened the book to where a thin ribbon marked a page. Standing with his legs pressed against the front of Ginny's chair, he made it impossible for her to stand.

Blake snorted in disgust as he read a verse aloud from the book:

Your heart you gave unto my keeping -
No words more fitly spoken,
Than the depths of love poured from your soul,
Contained in one sweet token.

"What would you know of love, Ginny? Hmm? What would you possibly know about love?" Blake asked, tossing the book onto her lap and turning his cold gaze on her in full force.

Shocked beyond the ability to speak, Ginny looked up at him with her mouth half-open, trying to think what would make Blake act so strange, so angry.

That's when she noticed the flyers in his hand. When she reached out to take them, he slapped the stack of paper on the arm of her chair, making a startled whimper escape her lips. He looked, for all the world, like he wished he could have beaten her about the head with them.

"What right do you have to go around town spreading rumors and ordering flyers? What right, Ginny?" Blake demanded, shoving the flyers in her face.

"I... well, I thought..."

"No. You didn't think. As usual, you just rushed headlong into some brilliant idea you dreamed up without stopping to think what you were doing or how it could hurt others." Blake ran a hand over his brown hair and released a sigh. "Thanks to your meddling, half the town now thinks I'm destitute and in need of work. Next thing you know, they'll blame my lack of income on my shoddy craftsmanship."

"Blake, I'm sorry. I didn't mean... I just wanted to help." Close to tears, Ginny's bottom lip quivered. "You do such beautiful work, I just wanted to let everyone know they have a talented carpenter and wood craftsman in their midst."

"Then why did you make it sound like I'm nearly homeless? The way I heard it, you went all around town trying to drum up business so I wouldn't starve this winter. Whether I need the work or not is none of your affair." Incensed, Blake yanked the twine off the flyers and threw them in the air.

As they fluttered down around Ginny, she swiped at the tears now rolling down her cheeks, sticking out her bottom lip in a pout that had charmed many a man, including Blake.

"I'm sorry," she whispered, trying to look contrite.

Blake glared at her with narrowed eyes, his jaw tightly clenched.

Leaning down, he braced his hands on either side of her against the arms of the chair, putting his face just inches away from her own. Jerking her head back, she had nowhere to go, trapped as she was between him and the chair.

When her eyes widened with astonishment and a hint of fear, Blake almost calmed his tone, almost tamped down his anger.

Almost.

Bending close, he could see three different shades of blue in her beautiful eyes, but he hardened his resolve and his heart. He took her proud chin firmly in his hand. "Just suck in that luscious little pout. You are well past the age to behave in such a childish manner, woman. It won't do you a bit of good with me, anyway. Not one little bit. You forget I know you too well."

"You don't know me at all," Ginny tried to protest, but Blake gave her chin a gentle shake.

"Fool yourself all you like, but we both know the truth. You, however, don't know a thing about me. Not a blessed thing. Don't you ever do something like this again. Do you hear me? I don't need your so-called help. I don't need your interference with my work and I most certainly don't need you. Stay out of my business you nosy little ninny!"

Ginny fought against his grasp on her chin so Blake held on a moment longer before standing upright and stalking back down the hall.

Entering the kitchen, he didn't slow his step, tipping his head at Filly and muttering "thank you" as he slammed the door behind him.

Stunned by his behavior, Filly rushed to the library to find Ginny on her knees gathering up the flyers strewn about the floor.

"Ginny?" Filly asked, taking a tentative step toward the girl. "Are you well?"

"No! That horrid man! He's so... he is such... Oh! I think I loathe him entirely!" Ginny slammed the flyers onto Luke's desk and picked up the book of poetry from the floor where it had fallen without her notice. Throwing it down, she stomped on it.

Filly took her hand and led her back to the kitchen, making them both a cup of tea. Sitting at the kitchen table, Ginny wiped at her tears and took a cleansing breath as Filly slid a plate of molasses cookies her direction.

"Want to talk about it?"

"Not particularly."

"Is there anything I can do to help?" Filly asked, taking a sip of her tea, assuming with enough time, Ginny would tell her what happened to upset both her and Blake.

"I don't believe so," Ginny said, toying with a cookie. Taking a deep breath, the words seemed to spill out before she could stop them. "I may have made an effort on Blake's behalf to generate some business and ordered flyers to post around town advertising his woodworking talents. The ungrateful wretch accused me of meddling in his affairs and he… he…"

Ginny dabbed at the tears freely flowing again.

"What, Ginny?" Filly prompted, handing Ginny a fresh handkerchief from her own pocket. "What did he do?"

"He called me a nosy little ninny." Ginny sobbed as she crossed her arms and laid her head on the table.

Trying not to smile, Filly walked around the table and gently rubbed Ginny on the back, offering soothing words. She was still standing there when Luke came in the back door. His words of cheery greeting died on his lips as he took in his distraught sister and somewhat amused wife.

Raising an inquisitive eyebrow at Filly, she mouthed "later" and gave Ginny an encouraging pat on her shoulder, suggesting she go freshen up before dinner.

Filly rushed to get supper on the table and was hurrying to take a casserole from the oven when she felt Luke's arms around her waist, and his breath warm by her ear.

"What disaster has befallen Ginny this time?" Luke asked, knowing the girl was given to theatrics when life didn't go just as she wished.

"Apparently, she took it upon herself to go about town encouraging people to do business with Blake, since he is so nearly destitute, or so the story went that she shared with everyone. She even went so far as to have Mr. Daily print up a stack of flyers to advertise Blake's business. Needless to say, he was furious." Filly tried to keep from smiling as she thought about Blake setting Ginny straight. The girl had not received many reprimands in her lifetime.

"Since when did Blake become nearly destitute?" Luke asked, finding humor in the situation. Of all the people he knew, Blake was the least likely to ever be destitute. He did feel sorry for his friend, though, knowing his sister could be unbelievably annoying. "Remember, I'm his banker."

"I never thought for a moment he was, but apparently Ginny equates his trade with being poor." Filly kissed Luke's cheek as she put biscuits on a plate then set it on the table. "I think the flyers are still on your desk in the library."

"Then I'll be sure to take a look after dinner." He washed his hands and waited for Ginny to reappear so they could eat. When she didn't immediately return, he stared impatiently at the kitchen doorway.

"Ginny! Would you please hurry it up before it's time for breakfast?" he called down the hall, hungry and ready to sit down to his dinner.

"Must you yell like a heathen?" Ginny asked, breezing past him into the kitchen, brooding and clearly out of sorts.

"As a matter of fact, I must." Luke seated Filly and purposely let Ginny seat herself at the table. "After dinner, you'll be spending some time with me in the library."

Ginny and Filly both turned questioning looks his direction, but he just smiled.

Following the meal, Luke took Filly's hand and waited for her to get to her feet before announcing that it would be good for Ginny to clean up after dinner and do the dishes by herself since Filly had a long, tiring day.

She and Filly both started to protest. He gave Ginny an authoritative glare and silenced Filly by playfully swatting her backside as he nudged her out the kitchen door.

Going to the parlor, Luke stoked the fire and sat on the sofa with his wife. She picked up the newspaper and started to read, but before she'd made it through the first page, she found herself seated across Luke's lap while he placed teasing kisses along her neck.

"What if Ginny comes in?" Filly whispered, enjoying Luke's attentive caresses.

"What if she does?" Luke nuzzled her ear, not caring what Ginny thought. "My dear little sister can just stew in the mess she made while she does the dishes."

Irritated with Luke for his high-handed ways, Ginny cleared the table, put away the leftover food and hurriedly washed the dishes, wondering what he wanted to discuss in the library. Dreading further reprimands from him, she felt her stomach tighten with anxiety.

Finished in the kitchen she dried her hands, took a deep breath and prepared to battle her brother.

Stomping down the hall to the parlor, she let out an exasperated sigh to see Luke and Filly involved in a passionate kiss as they sat before the fire.

"Must you two always be pawing at each other so? It is positively indecent. Mother would have apoplexy if she were here," Ginny said, fisting her hands at her hips and glaring at Luke defiantly.

"Must you skulk about?" Luke asked, releasing Filly who quickly jumped to her feet, her face a bright shade of red as she made some excuse about needing to check something upstairs and fleeing from the room. "You forget, you ungrateful little urchin, this is my house, my wife, and I'll kiss her anytime I feel like it, regardless of your thoughts on the matter."

If she hadn't seen his teasing smile, Luke's harsh words would have stung. "Don't be a jealous old hag, Ginny Lou. Can't you just be happy I found the perfect woman for me?"

"I am happy for you, Luke. For you and Filly." Ginny squeezed his arm as they walked down the hall to the library, meaning what she said. "She's everything Dad and Mother claimed her to be and more. Why don't I remember her from our school years, though? She's not that much older than me."

"You were always so involved with your group of friends, I don't think you paid any attention to the other children." Luke hoped his answer satisfied his sister. The last thing he wanted was for her to know Filly's father, the town drunk, imprisoned her on his farm when she was fourteen. Two years ago, Luke went out to the farm to collect payment on a loan and ended up accepting Filly in a crazy scheme her father made to cancel his debt.

She was the best bargain he'd ever made.

Although his parents knew the truth, very few people in town connected lovely Filly Granger with drunken Alford Booth. Luke planned to keep it that way. Other than his assistant, Arlan, the sheriff and his deputy, Chauncy and Abby Dodd, George and Aleta Bruner, and Blake Stratton, the rest of the residents of Hardman had no idea about Filly's background.

Most everyone agreed Luke had a beautiful, kind-hearted wife who loved him to distraction, regardless of how she came to be at Granger House.

If Ginny found out the truth, Luke worried what she'd do with it or how she'd treat Filly. He hoped she'd matured enough she wouldn't judge his wife, but something whispered that Ginny hadn't quite grown up that much, yet.

The proof of that sat in a stack of flyers on his desk. Picking up the papers, Luke read the advertisement, admitting that it merely stated the many things Blake was capable of creating without making it sound like he was destitute in any way. It did leave a person thinking he was looking for work, though.

Straightening the stack, he replaced it on his desk and motioned for Ginny to take a seat. Settling herself in a chair across the large desk from Luke, she wished he'd get to the point of her summons to the library. Her foot bumped against something and she bent to pick up the book of poetry she'd thrown earlier. Stuffing it down in the chair beside her so Luke wouldn't notice it, she gave him her full attention.

"I see you've been busy arranging things that aren't necessarily of your concern," Luke said, looking pointedly at the flyers.

"Well... I..."

"Now would be a good time to sit quietly, Ginny."

Luke didn't raise his head, instead picking up a pen and a sheaf of paper. He started writing rapidly while asking Ginny questions about things she'd done in the past few years, what types of activities she enjoyed, beyond shopping and interfering in other people's lives, and what skills she possessed in addition to pouting and charming men.

Irritated with her brother and his insulting comments, she knew making him further annoyed wasn't going to help things and wisely kept her thoughts to herself.

"What are you doing, Luke?" Ginny asked, sitting forward as Luke pulled out another clean sheet of paper and began writing again. She could see the first piece of paper appeared to be a list of some sort.

"According to what you just shared, your skills include furthering the suffragette movement, writing letters of complaint to political figures and government officials, embroidery, painting landscape scenes, playing the piano, and fashion. You obviously have some skill in creating advertisements, spinning tales, and the ability to spread news." Luke leaned back in his chair and grinned at his sister. "Unless you plan to play the piano at the saloon, become a fixture in front of the sheriff's house, or terrorize Abby's customers with fashion critiques, I would advise you to apply for a job with Mr. Daily."

Ginny's jaw dropped and she stared at her brother as if he spoke in some unknown tongue.

"Are you serious, Luke?" she asked then decided he was teasing. "Is this one of the times when you infuriate me and then I figure out you're only being ornery?"

"No." Quiet filled the room. The only sound Ginny heard was the rustle of her skirts as she shifted nervously in her chair. Luke broke the stillness by drumming his fingers on his desk.

"But, Luke…"

"Before you go from indignant to hysterical, just hear me out." His icy blue stare pinned her to her seat. "You obviously have way too much time on your hands. You have little interest and even less aptitude for learning any domestic arts. I know for a fact you aren't doing anything around here despite the fact my wife continually makes excuses for you. You're too temperamental to work with the public and there aren't any suffrage committees around

Hardman for you to spearhead. Mr. Daily needs a part-time reporter and I think, with your education and experiences, you'd do a good job."

Luke watched her gaze flit from her lap to the fire crackling in the fireplace across the room. Seeing her lip begin to protrude in a pout, he lost his temper. "Dang it, Ginny, you need to do something useful. Filling your day with idle chatter, stirring up trouble for our friends, and lazing away entire afternoons by the fire isn't acceptable. It's your choice if you want to remain single and 'unfettered,' as you call it, but it's long past time for you to take responsibility for yourself and stop acting like a child."

"That is ridiculous. I do take responsibility for myself," Ginny said defensively, raising her chin slightly.

"Really?" Luke tried not to laugh at the serious expression on her face. "Is that what you call receiving a monthly allowance from Dad? It's more than most men around here earn in a year. What do you do with that money, Ginny? Hmm? I'll tell you. You squander it on clothes and frippery, and useless pursuits. If you want to be your own person, shape your own future, you really need to stand on your own two feet."

Shocked by Luke's words, Ginny didn't know what to say. Beyond the point of tears, she was angry. Still miffed from her confrontation with Blake, she wanted to know what gave Luke the right to speak to her so. Even if he was her brother, even if what he said was true, she didn't appreciate his lecture.

"Knowing you, you're sitting there mad at me and thinking about your options of leaving and going somewhere else. Before you make any rash decisions, please consider the fact that you are welcome to stay here with Filly and I as long as you like. You've been given an opportunity to stretch and grow as a person without Mother or Dad here to shelter you. I'd like to see you take advantage of it and use it to your benefit. You're smart, Ginny Lou, sometimes too smart for your own good. Don't waste your intelligence by flitting your life away. Do something meaningful with it, something worthwhile."

"What do you suggest, then?" Ginny asked, refusing to raise her gaze from her lap to her brother's face, somewhat mollified by Luke telling her she was smart.

"I suggest you think about what I said. If you are agreeable, we can discuss a plan in the morning over breakfast." Luke rose to his feet and walked her back to the parlor where Filly set down a tray with tea and slices of gingerbread cake.

"Be the person God intended you to be, Ginny," Luke said and kissed the top of her head before crossing the room and taking a seat next to his wife.

Chapter Five

Infuriated by Ginny Granger and her intrusive behavior, Blake stalked away from Granger House and marched through town, oblivious to the world around him.

It was almost dark when he stomped up the steps to his house and threw open the door. As he jerked off his coat and hat, he realized his horse was still in a stall in Luke's barn. Luke insisted he leave the horse in the barn while he worked at their house, since he was there for the entire day.

There was no earthly way he was walking back to get Samson at this hour.

Not only was it dark and cold outside, he'd rather crawl back to town on his hand and knees than spend one more minute with that spiteful, meddling woman.

Thinking again of how alluring she looked sitting in the big chair by the fire with her feet curled under her and the glow from the flames highlighting her hair, Blake marched to the sink and splashed cold water on his face.

She was like some incurable disease, worming her way under his skin. It was bad enough she tormented him during his waking hours with her tempting smile and captivating fragrance, but at night she haunted his dreams. The sound of her voice, the feel of that wild, curly hair between his fingers, her silky skin, and enchanting blue eyes filled every moment of his slumber.

He thought he'd finally conquered his longing for her. It took years for the gaping wound in his heart to heal, for thoughts of her to bring something besides acute, intense pain. Just when he finally felt free, she had to go and fall at his feet off the stage.

Recalling the look on her face as the driver tossed her bag and knocked her into the mud made him chuckle. Someone needed to knock her on her bustle every so often. She was entirely too full of herself.

What kind of lunatic would want to spend a lifetime saddled with a woman incapable of minding her own business? One so selfish and frivolous? She was maddening, at the very least.

Ginny rarely thought about how her actions would affect others, blindly plunging ahead and doing whatever she pleased.

Refusing to acknowledge she may have only been trying to help him, he fought down any softening of his anger toward her. The woman needed the wind knocked from her sails. She needed to discover she didn't know everything. She needed to realize she could be wrong.

What she really needed was a strong man to take her in hand. A man to hold her, kiss her, and love her until she forgot about everything else.

The direction of his wayward thoughts made him groan.

Blake fried ham and eggs for dinner, sitting at his table trying to think of anything but the fair-haired woman who breezed into town and turned his world upside down.

Washing his few dishes and putting them away, he lit a lantern and went out to tend to his stock. When his father returned to England, he left behind his horses. Although Blake sold several, he kept the best horses for breeding of future stock.

A large dark head bumped his shoulder over the door of a stall, almost knocking him off balance.

"Romeo, you brute, I'll thank you not to tip me over," Blake admonished the big stallion as the animal bobbed his head, looking like he was laughing. Filling the horse's water bucket and tossing hay into the feed bunk, he took a minute to rub the horse's massive neck and scratch behind his ears.

"Why must women, that woman in particular, be so taxing and exasperating?"

The horse shook his mane and made a sound Blake took as agreement.

"You don't have any problems with females, do you boy? Nope. You show up, have a good time, then come back here to a life of leisure." Blake grinned as he rubbed Romeo's nose. "Be glad you are a horse and not a human."

Finishing his chores, Blake returned to the house and decided to write a letter to his parents. He tried to keep it light and interesting, but found himself writing of Ginny coming back to town and her having the newspaper office print flyers without asking him.

Sitting back in his chair, he thought of the look on Ginny's face when he leaned close and called her a nosy ninny. Her eyes begged him for a kiss every bit as much as that rosy mouth of hers.

He wondered if she was more frightened at the prospect of him actually taking liberties with her lips than she was by his anger.

After the way he spoke to her, he supposed it would be a while before she'd talk to him, let alone stick her nose in where it didn't belong.

He'd ignore her altogether, but it would be difficult since he had at least another day of work at Granger House.

Finishing his letter, he addressed an envelope then sealed it inside. Knowing he was too wound up to sleep, he went to his workshop and took out a project he was working on for Chauncy. The pastor asked him to build new pews for the church before Christmas, and those he would have done in plenty of time.

The piece before him would be a new lectern for the pastor. The man had no idea Blake was making it, which was part of the fun. Blake planned to deliver it to the church in time for the Christmas Eve service.

The scene he was carefully carving depicted a star dancing above a flock of sheep, watched over by shepherds. In the background would be a barn with a barely visible manger in an open door.

Smiling as he carved the head of a lamb, Blake hoped the pastor would like his gift. He knew the precious gift of the babe in a manger was one of Chauncy's favorite talking points during his sermons.

Blake thought of that babe, so innocent and small, yet destined for great things — things beyond the human mind's ability to comprehend fully.

Thinking of Joseph and Mary, a lowly carpenter and his wife, Blake pondered the heart of Joseph. His thoughts eventually brought him back around to Ginny and he felt a stab of guilt about speaking so harshly to her.

Convicted by his temper, he realized he probably should apologize, even if the woman sorely tested his patience and drove him to distraction.

Walking into town before the sun fully filled the morning sky, Blake waved at Chauncy as he hurried from the church toward the parsonage.

"Morning, Blake. What brings you out so early today?" Chauncy called as he stopped by the parsonage front walk.

"I forgot my horse at Luke's place. I want to take him to the livery for his morning feed before he feels like I've completely abandoned him."

Chauncy was aware Blake made some repairs at Granger House. Luke wanted the flooring and paneling to exactly match, so it was taking him time to make sure each piece looked perfect, but those were the types of projects he enjoyed the most. There was nothing like a challenge to pique his interest and stoke his creativity.

Chauncy laughed at him, reaching out to slap his back. "Come in and have breakfast before you go over. Abby always makes plenty and I know Erin will be thrilled to see you."

"I don't want to impose." Blake took a step away from the pastor, looking down the street in the direction of Granger House.

"You're not imposing if I insist." Chauncy threw an arm around Blake's shoulders, turning him toward the front door. "I think Abby was making pancakes this morning."

After eating his fill of Abby's hearty breakfast, he visited with Chauncy and bounced Erin on his knee while enjoying a second cup of coffee.

He set Erin on her feet, thanked Abby for the meal, and stood, putting on his coat and picking up his hat.

"Me go wif Unca Bake." Erin tugged on the hem of his coat and gazed up at him with big blue eyes in her cherubic little face. Her smile revealed pearly little teeth. The emphatic nod of her head as she talked set her dark curls bobbing. "Pease? Me go wif Unca Bake."

Blake looked from Chauncy to Abby who stood shaking their heads. "It's cold outside this morning, honey. You better stay inside with your mama where it's warm," he said hunkering down and holding one of the little girl's tiny hands in his own.

"I gots a coat," Erin said and ran to the door, pointing to her coat and scarf.

"Erin, you let Blake be on his way. He has work to do today and doesn't have time for you to be underfoot," Chauncy said, walking toward the child.

Blake took in her moist eyes and pouty lip, trembling with unshed tears. His heart turned to mush.

"Tell you what, Miss Erin, if your mama and daddy don't mind, you can go with me to get Samson. I need to take him to Mr. Douglas at the livery and get him some breakfast then I can bring you home. How would that be?" Blake asked, hoping Chauncy and Abby wouldn't mind him taking Erin out for a few minutes.

"Pease, Daddy. Pease? Me go wif Unca Bake!" Erin begged. When Chauncy took down her coat and held it for her, she squealed with glee. Abby wrapped the scarf around her little head and neck then secured her mittens in place before giving Blake a look that said he still had time to back out. He nodded his head and smiled down at the charming child.

"Shall we go?"

"Yep! Tank you, Daddy." Enthusiastically hugging her father's leg, Erin held her arms up to Blake.

He swung her into his arms and tipped his hat at Abby before opening the door and strolling down the walk, toward the edge of town.

Erin kept up a lively chatter as he walked and they stopped to look at two birds sitting on a tree limb then studied the way the sun melted frost from the boardwalk.

As they approached Granger House, Blake waved at Luke when he strode out of the barn.

"What are you doing with Blake, sweet girl?" Luke asked as Erin leaned over for him to take her.

He tossed her gently in the air and kissed her cheek.

"Hi, Unca Wuke! Unca Bake an me feed him horsey." Erin hugged Luke around the neck.

"I already fed ol' Samson, so why don't you two come to the house. Have you eaten, Blake?" Luke asked, tickling Erin as they walked toward the kitchen door.

Both men smiled at the little girl's giggles as she tried to wiggle away from Luke's fingers.

"I ate breakfast with Abby and Chauncy. Miss Erin wanted some fresh air and decided she would help me take Samson to the livery for his breakfast. I apologize for leaving him here last night. I didn't even realize what I'd done until I arrived home," Blake said, chagrined by the admission. "May I pay you for the feed?"

Laughing, Luke slapped him on the back good-naturedly. "Absolutely not. I feel like I should apologize for Ginny. She means well, I think, but that girl... I've given her some things to think about and starting today, I hope she plans to turn her excess energies toward more fruitful endeavors."

"Thank you, Luke. No apology necessary on your part." Blake stamped his feet and wiped them before stepping into Filly's clean kitchen. "I should probably offer mine to your sister, though. Between raising my voice and losing my temper yesterday, she probably thinks the worst of me."

"Let her simmer for a while. She could stand to learn a lesson or two." Luke grinned as he divested Erin of her scarf, mittens and coat. "Now, young lady, let's go see if we can find your Aunt Filly."

Before Luke could grab her hand, Erin took off running toward the front of the house calling for "Aunt Fiwwy!"

Luke shook his head and hung his outerwear by the door. "Will you be able to finish the woodwork this week?" Following Blake down the hall and up the back stairs, the men stood looking at the progress he'd made in replacing the ruined wood.

"If I don't finish today, I will definitely complete the project tomorrow." Blake set his hat and coat on a chair and picked up a piece of smooth wood. "At least I should as long as I don't have any further distractions."

"I don't think you'll have to worry about Ginny today, but Erin might be another story. I'll take her home on my way to the bank," Luke said, admiring the fine quality of Blake's work.

"I'd be happy to run her home. I certainly didn't mean to interrupt your morning or Filly's, for that matter." Blake started toward the stairs. Luke waved him back to the room.

"We don't mind having her here, not at all. We'll make sure she gets back home. Eventually." Luke clomped down the stairs. Blake heard Erin's giggles and smiled as he returned to his work.

Concentrating on his efforts to finish the project, he heard pattering steps and looked up to see Erin run in the room. Before she could grab a sharp tool or trip on a piece of wood, he scooped her up and kissed her rosy cheek.

"Did you come up by yourself?" he asked, smiling at the lively child.

"No. Ginny comed." Erin bounced in his arms.

Blake noticed Ginny standing in the doorway watching him, looking lovely as always. The pale blue suit she wore featured dark gray trim and accented the blue depths of her eyes.

"Miss Granger." He tipped his head her direction although he kept his face blank of emotion. Recalling the turmoil she created the previous afternoon made it easier to keep from uttering a word of apology for his outburst in the library.

"Mr. Stratton." She cast a frosty glare his direction. "My brother has requested I offer you a sincere word of regret for my misguided attempts at providing unsolicited assistance to your business enterprises."

Blake couldn't stop a grin from lifting the corners of his mouth. Stepping nearer to Ginny, he stood looking down at the pile of golden curls on her head and inhaled her light floral fragrance. "If that is your pathetic and quite artificial attempt at an apology, I suppose I shall have to accept. Is that really the best you can do?"

"Humph!" Ginny held her hands at her sides to keep from slapping the smirk right off Blake's face. How the man frustrated her! He left her annoyed and unsettled and... so wanting of his kiss yesterday. The feeling was just as strong now. Even more so as she watched the loving way he interacted with the little girl held in his arms. "Say your goodbye to Mr. Stratton, Erin. We need to get you back home."

The little girl frowned at Ginny before wrapping her chubby little arms around Blake's neck and delivering a sloppy kiss to his chin. "Bye, Unca Bake. Feed horsey morrow?"

"Another day, honey. We'll feed Samson another day. Okay?" Blake ran a gentle hand over her head of dark curls before kissing her cheek. "You go along with Miss Ginny now."

"Bye, Unca Bake!" Erin waved again as Ginny took her other hand and led her toward the stairs. He could hear the little girl chattering as they went. When Erin asked Ginny if she would kiss Blake, he heard, "Good heavens!" float into the room, making him chuckle.

He had no doubt Ginny needed a kiss.

Not just any kiss, though. One delivered by a man who loved her completely. A man who would give her his whole heart. A man who stirred her passion and captured her soul.

Blake wasn't sure how long it would take to convince himself he was the man for the job.

Chapter Six

As they stepped out into the chilly morning air, Luke carried Erin while Ginny strolled beside him, oblivious to the child's chatter as they walked toward the parsonage.

Her thoughts lingered on the man working in the upstairs bedroom at her brother's house. The sight of him holding Erin so tenderly did the most peculiar things to her heart.

A vision of a golden-haired child with an abundance of unruly curls and his soulful hazel eyes made the breath catch in her throat. Wanting to run from the room and far away from Hardman, the threat Blake represented to her plans and freedom made him far more dangerous to her than Nigel Pickford.

Nigel was a weak man she despised and looked at as an annoying bother.

Blake, however, was someone who held her admiration and respect, as well as her heart.

The realization of that fact caused her to trip on the boardwalk. Luke's quick hand to her arm was all that kept her from going to her knees. Her fingers crept to her pocket and ran over the little wooden token she'd placed there. She knew it was silly, but the heartfelt gift from Blake meant more to her than all the expensive belongings she possessed.

"Careful, Ginny, the sun hasn't melted all the frost yet this morning and the boardwalk can be slick." Luke studied his sister with a thoughtful expression as they neared the parsonage. "Are you well?"

"Yes, I'm fine. Just fine." Dismissively, she waved her hand at Luke as he opened the parsonage's back door and handed Erin to her mother. Abby invited them in for a cup of tea, but Luke refused, saying they had some business to attend to before he went to the bank.

"Are you sure you feel well, Ginny? Your face is pale." Concern made Luke remove a glove and press his palm to her forehead. She batted his hand away and kept walking. "I'm fine, Luke, but thank you for your concern."

"If you're sure, let's go see if you can dazzle Mr. Daily into a job," Luke teased as they neared the newspaper office and went inside.

Twenty minutes later, Ginny found herself gainfully employed on a part-time basis, starting that afternoon.

"Congratulations, Ginny Lou. You are officially on your way to being a fully independent woman." Luke smiled broadly as they walked to the bank. His big hand rested comfortingly on her shoulder.

Pleased that Luke didn't say a word while she spoke with Mr. Daily, she squeezed his arm and looked up at him with a happy expression, grateful for his support. From her experience, she knew most men thought women belonged at home, cooking, cleaning, and rearing children.

Her brother had always encouraged her to follow her dreams, be her own person, and think for herself.

Stopping suddenly, she looked at him. "Luke, thank you."

"For what?" Unaccustomed to Ginny expressing true gratitude, he could see the sincerity written across her face.

"I appreciate you encouraging me, albeit in a rather overbearing way, to pursue something worthwhile. Most men would condemn me to marriage and domesticity.

You've never once suggested that is what I should do with my life." Impulsively, she hugged her brother. "Thank you for that."

"You're welcome. You can ask Filly if you don't believe me, but I think everyone should have the opportunity to pursue their dreams, whatever they may be." Luke grinned wickedly as he looked down at her with twinkling eyes. "Besides, no man deserves to be sentenced to eating your cooking on a daily basis."

"You are every bit as horrid as you were as a boy. Now go to work, banker man. I'm going home to share my good news with your wife."

"I'm proud of you, Ginny," Luke said as he stepped into the bank.

Ginny brushed at the tears his words generated and hurried her step to Granger House, excited to tell Filly about her new job.

"Miss Granger, could you please come here a moment?" Ed Daily called as he sat at his desk, editing Ginny's latest article. With the Thanksgiving holiday approaching, she'd written a nice piece about the service planned at the church and the community potluck slated afterward.

Worried she'd have little talent for writing, Ed gave her a job because Luke asked him to take a chance on the girl. Surprisingly, she had a way with words, a quick mind, and produced whatever story he asked of her. She refused to learn to use the press, though, and often submitted articles he did not request.

However, both her writing and her discernment about what was appropriate subject matter for his newspaper were improving.

She'd been working for him about a week when she slid an article on his desk about Melanie LaRoux running off with some flimflam salesman passing through town.

While Ed thought the spiteful and cruel Miss LaRoux, a girl Luke courted until he married Filly, certainly deserved to have her latest turn of bad judgment plastered across his front page, he stayed far away from that type of news.

After explaining to Miss Granger why her article was completely unacceptable, she rewrote it in such a way that it conveyed the news without pointing fingers.

Although she would sigh and complain if he asked her to rewrite something, she did seem eager to learn and willing to keep working at a story until he was satisfied with the results.

"Yes, Mr. Daily?" Ginny asked, stepping into his office. She wondered what she'd done wrong now, because that seemed to be the only time Mr. Daily summoned her to his office. Learning more than she ever hoped to about writing and the newspaper business, she'd have told him weeks ago what she thought of his brusque manner except she enjoyed her work.

"I want to speak with you about your Thanksgiving article." Ed looked at her over the rim of his spectacles, maintaining a gruff expression.

"Yes? Did I misrepresent something? Leave out an important detail?" Ginny held out her hand to take back the copy and rewrite it.

Ed laid his hand over the article and leaned back in his chair. The smallest of smiles started forming at the corner of his mouth and he quirked a bushy gray eyebrow Ginny's direction. "Actually, you did everything perfectly. I wanted to commend you on a job well done."

"Oh." Caught off guard by the praise from her meticulous employer, she didn't know what to say. He'd picked apart every article she'd written. To hear a word of praise took her by surprise. Unable to respond immediately, she finally found her voice. "Thank you, sir. I appreciate that very much."

Ed nodded then cleared his throat.

"Don't let it go to your head, young lady," Ed admonished, then pointed his pencil at her. "I've got a new assignment for you."

"What exciting news will I be covering now? Did Mrs. Jenkins find out who made her a new rolling pin and left it in her henhouse, or maybe Mrs. Ferguson discovered who left the new cutting board on her back step?" Ginny fought the urge to smile, thinking about the strange stories some of the locals concocted. Imagine, thinking some mysterious person was going around leaving gifts for people.

"Actually, I want you to interview Blake Stratton. He's making new pews for the Christian Church and I'd like you to write an article detailing his work. I'll expect it to be on my desk the day after tomorrow." Ed dropped his gaze to his desk, shuffled some papers and motioned toward the door, indicating it was time for Ginny to leave.

"Yes, sir," she said, turning around so he wouldn't see her roll her eyes. The last person she wanted to interview was Blake. Since the day he'd brought Erin with him to the house, she hadn't spoken to him. At church, he somehow managed to escape before most of the congregation could get out of their seats. Other than catching a glimpse of him here and there about town, she managed to avoid him.

Apparently, he was ignoring her as well, since he'd refused the invitations Luke and Filly extended to him for dinner on numerous occasions. Insisting he join them for Thanksgiving Day, Ginny wondered how they'd pretend the other didn't exist when they would no doubt be seated in close proximity at the dinner table.

Instead of dreading it, Ginny decided to get the interview over with as soon as possible. She put on her hat and coat, wrapped her scarf, the same rich shade of blue as her eyes, around her neck, and tugged on her gloves. Picking up her reticule, a notepad and a pencil, she took a deep breath and sailed out the door.

Blake lived just a few miles out of town and since the sun was shining, she didn't mind the chilly bite in the air as she strolled in the direction of his place. She could have borrowed a horse from Luke or asked him to hitch up the buggy for her, but she was a little afraid of horses and much preferred to walk.

Breathing deeply, she inhaled the last lingering scents of fall floating on the afternoon breeze. Soon it would snow and jaunts on foot out of town would become impossible.

Approaching the Stratton place, Ginny watched smoke puff from the chimney in the house as well as what had to be Blake's workshop. Veering away from the house, she rapped on the door of the workshop and heard Blake's voice rumble for her to enter.

Gently pushing the door open, she gasped at the tools and furniture filling the large space.

Ornately carved chairs, unique side tables, a beautiful bedroom set and seven church pews sat finished on one side of the building. A large workbench ran along one wall and another pew sat in an open area where Blake sanded down a corner to make it smooth for the many hands that would run over it in the coming years. Although simple, the benches were sturdy and solid, made of beautiful oak wood.

"Blake, how wonderful!" Ginny exclaimed, stepping over to examine some of the chairs and tables. A rocking chair, quite similar in coloring to Filly's head of lovely curls, captured her attention and she couldn't keep from reaching out and running her fingers over the wood.

Delicately carved roses and vines highlighted the wood along the back and decorative rings ornamented the spindles along the sides.

"May I?" Ginny asked, looking at Blake for permission to sit in the chair. At his nod, she carefully sat on the seat, scooting back and relaxing with the smooth rocking motion.

Several moments of quiet lingered while she rocked and Blake continued to sand the corner of the pew.

When he finally looked her direction, she'd removed her coat and hat, looking so beautiful and excessively comfortable in his workshop. He'd missed being near her, even if she did infuriate and invigorate him beyond reason.

Unobtrusively glancing at her, he noticed her rosy cheeks, flushed from the cold air. Her pink lips practically begged for a kiss. He wondered if they'd taste as sweet as they looked.

As teens, he'd brushed her lips a time or two, but nothing he'd consider a real kiss. Even the goodbye kiss they shared a decade ago had been an innocent kiss from a boy experiencing his first love for a naive young girl.

Suddenly overwhelmed with the desire to sample her lips, he set down his sandpaper, brushed off his hands, and walked over to where she sat looking around at his many projects.

A shipment was ready to send to his parents, and he was more than halfway finished with the church pews. Most of the orders he had from locals wanting to surprise loved ones with Christmas gifts sat finished, ready to deliver.

Although she didn't know it, the chair she occupied would be delivered to Granger House as a gift to Filly from Luke. Ginny hadn't noticed it yet, but the back of the chair had one heart in the center with Luke and Filly's initials intertwined through it.

Because they were such good friends, he'd labored excessively over getting every detail perfect.

"Like that chair?" Blake asked, hunkering down near Ginny, rubbing his hand over the cool wood of the arm. His fingers stopped mere inches away from where Ginny's fingers rested.

"As a matter of fact, I do." She smiled at him with an odd light in her eyes. "I knew you had talent, Blake, but this is amazing. You are indeed a uniquely talented craftsman. If you moved to a large city, you could become famous."

"I've no desire to move to a large city or become famous." He shook his head. If Ginny knew who he really was, she'd also know his furniture was somewhat famous and coveted, at least in London and the surrounding areas. He stamped his pieces with the head of a fox and lettering that read "Roxbury House," as a tribute to his father's family. Many people were acquainted with the name and style of his work, even if the creator behind the pieces remained anonymous. That's how Blake intended to keep it.

Between the warmth of the room and Ginny's soft floral fragrance floating around him, Blake began to forget all the reasons he needed to stay away from her.

Moving to push himself upright, the chair rocked forward placing Ginny's lips just a breath from his own for the longest second of Blake's life.

Unable to stand the wanting, the longing, to taste her lips, Blake leaned down and gripped her arms in his hands, pulling her out of the chair and against him.

A little gasp escaped her lips as she stared at him with wide blue eyes. Gazing into the beautiful pools, he saw something flicker there, something that looked unmistakably like desire.

"Genevieve," he said in a raspy whisper, brushing his work-roughened hand across her cheek, absorbing the feel of her satiny-smooth skin.

Bending his head, he pressed his lips, moist and warm, to her neck. Shivers wracked through her in response as she leaned against him and he drew her closer to his chest. As he kissed his way along her jaw, he thought he heard a quiet moan and couldn't decide if it came from her or him.

He gazed once more into her eyes. Her lashes fluttered against her cheeks appealingly and he gave in to the need to lay claim to her mouth, pressing his lips to hers lightly at first. When her lips moved beneath his, he deepened the kiss and felt consumed by a raging flame, beginning from where his mouth caressed hers to the top of his head and all the way down to his toes.

As he rubbed fingers along her back, her hands slid up his arms and wrapped around the back of his neck, pulling him nearer.

Blake realized he'd done a good job of kidding himself the last ten years, convincing his mind and heart he was over this girl, that he no longer wanted or needed her in his life.

One taste of those divinely sweet lips just proved otherwise. Now that he'd savored a sip of her wonderful nectar, he knew he'd never be satisfied until he could drink of it freely, frequently.

Without a doubt, Blake wanted Ginny. Needed her. Loved her.

His concern was that she wouldn't ever feel the same. How could she when she never wrote him a single letter and sent his all back unopened?

Aware of his need to calm his fevered brain, Blake instead lost himself in the extraordinary sensations stirring from his midsection. He met Ginny's seeking lips with another ardent kiss.

As she pressed against him, pressed into him, all ability to think rationally fled.

"Genevieve." His husky voice further addled her thoughts while he delivered rapturous kisses along her jaw before returning his attention to her mouth.

Picking her up in his arms, he kept his lips locked on hers as he started toward the door, not even aware of what he was doing.

"Blake, stop." Ginny wriggled in his embrace. "Please, stop."

When he looked down at her with a confused glance, Ginny kissed his chin and pushed against him until he set her on her feet.

"What's wrong? I was under the distinct impression you weren't averse to my attentions," Blake said, dropping his hands and taking a step back, away from temptation.

"I'm not... I wasn't..." Ginny said, flustered. One moment she'd been sitting in the wonderful rocking chair admiring Blake's handiwork and the next she was being kissed more thoroughly and passionately than she'd ever dreamed possible.

Entranced by the fervent interlude, she didn't want to think about anything except how right it felt to be held in Blake's strong arms. His masculine scent teased her senses every bit as much as his mouth teased her lips.

When he swept her into his embrace, Ginny didn't think she'd ever felt so secure, so cherished, so loved.

Oblivious to anything but the man she loved and the way he made her feel, when Blake bent to open the door to the workshop she realized things could quickly get out of hand. Although part of her wanted him to keep right on kissing her, another part knew they had to stop.

As he stepped away from her, she felt chilled and so oddly alone. Looking at her hesitantly when she reached a hand out to him, he finally captured it between both of his.

"Blake, I most certainly was enjoying your attentions but I was concerned things were about to get... that is, to say..." Ginny searched for the right words and found herself at a loss. The tantalizing pattern Blake's finger traced across her palm made her thoughts scatter again while her jellied knees threatened to give way beneath her.

"It's okay, love." Blake pulled her to his chest and kissed her cheek, giving her a grin that was all male flirtation. "You're correct, of course. Had you not put a stop to my amorous intentions, we'd be in the house and I'd be ravaging more than just those scrumptious lips of yours."

Although his words pleased rather than shocked her, she felt obliged to smack his arm and give him a disapproving stare. "Mr. Stratton, that is no way for a gentleman to speak, think, or behave."

"No, ma'am, it isn't, but no one ever said you're dealing with a gentleman."

Before she could reply, Blake spun her around and wrapped his arms around her, engulfing her from behind while he placed wet, sloppy kisses all over both sides of her neck, making her squeal with laughter.

Stopping so she could catch her breath, Ginny looked at him over her shoulder. "I stand corrected. You, sir, are not a gentleman. Not in the least."

"I'm positively thrilled we've got that straightened out. I wouldn't want you to hold any mistaken beliefs about my character." Blake swept her back in his arms and kissed her as he spun around a few times.

Dizzy, both from his kisses and his playful antics, Ginny clung to him when he finally set her back on her unsteady feet.

Holding onto her arms until he could see she'd regained her balance, Blake led Ginny to a chair then hunkered down beside her.

"Now, I know for a fact you didn't come out here just to test my ability to keep my lips to myself, although you've sorely needed my attentions for a while," Blake teased, unable to keep from touching her. He ran a finger along the fine line of her jaw and trailed it across her puffy, pink lips. Taking a deep breath, he inhaled her soft fragrance, letting it soak into his soul.

Distracted by Blake's attention, Ginny searched her scrambled thoughts to recall why she did need, in fact, to see Blake. Recalling Mr. Daily's request for an article about the new church pews, Ginny attempted to return her focus to her job.

"Mr. Daily asked me to write an article about the new church pews you're making," she said, waving a hand to the finished pews lined up against one wall.

"So it wasn't my charming personality or dashing good looks that brought you out here today?" Blake asked, his tone teasing although he had hoped something more personal than a story for the newspaper prompted her visit.

"No." Ginny rose to her feet and retrieved her notepad and pencil from the rocking chair where she'd dropped them. "If you don't mind, I'd like to ask a few questions."

"Go ahead." He motioned to a set of chairs and a small table. With his thoughts entangled in the passionate kisses they'd just shared, he struggled to remember his full name, let alone any other pertinent details.

How could Ginny sit all prim and proper, acting for all the world like his kisses meant nothing to her? Like they hadn't left her heart pounding, her head swimming, and an unquenchable desire stirring inside her?

Answering her questions, he showed her the pews while she began drawing a simple sketch. His patience stretched thinner and thinner with each passing minute.

She talked to him as though he was a perfect stranger instead of the man who'd come unbelievably close to carrying her off to some amorous interlude just a few minutes ago. Consumed with her, he still wanted her, still desperately wanted to drink repeatedly from those wonderfully sweet lips.

All business, she maintained her cool façade while firing off questions, taking notes, and drawing a sketch of the pews.

Irritated tremendously, Blake, who rarely lost his temper, wanted to ram his fist through something. Her detached, calm demeanor would push him beyond the edge of reason in short order.

Finishing her sketch, she began gathering her things. He held her coat while she slipped it on and her fragrance ensnared his senses once more. Incapable of stopping himself, his fingers brushed lightly across the skin of her neck before she wrapped a scarf around her throat and pinned her hat in place.

Yanking on her gloves, she bid him good day and hurried toward the entrance to his workshop.

"I'll see you home," Blake said, taking her arm and pulling her to a stop before she opened the door.

"I'm perfectly capable of seeing myself home." Ginny couldn't make eye contact with Blake. If she did, the urge to kiss him again might completely overtake her. Her longing to be with him was irrational and unacceptable.

"No one said you weren't capable. However, it's getting late so I'll see you home." Blake tugged on his coat and slapped his hat on his head. "Wait here while I hitch the wagon."

Annoyed, she glared at the door he closed in her face and waited just long enough for him to enter the barn before she jerked it open and took off in the direction of town at a brisk pace. She couldn't trust herself to spend five more minutes with Blake let alone a trip to town. For self-preservation, she had to leave as quickly as possible.

"Ginny, you get back here!" Blake yelled as he glanced out the barn door and witnessed her hasty retreat in the direction of the road.

Picking up her skirts with both hands, she broke into a most unladylike run. She hadn't gone far when a stitch in her side made her stop and bend over in an attempt to suck air into her deprived lungs. The thundering of hooves behind her let her know Blake approached.

"You are the most intractable female I've ever encountered, Miss Granger." Blake glared down at her from the back of his big stallion, Romeo. Already infuriated by her obvious disinterest in him or exchanging more kisses, her running off fanned the sparks of his already kindled anger. "Since you won't wait while I hitch the wagon, you can just ride with me."

"No thank you, Mr. Stratton. I appreciate the offer, but I must respectfully decline." Ginny struggled to stand upright, and pressed a hand to her side as she began walking in the direction of Hardman. "Have a lovely evening."

Blake took off his hat and ran his hand over his head while drawing in a few calming breaths. What he really wanted to do was paddle Ginny's backside. He had a notion she'd received all too few spankings in her lifetime. Slapping his hat back on his head, he urged Romeo forward.

Walking as fast as she could with the stitch in her side, Ginny had gone about twenty feet when she felt hands grasp her upper arms and pull her onto the horse.

"My stars! I've never been manhandled like this in my entire life. I insist..." Ginny spluttered, struggling against Blake's strong arms.

"Maybe it's about time you were, then." Blake pressed his mouth to hers, effectively silencing her. He kissed her without a hint of softness yet she returned his ardor and pressed closer to him.

Realization finally penetrated the fog in her head and she pulled back. She would have slapped the devilish grin off his handsome face if she hadn't been afraid of falling off the horse. Perched across Blake's legs, safe in his arms, she didn't want to take any chances. Clinging to him with a death grip on the front of his coat, she closed her eyes and tried not to panic.

"I won't let you fall," he said quietly, noticing her discomfort when he finally lifted his eyes from her just-kissed lips.

"I didn't assume you would." Her eyes connected with his probing gaze. That was a big mistake. His hazel eyes called to her, drawing her to him. She always thought if she looked close enough, deep enough, she could see what was in his heart and soul through his expressive eyes. Right now, the anger mixed with desire and longing both frightened and excited her.

Forcing herself to look away, her gaze traveled across his face, briefly noting the familiar mole on his cheek before resting on his lips. The temptation they presented was overpowering.

Fighting the urge to feel their warmth against hers once more, she tried unsuccessfully to capture her wayward thoughts. Turning her focus from the attraction snapping between them, she instead looked ahead toward Hardman.

"You can leave me here, Blake. No need to make a scene riding down Main Street," Ginny stated, as they neared the edge of town.

"Make a scene riding through town? Well, if that's what you want…" Blake kicked the horse in the sides and yelled, "Yah!"

Romeo reared once before bolting down the street at a breakneck speed. Ginny clapped one hand on top of her head to hold on her hat while the other continued grasping Blake's coat lapel for dear life. She could feel one of his strong arms wrapped around her waist, holding her securely against his chest.

Reaching Granger House, he reined the horse to a stop and hopped to the ground, still holding her close. Her chest heaved against him from their wild ride down the street. Blake thought he would be completely undone when her lips parted and she tilted back her head to look at him.

"Let's just make sure to create as grand a spectacle as possible." He captured her lips in a kiss every bit as sizzling as the first one they shared that afternoon.

Roughly pulling back, he set her down at the end of the walk and stepped away.

"Have a lovely evening yourself, Miss Granger." Blake mounted the horse and raced back through town.

Chapter Seven

"Oh! I hate that man!" Ginny stamped her foot and raised a clenched fist at Blake's back as he rode away from her before spinning on her heel and marching around the house to the kitchen door. The chilly air did little to cool her hot cheeks and smoldering thoughts.

Flustered by the direction her mind continued to wander, she felt irritable and energized all at the same time.

What had she been thinking to allow him to kiss her so feverishly and return his eagerness?

It was nothing short of insane to fall for the man when he obviously didn't care for her. His wild, rough melding of their lips confirmed her thoughts that he despised her.

For a moment — a blissful, wonderful moment — she thought she saw something flicker in his eyes that looked like love.

She'd been mistaken, though. After he shattered her heart ten years ago, she'd be stupid and crazy to hand it to him to break again.

Fingering the symbol of his love she kept in her pocket, she further annoyed herself by realizing she had once again reached for it. She found herself touching it often since she'd returned to Hardman. Almost as if by having the smooth wood against her skin, she was touching Blake.

Thinking of the way their bodies brushed when he held her so close, how their lips connected so intensely, how the entire world seemed to spin off kilter when he kissed her, she felt heat flame into her face and pool in her midsection.

Rebuffing him as she attempted to sail out the door after the interview, Ginny thought she caught a glimpse of regret or confusion on Blake's face. But that couldn't be. He was just toying with her and she knew better than to let it happen again.

Especially after the way he rode through town like a wild hooligan on that beast of a horse.

Stomping up the back steps, she slammed the door. Removing her outerwear without saying a word, she turned to find Filly and Mrs. Kellogg studying her. Walking to the sink, she busied herself washing her hands.

"Is everything okay, Ginny?" Filly asked, wondering what had her sister-in-law all worked up. The look on the girl's face was enough to let anyone know to give her a wide berth or be prepared for the consequences.

"No, I don't believe it is." Ginny's hands shook from her frustration and anger. How dare Blake parade her through town like a wanton woman on the back of his horse?

"Here, dearie, sit yourself down." Mrs. Kellogg motioned her to the table while Filly brought her a steaming cup of tea.

Breathing in the minty fragrance, Ginny took a sip of the slightly sweet brew and closed her eyes. No wonder Luke loved the woman to distraction. Who wouldn't? She always seemed to know just what a body needed to feel better.

"What on earth is wrong?" Filly asked, sitting beside her and holding Ginny's chilled hand in her warm one.

"Blake Stratton. That, or who, is what's wrong. The man is... he's..." Ginny tried not to let her temper boil over on Filly. "He's despicable, on a good day!"

"And what despicable thing has the boy done now?" Mrs. Kellogg asked, winking at Filly from across the table.

"Mr. Daily asked me to write an article about the new church pews he's building, so I walked to Blake's workshop to see them for myself and ask a few questions. He... he..." Ginny couldn't quite find the words to describe what he did. She couldn't possibly tell Mrs. Kellogg and Filly that his kisses caused something inside her to blossom, that his embrace melted the icy fortress she kept around her heart, and his eyes seared into her soul.

"What did he do?" Filly asked, knowing Blake would never behave inappropriately or in an untoward fashion. The man radiated kindness and a humble gentleness.

"He kissed me!" Ginny covered her face with her hands, thinking she might die right there in the kitchen. Heat flamed into her cheeks as she recalled how much she'd welcomed and participated in each and every kiss Blake lavished on her.

"No! Say it isn't so," Filly teased, trying not to grin too broadly at Ginny's distressed face.

"On top of that, he insisted on bringing me back to town and practically abducted me, making me ride across his lap on that horrid beast he calls a horse, racing like a madman right down the main street of town for any and all to see." Ginny could only imagine the sight they made with her skirts blowing up and her mouth gaping open in shocked surprise.

"Well, I'm sorry I missed that." Mrs. Kellogg smiled as she gathered her things. Kissing both girls on their cheeks, she breezed out the door.

"I realize you find this amusing, but his behavior was completely unacceptable and uncivilized." Ginny wanted to beat her fists on the table or throw one of the plates across the room. Blake was so infuriating and so... so... handsome and strong and masculine.

"Ginny, before you work yourself into a..." Luke's arrival interrupted Filly's statement.

"Did I see you ride through town across Blake's lap like the hounds of Hades were chasing you?" Luke asked, tossing his hat and coat onto the pegs by the door as he grinned at his sister. He took in the disheveled state of her hair, red cheeks, and the anger snapping from her eyes as he waited for her response.

"Yes, you did," she ground out, glaring at her brother.

"Looked like you both were having a fine time." Luke walked over to the sink and washed his hands. He cringed when Ginny's hands slapped the top of the table and she screamed, "Men!" Her footsteps thudded against the floor as she stomped down the hall. The slamming of her bedroom door echoed into the kitchen.

"What did I say?" Luke asked innocently as he dried his hands.

Shaking her head at him, Filly hid her grin by tipping down her chin as she put hot rolls in a basket and set it on the table. After taking a pot roast from the oven, she set it on a platter and started to carve it when Luke removed the knife and fork from her hand, pulling her into his arms.

A grin worked up the corners of her lips and traveled to her bright green eyes as she looked into his face. "You know any mention of Blake gets her all worked up," Filly whispered, leaning against Luke's solid chest.

"I know. Why do you think I hurried home so quick and brought it up?" Luke gave his wife a wicked smile before nuzzling her neck. "You should have seen them. Blake was riding that big ol' stallion of his and Ginny sat across his lap with a look of terror on her face, as if he was racing headlong into the end of the world. It does her good to have her bloomers ruffled once in a while and Blake seems to be the man for the job."

"You're ornery, Luke Granger." Filly started to push away from him. "Ornery and a big tease."

"Yep, and don't forget it." He playfully swatted Filly on her backside as he went down the hall to coax Ginny out of her room for dinner.

"We need one more place setting, Ginny. Would you mind adding it, please?" Filly looked over the big dining room table awaiting the Thanksgiving meal they would soon serve their friends. Set with their best china and crystal, the table sparkled in the glow of the many candles nestled down the center of the table. Bowls of nuts, apples, and pinecones were interspersed among the candles, making a festive table adornment for the holiday.

"Please tell me that awful man is not joining us for dinner." Ginny shot a pleading gaze Filly's direction. It was bad enough she somehow found herself sitting next to Blake at the church service, but to have to endure his company further was more than she wanted to contemplate.

Between his masculine scent and the warmth of his presence penetrating her defenses at Chauncy's Thanksgiving service, Ginny could barely think straight. The thought of spending the day with him at Granger House as a guest was too much for her to bear.

"If you're referring to Blake, then, yes, he'll be joining us. You know he is anything but awful. He's a very nice hard-working man with a good and giving heart." Filly grew weary of Ginny's unflattering descriptions of their friend. Blake was kindness itself, often doing things to help others. Humble, generous, caring, and trustworthy were just some of the words Filly could think of to describe the man. He was one of the few people in Hardman Luke trusted to know about her true identity.

Although Blake was out of the country visiting his parents when she and Luke wed, upon his return to Hardman a few months later, Filly discovered a good friend in the gentle man. It was obvious he, Luke, and Chauncy had been friends for years and enjoyed teasing each other mercilessly.

With the three of them gathered around her Thanksgiving table, it should prove to be an interesting day, especially if Ginny continued to call him names and scowl at him.

"Do you think, just for today, you might put aside your unflattering descriptions of Blake and try to suffer his presence here as our guest?" Filly asked, giving Ginny a pointed look.

Releasing a long-suffering sigh, Ginny added one more place setting and nodded her head. Although she wouldn't admit it, some little part of her hoped she'd find herself seated next to Blake.

Luke invited the Bruner family to join them, along with the Dodd family, his assistant Arlan, and Blake.

"I'll do my best." Ginny walked back into the kitchen where Luke attempted to snatch a piece of pumpkin pie.

"Drop that fork and step away from the pie." Filly stared at Luke in exasperation. "You are far worse than an undisciplined child. Can't we leave the kitchen unattended for five minutes without you sneaking in here?"

"Nope." Luke grabbed his wife by her apron strings as she tried to breeze past him and pulled her into his arms. When she started to push against him, he launched into a lively dance across the kitchen floor, making Filly laugh and Ginny smile.

"What are we going to do with you, crazy man?" Filly asked, slightly breathless from Luke's antics when he finally stopped the dance.

"Give me a piece of pie to stay out of the way?" He suggested, waggling his eyebrows while tipping his head in the direction of the pie on the counter.

"Was he always this insufferable, Ginny?" Filly asked, cutting Luke a large wedge of pie and pouring him a glass of milk.

"I'm sure he never behaved this way at home, but only because Mother wouldn't allow it." Ginny grinned at her brother as he kissed Filly's cheek and wandered off in the direction of the library.

"Do you have fun memories from Thanksgiving holidays when you were a child?" Filly asked as the girl attempted to help with meal preparations. Ginny had learned quite a bit about cooking since she'd come to stay with them even if she still had no desire to attempt to cook anything on her own.

"We always had a cook, you know, so I remember sneaking into the kitchen and the cook would give Luke and I samples of what she was making. Then Mother would catch us and we'd be forced to sit in the parlor reading or playing the piano. Luke often escaped outside. One Thanksgiving he was gone for what seemed like hours. Father finally went searching for him and found him sitting next to Chauncy at the Dodd family's table, enjoying a meal there. Father dragged him home and Luke slid right up to the table and ate another meal." Ginny smiled at the memory. Luke was always so full of fun and charm, Ginny thought he got away with a lot more tomfoolery than she'd ever thought about pursuing. "He and Chauncy were as thick as thieves. Blake joined in sometimes, when he wasn't busy out on the farm with his parents. He always seemed to be quiet and subdued compared to the other two."

"That's because Luke and Chauncy are so boisterous." Filly thought the two men often acted more like mischievous little boys rather than the town banker and minister of the Christian Church.

"That they are." Ginny agreed, glancing out the kitchen window to see the Dodd family walking up the back steps. Erin squealed and hugged Bart around his scruffy neck. When the dog licked her face, Abby glared at Chauncy and he picked up his daughter before knocking on the door. "Speak of the devil..."

Filly turned and wiped her hands on a towel as Abby, Chauncy, and Erin trooped inside. After removing their outerwear, they exchanged hugs then Chauncy snatched a piece of fudge from a plate on the counter before going in search of Luke.

Abby insisted on washing Erin's face to remove the dog slobbers. Setting her back on her feet, Erin wrapped a little arm around Filly's leg and refused to let go.

"You know, Erin, I bet you could sit at the table and help me with a project," Ginny said, trying to find something that would entertain the little girl so Filly could work unhampered by the child's clinging. "You climb up on a chair and I'll be right back."

Abby seated Erin at the table, boosting her up by placing a few books in the chair for her to sit on.

Ginny hurried back and sat next to the little girl, placing several sheets of paper and a box of Franklin Crayons on the table. Erin studied the colorful sticks with interest and watched as Ginny picked up one and traced her hand on a sheet of paper.

"Let's make turkeys for everyone, Erin," Ginny said, adding feathers, an eye, and wattle to the bird she created.

The little girl clapped her hands with delight and grabbed a crayon in each chubby fist.

"Here, like this." Ginny took Erin's hand in hers and helped the child trace her hand.

"Do more! More!" Erin begged when they finished the first one.

"Yes, ma'am," Ginny said, looking up at Abby and Filly with a grin. Although she'd always thought children a nuisance, it was easy to love Erin. The child was bright, engaging, and refused to be ignored.

Concentrating on helping Erin, Ginny didn't even look up when a knock sounded at the back door. She felt the breeze of cold air when the door opened and closed then Blake's manly scent drifted around her and she snapped her head up to find his gaze resting intently on her.

Unsettled by his presence, she pretended to be busy, giving him a brief nod of her head in acknowledgement and continued in her efforts to help Erin.

The child, however, was happy to see one of her favorite people and jumped off the chair, running over to Blake with outstretched arms.

"Unca Bake! Ride horsey wif you?" Erin asked as he picked her up and kissed her cheek. She wrapped her little arms around his neck in a tight hug and Ginny felt a sudden jealousy that she couldn't do the same, especially when Blake tenderly patted the little girl on the back, then ran a gentle hand over her dark curls.

"Not today, sweetheart. It's far too cold outside for a little miss like you to go for a ride." Blake set Erin on her chair and studied the turkeys she and Ginny crafted. "Are you and Miss Ginny making turkeys?"

"Yep. Wanna hep?"

"No thank you, Erin. I don't know how to draw a turkey. I'm sorry." Blake wanted to escape somewhere far away from the petite woman seated at the table who tormented him with her very presence.

Opening the door and seeing Ginny's golden head bent over Erin's dark one, both covered with wild curls, did something strange and foreign to his heart. It was like a vision from the future, picturing Ginny with a fair-haired daughter.

Their daughter.

That thought caught him off guard and made his head swim while his heart began galloping madly.

The woman hadn't spoken to him since the day he raced her through town across his lap on Romeo. She'd glared at him at every opportunity and yesterday at the church service she held her skirt away from him as if he'd soil it by association when his leg brushed against hers in the crowded pew.

"Pease, Unca Bake? Make turkey wif me?" Erin asked, looking up at him with those big blue eyes that got him every time.

"Just a minute, sweetheart." Blake handed Filly his contribution to the meal then removed his coat and hat.

Filly looked at him with an excited smile.

"Are these the chocolates you shared last spring?" she asked, opening the lid and peeking inside the box. His parents sent the delicious candy for Easter and he'd just received another box a few days ago.

Not wanting to attend the Thanksgiving meal empty-handed, he'd forced himself to leave the box unopened so he could share the treat with his friends at Granger House.

"They are, indeed." Blake was glad he'd been able to bring something Filly appreciated. "I think you should sample one, just to make sure they traveled well through the mail.

"Only if the rest of you join in." Filly eyed the candy in her hand.

"No, go ahead, Filly. I don't want to spoil my dinner." Abby nudged her friend with her elbow.

"Well, if I must be the one to sacrifice a little room for dinner, so be it." Filly grinned as she chose a candy and popped it in her mouth. Her eyes glowed with a bright satisfaction as she set the candy near the pies and went back to her meal preparations.

Blake took a seat across from Ginny at the table.

"How should I proceed?" Blake asked, watching as Ginny helped Erin draw another turkey by tracing her hand.

"Just pick up a crayon and trace your hand," Ginny said, handing him one from those scattered on the table.

Blake picked it up and purposely pretended he couldn't make the simple motions of tracing his hand.

"I don't think my fingers are made for this type of work," he said, looking at Erin then Ginny, holding up a horribly lopsided turkey.

Erin giggled and pointed at his turkey while Ginny shook her head.

"You can't possibly be that doomed to failure, Mr. Stratton." Ginny handed Erin a green crayon to scribble in feathers.

Slowly walking around the table, Ginny leaned around Blake and took a clean sheet of paper from the stack she'd brought from her room. She set it in front of him, picked up a brown crayon, and looked at him like a teacher tasked with handling a hopelessly incompetent student. "Give me your hand."

Obeying, Blake lifted his hand to the table, placing it on the sheet of paper.

Ginny leaned over his shoulder, bracing herself with her left hand against his back. Heat and some odd tingling sensation sizzled from her palm up her arm, making her fight back a shudder.

Brushing against him, she placed her right hand over his and traced his left hand on the paper. Blake looked into her face and for a moment, she found herself entranced, at a loss to take even a shallow breath. The look in his eyes let her know he was fighting a battle as well.

Every place their skin connected, even through the layers of their clothing, made Blake feel like he was on fire. Ginny's delicate fragrance flooded his nose, making his thoughts muddle. Turning his head and looking up, his lips came dangerously close to hers.

His mouth began watering at the thought of kissing her incredible pink lips. Although she acted indifferent, he sensed a shift in her stance, especially when her gaze collided with his.

"See, it's not so difficult." Her eyes locked on his mouth as she stood, unable to move.

Neither of them noticed Abby and Filly casting each other knowing glances as they hustled from the room with food to place on the table. Erin babbled to herself as she colored another turkey.

Caught up in some sort of spell, Blake didn't know when his hands reached up and encircled Ginny's waist and pulled her onto his lap or how his fingers twined into her hair.

He was fully aware, however, when their lips connected in a fiery clash, making heat burn throughout his body with a smoldering force.

"Unca Bake kissin' Ginny," Erin giggled, pointing her crayon at them from across the table. "Kissy, kissy."

"My stars!" Ginny jumped to her feet and hurried back around the table to sit next to Erin. Befuddled, she patted her hair, pushing in loosened hairpins, and tried to calm her erratic breathing.

"Unca Bake kiss me!" Erin demanded, holding her arms up to him as he stood from the table, needing to put distance between him and Ginny before he did something unthinkable like ravage her right there in the kitchen.

Blake picked up the child and noisily kissed her cheek before poking her tummy playfully, making her giggle again. "You finish helping Miss Ginny make turkeys, Erin. I'm going to go visit with your daddy."

"I come wif you." Erin wiggled to be set down. Blake set her on her feet, but she reached up and took his hand. "Go see Daddy and Unca Wuke."

"Yes, ma'am." He smiled at Abby and Filly as they returned to the kitchen, both grinning at him like he'd done something humorous. He didn't see anything amusing in his inability to retain his good sense or composure around Ginny. Nothing at all.

Following Erin as she ran toward the parlor, he hoped the girl refrained from saying anything to Luke and Chauncy about his encounter with Ginny in the kitchen. Otherwise, he was in for an earful of their ribbing.

Chapter Eight

"That was very nice of you to keep Erin occupied, Ginny," Abby said as Ginny put away the crayons and paper.

"It was nice of you to occupy Blake, too." Filly's eyes glowed with humor. "I think you thoroughly distracted him with that kiss."

Blushing, Ginny glared at her sister-in-law and shook her head. "It was... it didn't mean... I wasn't..."

"I understand." Filly gave Ginny's shoulders a squeeze. "Although next time, you might want to wait until Erin isn't watching. She's already tattling to Luke and Chauncy about you kissing Blake."

Ginny groaned, knowing her brother would make at least one embarrassing comment at some point, most likely when all the guests joined them for dinner. He possessed a rare talent for finding the most inopportune time to humiliate her.

"Why don't you help us and it will take your mind off a good-looking carpenter with tempting lips." Abby motioned for Ginny to join her and Filly in putting the final touches on the meal.

The three of them hustled to dish up the food while Luke greeted the rest of their company at the front door.

Once guests removed their outerwear and exchanged friendly greetings, everyone converged in the dining room where Ginny thought the table might buckle beneath all the delicious-looking food.

Lively conversation prevailed throughout the meal. Although Luke insisted Ginny sit next to Blake, the two of them somehow managed to keep from even brushing so much as their sleeves together as they sat side by side.

Waiting for their meal to settle so they'd have room for dessert, Luke suggested everyone share something for which they were thankful.

When it was Ginny's turn, she realized there were many things that filled her with gratitude. Tears loomed in her big blue eyes as she looked first at Luke, then Filly. "I'm thankful to be here in Hardman. It was my home for many years and I didn't realize until I came back how much I missed it here. I'm thankful to Luke and Filly for opening their home to me and to Luke for giving me the sister I always wanted. I'm also thankful to be surrounded by good friends and all this good food."

Amid cheers of agreement, Blake looked at Ginny with an odd glint in his eye.

"Since it appears to be my turn, I'll keep it brief by saying I'm grateful for friends, both old and new." Blake raised his glass in a toast. "Thank you for being faithful and true."

Filly and Abby served dessert then Luke and Chauncy declared the men would clean up the dishes, while the women put up their feet and rested after preparing such a wonderful meal.

Knowing it was pointless to argue, Filly took Erin by the hand and the women sauntered to the front parlor. They laughed and talked while the men's rowdy banter floated down the hall from the kitchen.

"Are you sure they don't need some help?" Aleta Bruner asked, craning her neck to see into the dining room across the hall where her husband and son were helping clear away the last of the dishes.

"They'll manage." Filly knew Luke would chase her out of the kitchen if she tried to help. Worse, he might decide to waltz her around in front of their guests, or steal a few kisses.

Sensing the direction of her sister-in-law's thoughts, Ginny looked at Filly and grinned, nodding her head.

"Would you ladies like a spot of tea?" Blake asked, bringing in a tray with tea service. With his British accent, he could pass as a butler in the grand Granger House.

He'd seen many fancy homes and estates in his life, but he'd never found a parlor as inviting or as pleasing as the one the women sat in now. Decorated in shades of green and cream, the room was a cozy haven for all who lingered there. Glancing at the females sitting around the room, his eyes wandered to Ginny. She sat on a low chair by the fire, holding a picture book for Erin.

"We'd love some, kind sir." Filly motioned for Blake to set the tray on the low table in front of the sofa.

Glancing at the women as he set down the tray, he saw a look pass between Filly and Abby that he knew meant trouble. Convinced he was about to be drawn into something he wanted no part of, he began backing slowly toward the door.

"You ladies enjoy your tea." Blake attempted to hasten his escape, only to have Erin run over and wrap her arms around his leg, putting a halt to his retreat.

"Unca Bake, tea party wif me?" Erin asked, smiling up at him with those big eyes again. He'd been drawn into the little schemer's mischief once already today and wasn't interested in being further disgraced. Erin made sure everyone knew he'd been kissing Ginny. Luke and Chauncy tormented him until he thought he might have to miss the meal rather than take more of their teasing.

"I need to go help in the kitchen, sweetheart." Blake picked up the little girl and returned her to Abby. He was almost to the door when he heard the women giggling and looked over his shoulder to see Ginny being shoved his direction.

"Apparently, they aren't able to drink their tea without sugar." Ginny scowled at Filly and Abby as she left the parlor with Blake and walked slowly down the hall toward the kitchen.

"But there is sugar on the tray. I put the sugar bowl there myself." Blake realized Abby and Filly were up to no good.

"I see." Ginny stood in the hall, tapping her foot in irritation.

"Since everyone seems to be conspiring to force us together today, including Erin, what do you say we go for a walk?" The hopeful expression on his face wasn't lost on Ginny and she nodded her agreement. He returned to the kitchen to get his hat and coat while Ginny fetched hers from her room. Rather than risk being seen walking out the door together, Ginny suggested they meet at the end of the walk.

Making an excuse about needing fresh air, Blake left the men sitting around the kitchen table drinking coffee and snacking on pie while he hurried out the back door.

Reaching the fence around the yard, he didn't have to wait long for Ginny to quietly open the front door and hurry toward him.

"I feel like I'm skipping school," she said, grinning up at him as they started walking toward Luke's barn. The last thing either of them wanted was to encounter someone who would comment on their outing together.

"Are you warm enough?" Blake asked, looking down at Ginny with his hands stuffed in his pockets. The sun was shining and the air was still, but cold.

"Just a little chilly." She turned her blue eyes up at him with a look that hinted an invitation.

Placing his arm around her shoulders, he drew her closer to his side as they walked along. "Better?"

"Not quite." She reached out to clasp his other hand in hers. The movement pressed her closer against his side and Blake couldn't think of anywhere he'd rather be right at that moment.

When she gave him a cheeky grin, he felt his heart trip around in his chest. They wandered out to where the creek ran through Luke's property. Blake brushed off a fallen log and set his snowy white handkerchief on it. Ginny nodded her head in appreciation then took a seat.

He sat close beside her, fighting the urge to take her in his arms and kiss her until they both forgot all the reasons they didn't belong together.

"About the other day, Ginny," Blake started to say, ready to apologize for forcing her to ride through town with him. He could have apologized for kissing her, repeatedly, but he wasn't a bit sorry about doing it.

His brain stopped working when Ginny placed her gloved fingers against his mouth.

"Don't, Blake. We both let things become more… involved than we planned. No need to apologize." Desperately, she wished Blake would make some move to get that involved again. She'd hardly slept a wink since going out to see his workshop the other day.

Every time she closed her eyes, the look of wanting on his face played over and over in her head. His enticing scent beckoned to her and she dreamed she could feel his strong, muscled arms surrounding her. Lost in her fantasies of Blake, sleep became the last thing on her mind.

"We won't speak of it again, then," Blake said, glad Ginny no longer seemed to be angry with him.

To put her at ease, he asked her about her job at the newspaper, if her parents were well, and her plans for the Christmas season. She inquired about his woodworking projects, if he'd heard from his parents recently, and when he planned to see them again.

They were visiting quietly when they looked across the creek to find four wild turkeys studying them.

Ginny had never seen wild turkeys before and sat quietly watching them. The birds appeared so proud and regal, the artist in Ginny wished she had a pencil and pad handy so she could draw them.

Leaning close to Blake, she whispered, "Aren't they wonderful?"

He turned his head to agree and found his lips all but touching hers. Despite his good intentions, he could no more keep from kissing her than he could from drawing his next breath.

Taking off his glove, he slid his fingers along her cheek, caressing her jaw and chin before working his hand into her golden hair.

"Blake," Ginny whispered, turning her head and planting a soft kiss to his wrist. That simple touch ignited a roaring fire in him that made him want to do much more than give Ginny just a kiss or two.

With a deep groan, he picked her up and set her across his lap, lowering his mouth and kissing her deeply with an eager intensity. Hurriedly yanking off his other glove, he somehow managed to pull all the pins from her hair without breaking the heated blending of their lips.

As he lifted his head, he drank in the sight of her glorious wild locks falling down her back and across her shoulders. He captured her mouth again, stealing both her breath and her resolve to stay away from him.

When he stopped to draw in a lungful of air, Blake buried his face in her curls, memorizing the texture of her tresses, the silky feel of the strands, the floral scent that ensnared his senses. He'd loved her hair when they were younger and the fascination seemed to have intensified with age. Right now, soft beams of light floated through the trees, highlighting sections of her hair until it looked like liquid gold.

Ensnaring Ginny with another kiss, he drew her even closer against his chest, wishing nothing would ever come between them again.

She shifted and a hard lump in her pocket pushed against his thigh.

"What's in your pocket, Genevieve? I've felt it there before." Blake wondered what Ginny carried around with her. He'd noticed her nervously rubbing her hand over something in her pocket numerous times. When he kissed her the other day, he could feel a small lump pressing against him and was curious as to what it could be.

"Something special." She blushed as she pulled his face down to hers for another kiss, doing her best to distract him.

"Let's see it then." Temporarily, Blake let her sidetrack him as her lips grazed his jaw before returning to his questions. "Please, I want to see what it is that's special to you."

Ginny shook her head, burying her face against his neck. Blake groaned to keep his self-control with her breath blowing warm and tempting across his neck, sending his temperature soaring regardless of the chill in the air.

"Come on, love, let me see." Blake lifted her chin with his finger and kissed her softly, hoping to coax her into showing him her treasure.

Ginny stuck her hand in her pocket and pulled out something that she kept tightly clenched in her fist. "I've had this for almost ten years and I take it everywhere with me. It's my most precious possession."

Blake kissed her fingers and she slowly opened her hand. Feeling the air whoosh out of his lungs, he grabbed the carved wooden heart and ran his finger across the smooth wood.

Tied on a frayed red ribbon, Blake held it up in the afternoon light, recognizing every detail of the Christmas token he made for Ginny and gave to her the day she left town. It was a symbol of his love for the girl. He'd literally given his heart into her keeping that day.

If it was her most precious possession then why had she ignored him for the last decade?

Staring at her in confusion, Ginny smiled and took the heart from his hand, holding it by the ribbon on one delicate finger.

"Do you remember the day you gave this to me?" she asked, recalling every detail from that afternoon when Blake gave her the heart. She could remember the color of his shirt, how he'd ridden into town bareback, in a hurry to catch her before she could leave. He smelled of horses and wood and uniquely him. That scent had stayed in her memory every bit as much as the heart had stayed in her pocket.

Blake nodded his head, reliving the emotion of that day. He recalled thinking if Ginny had cut open his chest and removed his heart, it couldn't have been any more painful than watching her leave on the stage. She leaned out the window and waved at him until the road carried her over the hill and out of sight.

"You were so polite, bowing to my parents and asking permission to speak with me for a moment before we boarded the stage. Then you dragged me behind the livery and handed this to me." Wistfully, Ginny looked at the heart. "You told me that you were giving me your heart for safekeeping until we could be together again. You said..." Ginny's voice cracked. "You said you... loved me."

"I did, Ginny. I loved you with all the love a boy of seventeen has to give. It almost killed me when you left. I wanted, more than anything, for you to stay." Blake stared at the heart and the woman holding it. Suddenly, he needed answers to the questions he'd waited so long to ask. "Why, Ginny? Why did you send back my letters unopened? Couldn't you at least have possessed the decency to tell me you'd met someone new, or that you were no longer interested? It would have been better to hear that than know you cared so little, you didn't even open my letters."

"What letters?" she asked, sitting up and looking at Blake with a narrowed gaze. She would have devoured even the briefest of notes from him, had he bothered to send any. Crying herself to sleep for months, she missed him more than she'd ever imagined it possible to miss another human, but when weeks turned into months, she realized all she had left of Blake was the little wooden heart he'd given her. A simple token that seemed heartfelt at the time he pressed it into her hand.

"I wrote you once a week for months. I never heard a word back from you. Then that following summer after you left, I received a box with all my letters neatly tucked inside. They'd never been opened." He set Ginny back on the log, his amorous mood effectively cooled by their discussion.

All the pain and despair he felt then returned with a vengeance. The distance of her being in New York and him in Hardman had never been a concern. It was the fact that her mother thought he was unworthy and Ginny seemed to agree with Dora.

"I never received your letters, Blake. Not a one," Ginny said, dumbfounded. "And you never answered mine."

"Because you never wrote any." Swiftly rising to his feet, he paced back and forth along the creek bank. "Don't pretend you did, Ginny, just to save my feelings. I'm long past that. What I can't figure out is why you kept that ridiculous heart. I didn't mean anything to you, so why keep it? Why lie and say it's your most 'precious possession?'"

Ginny stared at Blake, unable to speak. How could he possibly think she'd never had any feelings for him, that she didn't still have feelings for him? She'd loved him completely. Instead of fading, the years had only intensified the love she felt for him. If she'd had any doubt of it, seeing him again, being held in his arms, had made that point undeniably clear.

"How dare you?" she huffed, jumping to her feet and grabbing Blake's arm, forcing him to look at her. "How dare you accuse me of lying about something that meant so much to me!"

"Is that why you took my heart with promises to write, to return to me as soon as your parents would allow, and I never heard from you again? Ten years is a long time, Ginny." Blake removed his hat and ran his hand through his thick brown hair. "It's a long time to wait and wonder, to hope and wish, only to realize you never cared at all."

"Blake, why do you think I kept the heart all this time? Why do you think I take it everywhere with me?" She was desperate to make him understand what she felt for him, what she'd always felt for him.

"How would I know?" Blake asked, defensive and brooding. "Why don't you explain it to me? Maybe then I'll understand why you took my heart with a promise to love me then tossed it away without so much as a single word of explanation."

Hurt and angry, Ginny lost the tenuous hold she had on her temper. Slapping Blake across the cheek, she stamped her foot and waved the wooden heart in his face.

"How could I love someone with such a thick head? You're an impossible, completely infuriating boy who never grew up!" Ginny took a step back and grabbed his hand, dropping the token that stood for their love into his palm.

"You wanted your heart back? Is that the problem? Well, here you go. It's yours to give to whomever you like because I certainly won't need it any longer."

Ginny marched indignantly toward the house. Blake looked from the heart in his hand to Ginny's retreating form and wondered what had just possessed him to push her into such a fit of fury.

"Ginny, wait!" He rushed to catch up to her. When she kept marching, he grabbed her arm to stop her. "I'm sorry. Please, let's talk this out."

"I'm completely through speaking with you, Mr. Stratton. There isn't anything further I wish to say to you now or in the future, other than goodbye." Ginny picked up her skirts and ran toward the house.

Tears rained down her cheeks, but she blindly ran on, stumbling twice and catching herself before she fell to her knees. She hoped Blake would catch her, take her in his arms, tell her he was sorry and everything would be fine.

Instead, she rushed to the house, knowing he stood watching, letting her leave like he had all those years ago.

Chapter Nine

"Ginny, I was hoping to catch up to you today."

Turning, Ginny smiled at Abby Dodd as the woman hurried up to her carrying Erin on one slim hip.

"How are you today, Abby?" Ginny asked, taking Erin when the little girl held out her arms and smiled.

"I'm fine, but so busy with Christmas just a few weeks away. Between people wanting new dresses, duties at the church, and the children's Christmas program, I'm feeling stretched a little thin these days." Abby took Erin back when the child tried to yank the lovely plume off Ginny's best hat.

Although the sun was shining, the air was bitterly cold as they stood on the boardwalk in front of Abby's store.

"Do you have a moment to come in?" Abby asked, quickly unlocking the door and motioning Ginny inside.

"Certainly." Ginny walked inside the store and admired Abby's beautiful displays. The shop carried everything a well-dressed lady could need or want to feel fashionable. Ginny was quite surprised Abby was able to stay up on current fashions, buried as she was in the middle of nowhere.

Fingering a beautiful pale blue silk gown, Ginny turned to see Abby watching her.

"That color would look stunning on you with your hair and complexion." Abby moved to take the dress out of the display for Ginny to try on.

"Thank you, Abby, but I'll not be trying on dresses today, no matter how pretty they are." Ginny fingered the silk one last time before turning her attention to where Erin played with a box full of toys in a sunny corner. "Now, about what did you wish to speak with me?"

"I know you're working part-time at the paper, but I was truly hoping you'd have some time to help me with the children's Christmas program. I've got the costumes made, but I need some help with the practices. Luke mentioned that you have some experience with plays and thought you might enjoy it."

"Oh, well... I... um..." Ginny didn't know the first thing about running a children's church program but she had participated in a few plays during her school years and goodness knew she'd attended more than her share of incredible performances all around the world. She did have spare time on her hands, more than she knew how to fill.

It was in those spare moments that thoughts of Blake made her heart ache fiercely. She'd thought about going to see him numerous times, but decided to leave well enough alone. He'd made his position regarding her perfectly clear.

Daily, she reached for the heart she'd carelessly returned to him in a fit of anger, fingering her empty pocket. She wished she had the comfort of the smooth wood against her palm. It was her last tie to him and now it was gone.

Maybe working with the children and attempting to get into the holiday spirit would do her good. It certainly couldn't hurt.

"I'd be pleased to help, Abby," Ginny finally said, offering the woman a warm smile. "When do I need to start?"

"We asked the children to come for the first practice Thursday after school. After that, you can work out a practice schedule with Chauncy. I'll be available, of course, if you need anything, but between the store, Erin, and making sure the costumes are ready, I really didn't feel like I could do the program justice." Abby squeezed Ginny's hand in relief. "I so appreciate your willingness to help."

"I appreciate you thinking of me. I'll be at the church Thursday afternoon, then." Ginny walked to the door.

Erin rushed over and threw her arms around Ginny's legs. "Bye, Ginny!"

"Goodbye, Erin. You be a good girl." Ginny waved at Abby and her precocious child as she hurried to the mercantile to finish her errand for Filly.

The woman announced last night at dinner she wanted to start decorating the house for Christmas. Luke groaned and mumbled something about breaking his back dragging trunks from the attic, but this morning he was clearly as excited as Filly as he carried them down the stairs and left them in the parlor.

Filly needed red ribbon for trim and asked Ginny if she'd mind running to the store to pick up several yards.

Glad for an excuse to be outside in the fresh air, Ginny entered the Bruner's mercantile and took a moment to look around, inhaling the scents of spices and leather.

Wandering back to the dry goods area, she found a spool of red ribbon and decided to purchase the entire thing, not wanting Filly to run out. She had a few projects of her own she wanted to work on and looked forward to helping her sister-in-law festoon Granger House for the holidays.

Noticing Aleta busily assisting a customer at the counter, Ginny spent a few minutes looking around the store. Her gaze landed on a box of her favorite chocolates and she decided to splurge. Luke loved sweets every bit as much as she did and she knew Filly would enjoy the treat as well.

Aleta smiled and waved her over as the last customer left.

"How are you today, Ginny?" Aleta asked as Ginny set the ribbon and candy on the counter.

"Just fine, Aleta. Thank you for asking. I hope this day finds you well," Ginny said politely, paying for her purchases. She noticed Percy run in from the back room and dance excitedly off one foot to the other, waiting for his mother to acknowledge him. "How are you, Percy?"

"Fine, Miss Granger." Percy eyed the box of candy on the counter. "Ma, can I run over to Tommy's house? His pa brung home a new horse and Tommy said he ain't never seen anythin' as wild as him. He already done bucked off three men and one broke his arm."

"I suppose so." Aleta gave Percy a motherly glare while Ginny opened the box of chocolates and offered him one. He snatched it with a grin and turned his attention back to his mother. "But you stay away from that horse and be back before the hour is up. I have three deliveries for you to make when you return. And for goodness sakes, learn the proper English your teacher tries so hard to drill into your head."

"Yes, Ma!" Percy yelled, flinging open the front door. "Thanks, Miss Granger!"

When she held the box of chocolates out to Aleta, the woman gratefully accepted a candy. Ginny selected one, popping the entire thing in her mouth. She choked on it when she heard Blake's rich voice greeting Percy as the boy ran around him and down the boardwalk.

Discreetly coughing while attempting to quickly chew and swallow her mouthful of candy, Ginny looked like a fish trying not to gulp water.

Aleta smirked and nodded her head toward Blake as he stepped up beside Ginny and stood at the counter.

Ignoring him wasn't an option, so she held a gloved hand in front of her mouth and chomped her candy in a most unladylike manner. She would never again stick a whole piece of candy in her mouth, especially not in a public place. Whipping a handkerchief from her reticule, she dabbed at her lips as she swallowed.

Blake stared at her with an amused expression on his exceedingly attractive face.

"Chocolate?" she asked, holding out the box to him. He grinned and took a piece, his eyes never leaving her face.

Biting into the treat, he finished it quickly then continued to stare at her with a teasing light in his eye and a devilish tilt to his lips. Slowly removing his gloves, he set them on the counter.

"You missed a spot, Miss Granger." Blake reached down and wiped a bit of chocolate from the corner of her mouth. Instead of wiping his finger on his pants or a handkerchief, he licked it, never taking his eyes off hers.

Shocked by his actions, Ginny slapped the lid on the box of candy and started backing in the direction of the door.

"Don't forget your ribbon, dear." Aleta held the spool of ribbon out to Ginny. She took a step forward and grabbed it, then hurried out the door, toward the safety of home.

Blake watched her go, trying to remember what it was he came in the mercantile to purchase. His thoughts scrambled in his head the instant he saw Ginny, looking so lovely in a cream and blue gown with a dark blue coat and snappy little blue hat.

It didn't matter where he went in town, she seemed to be there. If she wasn't working on an article for Ed's newspaper, she was running an errand for Filly or helping Luke with something. Managing to avoid being close to her, today was the first time he'd been near enough to smell her light fragrance and study the way the sun spun gold into that crown of glorious hair.

Amused by her mouthful of candy, he wanted to laugh as she stood frantically trying to chew it so she could speak.

When she turned to him with that bit of chocolate clinging to the corner of her mouth, it took every ounce of control he possessed not to bend down and kiss it away.

He was still mad at her for the things she said Thanksgiving Day and slapping his cheek, but he missed her with every breath he took. His heart hurt more now than it ever did when she'd left him ten years ago. It seemed ironic the pain increased the second she returned the hand-carved heart he'd given into her keeping. He couldn't believe she'd held onto it, cherished it, all these years only to toss it back at him in a fit of anger.

He wondered what she meant about writing him letters and never receiving his. If he thought the two of them could sit down and have a rational conversation without either losing their temper or winding up locked in a passionate embrace, he'd go pound on the Granger's door and insist she speak with him.

Finally remembering what he came to the store to purchase, he quickly paid Aleta for a handful of pencils and a stack of paper before turning to leave the store. He'd taken just a few steps down the boardwalk when Chauncy Dodd came out of his wife's store carrying little Erin on his shoulders.

"Unca Bake! Unca Bake! See me ride Daddy!" Erin pounded Chauncy on the head as she bounced from her lofty position.

"I see you indeed, sweetheart." Blake laughed as Chauncy rolled his eyes at his daughter.

"Now, see here, young lady. Don't pound your father to death, please." Chauncy grinned as he greeted Blake.

As they walked down the block, they visited for a few minutes before Chauncy snapped his fingers and grabbed Blake's arm. "Say, Blake, would you have time to help a few afternoons with the children's program? I'm tied up with getting other things ready for the Christmas service and Abby is about at wit's end trying to fill all the holiday dress orders and keep an eye on Erin along with making costumes for the program. If you have time, we'd really appreciate the assistance."

"I suppose I could help." Not overly excited at the prospect, Blake was already burning the midnight oil trying to complete all the last minute holiday orders before Christmas Eve. "What do I need to do?"

"The first practice is Thursday. You mostly need to help keep the children organized and we might need to construct a few props for the program. "

"I can do that." Blake shook the hand Chauncy offered then squeezed Erin's hand as she waved it at him. "I'll see you Thursday."

Chauncy waited until Blake was out of earshot to laugh. "He'll see someone Thursday, Erin, my girl, but it won't be me."

Chapter Ten

Standing back and studying their handiwork, Filly and Ginny smiled at each other with satisfaction. After throwing themselves into decorating Granger House for the holidays, they were finally finished.

Garlands draped across the porch, a big wreath hung on the front door and greens with red berries filled pots leading up the steps. Ropes of greenery twined around the posts and even the doghouse featured garland along the edge of the roof.

At the sound of boots clomping down the boardwalk behind them, they turned to see Luke approaching. Bart barked and ran around his legs, excited his master was home.

"Ladies, the house looks marvelous," Luke said, patting the dog then wrapping his arms around Filly and kissing her cheek. "Did Saint Nick visit early?"

"Don't be absurd, Luke," Ginny scolded, although pleased he noticed and appreciated their efforts to make Granger House look festive. "You know he won't come until December twenty-fourth and the odds of him coming here are purely up for speculation. We all know you aren't a very good boy."

"Did you hear that, Filly, darlin'? She's accusing me of running off Santa." Dramatically, Luke slapped a hand to his chest, affecting a wounded appearance.

"Maybe you better plan on coal in your stocking this year," Filly teased, then let out a squeal as Luke tickled her sides and nuzzled her neck.

"If I'm going to be branded as naughty, I might as well act the part." He turned Filly around and planted a long, involved kiss on her surprised mouth.

"Can't you two at least do that inside, where half the town can't gape if they look this direction?" Ginny asked, marching down the front walk, amused by Filly's red face and fruitless efforts to get away from Luke's grasp.

"Let them gawk all they want. You act like they've never before seen a man besotted by a beautiful woman." Luke chased Filly as she raced past Ginny and in the front door.

Shaking her head, she walked inside where the smell of cinnamon and bayberry filled the air with a wonderful, welcoming scent.

As she recalled holidays spent at Granger House during her childhood years, Ginny didn't think the house had ever looked or smelled so festive and inviting. Filly truly was talented at turning a house into a home.

When they sat down to dinner, Luke kept up his teasing throughout the meal and after the last dish was dried, the three of them retired to the parlor.

Accustomed to Luke and Filly's evening debates, Ginny often took Filly's side just to annoy Luke. It made the evenings pass quickly and it was fascinating to hear their differing opinions. They discussed ideas and topics without fear of ridicule or belittlement. There was no anger in their words, just lively opposition that was fun to listen to as they each tried to prove their point the most sound.

Despite their pleasure in debating one another, anyone could see how devoted they were to each other, how very much in love.

She'd never heard the two of them fight or argue in the almost two months she'd stayed with them and stopped to contemplate the fact. They didn't always agree but they seemed to discuss their opinions openly, without judgment.

Her parents, while completely devoted to each other, didn't have a relationship Ginny wanted to duplicate. Up until the last few years, her mother always got her way. Always. Regardless of the consequences, her father bowed to her mother's whims and will. While they seemed to be taking on more of a balanced relationship, she knew her father still often gave in to her mother's bidding.

To her, it seemed Luke and Filly treated each other as equals. Oh, there was no doubt Luke was the head of the household, but he listened to Filly, respected her, and gave her ideas consideration.

Glad her brother had chosen such a perfect woman for him, she hoped if she ever did wed to have the same kind of partnership she saw in Luke and Filly. She didn't want just a husband. She wanted a confidant, a friend, and a lover.

Thoughts of a lover brought images of Blake to mind and caused her to shift restlessly in her chair. Forcing herself to gain control of her thoughts, she turned to look at her sister-in-law.

"Did you see the article about America's first auto race?" Filly asked as she finished reading the paper and set it on a side table.

"I did." Luke looked at Filly over the top of the book he was reading. "Wouldn't it have been fun to be there to see it?"

"I don't know." Filly thoughtfully considered the possibility. "I assume since it was in Chicago, it would have been cold, and it did say there was snow on the ground. I'm surprised the Duryea won."

"Why does that surprise you? Because it was a gasoline powered auto?" Luke asked, curious to his wife's thoughts. She always had such an interesting way of looking at things, it never ceased to entertain or surprise him.

"No, because it was only the second Duryea built. I assume many bets were placed on one of the Benz autos winning, since they were sponsored by Macy's." Filly studied Luke, waiting for him to disagree with her opinions.

"As much as I'd love to argue the point, my thoughts are the same as yours. Who would have thought a car Frank Duryea built himself would win the race?" Luke smiled at Filly before turning to his sister. "What about you, Ginny Lou? What car would you have bet on?"

"I don't make bets." With a haughty tilt of her head, Ginny pretended to study her no longer perfectly manicured fingers. "However, in this case, I would have put my money on the vehicle entered by H. Mueller and Company because it won the consolation competition held a few weeks before the actual race."

"Have you ridden in an auto, Ginny?" Filly asked, knowing her sister-in-law had many adventures she'd only dreamed of experiencing.

"Yes, I have. Many times." Ginny recalled all the boys and men who had given her rides, trying to impress her. As much as she disliked horses, she thought she preferred a buggy, though. The autos went too fast, often had strange smells, and never failed to whip her hair into an uncontrollable mess. "Nigel has an auto that he drives everywhere, even the two blocks to church. It's absolutely ridiculous."

"I wonder when we'll see an auto here in Hardman?" Filly asked. With the way the streets turned to soupy mud in the spring, it would be impossible for a vehicle to travel through the muck.

"Probably not until one of the upstanding citizens has one shipped in." Ginny offered her brother a cheeky grin. "Shouldn't the banker be the first to plunge into that sort of investment?"

"I think the doctor should be the first." Luke was in no hurry to abandon his horses for a motorized vehicle. "Or maybe the pastor of the Christian Church."

Ginny and Filly laughed, knowing there was no way on earth Chauncy would willingly climb behind the wheel of an automobile.

"Speaking of Chauncy, I heard you're going to help with the children's program, Ginny," Luke said. Although he expected Ginny to continue to behave in her usual spoiled manner after he gave her the choice of staying or leaving, she had worked very diligently on changing her self-indulgent ways.

She'd made remarkable progress in the last month and he felt proud of her for even trying. When Chauncy and Abby mentioned she was helping with the children's program at church, Luke couldn't have been happier.

"Abby asked if I could help. She's got her hands full with Erin, her store, and the usual Christmas festivities." Ginny glanced from Luke to Filly. "The first practice is tomorrow after school. I was wondering, Filly, if you could make some cookies for the children. I thought that might help win them over."

"I'd be happy to." Filly smiled warmly, mentally thinking about what recipe the children might enjoy the most. "If you need help with anything, just let me know. I'm watching Erin tomorrow, but can certainly offer my assistance with whatever you need."

"Thank you. I appreciate that. Chauncy will be there and Abby is working on costumes, so I'm sure we'll be fine." Ginny smoothed a hand down her skirt to her pocket, remembering Blake's heart was no longer there. As her fingers brushed her dress, the rustle of paper reminded her she'd picked up a letter for Filly at the post office on her way home from the newspaper.

"I forgot earlier, but you had a letter come today," Ginny said, passing an envelope to Filly.

"Who's it from, darlin'?" Luke asked, watching Filly's face light with happiness. It slowly faded as she sent a cautious glance at Ginny before looking at Luke.

Sensing her unspoken question, he offered an encouraging smile and nodded his head slightly.

"My father," Filly said quietly, stroking the envelope in her hand.

"Where is your father?" Ginny asked, curious. Her mother mentioned in passing that Filly's mother had died years ago and her father was gone. She didn't know if gone meant deceased or not in the area. At the time her mother brought it up, she hadn't cared enough to ask more questions. Realizing she should have asked weeks ago, she was genuinely interested in knowing more about Filly's family. "I don't believe you've mentioned him before."

"Alford has been gone for a while." Luke hoped Ginny wouldn't react badly to finding out the truth about Filly's father.

"Gone where?" Ginny asked, looking from Luke to Filly. They were both behaving oddly, casting each other careful glances.

"Prison."

Ginny watched Filly fiddle with the letter on her lap, nervously picking at the envelope she had yet to open.

"Did you say prison?" Ginny asked, keeping her voice calm. A million questions rushed through her mind as she sat waiting for Filly or Luke to offer an explanation.

"Yes. My father, well, he um..." Filly struggled to find the right words. "Two years ago, on Christmas Eve,

SHANNA HATFIELD

he threatened to shoot Luke and your father, planned to kill me, and ended up shooting the deputy."

Breath whooshed out of Ginny's lungs and she sat numbly staring at the other two occupants of the room.

"Chauncy tackled him before he did too much damage, but we all felt it best if he spent some time in jail," Luke said.

"And no one thought I needed to know that at the time?" Ginny asked, incredulous that the family kept something like that from her.

"You were on your European tour and honestly, you wouldn't have taken the news well." Pointedly, he glared at his sister.

"True as that may be, someone still should have told me." Ginny stared at Luke then looked inquisitively at Filly. "So you grew up here? In Hardman?"

"Yes, I went to school here until my father made me stay home. You were a few years younger than I was. I went by Philamena, then. Philamena Booth."

"I do remember you, Filly. You were such a pretty girl, even then." Ginny smiled at fond memories of school days. Remembering what a lovely, lively girl Filly had been then, she was surprised she hadn't made the connection.

Luke cleared his throat. "You see, Ginny Lou, when Filly was fourteen her mother died in childbirth. Her father couldn't cope with the loss and held her prisoner on their farm from then until just before I married her. He drank all the time and did things we'd all like to forget. When he realized how close he came to killing Filly, he begged for a second chance. His time in prison sobered him up and when he was released last summer, Chauncy found him a job working as a groundskeeper at a large church in Portland."

Ginny looked at Filly who nodded her head and brushed at the tears rolling down her cheeks.

"We've been to see him twice and he's doing very well." Filly opened the letter and let the thin pages rest on her lap. "He's trying so hard to be a good man again."

Quickly getting to her feet, Ginny hurried to the sofa and wrapped her arms around her sister-in-law. "I'm so sorry, Filly. I had no idea."

"I'm sorry we didn't tell you sooner." Filly hugged Ginny as they both brushed at tears.

"I was concerned how you would react to the details, Ginny." Luke studied his sister. From all indications, the girl was finally growing up and becoming the person he always knew she could be.

"What did you expect me to do? Think Filly was somehow tainted from her father's misdeeds? Stare down my nose at her?" Ginny asked, knowing that was exactly how she would have reacted had she known when she first arrived in town. "In case you two have forgotten, I'd have to climb on a chair to do that. Filly's almost a foot taller than me!"

They all laughed then Filly read them her father's letter. He described how pretty the church looked with all the Christmas decorations and how much he enjoyed watching the hustle and bustle of holiday shoppers. He finished the letter by sending his love and prayers for them all.

"Maybe we can visit him in January. Things are usually slow around town then," Luke said, smiling at Filly.

"Speaking of visiting, when are Mother and Dad expected to grace us with their presence?" Ginny asked, both looking forward to and dreading seeing her parents. She'd only written them a few times since arriving in Hardman, relying on Luke and Filly to keep in touch with them.

"Dad said they'd be here on the twentieth," Luke said, hoping his mother was maintaining her kinder, gentler attitude toward life. When she first met Filly, she'd treated his wife like an outcast and said many unkind, hurtful things to her, the least of which was that she thought Luke could have made a much better choice for a spouse and how Filly was wholly unacceptable.

The day Alford tried to kill his daughter, Dora took Filly into her arms and heart. From then on, she referred to her as a daughter.

"Are we ready for Dora?" Ginny asked with a sassy grin, knowing how demanding and trying her mother could be.

"As ready as we'll ever be," Luke laughed, winking at Filly.

"You two should be ashamed. Dora is trying to… well, to not be so…" Filly searched to find the best way to phrase her comment.

"Oh, just tell it like it is. She's trying really hard to not be like herself." Ginny patted Filly's hand as she smiled. "Although I must say, the improvements have been wonderful. First, you went to work on mother and now me. In another ten or twenty years, you might even have Luke whipped into shape."

"What's wrong with me?" Luke asked, sitting up in his chair and glaring at his sister. "You're the one who was Mother's pet project."

"Don't I know it," Ginny said, stifling a yawn. Thinking about working with the youngsters at the church coupled with the impending arrival of her parents made her exhausted. "I have no doubt tomorrow will be a long day, so I'm going to bid you both good night."

"Night, Ginny. Sweet dreams," Luke and Filly called as she left the room.

After going to the kitchen for a drink of water, she remembered she wanted to ask Luke something and went back to the parlor. She wasn't surprised to step in the room to find Filly on Luke's lap and the two of them involved in a passionate kiss.

Backing quietly out of the parlor, she grinned as she went down the hall. If her brother, who avoided marriage like the plague up until the moment he decided to wed Filly, could fall so hard and deeply in love, maybe there was hope yet for her.

Chapter Eleven

Rushing home after finishing at the newspaper office, Ginny raced up the back walk and tripped over the dog as he lounged across the top step.

"Bart, you need to find somewhere else to sleep away the day," Ginny grumbled as she stepped over him and hurried in the back door. Throwing her things down on the table, she asked Filly to pack cookies into a basket for the children while she changed her clothes. Forgetting to stay away from the press while it was running, flecks of ink now dotted both her skirt and blouse.

Grabbing one of her favorite wool gowns, she pulled it on and quickly fastened the pearl buttons decorating the front. Rather than making time to take down her hair and comb it, she snatched a ribbon from a dresser drawer and tied it around the wayward curls that escaped their confines earlier in the day.

She raced back to the kitchen, donned her coat and hat, yanked on gloves, grabbed a notebook and pencil, then snatched the basket Filly placed on the table as she ran out the door.

Briskly walking down the boardwalk into town, she made it to the church in record time. She stood outside the door a moment to catch her breath before going inside and tucking her gloves in her coat pocket.

At the front of the sanctuary, she set the basket and the rest of her things on the front pew. The church was warm, so Ginny knew the pastor had to have been over to stoke the furnace and heat the building. As she removed her hat and coat, she heard the school bell ring outside, signaling the end of classes for the day.

She noticed Blake had delivered some of the new pews. By Sunday, he would have them all replaced.

Stepping up to one, she ran her hand over the smooth wood, admiring his handiwork. Although simple in design, the pews would last for years and years to come.

Critically studying the front of the church, Ginny could picture a simple set for the program. Maybe one of the parents could help produce one. Luke mentioned they didn't have any props for the play other than the costumes for the children and a few live animals they brought in for the nativity scene. It seemed someone brought a goat instead of a sheep for the program the previous year and the animal destroyed most all the props in a fit of terror induced by the clapping at the end of the program.

Humorously recalling the year Luke and Chauncy turned mice loose during the Christmas Eve service, she hoped she wouldn't have any ornery little boys to handle in the group this year. She laughed, remembering the chaos that erupted after the mice scattered through the church. Her mother was one of the women who jumped on a pew and refused to come down until her father carried her outside.

"I think I missed the joke," Blake said from directly behind her, making her scream and whirl around to face him.

"My stars! You could scare a body half to death sneaking up like that." Ginny held her hand to her chest while her heart beat wildly. She thought its rapid thumping had more to do with Blake than the fact he'd caught her unawares. "What are you doing here?"

"I could ask you the same question." Blake thought Ginny looked like a summer flower in her pink gown with rosy cheeks and that head of golden hair. A pink ribbon she'd tied around her head to keep the curls out of her face just made him want to reach out and remove it, along with all her hairpins.

Remembering how beautiful all that hair looked down made his throat so dry he could barely swallow.

"Abby asked me to help with the children's program." Ginny glared at Blake. Why did he have to look so altogether appealing?

He wore denim pants, a green shirt that brought out the green flecks in his hazel eyes, and a tan coat that accented the breadth of his shoulders. He smelled of leather, wood shavings and man — an enthralling combination. His hat dangled from long, capable fingers and a bit of sawdust clung to the toe of one boot. Blake was so much more... virile than anyone she'd come across since she'd left Hardman as a girl.

When Blake chuckled and sank down on a pew, shaking his head, she tapped her foot impatiently.

"Chauncy asked me to help with the program as well. Isn't that interesting?" Blake set down his hat and removed his coat.

Annoyed with Chauncy and Abby for their scheming, she was even more annoyed with herself for being pleased their efforts resulted in Blake spending time with her. She doubted he would have done so otherwise.

"Looks to me like they either really need our help or have decided to get involved in something that isn't any of their business," Blake mused, walking to Chauncy's lectern and picking up the script for the program. Chauncy mentioned he'd leave it there.

"I think we should assume they are busy and truly need the assistance," Ginny said, noticing Blake was looking through the program. Since there was only one copy, she moved closer to him so she could see the information as well. He held it out so they both could read it and discussed a few details before the children poured in the door, led by Percy Bruner.

"We're all here, Miss Granger," Percy announced as the children sat in pews, anxiously awaiting instruction.

"Very well, children," Ginny said, passing around the basket of cookies as she and Blake learned who participated in the play the previous year and who wanted what part this year.

Making assignments, the children took their roles in the program seriously and set to work learning their parts.

One of the shepherds made it known he preferred to be a wise man and one of the angels burst into tears when the innkeeper pulled her braid, but other than that, the first practice went well.

"Let's set the next practice for Monday after school. That gives us almost two weeks before the program," Ginny said, looking to Blake for agreement. He nodded his head and smiled at the youngsters before they ran out the door for their respective homes.

"Perhaps we can practice Mondays and Thursdays," Ginny suggested as she and Blake tidied up after the children. There was one cookie left. Blake snatched it from the basket and took a bite.

"How do you know I wasn't saving that one?" Disapprovingly, Ginny stared at him.

He grinned and held the cookie out to her. "Want a bite?"

"Not now that you've slobbered all over it." She wanted not just a bite of the cookie, but also a taste of his tempting lips.

"You didn't seem to mind my slobbers a few weeks ago." Blake gave her a heated look. "Besides, you have access to Filly's cooking all the time. The rest of us have to take what we can get when it's available."

"How do you know Filly made the cookies?" Ginny asked, irritated at her feelings for Blake almost as much as she was by his teasing.

"Because I've had her kisses before." Blake brushed the crumbs from his fingers and slipping on his coat.

Quirking an eyebrow at him, Ginny shook her head. "You better not let Luke hear you say that."

"You know perfectly well I was referring to the cookies. I like them best when she adds in coconut."

Ginny continued to look at him with a calculating stare. He picked up her coat and helped her put it on then politely waited while she fastened the hat on her head, pulled on her gloves and gathered her things.

"Will Saturday morning about nine work for you?" Blake asked as they walked to the door.

"What on earth are you talking about?" Ginny asked, stopping to glare at him again, confused. She did not intend to see him Saturday.

"If we're going to get props ready in time for the program, I can't do it all myself. Come to my workshop Saturday morning and we'll work on it. Ask Luke and Filly to join us if you like," Blake said, standing at the door waiting for her to move from her position several feet away.

As much as she hated to admit it, they did need some props and Blake was the likely candidate to build them. How did she let Abby talk her into this? Shaking her head, she marched up to Blake. "Fine, I'll be there Saturday, but you better have everything ready to go and not plan on dilly-dallying around. I'll see if Luke and Filly will come, too."

"I'll provide lunch, in thanks for the great sacrifice of your time and contribution of your efforts." Pleased at how easily Ginny went along with his plans, he wondered what else she'd agree to. Despite his head telling him to stay far away from the beautiful woman, his heart urged him to draw closer. After their fight Thanksgiving Day, he had plenty of time to replay every word from that painful conversation. He realized they both still had feelings, deep feelings, for each other.

His heart knew down in its depths that Ginny cared more than she was willing to admit. Given enough time and opportunity, he hoped she'd fall in love with him again. Only this time as a woman falls in love with a man.

"If that is an enticement you use to woo women to your workshop, you might endeavor to apply a different approach." A cheeky smile lit her face as she started out the door.

"Does this work better?" Blake asked, reaching out and grabbing her arm before she stepped outside. He licked her cheek and laughed at the appalled expression on her face before pushing her outside and shutting the door behind them. As he settled his hat on his head, he gave her a devilish grin. "Perhaps you'd rather have my slobbers after all."

Furiously wiping at her cheek, Ginny bit her lip to keep from grinning. Blake was as fun and playful as he'd been as a boy and she loved receiving his attention, even if it was slobbers on her cheek. Watching him walk around the corner, whistling what sounded like *God Rest Ye Merry Gentlemen*, she couldn't help but smile.

Maybe she still had a chance at winning back his heart.

Walking home with a lively step, she'd barely closed the kitchen door when Erin grabbed her around the knees, hugging her tightly.

"Hi, Ginny!" Erin gazed up at her with a happy grin.

"Hello, Erin. Where are you going?" Ginny asked, noticing Erin wore her coat and had mittens on her hands. She forgot Filly watched the little girl all day. She must have been napping when Ginny made her whirlwind trip home to change her clothes.

Filly hurried into the kitchen, looking flushed and tired. "How was practice?" she asked, tugging a knit cap over Erin's curls and tickling the little girl beneath the chin.

"Fine." Ginny grinned at Erin's giggles. "I can take her home since I'm already dressed for the outdoors, if you like."

"That would be so helpful and very much appreciated." Filly wrapped a scarf around Erin's neck then kissed her rosy little cheek. "Ginny's going to take you home, Erin, but I'll see you at church Sunday, if not sooner. Okay, honey?"

"Yep!" Erin hugged Filly one last time. "Wuv you, Aunt Fiwwy."

"Love you, too, sweetheart." Filly waved as Ginny took Erin's hand and helped her down the steps.

"Did you have a good time with Aunt Filly?" Ginny asked as Bart walked beside them, trying to lick Erin's face as they strolled along. Glaring at the dog, he ignored her silent reprimand and looked at her with a lopsided doggy grin, continuing to saunter next to the child. The hand Ginny wasn't holding entwined into the dog's fur.

"Yep. I make cookies for Unca Wuke," Erin said, dragging the toes of her boots in the snow.

"You did? What kind did you make?" Ginny asked, fighting the urge to pick up the child and rush her home. She knew the fresh air was good for the little one, as well as the walk home.

"Wasses."

"Molasses?" Ginny tugged gently on Erin's hand when the child stopped to stare into a mud puddle on the street. As quick as the little imp could be, it would only take a second for her to jump in the puddle and start splashing.

"Yep, wasses. Unca Wuke wikes dem."

"So he does."

"You my aunt, too?" Erin asked, trying to figure out how everyone fit into her little world.

"I suppose so, since I'm Luke's sister. Would you like to call me Aunt Ginny?"

"Yep. You Aunt Ginny and him Unca Bake." Erin pointed across the street where Blake exited the mercantile.

Rather than correct the child, Ginny swung her up into her arms and hastened on toward the church. The last thing she needed today was another encounter with the teasing, good-looking carpenter.

Tapping on the back door of the parsonage, Ginny opened it and set Erin down. Abby was wearing her hat and only had one arm out of her coat sleeve when they walked in, but bent to take the little girl in her arms, lavishing her with hugs and kisses.

"Were you a good girl for Aunt Filly today?" Abby asked, as she set Erin down and quickly finished removing her coat and hat while Ginny started removing Erin's many layers.

"I good, Mama. I hep Aunt Fiwwy make cookies."

"You did?" Abby said, smiling at her child. "Were they good?"

"Yep. I ated this many," Erin said, holding up two fingers.

"My goodness," Abby said, hugging Erin then setting her down. "Did you save room for your supper?"

"Yep, got's room," Erin said, sticking out her tummy and patting it.

Just then, the sound of the front door opening floated to the kitchen along with Chauncy's cheerful greeting. Erin scampered down the hall to her father and Ginny shook her head at Abby.

"I'll thank you and Pastor Dodd to cease any further matchmaking efforts on my behalf," Ginny said, trying to look stern.

"Us? Why, dear girl, whatever are you talking about?" Abby attempted to feign innocence.

"You know what I'm talking about. You two should be ashamed of yourselves, using the children's Christmas program as a ploy to throw me together with Blake. It's shameful!" Ginny wasn't nearly as upset as she led Abby to believe. "Unless you want me to leave you to run that program yourself, you and Chauncy better squelch any romantic notions you're contemplating regarding Blake and I."

"What's all the jabbering going on in here?" Chauncy asked as he stepped into the room carrying Erin on his shoulders.

"I'm well aware of your scheming and I won't tolerate further interference in my romantic inclinations, or lack thereof." Ginny narrowed her gaze at Chauncy when he stood looking at her with a ridiculous grin on his face.

"To paraphrase, you're telling us to mind our own business. Is that it?" he asked, setting Erin in her high chair and giving her a cracker to nibble.

"Exactly." She yanked on her gloves and turned toward the door.

"You know, that's kind of funny," Chauncy said, causing her to glance over her shoulder at him. "Blake just told me the same thing."

"Humph!" Ginny marched out the door and pulled it shut behind her. The thought of Blake going to Chauncy and telling him he didn't appreciate having to work with her made her angry, especially after his childish behavior.

What kind of man licked a woman on the cheek, anyway? It was utter nonsense.

Forgetting the dog followed her to the parsonage, she jumped when he brushed against her leg as she waited for a wagon to pass so she could cross the street.

"Bart, you lunkhead," Ginny scolded the dog. When he sat staring at her with a pitiful look on his face, she rolled her eyes and rubbed her hand over his back then gave him a brief scratch behind his ears. "I'm sorry. I shouldn't have snapped at you. Now, let's go home."

The dog barked and ran around her as they finished the walk home. Bart ran to his house and slurped noisily from a bowl of water while Ginny tried to wipe off the snow clinging to her boots before going in the back door.

"There you are," Filly said with a smile as Ginny removed her gloves and coat then hung up her hat. "We're just about ready to eat. After you wash up, would you mind telling Luke supper's ready. He's in the library."

"Certainly." Ginny washed her hands in the bathroom then stuck her head around the library door. Luke sat at his desk, his attention locked on the account book in front of him. "Time for dinner, brother dear."

"Thanks, Ginny. I'll be right there." Luke finished writing a number in the book then stood from the desk. He was dressed in work pants and a wool shirt with scuffed boots on his feet.

Tall like their father, Ginny thought Luke very handsome, even if he was a bothersome, sometimes overbearing older brother.

"What does mother think of your western attire when she visits?" Ginny asked, pointing to his denim pants.

"She rolls her eyes and makes a fuss, but then I offer to let her do the chores and it shuts her right up, every time."

Ginny laughed as they walked inside the kitchen. Luke kissed Filly's cheek and seated her at the table before taking his chair.

Enjoying a tender beef roast with mashed potatoes and gravy, Luke was in a jovial mood as they sat visiting after the meal was over.

"I need to finish the chores." Luke stood and reached for his hat and coat.

"Before you do, I wanted to ask if you'd both have some time to spare on Saturday." Ginny carried dirty plates to the sink, casting a glance at her brother.

"What do you need, Ginny Lou?" Luke asked, buttoning his chore coat and fishing in his pocket for his leather work gloves.

"Chauncy asked Blake to help with the Christmas program and he's making a few props. He thought if we all worked on the project Saturday, we should be able to get most of them finished," Ginny said, still aggravated the pastor and Abby tried to force her and Blake to spend time together, even if they were chaperoned by two dozen children.

"We'd be happy to help." Filly looked to Luke for agreement.

He nodded his head and opened the back door. "Tell Blake we'll bring lunch."

"Thank you," Ginny called as Luke shut the door behind him. "Blake offered to cook, but I was hoping we could take food."

"I'll put together a picnic lunch. How does that sound?" Filly gave Ginny a quick hug around her shoulders as they finished clearing the table and started working on the dishes.

"That would be wonderful. I thought I'd take my paint supplies, that way I'd have them on hand in case we want to paint a scene, or anything."

"I've seen some of your artwork, Ginny. You're quite talented."

Ginny blushed, pleased by the compliment. She'd always loved to draw and paint, but never gave it much thought. She just did it for fun.

"Thank you. I wouldn't go so far to say there is any talent involved in what I do, but it gives me pleasure. Mr. Daily printed a few of my drawings to go along with my articles."

"I noticed that. The drawing you did of the new church pews was especially nice. Oh, and the one of Mrs. Ferguson's missing cat."

"That cat." Ginny shook her head. "Did you hear he got stuck in the LaRoux's coal chute? That's where he was all that time."

"I bet he was a dirty little thing when Mrs. Ferguson finally got him home," Filly said with a laugh, picturing the bedraggled feline. Bringing the conversation back around to the church program, she asked Ginny about the practice.

"Percy wanted to be the innkeeper but he can't seem to leave the poor little Jenkins girl alone," Ginny said, drying plates and putting them away. She wasn't looking forward to hearing a lecture from her mother about her work-reddened hands.

Initially, she was mad and insulted when Luke insisted she help around the house. She quickly learned she enjoyed visiting with Filly while they did the dinner dishes and tidied the house, even if she didn't enjoy the work. At least now, she knew how to wash clothes, keep a floor clean, and a sink shiny. Even if her cooking skills hadn't improved greatly, Filly taught her to make a few very basic things. If she ever had to take care of herself, at least Ginny thought she wouldn't starve.

"That's because he likes her," Filly said with a knowing smile. "You should have seen him the year Erin was born. Percy played Joseph and Anna Jenkins played Mary. They were adorable."

"I'm sure they were, but if Percy doesn't quit pulling on her braid, the poor child will be bald. It's just wrong for the angel in the program to constantly be in tears." Ginny wondered if the Bruner boy could behave himself at least during the program.

"Have Blake speak with him. I'm sure he'll listen," Filly suggested, wiping off the table and rinsing out the rag.

"I guess we can try, otherwise, I'm not sure what we'll do." Ginny thought the children all seemed to like Blake. As good as he was with them, she wondered where he'd gotten any experience. Then again, he and Erin seemed quite fond of one another. Either that, or he was just naturally gifted in relating to them.

Recalling his boyish lick to her cheek, she decided maybe it was his ability to relate to them so well, since he could act entirely childish when the mood struck.

"Is there anything else we need to take to Blake's Saturday?" Filly asked, drawing her from her musings.

"No. He'll have all the tools and supplies necessary, I'm sure."

"Are you comfortable working with Blake on this? If not, I could talk to Abby about filling in or finding someone else," Filly said, knowing Ginny and Blake were trying to avoid each other. Secretly, though, she thought Abby and Chauncy quite clever to throw the two stubborn people together. Someone had to do something or those two would never make up and move forward with their relationship.

"I'm fine. Perfectly fine. We are, after all, adults and as such, capable of putting aside our differences for the good of the children and the Christmas program," Ginny stated, trying to convince herself as well as Filly.

"Not only that, but I'm sure it isn't much of a hardship to have to spend extra time with that very nice-looking man right beside you." Filly rushed out of the kitchen before Ginny could throw a soggy dishtowel at her.

Chapter Twelve

"You do amazing work, Ginny." Blake admired the scene she painted of a star glowing through a dark blue night sky. They could use it for both the shepherds and the wise men portion of the program. He noticed a few of her sketches in Ed's paper, but had no idea she could paint.

Recalling how much she liked to draw when they were younger, her talents didn't come as a surprise. Stepping beside her, he looked over a more detailed scene she'd finished earlier, impressed by her efforts.

Ginny set down the brush in her hand and studied her work, unsettled by Blake's nearness, by his scent permeating her senses and rendering her witless.

While Luke and Blake built a manger and a few other props, she and Filly worked on painting scenes. This was the last one. Filly filled in the large areas with color while Ginny added the details. The four of them made a good team.

Except now, one member of that team made her stomach flutter nervously and her hand tremble.

"Thank you. It's something I enjoy." She wiped her hands on a rag. It was impossible for her to paint anything with him standing so close. She needed space, maybe some bracing December air. "Is everyone ready for lunch?"

"I think so. Filly and Luke went into the house to wash up and set out the food. I told them we'd be right there." Blake fought the urge to pull Ginny into his arms and kiss her repeatedly. Her lips looked so soft and lush, he wanted to see if they tasted as delectable as he remembered.

Lifting a finger, he toyed with a stray curl near her cheek, rubbing the silky strands between his fingers. Ginny closed her eyes and swallowed hard before looking at him with warmth in her blue gaze.

He took a step closer to her. A smudge of blue paint accented her left cheek and splatters covered the front of the big apron she wore over a plain dark blue dress. She could have been dressed in a flour sack and Blake still would have found her beautiful. Her light fragrance floated around him, drawing him into a place he didn't know if he was capable of leaving and wasn't sure he wanted to.

When she continued to stare at him, unmoving, he took out his handkerchief and wiped at her cheek.

"Oh," she said, in surprise, taking the handkerchief from him and roughly scrubbing her skin. "I didn't realize I had paint all over me."

"You don't. Just a little spot." He retrieved his handkerchief and gently wiped the last of the paint away before kissing her reddened cheek. "No need to rough up something so lovely."

Blushing at his compliment, Ginny searched for a diversion from her all-consuming interest in Blake. She could feel his warmth soaking into her, even though he stood with several inches between them.

As she glanced around, she noticed many of the pieces filling his shop on her previous visit were gone.

"Where did everything go?" she asked, waving her hand around at the large, empty space.

"I sent a shipment to my folks a few weeks ago. Several people have picked up their Christmas orders and the pews are at the church. That emptied much of the space." He was glad to have a little room to work, especially as they constructed the bigger pieces for the Christmas program. Once the paint dried, he'd use the wagon to haul everything to the church.

"Where's that lovely rocking chair? Don't tell me it's gone." Ginny didn't see it anywhere.

"It's a Christmas gift." Blake didn't want anything to spoil Luke's surprise for Filly. When he knew they were coming for the day, he wrapped it in a blanket and hid it in his barn.

Ginny walked around, looking at the beautiful furniture Blake crafted. She knew in addition to that, he could be found putting up a barn wall or doing home repairs, like he had at Granger House. He seemed to be willing to do most any type of wood project.

Covertly glancing at him from beneath her lashes, she studied his firm chin, sculpted mouth, and eyes that shone like windows into his heart. There was no denying he was handsome. Nor could she deny he was a kind, good man. One other people looked to with respect.

"I suppose we better go in for lunch or Luke will be vocal in his assumptions about what we're doing out here." Ginny walked to the door but Blake beat her there, holding it open for her.

"If we run fast, we shouldn't get too chilled before we reach the house." He grabbed her hand and pulled her across the yard into the warmth of his home.

Filly and Luke looked up from where they were setting food on the table and grinned.

"There you two are," Filly said, giving Ginny a knowing look. "If you wash up, I think we're ready for lunch."

"Everything looks wonderful, Filly," Blake said, pumping the handle at the sink for Ginny to wash her hands. Although she was used to the finely appointed

Granger House, things were somewhat primitive at the Stratton household.

After washing his hands, he seated Ginny at the table, offered thanks for the meal and looked around the table expectantly. Fried chicken, potato salad, pickles, baked beans, biscuits, and canned peaches made him think of summer.

"Ginny and I thought a picnic lunch would be fun. Since it's too cold to eat outside, we can at least enjoy a picnic meal," Filly said, passing the butter and jam to Luke to go along with his biscuit.

"This is perfect." Blake looked forward to sampling the food before him. He'd yet to eat anything Filly made that wasn't delicious. Luke was a very lucky man.

Thinking about Ginny and her inability to cook, he realized whoever won her hand had better be prepared to do the cooking or resigned to eating in town. Stifling a laugh at the image of Ginny standing in his kitchen trying to make biscuits, he grinned as he passed her the platter of chicken.

"What's so funny?" she asked, wondering what made him look so happy.

"You," he said, then took a bite of his chicken. The crispy skin, cooked to golden brown perfection, was even tastier than he anticipated.

Ginny and Filly carried most of the conversation while he and Luke enjoyed the meal. Filly brought out a pie for dessert and Blake was glad he hadn't eaten the last piece of chicken. If he had, there'd be no room in his belly for the sweet treat.

He and Luke talked about crops and cattle, comparing prices from America to England on a variety of topics as they ate dessert.

Ginny and Filly started washing the dishes while the men finished their coffee. Looking over at her sister-in-law, Ginny watched Filly clutch the edge of the sink in a white-knuckled grip.

"Filly, are you feeling well? Your face is so pale." Ginny grabbed a dishtowel, quickly dried her hands, and placed her palm to Filly's forehead. "You don't feel warm."

"I'm just a little lightheaded." Filly swayed slightly on her feet.

Frantically turning to the men, Ginny flapped her hand at Luke, getting his attention, while keeping the other arm wrapped around her sister-in-law.

"Something's wrong with Filly," she said, trying to steady her. Filly was so much taller, Ginny struggled to stay upright with the added weight against her petite frame.

Luke and Blake both rushed over. Luke wrapped his arms around Filly and she leaned against him, taking shallow breaths.

"What's wrong, darlin'? Does something hurt?" Luke asked, his voice revealing his worry and concern every bit as much as the look on his face.

"Nothing hurts. I just feel dizzy and a little queasy." Filly closed her eyes as she leaned into Luke's strength. "I'll be fine in a moment."

"Has this happened before?" Luke asked, wondering what was wrong with his wife. His mind flew to a dozen scenarios, all ending with some tragic diagnosis.

"A time or two." Filly opened her eyes and glanced at Luke. "It will pass in a minute."

"I don't care if it does. I'm taking you to see Doc." Luke stared at his wife. Ginny offered to help put on her coat while Blake ran outside and hitched Luke's horse to the sleigh, bringing it around to his front door.

Luke carried Filly outside as Blake bounded up the steps. Her head slumped against Luke's shoulder and her hands rested limply around his neck. "I'll be fine, Luke. Please stop fussing. Just take me home."

"We'll see. I told you to slow down. Between cooking and cleaning and decorating for Christmas and watching Erin and who knows what else, I think I mentioned just yesterday you were doing too much and wearing yourself out," Luke chided as he set her in the sleigh and pulled a warm blanket over her legs. Turning to Blake, he shook his hand. "Would you mind bringing Ginny home later?"

Blake nodded and turned to see Ginny rush up beside him, hugging her arms around herself to keep warm. He forgot they left their coats in the workshop. "I'd be happy to," he said, glad for the opportunity to have Ginny to himself for an hour or two, but concerned about Filly.

Always full of energy and fun, she seemed fine while they were eating. He hoped whatever upset her was just a passing ailment. "Get Filly home and take good care of her."

"I plan on it." Luke urged the horse off at a trot. Filly leaned against Luke's side as he wrapped an arm around her and held the reins with his other hand.

When Ginny shivered next to him, Blake rubbed his hands up and down her arms, causing something charged and heated to pass between them. "Let's get you back inside before you freeze."

Ginny hurried back up the steps and returned to the sink where the dishes waited. Blake dried as she washed then she packed Filly's dishes into one of the baskets they'd used to bring the food to Blake's and looked around the tidy kitchen.

"The house looks the same," she said, noting not much had changed since the days when she used to visit with Blake. She'd eaten many meals with his parents at the simple table in the kitchen. They were both gentle, friendly people who always made her feel welcome.

"With just me here, I didn't see the need to do much other than keep it clean." Blake glanced around his home. The large kitchen and spacious front room filled the front of the house while two bedrooms made up the back. It wasn't large, by any means, but it was solid and warm and it was home. The only one he'd known since he was six years old.

"I like it." Ginny realized living with Blake in poverty sounded like a much better prospect than residing in riches with anyone else. "I always liked being here."

"My parents liked you, too." Blake made sure his parents knew Ginny was back in Hardman as well as how he felt about her return. He also knew their thoughts on the subject.

"Remember the time your dad pretended he found a mouse in the stew?" Ginny asked, laughing as she recalled how Sarah screamed and jumped up on her chair when the stew- covered rodent ran across the table and Blake shooed it out the door, laughing so hard he could barely stand up.

Ginny knew for a fact Robert hated stew and deliberately dropped the mouse in his bowl. She'd seen him do it. When he winked at her with a smile so like Blake's, she refrained from saying anything to Sarah when she demanded to know how the mouse got into his bowl.

Blake chuckled. "Yes. Father took us all to town and we ate dinner at the restaurant. Mother never made stew again."

"That's probably a good thing." Laughter filled her eyes as she placed a hand on Blake's arm and smiled. "They were always so fun to be around, Blake. I appreciated them including me as often as they did in your family."

Blake just nodded his head and wrapped a blanket around Ginny's shoulders as they walked out the back door to the workshop.

Ginny returned to her painting and Blake completed the last of the props for the set. Stretching her back when she finished, Ginny looked around to find Blake watching her in the afternoon silence.

Blushing under his intense scrutiny, she wiped her hands on a rag, bundled into her coat, and took her supplies to the house to rinse off her brushes.

Blake muttered something about hitching a horse to the wagon and left her alone in the kitchen.

Quickly cleaning her brushes, she packed her supplies in her basket and gathered the ones Filly left behind. When Blake returned, she could see the sky turning dark and ominous.

"Looks like we're about to get some snow." Blake stood by the stove and warmed his hands. In his preoccupation with Ginny, he left his gloves by the door and almost froze his fingers while harnessing the horses.

"I suppose it's a good thing I'm ready to go home, then." Ginny wrapped her scarf around her head. She hadn't bothered with a hat, knowing by the time they arrived at Blake's, her hair would be a wild mess anyway.

Blowing at a curl that insisted on springing out of its confines by her eye, she felt Blake's cool fingers brush it away from her face.

"That one giving you trouble, love?" he asked, with a look on his face that made Ginny's insides heat and her legs feel as weak as a newborn colt.

Unable to speak with him standing so close, she nodded her head. Blake placed a hand on either side of her face and tipped her head up so she was looking at him. Their eyes locked and all she could think of was how much she wanted to kiss him.

As though he read her thoughts, his lips lowered to hers, offering her a sweet, gentle kiss.

Ginny stood on her tiptoes and wrapped her arms around his neck, pulling him closer. Although they both wore coats, she was sure she could feel the mad thumping of his heart keeping time to her own.

"Kiss me, Blake, like you mean it," she whispered, unaware the words had come out of her mouth, instead of floating around in her head. "Like you want to."

"As you wish." Blake held her tight as his lips took hers in a demanding, consuming kiss. He captivated her, claimed her with that kiss.

Ginny knew then she belonged to him. She didn't care about being an independent woman. She didn't care about the suffrage movement or any of her many causes. She didn't care about New York or Nigel or anything other than being with Blake. She wanted to be with him forever.

"Genevieve, what have you done to me?" Blake asked, convinced she'd cast some spell over him. His best intentions to leave her alone and keep his heart safeguarded were of no importance when he held her in his arms, when she placed herself there so willingly.

Wanting to get rid of the coats and many layers of clothes separating them, Blake instead tugged Ginny's scarf around her neck and kissed her cheek.

"Let's get you home while I'm still willing to take you." With a wicked smile, Blake gave one last lingering thought to having his way with the beautiful woman in his arms.

"Mr. Stratton, you are quite scandalous at times." Ginny tried to sound offended, but couldn't keep from grinning at him.

"So you continue to tell me." He picked up the baskets and carried them to the wagon. He set them in the back then picked up Ginny and swung her onto the seat. Climbing up, he carefully draped a blanket over her, spending far more time than was necessary tucking it in around her.

"You'll suffocate me if you're any more thorough in your endeavors to ensure I'm properly shielded from the wind and cold," she said dryly, enjoying his attention focused solely on her.

"Don't want Jack Frost to nip anything." He smacked the reins lightly on the backs of the horses.

"I believe that would be impossible at this point." Her gaze drifted skyward as snow began to fall. It was a lovely way to end the afternoon. The flakes were big, fluffy, and full of promise.

The two of them were silent as they made the short ride into town, lost in their own thoughts.

"I hope Filly will be fine," Blake finally said, breaking the silence as they drove down Main Street.

"I'm sure she will be. Luke's probably correct. She's on the go from the moment she gets up in the morning until Luke makes her stop for the night." Ginny knew her sister-in-law worked very hard to make Granger House a welcoming home.

There were dozens of little things Filly did to make the house comfortable and inviting that both Ginny and Luke took for granted.

Suddenly coming to that realization, Ginny decided she'd do a better job of helping Filly. She'd talk to Luke about it, too. He really should hire some full-time help because that monstrous house was a lot for one person to care for, even with Mrs. Kellogg's efficient help a few days a week.

"Thank you for the ride home, Blake." Ginny glanced at the snow that was now falling in earnest. "Will you be able to get home before the snow worsens? I don't want you to get lost in a blizzard."

"Don't worry about me." He set the brake on the wagon and ran around to help Ginny down from the seat. After grabbing the baskets from the wagon bed, he walked her to the kitchen door then saw her inside. Luke was there, lifting the teakettle off the stove.

"How is she?" Ginny asked as she removed her scarf and gloves.

"Better. She refused to go the doctor, stubborn woman that she is." Frown lines creased Luke's forehead as he poured hot water into a teapot. "She agreed to rest in the parlor, though, so I'm making some tea. Would you like to come in and warm up, Blake?"

"No, thank you, but I appreciate the offer." Blake rewrapped his scarf around his neck. "I believe I better head home before the storm hits,"

"Storm?" Luke asked, raising his gaze to take in the dark sky and swirling flakes falling outside the kitchen window. "Looks like it might settle in and snow for a while."

"That's my assumption." Blake tipped his hat and gave Ginny a look that made her feel like he'd reached out and touched her soul although he hadn't so much as brushed her hand.

"I'll see you all at church tomorrow." He hurried out the back door. Quickly patting Bart and telling him to be a good dog, he swung onto the wagon seat and hustled home.

After driving the wagon out of the weather into his barn, he unhitched his team and cared for them before he returned to his workshop. Oddly energized and restless after being with Ginny, he needed something to keep his hands and mind busy for a while.

Chapter Thirteen

Blake ran his hand through his hair and looked at Ginny in exasperation as she tipped her head toward Percy Bruner.

Resigning himself to doing her bidding, he asked the boy to take a walk with him before they began practice for the Christmas program.

"Where are we going, Mr. Stratton?" Percy asked as they stepped outside into the nippy afternoon weather. Although it stopped snowing, it was bitterly cold outside.

"For a quick walk." Blake glanced down at the boy. His cap sat at a rakish angle on his bright red head and a missing tooth gave him an even more mischievous appearance than normal.

"Why are we walking?" Percy asked, stuffing his hands in his pockets, trying to emulate the way Blake strode along the boardwalk. "It's freezing out here."

"Yes, it is, so I'll keep this brief," Blake said, turning the corner and walking down a side street past the barber shop. "We all need to do our very best to make this program a success. Wouldn't you agree, Percy?"

"Yes, sir," Percy said, wondering why Mr. Stratton was talking to him about the program and why they were walking around town in the cold.

"Good. Would you say doing your best includes helping others do their best?" Blake asked, hoping he was going to be able to express his thoughts to Percy in a way the boy understood he and Ginny wouldn't put up with more nonsense where the Jenkins girl was concerned.

"Yes, sir," Percy answered, looking confused and a little worried.

"Very good, Percy. Then I'll expect you to do your best with the program from here on out." Blake stopped as they turned another corner and stood in front of the boarding house.

"But, sir, I've been doing my best." The boy was clearly upset that Blake thought otherwise. His mother helped him practice his lines several times so he wouldn't forget them the night of the program. He was excited about being the innkeeper and wanted to be the best one they'd ever had in a play at the church.

"Are you sure about that?" Blake asked, motioning for Percy to take a seat on a bench.

"I… I think so." Percy tried to think of anything he'd done that could have gotten him into trouble. He hadn't brought anything to the practices he shouldn't, hadn't played any jokes on anyone, and he even refrained from pushing that bully Jimmy Jenner into a snow bank when he tripped one of the younger girls intentionally.

"Pulling Anna Jenkins' braids and making her cry isn't exactly doing your best, Percy." Blake stared pointedly at the boy.

"Oh, that." Relieved Mr. Stratton wasn't upset about something important, Percy grinned. He and Anna were friends, but she threw the biggest fit when he messed with her dumb old braids. That was precisely why he did it at least three times a day.

"Yes, that." Blake settled a strong hand on Percy's young shoulder. "From now on, Miss Granger and I would appreciate it if you would cease your inclinations to pull her hair, tease her, or otherwise torment her during practice and most certainly during the program. A smart, strapping lad like you needs to watch out for the women folk, not make them cry."

"Well, shoot, that ain't gonna be no fun." Percy glanced up to see Mr. Stratton was serious. With a long-suffering sigh, he nodded his head. "Yes, sir."

"Very good, young man." Blake stood and held out his hand to Percy. "Shall we shake on it?"

"Yes, sir!" Percy beamed, pleased Blake treated him like a grown up instead of a little kid.

Returning to the church, Percy ran over to the Jenkins girl who winced, ready for a tug on her braid. Instead, Percy whispered something to her that made her smile shyly.

"Miss Granger, I do believe it's past time to carry on with the practice." Blake smiled at her with a satisfactory nod as he removed his coat and hat, leaving them on a pew.

Ginny was flabbergasted when Percy spent the rest of the rehearsal behaving like a perfect gentleman. He looked to Blake several times for approval and received the man's encouraging nod and smile. She had no idea what Blake said to the boy, but the change was notable.

Abby arrived before the children went home and quickly fit their costumes with Blake and Ginny's help.

Cleaning up scattered papers and cookie crumbs, Blake left Abby and Ginny discussing alterations to costumes, saying he had a delivery he needed to make before dark.

"How are you?" Abby asked as she and Ginny folded the last of the costumes.

"Fine. The children are actually fun to work with," Ginny said, smiling as she thought of some of the things the children did and said that were particularly amusing.

"Blake even got Percy to stop pulling poor little Anna Jenkins' hair."

"Really? That is quite an accomplishment. From what I hear, it is a daily occurrence," Abby commented, looking up when Chauncy walked in with Erin.

"Mama! Me hep Daddy!" Erin said, running to Abby and hugging her knees.

"You're a big helper, aren't you?" Abby said, picking up her daughter and placing kisses on her rosy cheek.

"Yep. I hep good. Hi, Aunt Ginny!" Erin noticed Ginny slipping on her coat.

Ginny smiled at the lively child. "Hello, Erin."

"Where Unca Bake?" Erin looked as though she expected the man to magically appear since Ginny was there. The connection she made between Ginny and Blake didn't go unnoticed by any of the adults in the room.

Chauncy coughed to hide his laugh and Abby smiled broadly. "Uncle Blake had to make a delivery," Abby said.

"Me go wif you." Erin held out her arms to Ginny.

With a shake of her head, Ginny finished buttoning her coat and pulled on her gloves. "Not this time, sweetheart. I'm going home and it's cold outside. You better stay with your mama and daddy."

"Okay," Erin said, laying her head on her mother's shoulder and turning sad eyes toward Ginny.

Gently kissing the little girl on her cheek, Ginny ruffled her curls, gathered her things, and waved as she walked out the door.

As she walked home, she thought about how much she enjoyed living in Hardman. Although her original intention for visiting was to escape Nigel's unwanted attentions and give herself a peaceful holiday without any expectations, she was glad Luke insisted she get involved in the community.

SHANNA HATFIELD

She missed a few conveniences from the big city, but realized she was happier in Hardman than she'd been at any time during the last ten years.

It felt like home.

She didn't want to admit it, but a part of that feeling came from the fact it was where Blake Stratton resided.

Sighing as her hand reached for the heart in her pocket that was no longer there, she wished she knew what he was thinking where she was concerned. At times, she was convinced he still cared for her, still wanted her, then other moments he seemed so aloof and distant.

One thing was for certain — she was through meddling in his business. She'd learned that lesson well enough the last time. It appeared he didn't need her assistance, anyway, with his workshop full of orders and people constantly requesting his work.

Glad he was busy and content, she rubbed Bart's ears and scratched his head as he followed her down the walk and up the steps to the kitchen.

As she opened the door, the mouth-watering aroma of fresh bread and roasted meat greeted her, making her realize she'd worked up quite an appetite since lunch. Before she could close the door, Bart ran by her legs, all but upending her.

"That dog is an ill-mannered beast." Ginny frowned at the canine when he hurried to Filly, rubbing against her legs and whining.

"Did you hear that, boy? She called you a beast." Filly looked at the dog with a kind smile. "Is that worse or better than your usual title of lunkhead?"

Bart wagged his tail and continued pressing his head against Filly.

"He was acting strange when I came up the walk, like he wanted attention." Ginny tried to drag the dog back outside, but he refused to budge from his spot next to Filly.

"I guess he doesn't want to go." Filly took a ham bone still covered in meat from the icebox and gave it to the dog. He plopped down by the stove and gnawed his treat. "Maybe he's just cold. It is chilly out."

"Maybe." Ginny was glad her mother wasn't there to see the dog in the kitchen. Dora would pitch a royal fit.

After setting the table, Ginny turned around to find Filly once again white-faced and swaying on her feet.

Quickly guiding her to a chair at the table, she got her a drink of water and a cool cloth for her face.

"Are you sure you shouldn't go see the doctor?" Ginny asked, wondering when Luke would be home. If he saw Filly looking sick again, he'd probably carry her all the way to the doctor's office despite any protest the woman might offer.

"I'll be fine in a minute. Luke's probably right. Things have been so busy trying to get ready for Christmas and your parents coming to visit and watching Erin. I'm sure I'll be fine after the holidays." Filly sipped the water and held the cool cloth to her warm forehead.

"Well, you better hurry up and feel better, because Luke's coming up the walk." Ginny caught sight of her brother as he strolled up the back steps.

"I'll be right back." Filly stood and rushed from the room.

"No tattling, Bart." Ginny grinned at the dog as Luke walked inside, humming a holiday tune.

"Hello, Ginny Lou! Did you have a good day?" Luke asked, removing his outerwear and looking around the kitchen for Filly. He noticed Bart with his bone and shook his head. "Bart, my boy, what are you doing in the house?"

"He ran in when I came back from the church and wouldn't leave. Filly finally gave him a bone to get him out from underfoot." Ginny removed the bread from the oven and set the pan on the counter to cool.

159

"Is that right, Bart? Are you being a nuisance?" Luke asked, ruffling the dog's ears.

Next to Filly, the dog was the best Christmas present he'd ever received. Supposed to be a surprise for him Christmas morning the year they wed, Bart made such a ruckus from his hiding place off the kitchen, Luke discovered his gift a little early. He hadn't minded though. He loved the dog and especially loved the girl who gave him the puppy.

Bart lifted his head and licked Luke's hand before returning to his bone.

"I suppose that means no," Luke laughed, deciding the dog wasn't hurting anything by the stove. Washing his hands, he looked at his sister, concern beginning to etch lines across his forehead. "Where's Filly?"

"She needed to… um… she's just momentarily… indisposed," Ginny stammered, avoiding eye contact with her brother as she began slicing the bread.

"Indisposed? What's that mean, exactly? She's not having another sick spell, is she?" Luke asked, throwing down the dishtowel on the counter and starting to march through the doorway leading to the rest of the house. "If she is, so help me, I'll take her to…"

"To what, Mr. Granger?" Filly asked, putting a hand to his chest as she breezed back in the room.

"Are you well, Filly?" Luke grasped her arms in his hands and stared into her beloved face.

"Fit as a fiddle." Filly kissed his cheek and hurried to set dinner on the table. "Now stop your fussing and tell me why your dog is behaving like a ninny."

Luke laughed and glanced at Bart. The dog abandoned his bone and continued looking fretfully at the back door. "That I can't explain."

Seated around the cozy table with their hot meal, they all three lifted their heads at a loud knock sounding at the back door.

Luke opened it to find Blake, Mr. Jenkins, and two other farmers standing on the steps holding guns.

"Gentlemen." Luke took an uneasy step back to allow them to enter the kitchen. Bart barked and ran to Filly's side, planting himself across her feet. "What's got you out on a cold night like this?"

Blake removed his hat and tipped his head politely toward Filly and Ginny. "Our apologies for interrupting your fine dinner, Luke, but there's been a little trouble with a cougar. He took down one of my colts this afternoon. I followed his tracks to Jenkins' place. He'd already made a few kills the past several days at some of the outlying farms."

Ginny's hand went to her throat, thinking of a wild animal harming one of Blake's horses. He loved them like they were part of his family. She glanced at Filly, who stared at the men wide-eyed while her fingers rubbed soothingly across Bart's head.

"Did you lose his tracks?" Luke asked, shrugging into his coat and fastening the buttons.

"No. The reason we're here is because the beast came around on the back side of town and his tracks lead out to the ridge above your cattle. We just wanted to let you know before you heard gunshots outside," Blake said as the other men nodded.

"I appreciate that. If you give me a minute to saddle Drake and get my rifle, I'll go with you." Luke slapped his hat on his head before turning to Filly and kissing her cheek.

"Keep Bart in here with you. I don't want him getting in the middle of something." Luke nodded to the two women before rushing out the door.

Filly turned her attention to the men standing in her kitchen. "Would you gentlemen care for a cup of hot coffee while you wait for Luke?"

At their nods, Ginny poured coffee while Filly quickly filled slices of bread with meat and handed each man a sandwich.

Filling Blake's cup last, Ginny brushed her fingers against his hand and gave him a look conveying both her sympathy and fear.

It took just a moment for Luke to hustle in the door, fetch his rifle and a revolver, and return to the kitchen.

"What are you gonna shoot with that revolver, Luke?" one of the men teased. "I don't plan on getting that close to the beast, myself."

"You never know." Luke tightened the gun belt around his hips. "I'd rather be safe than sorry."

Blake nodded his head at Luke, moving his coat to reveal the revolver he wore.

"Be careful." Filly threw her arms around Luke, ignoring the looks of the others as they ate their sandwiches. She kissed him on the lips then wrapped a scarf around his neck before he followed the other men outside.

Ginny hugged Filly, wishing she could have kissed Blake goodbye.

The two women decided dinner no longer held any interest for them. Putting away the food, they washed dishes in silence, interrupted by Bart's occasional whine as he leaned against Filly.

"You're a good dog, Bart. We should have known something was wrong when you wanted to stay inside," Filly said, rubbing the dog's head while sending up prayers for those outside to be safe.

The men decided to split into two groups. Jenkins and the two farmers rode up to the ridge where they'd spotted the cougar's tracks while Blake and Luke rode out to where Luke had his cattle pastured.

"Your colt gonna make it?" Luke asked, grateful the moon was bright, otherwise they wouldn't be able to see a thing.

"No." Angry, Blake mourned the loss of the horse. It was always hard to lose an animal, but especially one he'd cared for and gentled since it was born. "The cougar crushed his throat. It was bad."

"I'm sorry, Blake." Luke hoped they could find the cougar before it killed anything else.

"Me, too."

Although Blake wasn't much of a hunter, he could shoot a gun when the necessity arose. Tracking the cougar had been easy with fresh snow on the ground. They all wondered why it came back toward town, other than Luke had a pasture full of big, fat cattle that would be easy pickings.

From the vantage point of the ridge above them, the cougar could easily choose which target to hit and be on top of the animal before it knew what happened.

Riding through the evening quiet out to the edge of the herd, Luke and Blake refrained from speaking. Their attention focused around them, listening for any sound and watching for any movement that would signal the cougar was nearby.

Although they hoped to hear a telltale shot from the ridge, the evening remained eerily silent.

Blake glanced at Luke and he shook his head, agreeing that they should have heard something by now.

Luke motioned for them to ride in opposite directions around the cattle. Blake nodded and took off to the left. He hadn't gone far when he heard a low growl.

The impact of the cougar hitting his shoulder knocked him out of his saddle.

Heat and pain licked across his left arm as the animal's claws ripped into the sleeve of his coat, tearing at his flesh.

Swiftly grasping the revolver strapped to his right hip, Blake fired twice into the chest of the writhing beast pinning him to the ground. With one more guttural growl, the cougar stilled.

"Blake! Blake!" he heard Luke call as he raced his direction. "Are you okay?"

"I'm fine!" Blake yelled, trying to shove the creature off his chest so he could get to his feet. He felt the cougar dragged off his body and a hand reached down to help him stand. Grasping it in his right hand, he stood.

"Are you sure you're fine?" Luke tried to take in what happened by looking around him.

Blake nodded his head and studied the cougar. It was the biggest he'd ever seen. No wonder he felt like he'd been hit by a runaway wagon. Even in the moonlight, he could see huge paws and a massive head.

"Man alive, that thing is a monster." Luke studied the animal. The sound of hoof beats let them know the other three men approached.

"We heard the shots. Looks like you got him," Mr. Jenkins said, glancing from Luke to Blake.

"He's dead, alright." Luke noticed Blake clutched his arm. When he tried to look at the wound, Blake pushed at his hand.

"It's fine," he said, his words slurring a little. Blake felt light-headed, now that the excitement had passed. As he glanced at his arm, he could see something dripped into a puddle in the snow.

Blood. His blood.

"I think we better get you to Doc." Luke turned to the other men. "Just so you know, Farley, Blake took him out with his revolver."

"Well, I'll be," the man said, nudging the animal with the toe of his boot. "Guess you boys knew what you were doing."

"Guess we did." Luke looked around for Blake's horse. He stood, nervously pacing by his own. Whistling for Drake, Samson followed and between Luke and Mr. Jenkins, they helped Blake mount.

"Let's get you to the doctor." Luke waved a hand toward the cougar as he began riding off with Blake. "Would you gents mind doing something with that thing?"

"Be happy to," Mr. Jenkins said, tipping his hat at Luke as he and Blake rode toward town.

Filly and Ginny, who stood watching out the front window, saw two riders approach the house and ran out the door, Bart beside them.

"We heard shots. Did you find it?" Filly asked as Luke raised a hand her direction.

"Blake shot it. He wrangled with the cougar, so I'm taking him to Doc's office," Luke said as they rode by the house. "We shouldn't be gone long."

"My stars!" Ginny raced into the house to grab her coat then ran back out the door, following the men. She ignored Filly's calls to her to come back to the house.

Luke was helping Blake dismount when Ginny reached the doctor's office, out of breath from her dash through town.

"Run inside, Ginny, and see if Doc's around." Luke nodded toward the door as Blake tried to shake off his supporting hand.

"Really, Luke, I'm perfectly fine." Blake swayed as he took a step back toward Samson.

"Sure you are, but let's have Doc confirm your diagnosis." Luke sounded agreeable as he pushed Blake forward into the doctor's office.

Ginny stood there with the doctor, staring at the torn fabric of Blake's coat and shirt. Blood dripped on the floor and Doc quickly wrapped a towel around the wound.

"You just come on back with me, Blake. We'll fix you up in no time at all." Doc led him toward an examination room. "Luke, I might need your help."

"Wait here, Ginny, or go on home." Luke patted her arm then followed Doc down the hall.

Ginny sat for a few minutes in a chair, fidgeting. Standing to her full, diminutive height and rolling back her shoulders, she decided she had just as much right as Luke to provide assistance with Blake.

She marched into the room where Blake sat on an examination table. Bare to the waist, he sucked in his breath as Doc cleansed the wound and Luke supported his extended arm.

"Ginny, we told you to wait," Luke cautioned, tipping his head toward the door. "Out."

"I… um…" Ginny stuttered, completely distracted by the site of Blake's bare chest and arm. She had no idea men were so… ruggedly appealing beneath their shirts. Strong muscles and golden skin looked like nothing she'd ever imagined seeing.

Growing up with a brother, she'd not seen him bare-chested since he and Chauncy outgrew their habit of stripping off their shirts and pretending to be wild Indians as young boys.

No wonder girls went absolutely giddy over men who appeared to have muscles to spare, like the one currently sitting on the exam table with a face whiter than the snow outside.

Blake's gasp when Doc began stitching up the wound drew her from her stupor. "Is there anything I can do to help?"

"No." Blake turned his head to meet her gaze. His eyes pleaded for her to stay even though his tone told her to go.

"In that case, I'll just stand over here and distract the patient." Brightly smiling as she walked to Blake's other side, she began recalling silly things they'd done as children. Soon his thoughts were engaged in fun memories and not on the three deep claw marks the doctor stitched shut.

When he finished, Doc wrapped Blake's arm in a bandage. Luke ripped off the torn, bloody sleeve of Blake's shirt then helped him put it on while Doc gave him instructions for keeping the wound clean. He received the doctor's orders to check back in a few days to make sure it healed properly.

"Thanks, Doc," Blake said, slipping back into his coat and placing his hat on his head.

"That arm is going to hurt for a few days, so just take it easy, son." Doc glanced at Luke. "It might be a good idea if he didn't ride home to an empty house tonight."

"He'll stay at Granger House, of course," Luke said, and Ginny nodded her approval of the idea.

"We'll take good care of him." She ignored the frown Blake shot her from where he stood at the door.

"I'm sure you will," Doc said with a chuckle. "Just give him a good meal and a warm bed and he'll no doubt be fine tomorrow."

"Yes, sir." Luke opened the door and motioned for Ginny to lead the way. Luke took the horses by their reins and the three of them walked to Granger House. Blake should have ridden in his weakened conditioning, but his pride kept him from begging Luke to boost him onto his horse since he lacked the strength to pull himself up. Instead, he staggered along between Luke and Ginny.

While Luke put the horses in the barn, Ginny escorted Blake inside the house, insisting he go into the parlor and rest.

After he removed his coat and hat, Ginny took them to the kitchen and hung them by the door then asked Filly if they could make a tray of food to take into the parlor for the men.

Filly warmed food then arranged it on a tray while Ginny gathered things for tea and told Filly about Blake's injury.

Luke came in the door as they picked up the trays.

"Filly, darlin', I'm starved half to death," Luke said, hanging up his coat and washing his hands. Taking the tray from his wife, he planted a noisy kiss to her cheek and followed the two women to the parlor.

Blake sat in a chair close to the fire, his feet stretched out, head tipped back and eyes closed.

"Is he asleep?" Filly whispered.

"I don't know." Ginny whispered, setting down her tray and bending over Blake. Slowly leaning down, trying to see if he was still breathing, she yelped when he opened his eyes and kissed her cheek. Startled, she took a quick step back, tripped over a footstool, and landed in an undignified heap on the sofa.

"I'm awake." He sat up with a muffled groan, staring at Ginny. Doc didn't tell him his arm would feel like he'd pressed it into a pit of hot coals.

His whole body ached, but his arm seared with pain.

Graciously accepting the food Filly set before him, he listened to Luke tell the women about the cougar jumping out of the dark and knocking Blake from his saddle.

"He shot the thing before I could even get my bearings." Admiration filled Luke's voice.

Blake took a drink of the spicy tea Ginny poured for him. It was good and tasted like Christmas.

Thoughts of all the work he needed to finish before the fast approaching holiday made him hope his arm wouldn't bother him too much. Wishing he could be home in his own bed, he was grateful to Luke for offering him a place to stay for the night. Jenkins said he'd feed and water the stock on his way home so Blake wouldn't have to worry about his animals.

"I wouldn't mind if that is the first and last cougar I have to kill, at least at such close proximity," Blake said, trying unsuccessfully to ignore the pain in his arm.

Ginny shivered, thinking about how close Blake came to being seriously hurt. She'd read accounts of men being killed by cougars. The thick white bandage wrapped around his upper arm stood in stark contrast to the tan skin that glowed in the firelight.

Forcing herself to look somewhere other than Blake's bare, muscled arm, she turned her attention to the plate Filly held out to her.

Finishing their food, Filly and Ginny cleared away the dishes while Luke and Blake visited. Aware that their guest was exhausted and in pain, Luke told Blake he'd make sure the guest room was sufficiently heated, then left the room.

Sitting with his eyes shut, Blake could sense Ginny's presence near his chair before he felt her hand gently touch his shoulder.

"Blake?" she asked in a whisper. "Are you sure you're fine?"

"I will be tomorrow." He opened his eyes and stood. Taking a moment to let his head stop spinning, he mustered a smile for Ginny. "If you wouldn't mind showing me where you'd like me to stay, I think I'll turn in for the night."

"Certainly." Ginny walked down the hall. Rather than take him upstairs, Ginny headed for the guest room Filly had spent time that day cleaning and fluffing for the arrival of Dora and Greg. She didn't think Blake needed to climb the stairs and the guest rooms upstairs would be chilly, anyway.

"Here we are." Ginny motioned Blake into a large bedroom done in blue and burgundy. Luke was folding back the blankets on the bed while Filly set a glass of water on a table next to the elaborate headboard.

"Thank you all, so much." Blake was ready to fall in the bed and sleep for a week. Suddenly his eyes felt so heavy, he hoped he could keep them open long enough to remove his boots and pants.

"If you need anything, just ring this," Filly said, setting a small silver bell next to the glass of water. "One of us will come running."

"Thank you." There was no way he was ringing that bell. "Good night."

"Sleep well." Luke took Filly's hand and ushered her out the door. Ginny gave Blake a glance that made her eyes look as blue and bottomless as a mountain lake he'd once seen before she stepped out the door, closing it behind her.

Blake slid out of his shirt then sat on the bed, trying to remove his boots and having a hard time of it. Ready to give up and sleep with them on, he started to scoot back on the bed when he heard a tap on the door.

"Come in," he said, expecting it to be Luke.

Ginny stood there, looking so lovely the sight of her made his breath catch in his throat. The light from the hall cast a glow around her, highlighting the streams of golden hair cascading around her shoulders and down her back. A robe encased her form, but didn't keep him from being able to see the outline of soft curves.

"I thought you might have need of some aid." She stepped into the room and eyed his boots.

Almost ready to climb into her bed, she wondered how Blake would be able to undress himself with his injured arm and decided to see if he needed help. At least she kept repeating that excuse to herself as she walked down the hall and tapped on his door. It absolutely couldn't have anything to do with her desire to see him without his shirt on again. Trying not to stare at his exposed arm in the parlor had taken every bit of her concentration.

"Thanks." Blake studied his feet. "I thought I might have to sleep with them on."

Ginny laughed and the sound warmed his heart, reminding him of all the happy times they spent together. Happy times he hoped to have with her in the future.

"Let's see if we can get them off, shall we?" She picked up his foot and tugged on the boot. Yanking with all her might, she couldn't get it to budge.

"I think you need to turn around, Genevieve." Blake tried not to chuckle at the look of disbelief on her face at his suggestion.

She didn't say anything as she lifted her robe and nightgown, straddled his leg, and grabbed hold of his boot again. As she pulled on it, he placed his other foot against her backside and pushed, eliciting a gasp from her as the boot came off and she followed it down to the floor.

"My stars, Blake!" She shot him a stern glare over her shoulder. Picking up the other foot, they repeated the process, although Ginny caught herself on the edge of the dresser before she fell to the floor.

Slowly turning, she felt her gaze drawn to his and stood taking him in from his engaging eyes to his muscled chest and flat stomach. One thing was certain — a very beautifully formed man sat staring at her. "Will you require any further assistance?"

"Yes, actually, there is one more thing I need." His voice sounded serious as he scooted back and rested his head against the fluffy pillows.

SHANNA HATFIELD

"What is it?" Ginny asked, wondering if he needed help with his pants. If so, she'd have to get Luke because that was where she was drawing the line.

"Can you come a little closer?" Blake asked, motioning her to walk nearer.

Stepping next to where his head rested on the bed, she bent over, placing her face above his. "What do you need?"

"Just this." He lifted his right hand and entwined his fingers into her hair, pulling her face down to his until he could kiss her. A brief touch he meant to be teasing turned into something potent and filled with fervor.

Ginny lost herself in the wonderful sensations, placing both her hands on either side of Blake's face, exploring the feel of his stubbly cheeks against the soft palms of her hands.

Blake finally ended the kiss and looked at her with something in his eyes that made her want to keep kissing him all night.

Taking a step away from the bed, she held her fingers to her puffy, just-kissed lips and shook her head. "Anything else you need?"

"No, Ginny." Blake offered her a wicked grin. "Nothing you can take care of. Thank you."

"Good night, then." She backed into the hall and closed his door for a second time.

Quickly going to her room and climbing between the cool sheets on her bed, her cheeks felt hot enough to start a small fire. Restlessly staring into the dark, she hoped Blake had an easier time falling asleep than she would after that astounding kiss.

Chapter Fourteen

"Is everything ready, dearie?" Mrs. Kellogg asked as she put on her coat while Ginny and Filly bustled around the kitchen, preparing for the arrival of Dora and Greg.

"As ready as we can make it," Filly said, smiling at the plump grandmotherly woman who came in three times a week and helped her with laundry and cleaning. "Thank you for all you did today, and every day."

"You are most welcome." Mrs. Kellogg picked up a basket and opened the door. "Good luck!" she called over her shoulder.

Ginny and Filly laughed as the woman breezed outside, on her way home.

"You shouldn't be nervous, Filly. You know mother loves you." Ginny watched as her sister-in-law frosted a huge three-layer cake. As she finished an arrangement of greens and berries for the table, she was glad Luke told Filly at lunch not to bother setting the dining room table. They would add a chair to the small table in the kitchen and plan to dine there.

Grateful to escape the ordeal of setting the big table and carting the food to the dining room and back again, Filly hoped Dora wouldn't mind the informality.

With an hour left before the stage arrived, Filly and Ginny both rushed to their rooms to change their clothes and comb their hair.

Ginny almost ran into Filly as she came out of her bedroom into the hall. "What are you doing?"

"Just making sure the guest room is ready for your mother. Although I was happy to have Blake stay last night, we did have to remake the bed and dust again. I wanted to convince myself everything looks perfect."

Ginny studied Filly, since she sounded out of breath, although she appeared calm and well. Knowing her sister-in-law, she'd done half a dozen little things on her way up to change and another six on her way back to the kitchen.

She grinned and pushed Filly toward the kitchen. "Everything is perfect. Mother will be fine. Besides, she fusses just to have something to do, not because she's truly displeased. Luke and I figured that out a long time ago."

"I noticed that myself." Filly grinned then raised an eyebrow at Ginny. "I also noticed Blake left bright and early this morning. Couldn't you convince him to stay a little longer?"

"It wasn't for a lack of trying." Ginny's cheeks heated as thoughts of the kiss she gave Blake before he left that morning filled her mind. She wasn't sure how it happened, but after breakfast, she found herself alone with him in the kitchen while Luke saddled his horse and Filly concocted some reason to run upstairs.

Helping him slip on his coat, she was smoothing the fabric across his shoulders when he suddenly turned around and wrapped her in his arms, burying his face in the curls piled on top of her head.

"Ginny, love, why must you be so entirely tempting?" he asked, taking her lips in a heated, intense kiss.

Before she could string enough words together to come up with a response, he was out the door and down the walk.

Later, as she hurried through the cold to the newspaper office, she heard the town buzzing about the cougar Blake killed.

After discovering Mr. Jenkins left the body at the upholstery shop to be mounted, Ginny went to see it for herself.

The animal was bigger than she'd envisioned and looked fierce, even in death. Quickly sketching it, she took note of the two bullet holes in the animal's chest. Thinking about how close Blake had been to put those there made her say a prayer of thanks that he escaped with nothing more than a wounded arm in need of stitches.

Offering up multiple prayers of thanks through the day, she said one more as she filled glasses with water while Filly put potatoes on to boil, counting down the time until Dora and Greg Granger walked through the door.

When Luke arrived with their parents a few minutes later, she and Filly stood waiting, ready to greet them at the front entrance.

Dora engulfed her in a perfumed hug and Ginny stifled a laugh at her mother's hat. The assortment of flowers, lace, and bows stood at least a foot off the crown of the narrow brimmed hat, making the petite woman look top-heavy.

"Mother, where did you get that hat?" Ginny asked, winking at Luke as he rolled his eyes.

"Oh, isn't it something?" Dora asked, removing her coat and handing it to Luke before hugging Filly. "I was shopping with Mrs. Atwillinger one day and we saw it in the window. Of course, I snatched it up before she had the chance."

"What a pity," Ginny mumbled under her breath, thinking the hat a dreadful monstrosity. Whoever created it should be run out of business.

"What was that, dear?" Dora asked, hugging Ginny again.

"I said the hat is so pretty, Mother."

Greg coughed into his hand to hide his laugh and hugged his daughter.

"How have you been, Ginny?" Greg asked, stepping back to take a good look at his youngest child. With glowing cheeks and a twinkle in her eye, he didn't know the last time he'd seen her look so happy. "I think the Hardman air agrees with you."

"I believe it does, Dad." Ginny squeezed his hand.

Greg smiled at her warmly then turned his attention to his daughter-in-law.

"Filly, you get prettier every time I see you." Greg kissed her cheek and walked with her to the kitchen, asking about dinner. Luke and Ginny accompanied Dora to the guest room where Luke deposited a load of bags, promising to return with Dora's trunk.

Removing her hat and primping in front of the mirror above the dresser, Dora caught Ginny's eye and smiled. "I brought a few things from home I thought you might like to have."

"Oh?" Ginny asked, trying to think of anything she'd left behind she'd missed. Other than some of her clothes, piano sheet music, and the rest of her art supplies, she couldn't think of a thing.

"Yes, I'll get them for you later." Dora smoothed down the skirt of her gray and lavender striped dress. "Luke tells me you've been working hard at the newspaper and helping with the church program. He said Filly has even been teaching you how to properly run a household."

"Yes, Mother. It's been exciting and interesting. I'm enjoying being here very much," Ginny said, realizing how much she had enjoyed Hardman and being with Luke and Filly.

"I'm glad to hear that, dear. Now, tell me what wonderful thing Filly and you made for dinner?" Dora said, knowing from past visits Filly would make all their favorite foods.

"Filly made most of it, although I made the biscuits without too much of her assistance," Ginny said, linking her arm in Dora's and walking down the hall. Luke struggled to get past them with the trunk and they all laughed when he squeezed by.

"I love to hear the sounds of laughter in this house," Greg said as Dora and Ginny strolled in the kitchen. He leaned against the counter, contentedly munching a cookie while Filly sliced the chicken. Ginny hurried to help set the food on the table.

Exchanging pleasantries and visiting about plans for the next few days, Ginny learned Blake agreed to be their guest Christmas Day for dinner.

"You should see that cougar, Dad," Luke said, telling the story of their previous evening's adventures to his parents.

"It's huge, just like Luke said," Ginny added to the conversation, smiling at her father.

"You saw it?" Dora asked, dropping her fork in her mashed potatoes.

"Yes, Mother. I drew a sketch of it for the article in the newspaper. It's not every day a cougar is killed so close to town, you know," Ginny said, annoyed that Dora obviously thought she shouldn't have seen the big cat.

"Good gracious, Luke! What have you done to your sister?" Dora asked, turning a cool glare in the direction of her son. "You've always run a little on the wild side, but how could you corrupt your dear little sister so quickly?"

"He hasn't done anything, Mother," Ginny said defensively. "When I first arrived, Luke made it clear I was expected to do more than idly waste away my time, and encouraged me to find some worthwhile endeavor. I enjoy writing for the newspaper and sometimes draw sketches to go along with the articles."

"Good for you, Ginny," Greg said, smiling his approval. After Ginny spent two years flitting around Europe and came home even less interested in doing something purposeful with her time, he wondered what it would take to get her to open her eyes and realize life should be lived, not squandered.

It did his heart good to see her thriving in Hardman, although he had an idea part of her newfound happiness with life had something to do with the Stratton boy. Dora would have a fit to know Ginny was still in love with him, but Luke had mentioned he thought there was a possibility of the two rekindling the romance that ended a decade earlier.

That whole debacle had been Dora's idea, not Greg's. However, he loved his wife too much to tell her no when she insisted they move back to civilization, as she liked to call their home in New York.

"I'm proud of you, daughter. Very proud," Greg said, beaming at Ginny across the table.

"Thank you, Dad," Ginny said, swallowing back the tears that threatened to roll down her cheeks. It was the first time she could remember her father saying he was proud of her. Her mother had thrown around the word many times, like when Ginny looked nice for a party or attracted the attention of a wealthy boy, but not for anything she'd done that was worthwhile.

"I'm proud of all three of you youngsters," Greg said, pleased to have his family together for the holiday season.

"Thank you, Dad," Luke said, grinning at his father while his mother rolled her eyes and helped herself to another slice of chicken. "Although I think you are getting carried away to call us all youngsters. I'm an old man, now, you know."

"At what, the ripe old age of thirty-one?" Greg asked with a laugh. "You've got a long way to go to catch me."

"Speaking of catching you," Dora said, turning to look first at Luke then Filly. "When do you think we can look forward to being grandparents?"

Luke choked on the bite he was swallowing and Filly's face turned a shade of red that matched the strawberry jam Greg was slathering on his biscuit.

"Dora, honey, I thought we agreed not to discuss b-a-b-i-e-s." Greg glanced at his wife.

"We can all spell, Dad." Ginny hid her grin behind her napkin as Luke gulped water and Filly fluttered a napkin in front of her face. "Even it if isn't any of our business."

"Right you are, Ginny." In an attempt to divert the conversation to safer topics, Greg asked Luke about the bank.

After the meal, Dora and Greg joined Luke in the parlor by the fire while Ginny helped Filly with the dinner dishes.

"Sorry about Mother," Ginny whispered as she dried and put away plates. "She sometimes doesn't know when to be quiet."

"It's fine, Ginny. Her question just caught me by surprise," Filly said, her cheeks blushing again. "I... um..."

"Yes?" Ginny asked, amused by Filly's discomfort with the subject.

"Oh, never mind." Filly rinsed the last of the dishes and picked up a rag to wipe off the table. "How many more practices do you have before the program?"

"Two." Ginny hoped the students would be ready. "We'll practice tomorrow and then again on the twenty-third."

"If Luke or I can help, just let us know," Filly said, then looked thoughtfully toward the doorway. "The program is something your mother might enjoy. Would you consider asking for her assistance?"

"Maybe," Ginny said, bearing in mind how much her mother liked to share her opinions. She might ask her to attend practice tomorrow, just to see if Dora would like to get involved. "It would greatly depend on how much assistance she wants to provide."

Filly gave her a knowing nod of her head and the two women shared a laugh as they prepared a tray with dessert and tea to take to the parlor.

"You might suggest she leave that hat here. It could scare some of the children," Filly teased, remembering the wagon-wheel sized hat Dora wore the first time she met the woman.

Ginny nodded her head in agreement. "We'll have to make sure Abby sees it. I'm sure she'll be intrigued."

"Positively," Filly said as they entered the parlor to find Greg and Luke engaged in a lively discussion while Dora studied a sketchpad Ginny left on a side table.

"Are these your drawings, darling?" Dora asked, holding the sketches up for Ginny to see.

"Yes, Mother," Ginny said, trying to gauge her mother's reaction.

"They are quite good." Dora patted the sofa seat beside her. Rather than the landscapes Ginny used to draw, the pad was full of sketches of people. "Tell me all about the people in here."

Filly smiled at Ginny as she sat down next to her mother and discussed her drawings. "You know the Bruner family, Mother. This is Percy. The little boy stopped by with a delivery a few weeks ago. Dust covered him from head to toe and a cobweb clung to his cap. When I asked him what he was doing, he told me he dropped a dime in a crack in the boardwalk and crawled under it to retrieve it."

"He's an active little fellow, isn't he?" Dora commented, turning the page and recognizing Chauncy and Abby. The following page featured Erin's adorable face. "Tell me that isn't Erin. She can't be so big already."

"She's grown so much since you've last seen her, Mother," Filly said, leaning forward in her chair to glance across the table at Ginny's drawing. She perfectly captured Erin's sweetness and unique little spirit. "And she talks."

"Non-stop," Ginny added with a laugh. "You should hear how she talks about Unca Wuke and Aunt Fiwwy."

"Oh, I can't wait to see her," Dora said, clasping her hands beneath her chin then urging Ginny to continue turning pages. As they neared the back, Ginny tried to close the book but Dora took it from her. "I want to look at the rest of them, dear."

"But Mother, you..." Ginny said, then felt her cheeks flush as the last several pages revealed drawings of Blake.

She'd sketched him smiling, laughing, concentrating on his work, rubbing his hand along Samson's neck. Her favorite showed him gazing intently at someone only he could see, his eyes filled with depth and warmth, intensity and love. It was the way Ginny saw him when she closed her eyes — the way he'd looked at her numerous times in the past two months.

"Who is that man?" Dora asked, putting a hand to her throat. "Gracious, Ginny, he's certainly handsome. He almost looks... regal. Something about him seems familiar."

"It's Blake, Mother," Ginny said, wanting to snatch the book away from her mother. She hadn't shared those particular sketches with anyone. They were hers alone. Grateful she hadn't found time to sit down and draw a sketch of him without his shirt, she should have remembered to put the book in her room. There was no help for whatever her mother would say or think now. "Blake Stratton."

"This is Blake Stratton? He... I... oh." Dora quietly glanced from the sketchbook to Ginny.

"Let's have a look, daughter." Greg held out his hand for the book. Ginny gave it to her dad and watched him nod his head in approval. "He very much resembles his father, doesn't he?"

"I always thought so." Luke attempted to move the focus of the conversation a different direction. "Did you know his folks moved back to England?"

"Yes, I believe you told us that when they first left. Does Blake still have the horses?" Greg asked. He'd enjoyed going out to the Stratton place when Robert and Sarah lived there and talking horses with the man. He wasn't much of a farmer, but no one bred and trained horses like Robert Stratton.

"He does. Remember that old stallion Robert had? The big, black beast? Well, Blake kept his son and Romeo is in high demand these days." Luke winked at Ginny as Greg handed her the sketchbook and she held it on her lap. "He's even taken him on the train to some place in Washington to do his… um… duties."

"Is that right?" Greg asked. He and Luke discussed the horses while the women talked about Christmas menus and planned activities for the next few days.

When Greg and Dora announced it was time for bed, Ginny helped Filly with the dessert dishes before retiring for the evening.

"You might want to keep your sketches in your room." Filly handed Ginny the book after she left it on the sofa in the parlor. "You really are very talented and those drawings of Blake are truly special."

Blushing, Ginny nodded her head and wandered down the hall, hoping her mother wouldn't start listing all the reasons Blake was unworthy of her affections.

The truth of the matter was that Ginny felt entirely unworthy of his.

Chapter Fifteen

Ginny and Dora were setting the table for lunch when the kitchen door banged back against the wall and Luke ran in the room, looking wild-eyed and upset. He wasn't wearing his coat or hat and his hair looked like he'd shoved his hands through it, making it stand up in a tousled mess.

"Where's Filly?" he asked, frantically looking around the room, not seeing his wife anywhere.

"She's just..." Ginny started to say, but was interrupted as Luke ran to the doorway and yelled down the hall.

"Filly? Filly! Where are you?"

"Luke! Stop that this instant." His mother smacked at his arm and turned to look at Greg as he sauntered in the door and closed it behind him, carrying Luke's outerwear. He hung up his son's things on the hooks by the door then removed his own.

Dora turned back to Luke. "I didn't raise you to holler like a wild ruffian. Show some decorum."

"I don't have the time or patience for decorum right now, Mother." Luke shook off Dora's hand from his arm. "Where is my wife?"

"She ran upstairs for a minute, Luke. She'll be right down." Ginny wondered what had her brother in such a tizzy. He was usually calm and, since marrying Filly, most often in a good mood. He currently stood in the kitchen uptight and tense, looking like he might fly into a rage at any moment.

A tap at the back door interrupted further speculation as Greg opened it and admitted Blake.

"My apologies for stopping in unannounced, but I wanted to let Ginny know I took care of treats for the program practice today." Blake noticed the concerned looks on the faces of the people in the kitchen.

"Well, Blake, my boy, you are a sight for sore eyes," Greg said, slapping him on the back and shaking his hand. "How are you, son?"

"Very well, sir," Blake said, genuinely pleased to see Greg Granger. Like Luke, Greg was easy to get along with and frequently full of fun. He'd always been kind to him and his parents when he and Dora lived in Hardman. "It's a pleasure to see you and Mrs. Granger."

"Blake, you've grown since the last time I saw you." Dora was surprised when Blake took her hand, brushing the back of her fingers with his lips as he bowed in front of her, calling upon his finest manners. He couldn't have given the queen herself a more respectful or dignified greeting.

"Yes, ma'am. I suppose I have, but you are every bit as lovely as you were ten years ago. You don't look old enough to have two grown children," Blake said, hoping some flattery, even if it was true, would help grease Dora's wheels where he was concerned.

"I see your manners have improved as well," Dora said, blushing from his praise. "Would you care to join us for lunch? We were just getting ready to serve the meal."

"No, thank you. I didn't mean to impose. I just wanted Filly and Ginny to know they didn't need to bring cookies to the church this afternoon," Blake said, backing toward the door. Luke paced the floor, looking agitated and out of sorts, entirely unlike himself. "Is everything okay, Luke?"

"Yes. No. I don't know." Luke glanced down the hall again as he plowed a hand through his hair. It stood up even more than it already had been, giving him an almost demented appearance. "Where did you say Filly is?"

"Right here, Luke." Filly swept into the room and placed a hand on her husband's chest. Her bright green eyes glowed with humor. "Must you bellow about the house like a bull in the chute? I could hear you from upstairs blustering about."

Greg and Blake both laughed while Ginny shook her head and Dora stared at them.

"Yes, I must." Luke wrapped his arms around Filly and gazed intently in her eyes. "Mrs. Ferguson told Aleta Bruner who mentioned to Arlan she saw you at the doctor's office this morning. What's wrong? Are you gravely ill? Why didn't you tell me you were going?"

"Can we please talk about this later, Luke?" Filly asked, giving Luke a tight smile while tipping her head toward the four other people standing in the kitchen. "Now isn't the most opportune time for a discussion."

"No, I can't wait five more minutes. Tell me what Doc said," Luke begged. Tightening his grip around her, he looked at her in desperation. "Please, Filly, darlin'? I've got to know you're going to be fine. Please tell me now."

"Come with me." Filly walked down the hall and into the library with Luke hot on her heels.

Ginny looked at Blake and shrugged her shoulders while Greg washed his hands then helped Dora fill water glasses. After motioning for Blake to stay, Ginny almost dropped the platter she picked up to set on the table when Luke let out a whoop that she was sure people on the far end of town could hear.

"What on earth?" Dora stared in the direction of the library. Footsteps thudded down the hall and Luke rushed into the room carrying Filly in his arms. Her hair threatened to spill from its pins and her cheeks flushed brightly, but she looked quite happy.

At least for someone Luke had been convinced was dying just a few short minutes ago.

"Let me go, you crazy man." Filly laughed as she tapped Luke on the shoulder.

"Never." Luke swung her around the room before stopping by the table and setting her on a chair.

"Luke, I need to finish setting lunch on the table." Filly started to get to her feet.

Luke gently pushed her down and wagged a finger in her face. "You'll stay right there and then this afternoon you'll rest with your feet up and then…"

"Then I'll be completely bored and annoyed." Filly shook her head at her husband. "I'm not an invalid, I'm just…"

"Yes, Filly, dear? What are you exactly?" Dora asked, hoping her suspicions were correct.

"Go on, Luke, you tell them," Filly said, blushing again.

"We're going to be parents." Luke grinned from ear to ear. "We'll be welcoming a summer baby, so she says."

"Oh, darling, that's wonderful." Dora hugged Filly's shoulders then wrapped her arms around Luke before sitting down next to Filly and hugging her again.

"Mr. Granger, we're going to be grandparents!" Dora exclaimed, quite pleased with the news.

"Yes, Dora. I gathered that much," Greg said dryly, shaking Luke's hand and grinning at Filly.

"Congratulations to you both." Blake shook Luke's hand. He edged toward the door, not wanting to intrude on a special family time. Happy for his friends, he knew they'd be wonderful parents. Watching them with Erin, it was easy to see how much they would love a child of their own.

"Don't leave, Blake," Ginny said, reaching out and grasping his hand while Dora and Greg fussed over Filly. "Please stay."

"This is family time, Ginny. I really should go." Blake didn't want to leave, but felt he should.

"Oh, you might as well stay, Blake. There's plenty of food and we all feel like celebrating," Dora said, smiling at him with sincere warmth.

Blake worked to keep his jaw from dropping open. Dora Granger was nothing like he remembered from his youth.

She'd been judgmental and curt, looking down her nose at him when she acknowledged his presence at all. Ten years ago, he was convinced it was her decision to get Ginny out of Hardman and away from him that resulted in the family returning to New York.

Now she smiled at him like she not only accepted his presence, but also welcomed it.

"If you all are sure it won't be an imposition." He stood at the door, his hat held tightly in his hand.

"Absolutely sure." Luke slapped him on the shoulder.

While Blake removed his coat, Greg disappeared and returned carrying another chair. Ginny and Dora set the food on the table and Luke offered a very heartfelt and joyful prayer over the meal.

Blake was surprised to find himself sitting elbow to elbow with Ginny. Turning his head, he grinned at her as she handed him a platter of cornbread.

Something passed between the two of them when his fingers touched hers as he took the plate from her hands. Something he couldn't define or fully understand, but it made his gut clench and his heart pound.

"So, Filly, I assume the upcoming expansion of your family is the reason behind your recent bouts of illness," Blake said, looking at his hostess. Her face glowed and he thought she looked quite lovely. Almost as lovely as Ginny.

"Yes, the doctor said I need to slow down a little and get plenty of rest. Other than that, I should be just fine." Filly smiled at Luke and patted his hand. Now that he knew she wasn't about to die of some horrid disease, he was clearly on top of the world.

"I have four witnesses who heard what you said, Filly, so the first time I find you running yourself ragged, you are in big trouble," Luke teased, clasping her hand in his and kissing her fingers. He couldn't seem to keep from touching her through the meal.

"Please tell me you're not going to be an overbearing, fussy nag from now until the baby arrives," Filly said, making everyone laugh.

Luke didn't know what to say to that, making Filly and Ginny laugh all the harder.

"I'm not a nag." Luke pouted, shoving beans around on his plate.

"No, certainly not. And you've never been overbearing a day in your life," Ginny said, smiling sweetly at her brother. Blake joined in the laughter at Luke's expense.

"Why didn't you tell us sooner?" Dora asked, looking at Filly.

"I wanted to make sure with the doctor first and I thought it would make a lovely Christmas surprise," Filly said, looking around the table. "Since Mr. Impatient couldn't wait a few more days, now you all know."

Turning her gaze to Blake, Filly smiled at him. "And I apologize, Blake, for you being the unfortunate witness to such a personal conversation."

"No need to apologize. Between you, Chauncy and Abby, you've been my extended family since my parents left," Blake said, grinning at Filly. "Besides, Luke won't be able to keep this a secret for long. We could place bets on how long it will take for the news to be all over town."

"Here, now. There's no need for that," Luke said, frowning at Blake.

"I'll put a dollar in the pot," Greg said, grinning at his son. "I'd say there won't be a resident of this town who doesn't know the news by the end of the day tomorrow."

"Do you really think it will take that long? I'd guess by noon tomorrow everyone will know." Dora surprised them with her comment. At the shocked looks on their faces, she shrugged her shoulders. "What? Between Luke and Chauncy, once he knows, how could it possibly be a secret?"

"I think this is a good time to change the subject." Luke turned to Blake. "Do you need any help with deliveries or finishing projects now that your arm is injured?"

"I could use some help with deliveries, if anyone has time. I thought I'd make most of them before our last program practice. There are a few that need to wait until Christmas Eve." Blake nodded appreciatively at Luke.

"Dad and I can help you, can't we?" Luke looked to his father for agreement.

"Certainly. What are we helping with?" Greg asked, glancing from Luke to Blake.

"Blake makes furniture in addition to doing carpentry work. He has several Christmas orders that need to be delivered. When the cougar ripped into his arm the other night, he had to get three impressive rows of stitches," Luke explained to his dad. "He could use some help lifting the heavier pieces."

"Goodness!" Dora glanced at Blake and noted the bulge of a bandage beneath his shirtsleeve. "Doesn't it hurt?"

"Stings a little," Blake said, not willing to admit his whole arm still felt like it was on fire. He was so grateful to Luke for offering help with his deliveries. Thank goodness, the only project he had left to finish was a special one for Ginny. Working carefully, he should have it done in plenty of time to give it to her Christmas Eve.

"I should say so," Greg said. "Luke showed me the beast this morning. How close were you to that thing when you shot it?"

"Closer than I ever again want to be to anything with claws and teeth like that," Blake said with a teasing smile. He woke himself up twice the previous night with a vision of the cougar's face in his, its pointed teeth lunging for his neck. He supposed it was natural to have nightmares considering what happened.

"It gives me cold shivers just thinking about it." Greg playfully poked Ginny's arm.

It gave her shivers, too.

Every time she thought about how badly Blake could have been hurt, she wanted to wrap her arms around him and refuse to let go. She wondered what he'd do if she did.

Looking at him, he caught her eye and winked. Dropping her hand beneath the table, she reached out and squeezed his where it rested on his thigh. Heat zipped up her fingers to her arm and traveled straight to her heart. When he gently squeezed back, she smiled at him.

"What time does your practice for the program begin?" Dora asked, wiping her mouth with a napkin as she looked at Ginny.

"At two o'clock. A few of the children won't be able to make it since they live out of town, but we'll practice with the ones who can," Ginny said, suddenly wondering what Blake prepared for a treat. "Blake, you said you took care of the treats today, what did you plan to share?"

"I think I'll let it be a surprise for you as well, Miss Granger," Blake said, finishing his last bite of ham and not saying more.

"Would anyone like a slice of cake? There's plenty left over from last night," Filly said, starting to get to her feet.

"I'll get it," Luke said, jumping up and carrying the cake to the table. Ginny and Dora cleared away the lunch dishes and made room for the dessert.

After they finished the cake, Luke insisted Filly go to their room to rest for a while. When she refused, he swept her into his arms and carried her upstairs, ignoring her protests. Blake and Greg laughed at his fussing. They cleared the rest of the dishes from the table while Ginny and Dora washed them. The two men helped dry and by then Luke returned to the kitchen, looking a little battle weary.

"It's going to be hard to coddle someone so stubborn," he said, eliciting another round of laughter from his family and friend.

"Give her some room to breathe, son. You can't smother her," Greg cautioned, remembering how irritable Dora had been the entire nine months she was expecting Ginny.

"I guess," Luke said, noticing the kitchen was set to rights. "Thank you all for your help."

"You're welcome," Greg said, grabbing his coat and hat. "You and I were going to go visit my friend Douglas. Why don't we let Ginny and Blake go on to prepare the church for the children and we can walk your mother down in a few minutes?"

"That's a fine plan," Luke said, grinning as Blake helped Ginny on with her coat then slipped on his own and hurried her out the door.

"See you soon," Blake said, tipping his hat at Dora as he shut the door behind him.

Ginny held his arm as they strolled down the walk to the street and followed the boardwalk into town.

"If I didn't know better, I'd say your mother no longer hates me," Blake said, grinning down at Ginny. The scarf around her neck was the perfect color to set off her beautiful blue eyes. With rosy cheeks and her golden curls, he thought she could be some sort of winter sprite, especially with a smart little dark blue hat on top of her head.

"Mother never hated you," Ginny said, then looked at Blake and laughed. "Not more than she did anyone else here in Hardman."

He chuckled and continued their leisurely stroll toward the church. Stopping outside the door, they both stomped the snow from their boots before going inside.

Blake helped Ginny remove her coat before taking off his own and setting them on a pew. He'd already brought in his surprise and set it up front, out of the way.

Before the next practice, he'd have Luke and Greg help him bring in the props for the play and set them up so they'd be ready for the Christmas Eve service. He'd greatly enjoyed working with the children and spending the time with Ginny. He just hoped the youngsters had fun presenting the program.

Recalling how nervous the programs made him as a child, it was no wonder he always volunteered to be a shepherd. One who stood in the back and didn't have any lines. Although no one mentioned it, growing up he sometimes felt like an outsider with his British accent. He'd worked to rid himself of it over the years, but hints of it lingered and he sounded quite like the English viscount he really was when he got excited or lost his temper.

"Remember the year you were an angel and your mother decided you needed to float above the stage and tried to get a couple of the boys to pull you up on a rope?" Blake asked, thinking how ethereal Ginny looked in the costume with a halo and wings and her flowing blond hair.

Ginny laughed as she remembered the fiasco. "They used fishing line instead of rope and it broke before they even had me hoisted all the way up in the air. I fell on top of Chauncy. Wasn't he the innkeeper that year?"

"Yes, I believe he was," Blake said, sitting on a pew and tugging Ginny down beside him. "He tried to keep his balance and ended up shoving two of the wise men into the manger. Good thing all we had was a doll in that thing instead of a baby. No wonder there aren't any props left to use."

"Those were fun times, weren't they?" Ginny asked, turning to look at Blake and suddenly realizing how close they were sitting when she could feel the warmth of his breath on her cheek.

"Fun times," Blake muttered, reaching up to run his thumb across the delicate pink of her lower lip. So often, it stuck out in a pout, or tucked under the top one while she concentrated on something. Right now, it just begged for him to worry it with a kiss.

Lowering his head, their lips barely touched when the door opened and the sounds of children's voices filled the church.

"Practice time," he whispered, pulling back a respectable distance and turning to look at the children. Dora, Luke, and Greg followed the youngsters inside, smiling at the lively chatter.

"Mother, would you like to play the piano? I've been trying to play and lead the singing at the same time, but if you could play, it would be such a big help," Ginny said, knowing her mother would be more interested in helping if she had a specific job to do.

"Of course I'll play, dear," Dora said, removing her hideous hat and setting it on the pew with Ginny and Blake's coats. Dropping her voice to a whisper, Dora leaned closer to Blake. "Do the children get their surprise before or after practice?"

"Both," Blake said, grinning broadly as he opened a box filled with peppermint sticks. "They can have one now, and one on their way out the door. Would you like one, Mrs. Granger?"

"Maybe later," Dora said, smiling at him and going to the piano where she looked through the sheet music.

After a successful practice followed by a group of children anxious to have another peppermint, Dora and Ginny each took a piece of candy and sucked on their sticks as Blake walked them next door to the parsonage so Dora could visit Erin.

Tapping on the door, they waited just a moment before Abby opened it. As soon as Erin saw Blake, she ran to him. "Unca Bake! Me ride horsey?"

"Not today, sweetheart, but I brought you a treat," Blake said, handing Erin a peppermint stick.

"Tank you," Erin said, accepting the candy then leaning over for Ginny to take her.

"Do you remember my mama, Erin?" Ginny asked as the child shyly gazed at Dora.

Erin shook her head while sucking on her candy.

"Well, I remember you, sweet girl," Dora said, turning to Abby and smiling. "My gracious, she's grown so big and I can't believe she's talking so much."

"Oh, yes. She talks and talks and talks," Abby said, smiling at Ginny and Blake then turning to Dora. "Can you stay a while?"

"Yes, a few minutes," Dora said, removing her coat and hat. "Are you staying, Ginny?"

"I think I'll run home and see if Filly needs any help," Ginny said, handing Erin back to her mother. "Goodbye, Erin."

"Bye, Aunt Ginny," Erin said, waving the hand holding her sticky peppermint treat. "Bye, Unca Bake."

"Be good, sweetheart." Blake waved at her then tipped his hat at Abby and Dora before escorting Ginny out the door.

"Your mother seems to be quite fond of Erin," Blake said as Ginny held his arm and they walked toward Granger House.

"She is. For reasons none of us understand, she adores babies. As fussy as she can be, you'd think she wouldn't want a thing to do with them," Ginny said, waving to Mrs. Kellogg as she bustled out of the mercantile.

"Then she'll probably be beside herself when Luke and Filly's child arrives," Blake said, chuckling as he thought of Luke's behavior earlier in the day. "Although I'm not sure your brother will be willing to share."

"He did appear to be quite excited by the news, didn't he?" Ginny grinned as she thought of her unflappable brother being so distraught and disheveled. "I'm happy for them. I don't know when I've seen a couple so in love and devoted to each other. If I didn't love them both so much, I'd find it all quite sickening."

"That doesn't sound a bit romantic, not at all."

"Well, you wouldn't think it was so romantic if you had to watch your brother acting like a lovesick fool over the dinner table every night."

Blake laughed, steering Ginny around to the back door of Granger House where Bart sat wagging his tail, eager for attention. Blake obliged by thumping his sides, rubbing his head, and throwing a stick for him a few times before returning his attention to Ginny.

"Thank you, Ginny," he said, reaching out and taking her gloved hand in his.

"For what?" she asked, looking at him confused. He stood a few steps below her, which put her on eye and lip level with him. It was hard to concentrate on anything except how much she ached to kiss him.

"For including me today. It seemed a lot like old times, except now your mother doesn't appear to despise my very existence," Blake said with a teasing grin.

"You forget she's changed considerably since Luke married Filly. She really is a different person now, at least most of the time," Ginny said, glad her mother had changed for the better. In fact, Ginny thought both the Granger women were seeing things from a different perspective these days.

"I'll see you tomorrow at church," Blake said, realizing he needed to leave before he did something irrational, like drop the remainder of the peppermint sticks in the snow and wrap Ginny in his arms.

"I'll save you a seat," she said, learning forward slightly, her eyes keenly focused on Blake's lips. They were moving but she didn't listen to a word he spoke.

"Did you hear what I said, Ginny?" Blake asked, watching her eyes start to slide closed while her tongue moistened her lips. If she'd come right out and demand he kiss her, the invitation couldn't have been any more obvious.

"No," she whispered, wrapping her arms around his neck.

"Oh," Blake said, ignoring the voice telling him to step away. Instead, he pulled Ginny closer and plundered her mouth with his. She pressed closer against him and goodness only knew what would have happened if Luke hadn't slapped him on the back.

Ginny jumped away from him and would have fallen over Bart if Blake hadn't grabbed onto her arm.

"You better not let Mother see you out here doing that," Luke teased, tipping his head back toward town. Dora's hat was visible bobbing along beside Greg as they strolled down the boardwalk.

"It's definitely time for me to leave," Blake said, grinning first at Luke, then Ginny. "Until later, Genevieve."

Blushing, Ginny quickly nodded her head at Blake then rushed in the kitchen, Luke right behind her.

Removing her gloves, hat, and coat, she turned to Luke with a furious look. "Don't you dare say a word, big brother. Not. One. Word."

Holding his hands in front of him in an innocent gesture, he took a step away from her. "Me? Say something? Never."

"Very well," Ginny said, running a hand up to her hair to tuck in a few escaped curls.

"Just so you know, Ginny Lou, we all like Blake and think he's a really nice fellow."

"I appreciate that, Luke," Ginny said, patting his arm as they heard Dora and Greg approaching the back door. "Have you locked your wife in her room or can she come out now?"

"I'll go get her," Luke said, hurrying to remove his coat while Ginny lifted a spoon and stirred the soup cooking on the stove. "She was taking a nap when I checked on her a little while ago, or at least she was pretending to be asleep. Either way, she'll want to make dinner and I'm inclined to let her since you and Mother haven't quite mastered the fine arts of the kitchen."

"Oh, get out of here," Ginny said, turning around and shaking the spoon threateningly Luke's direction. "Don't you have a wife to harass?"

Chapter Sixteen

The family spent an evening in the parlor, chatting and playing a few games. Ginny volunteered to take the dessert tray back to the kitchen and Dora followed behind with the tea tray. "Ginny, darling, may I speak with you please?"

"What is it, Mother?" Ginny set the leftover pie in the icebox and washed the few dirty dishes.

"Will you come to my room?" Dora asked nervously while drying the dishes Ginny handed her.

"Certainly, Mother. Whatever is the matter?" Ginny wiped her hands on a dishtowel and linked her arm with Dora's as they walked down the hall.

After entering the large blue and burgundy room, Dora sat on the side of the bed and patted the spot next to her. Ginny sat beside her, wrapping her arm around her mother.

As she glanced across the room in the mirror, she noticed how much they looked alike. Both petite and short, they shared the same golden hair, although Ginny's had the tendency to curl with wild abandon, and blue eyes, as well as the shape of their mouth and chin. Luke, on the other hand, bore a striking resemblance to their father, except for his light colored hair and icy blue eyes.

"Blake's right, you know, Mother," Ginny said, pointing to the mirror. "You don't look old enough to have two grown children and especially not to be a grandmother."

"Thank you, darling. Isn't it so exciting Luke and Filly will finally welcome a baby here at Granger House?" Dora all but bounced on the bed, thinking about becoming a grandmother. She and Greg would have to plan an extended trip to visit when the baby arrived.

"It's not like they've been trying for ages, Mother. They've barely been married for two years," Ginny said, shaking her head at her mother.

"I know that, but I want a grandbaby to play with," Dora said, sticking out her bottom lip in a pout that Ginny knew well. She'd seen it in the mirror in her own reflection many times.

"And so you'll have one next summer," Ginny said, patting Dora's hand where it held hers on her lap. "Now, why did you wish to speak with me? I know it isn't about babies."

"No, Ginny, it isn't," Dora took a deep breath then slowly let it out. "Darling, I need to confess something to you. Something terrible I did years ago. I thought it was in your best interest at the time, but now, after seeing you with Blake, I'm not so sure it was the right thing to do at all."

"What is it, Mother? What did you do?" Ginny asked with an overwhelming sense of dread.

"Truthfully, there are two parts to this confession. The first is that I knew Blake loved you and you loved him before we moved back to New York. You were so, so young. You both were. I wanted you to experience life before you settled down. I didn't want you to find yourself trapped here in Hardman with the first boy you loved."

"But, Mother…" Ginny began to protest.

Dora held up a hand and silenced Ginny. "Let me finish, please. I also thought Blake wasn't worthy of you. You were so smart, Ginny, so talented and full of life, waiting for adventure. Blake's parents seemed hard-pressed at times to keep food on the table, living in that little house, trying without much success to farm. If it wasn't for the horses they raised, I think they would have been entirely destitute."

"They were never destitute, Mother," Ginny said, censure and irritation filling her voice.

"I realize that now, but back then I envisioned you living in squalor in some primitive one-room cabin with half a dozen children hanging off your tattered skirts."

Ginny couldn't help laughing at the picture that created. "My stars! You can be so dramatic."

"Regardless, I was sure that is what your future would hold if you didn't distance yourself from Blake. I finally convinced your father no good could come from staying in Hardman. I wasn't all that fond of living out here at the gateway to nowhere and I certainly wouldn't allow your opportunity for a happy future to be destroyed by what you thought was love."

"But I did love him, Mother. I loved him with my whole heart." Ginny brushed at a tear that rolled down her cheek. She knew their abrupt departure from town had something to do with her love for Blake. Something inside her always knew the truth even if her mind refused to accept it.

"I know you did, darling. It's quite obvious you still do," Dora said, furiously wiping at her own tears. "I'm sorry, Ginny. I had no idea the love you felt for Blake was so strong, so true. I'd like to think if I'd realized it then, we would have done things differently, but we both know I wasn't the same person I am now."

"I know, Mother." Ginny released a sad sigh. Looking back on what could have been wouldn't do anything but cause more hurt and pain.

"Which brings me to my second, and perhaps more painful confession," Dora said, getting to her feet and walking across the room. Opening a dresser drawer, she pulled out a box.

Rubbing her hand across the lid, she looked at Ginny with a plea for forgiveness written across her face. Setting the box on Ginny's lap, Dora removed the lid.

Staring down at a bundle of letters written in her own hand, Ginny sucked in a gulp of air. Lifting one out, she realized the box contained all the letters she wrote to Blake. Glancing at her mother with a look of hurt and confusion, she didn't know what to think.

"Mother?"

"Oh, Ginny, I know it was so wrong of me, but I couldn't bear the thought of you wanting to return to Hardman to marry that boy. I made sure not a single letter you wrote him made it out our front door. Likewise, I intercepted all the letters he wrote you. When they finally stopped coming, I bundled them all together and sent them back to him, unopened."

"How could you do such a thing?" Ginny asked, glaring at Dora. "I cried myself to sleep for months. Months, Mother! I thought he forgot about me. That he didn't care. Why just a few weeks ago, I accused him…"

Setting the box on the bed beside her, Ginny covered her face with her hands and wept. Dora wrapped her arms around her daughter and held her close as they both cried.

"I'm so sorry, darling. So terribly, terribly sorry. I don't know what to do to make this better," Dora said, pulling a handkerchief from her pocket and mopping at her face while Ginny wiped away her tears and stared at her mother with a look of anger and distrust.

Taking her daughter's hand in hers, Dora squeezed gently. "Blake has grown into a fine man, a good man. One we'd be proud to have as part of our family, even if he does seem to live a humble life."

"He is a good man, Mother. One of the best," Ginny said, sniffling as she mopped at her tears again. "He lives a humble life because he's a humble man. I've never met anyone like him. He is so generous, kind, and patient. According to Luke, he makes plenty enough money, he just chooses to live a simple life."

"Well, I'm glad when you marry him, you won't be poor," Dora said, offering Ginny a watery smile. "That is something I promised myself you'd never be, was poor."

"What makes you think I'll marry him? Do you really think he'd have me, Mother? As far as he's concerned, I ran away and never gave him another thought until I came back a few months ago," Ginny said, letting out a frustrated sigh. "If he's smart, he'd never speak to me again."

"Oh, I do believe that young man is plenty smart. That's why he's head over heels in love with you. Even your father commented on how smitten he seems to be with our beautiful daughter."

Dora brushed Ginny's unruly curls away from her face and kissed her cheek. "Please, Ginny, I have no right to ask, but I'm begging for your forgiveness. What I did was wrong and hurtful, and I'm very sorry."

Giving her mother a hug, Ginny kissed the top of her head. "I forgive you, Mother. It doesn't mean I'm still not mad at you or hurt by what you did, but I do forgive you. You had your reasons for your actions. I just hope someday Blake can forgive us both."

"Why would he need to forgive you? What did you do?" Dora asked, confused.

"I left him in the first place. If I'd thrown a big enough fit, you would have stayed. You wouldn't have forced me to go. If I loved him as much as I claimed to, I would never have left him behind," Ginny said, tears trickling down her cheeks again.

"Hush, darling," Dora said, wrapping her in a comforting embrace only a mother can offer. "You were fifteen. You needed to gain a little experience in the world before you figured out where you truly belong. I think you'll discover everything has worked out for the best."

"I hope you're right. I hope and pray you are correct."

Taking a chance that Blake would be home, Ginny bundled up in her warmest clothes and told her family she wanted to go for a walk.

As she picked up the box with her letters, Dora winked at her and Luke told her to say hello to Blake for all of them.

Shaking her head, she stepped outside into the crisp afternoon, grateful for the sunshine. Glistening on the mounds of snow, the sunny beams made it sparkle with icy diamonds. Ginny breathed deeply of the fresh air and strolled out of town.

Looking behind her, she noticed Bart tagging along and called to the dog. He loped beside her, slapping his tail against her leg while his tongue lolled out of his mouth, making him look slightly crazy.

"You are the strangest dog, you know that?" Ginny said, stopping to look for a stick and seeing one peeking through the snow on the side of the road. Tossing it for the dog, he barked and chased it down the road, retrieving it and hurrying back to her side.

They played fetch all the way to Blake's house. Her arm was tired of throwing the stick by the time they arrived and she knocked on his door.

Not hearing any movement in the house, she tapped on his workshop door and stuck her head inside, not seeing him there either.

Wandering to the barn, she heard the deep rumble of his voice and stepped inside.

As her eyes adjusted to the dark interior, she saw him in a stall brushing down Samson. Walking softly toward him, she realized he was humming a Christmas song as he worked.

Stepping around the end of the open stall door, she watched Blake work for a while before the horse nickered and moved her direction.

"Hi, Samson," Ginny said, holding out her hand and gently patting the horse's neck. He rubbed his face against her, just about knocking her down.

"Hey, boy, not so rough," Blake said, reaching out to steady her, while stepping between her and Samson. "I guess that means you've won him over."

"Now, if I can just work on his owner," Ginny teased, giving Blake a flirty grin. The look that swept over his face made her take a step back and her eyes widen.

"I think you've already worked on him sufficiently," Blake said, closing the stall door then wrapping his arms around Ginny and kissing her chilly cheek. "What brings you out in the cold?"

"I… um… there's something I need to discuss with you, Blake." She looked up at him with moisture filling her eyes. Swallowing twice, she willed away the tears, knowing that wouldn't make what she needed to say to Blake any easier.

"Let's go in the house where it's warm. I can make some tea," Blake said, taking her arm and walking her toward the door, noticing the box she carried in her hand. Bart sat waiting by the front step and Blake rubbed the dog's head before telling him to stay close to the house. Bart barked and flopped down on the porch.

"He's a funny dog," Blake said, helping Ginny remove her coat then taking off his before going to the sink and washing his hands.

Ginny looked around the front room while Blake made tea. He seated her on a worn but serviceable sofa and set down a beautifully carved wooden tray bearing a teapot, cups, sugar, and a few cookies.

"Mrs. Ferguson had me fix a hinge on a door yesterday, so my payment was in oatmeal cookies," Blake said, filling Ginny's cup with tea.

Accepting it with a nod, she remembered Blake's mother pouring tea from the same pot many, many times when she was a young girl.

"So, what would you like to discuss? It must be something important for you to walk out here when I just saw you a few hours ago at church," Blake said, trying to keep his tone light although something told him whatever Ginny had to say he probably didn't want to hear.

"I'll get to the point, Blake. The reason you never received the letters I wrote to you is that my mother made sure they never left our house. Last night she confessed confiscating them before they reached the mail, along with intercepting your letters," Ginny said, feeling the sting of tears prick her eyes. Taking a deep breath, she picked up the box from beside her and handed it to Blake. "I'm at least grateful she saved them so you can read them. Maybe now you'll understand how hard it was for me to leave you."

"Thank you, Ginny," Blake said quietly, looking at the stack of letters in the box. Something that had hardened in his heart suddenly melted and raw emotion flooded through him. "I appreciate you telling me that and bringing the letters."

"I'm so sorry, Blake. I had no idea Mother would do such a thing. She, of course, feels terrible about it now. She said... she indicated... anyway, she's very sorry."

"Of course she is. Otherwise she wouldn't have saved these and brought them to you," Blake said, running his fingers over the letters. Setting the box aside, he got to his feet and disappeared down the hall. When he returned, he held a bundle tied with a blue ribbon.

"I assume, then, it was your mother who returned these to me?" Blake said, holding out a stack of envelopes to Ginny, tied with one of her old ribbons. She remembered Blake stealing it from her hair one summer afternoon. He'd taken more than one and she wondered, suddenly, if he still had the others.

"So she said," Ginny whispered, clutching the letters he'd written so long ago to her chest. "You kept them?"

"Yes, although I attempted to burn them more than once. Every time I tried, something held me back and I'd retie them with that ribbon and put them back in a box for safekeeping."

"I'm ever so glad, Blake," Ginny said, feeling tears wet her cheeks as she set down her cup of tea.

"Me, too, Genevieve," Blake said, brushing away her tears with the pad of his thumb. "Don't cry, love, don't cry."

"Oh, Blake," Ginny said, throwing herself into his arms and sobbing against his chest. He murmured words of comfort and rubbed her back soothingly. When she finished, he handed her a white handkerchief from his pocket and watched as she wiped at her face.

"Better?" he asked, kissing one cheek, then the other. His lips trailed along her jaw, tasting the remainder of her tears in the salt on her skin. Moving to her lips, he kissed her so gently, so tenderly, she felt like weeping again.

"You must know by now, dear girl, that I love you," Blake said, his breath warm by her ear where his lips nibbled at her lobe.

"I love you, too, Blake," Ginny said, putting her hands on his face and pulling his head around so she could look in his eyes. "I never stopped loving you."

"That is good news, indeed, Genevieve," he said, turning so her back rested against his chest and his chin nestled on the pile of curls atop her head.

"Do you know you are the only person who calls me Genevieve?" Ginny asked, loving the way her name sounded when he said it with his light British accent. It made her feel like a princess.

"I do realize that particular fact and that is precisely why I use that beautiful name. I want it to be special when you hear me say it," Blake said, his finger brushing a tantalizing pattern along the exposed skin of her neck.

"Believe me, it's special," Ginny said, feeling a shiver of delight work its way from her toes to her head.

"Yes, I believe it just might be." Blake lifted her onto his lap and kissed her with such ardor Ginny thought she might die right there from the delight of it.

Regaining the tiniest glimmer of sense, she pushed a hand against his chest before he could capture her mouth with his again.

"I do believe it's time for me to go home," Ginny said, registering the look of disappointment in Blake's eyes.

"Since I can't seem to keep from kissing you, then I suppose you are probably right," Blake said, setting Ginny on her feet then rising from the sofa. "May I take you home?"

"That would be agreeable, Mr. Stratton, if it isn't an imposition."

"None at all, love. None at all," Blake said, kissing her thoroughly one more time before going to the barn and saddling Romeo.

When he returned inside to get her, Ginny was holding a sewing box he'd finished making the previous evening in her hands. He'd meant to deliver it on his way to church that morning and forgot.

"It's you," Ginny said, looking at him with wonder and surprise on her face.

"Yes, it's me. You've known me your whole life," Blake said, giving her an odd look.

"No, you're the one who's been leaving little gifts around town," Ginny said, setting down the sewing box that bore a tag with Aleta Bruner's name on it. Ginny was in the store last week when Percy and his sister were fighting over something and Alice pushed Percy over. He happened to fall on his mother's sewing box, smashing it beyond repair. Aleta was quite upset about her children destroying something that had been a keepsake.

"What are you talking about?" Blake asked, unable to look Ginny in the eye and deny her claim. He enjoyed making little surprises for people. It was great fun for him to hide the items somewhere they'd be sure to find them, but not know who provided the gift.

"I'm talking about you making Mrs. Jenkins a rolling pin and Mrs. Ferguson a cutting board and who knows what else," Ginny said, wrapping her arms around him and hugging him tightly. "You really are such a good man, Blake. I think you're one of a kind."

"According to my mother, one was more than plenty," Blake said, kissing the top of her head then helping her on with her coat. "You... um... won't share your discovery will you?"

"Of course not," Ginny said, squeezing his hand as they walked out the door. "At least I won't as long as you let me know when you hide the sewing box for Aleta. I'd love to see her face when she finds it."

"I think that can be arranged," Blake said, standing beside Ginny as she stood looking up at his big stallion, Romeo.

"Where's your wagon?" she asked, not thrilled at the prospect of riding the huge horse back to town, even if it did mean riding close to Blake.

"Here, now. Where's your sense of adventure?" he asked, swinging into the saddle with ease. "Give me your hand and I'll pull you up."

Blake held gloved fingers out to Ginny and moved his foot out of the stirrup. Lifting her skirts, she placed her foot in the stirrup and grasped his hand, expecting to swing up behind him. Instead, Blake pulled her in front of him, holding her across his lap, nestled against his chest.

"You are determined to make a spectacle out of me, aren't you?" Ginny asked with a cheeky grin, thrilled at the feel of being in Blake's arms while Bart woofed from the top step of Blake's porch.

"I do what I can," Blake teased, kissing her lips followed by her nose before calling to the dog. "Come along, Bart. Let's head to town, old boy."

The dog barked and ran ahead of them, as if he was showing Blake the way.

Blake rode around town, trying to shield Ginny from receiving too many curious stares as she sat across his lap. Stopping at the end of the walk at Granger House, Ginny reached up and pulled Blake's head down for one more incredible kiss. Scorching heat flamed through her as his arms tightened around her and she was kissed more thoroughly than she'd ever imagined possible.

The horse shifted beneath them restlessly, causing Blake to pull back just enough that she could see the longing in his eyes.

"I believe Romeo has decided it's time for me to be on my way," Blake said with a hint of humor. Leave it to a horse named after a romantic character to put an end to his little interlude with Ginny. It was probably for the best. If they kept kissing each other like it was the last one they'd ever share, Dora would no doubt come outside and set him on his ear.

After giving her a peck on the cheek, he gently set her on her feet, tipped his hat, and started to ride away.

Watching him, she waved when he turned around and grinned. "I love you, Genevieve Granger!"

Playfully blowing him a kiss, she ran around to the back door, tripping over Bart. Telling him to stay out of the way, she was grateful to find the kitchen empty when she stepped inside. Flinging off her outerwear and tossing it on a peg, she hurried to her room, shutting the door quietly behind her.

Curling up in the chair beneath the window, she took a breath, ready to read Blake's letters. A tap at the door made her frown, especially when Dora stuck her head in the room.

"Is everything all right, darling?"

"Yes, Mother. Blake gave me the letters he wrote and I just wanted to be alone for a while to read them," Ginny said, looking at her mother with a raised brow, hoping her mother would take the hint and give her a few moments of solitude.

"Then we'll certainly leave you alone, dear," Dora said, closing the door.

An hour later, she and Filly both stood outside Ginny's door, listening to the girl sob, wondering if they should go in or leave her alone.

"Leave her be," Greg said quietly as he put a hand on their shoulders, guiding them toward the kitchen. "Sometimes you girls just need a good cry."

"Is that so, Mr. Granger?" Dora asked, eyeing her husband speculatively. "How did you become so smart and well-versed in women?"

"By marrying you, dear," Greg wisely said, kissing Dora's cheek before wandering off in search of Luke.

The four of them were about to sit down to dinner when Ginny walked into the kitchen, her eyes red and puffy from crying, but a look of contentment and happiness on her face.

"Better now?" Dora asked, rubbing Ginny's back as she took a seat at the table.

"Yes, Mother. Much," Ginny said, looking around at the meal and realizing she was feeling much better — and very much in love.

Chapter Seventeen

"I can't thank you enough for your strong arms and backs today," Blake said to Luke and Greg as they helped him carry in props for the church program.

They spent the better part of the morning helping him deliver orders around town and to a couple of outlying farms. The few pieces he had left to deliver the following day were light enough he could move them without putting any strain on his arm.

Forgetting about the stitches yesterday when he'd tugged Ginny up on the horse in front of him, five popped and bled impressively before he decided he better have the doctor look at them.

Receiving an earful from Doc about taking it easy and being careful, he had a fresh bandage around his arm and a threat to have the limb amputated if he couldn't behave himself.

"Heard you were at Doc's first thing this morning," Luke said as he carried in the new manger Blake constructed.

"Yeah. Popped a few stitches yesterday," Blake said, carrying in the star scene Ginny painted.

"What are you doing packing all this around today, then, son?" Greg asked, taking the scene from Blake and leaning it against the wall, behind the lectern at the front of the church.

"Spreading Christmas cheer," Blake said with a grin, going back out to the wagon for the last load.

"He's a hard worker," Greg mumbled to Luke as they trudged back outside.

"And hard-headed," Luke said, taking one end of a prop that looked like a barn wall. He and Blake carried it to the front of the church and left it with the rest of the props.

"When are the ladies coming to decorate?" Blake asked, picturing how things would look with the curtain Ginny wanted to put up for the program and the festive touches he was sure Filly and Dora would add.

"Right after lunch. You might as well come home with us and have a hot meal," Luke said, slapping Blake on the back as they returned outside.

Abby approached from the direction of her store with Erin chattering along happily beside her.

Spying two of her favorite people, Erin squealed and ran toward the men. "Unca Wuke! Unca Bake!"

"Hi, honey," Luke said, picking her up and kissing her cheek, and getting a tight hug before passing the wriggling little girl to Blake.

"Hello, sweetheart. Are you helping your mama today?" Blake asked, kissing her cheek and looking to Greg to see if he wanted to hold the child. Greg nodded but waited to see what Erin would do.

"Yep. I hep. Hi, Papa," Erin said, reaching out to Greg. He and Dora spent a considerable amount of time becoming reacquainted with her the previous afternoon while Ginny went for her walk. Erin started calling him Papa, for whatever reason. He wasn't going to argue.

"Are you being a good girl today?" Greg asked, studying Erin's face with feigned scrutiny.

"I good," Erin said, poking her mitten-covered hand at her chest, making all the adults laugh.

"Well, in that case," Greg said, digging in his pocket and pulling out a lemon drop, handing it to the child.

"Tank you," she said, kissing Greg's cheek then wiggling to be set down.

"Candy, Mama," Erin said, holding her hand up to Abby before popping the sweet in her mouth.

"Thank you," Abby said, smiling at the men. "Are the girls still planning to decorate after lunch?"

"Last I heard," Luke said, nodding his head.

"Wonderful. Our little busybody will be down for a nap and Chauncy should be back by then, so we can both help," Abby said, grinning as Erin grabbed her hand and tugged in the direction of the parsonage door. "We'll see you soon."

Greg chuckled and shook his head. "Busybody is right. My, how that sweet little thing has grown. Just think, Luke, by this time next year, you'll have your own baby to fuss over."

"Yes, sir," Luke said, grinning broadly. "He'll be a welcome addition to our little family."

"He?" Blake asked, innocently. "You put in a special order, did you? Know for sure it will be a boy?"

Luke glared at him while Greg laughed and thumped him on the shoulder.

"It could very well be a girl," Greg said as they climbed in Blake's wagon and he drove the short distance to Granger House.

"I know that, but I'd kind of like it to be a boy," Luke said as Blake stopped the wagon by the barn. Together they unhitched the team. Since Blake would be in town until late afternoon, Luke offered to keep the horses in his corral so they wouldn't have to stand hitched to the wagon for hours on end.

"Are you going to impart that information to your wife?" Blake asked with a teasing smile as they led the horses to the gate and Luke tossed a few forkfuls of hay over the fence.

"Not on your life. I value the peace of my home too much," Luke said, making Greg laugh again.

Finishing with the horses, Luke stopped Blake before they walked in the house and discussed arrangements for picking up Filly's rocking chair.

Blake planned to drop off the chair at the bank the following morning when he made a few final deliveries then he'd join the Granger and Dodd families as they trekked out to cut down Christmas trees. Blake hadn't felt so much like part of a family since his parents moved back to England.

Sitting down for one of Filly's delicious meals, the conversation around the table was lively. As soon as they finished and cleaned up the dishes, they all walked to the church to put up decorations. He, Luke and Greg each carried garlands and wreaths while the women carried candles, red ribbon, and a basket of what Luke called "frippery."

Abby and Chauncy met them at the church door.

"Nice of you to show up to help," Luke said, giving Chauncy a playful shove. "Where were you when we were unloading all the props?"

"Visiting Mrs. Heming," Chauncy said, taking a handful of the garlands Luke held out to him. "She slipped on the ice a few days ago and broke her leg. She's staying at the boarding house since she lives so far out of town and she's all alone."

"How is the poor dear?" Dora asked, setting down the basket of candles she carried. The scent of bayberry drifted up to her nose, making her smile at the pleasant nostalgic fragrance.

"As well as an eighty-year-old with a broken leg can be," Chauncy said, smiling at Dora then looking around the group. "If you ladies will just tell us what you want done, we'll get to work."

Abby and Dora took charge of decorations while Ginny and Filly directed the men in setting up the props for the program. Abby had Chauncy bring over all the costumes and set them behind the curtain they erected to hide the program area.

Finishing with the decorations, they all decided the church looked quite festive. Garlands draped across the front of the church, wreaths hung on the doors and candles sat in the windows, where they would send out a welcoming glow the following evening. Red bows draped the ends of each pew and a big basket of greens with holly sat near the lectern.

Admiring their hard work, the sound of childish laughter signaled the arrival of the children for their final program practice. Greg, along with Luke, Filly, Chauncy and Abby decided to stay and watch. Abby wanted to make sure all the costumes fit properly and Filly helped get the right outfits on each child.

Dora sat at the piano while Blake and Ginny encouraged the children and offered assistance when one of them forgot their line. Practice went smoothly with the adults clapping and cheering. Percy kept his hands to himself and Anna Jenkins smiled at him the whole time.

The youngsters were nearing the end of the practice, singing *Away in a Manger* with their little voices blending in harmony, when the church door swung open and a small man charged down the aisle, grabbing Ginny's arm before anyone could stop him.

"Unhand me," Ginny said, turning to see what buffoon had not only interrupted the children, but also bruised her arm with his tight grip. Her jaw dropped as she looked into the pinched, pale features of Nigel Pickford's face.

Gathering her wits, she wrenched her arm away and took a step back. She felt Blake's presence behind her and noticed Luke and her father hurrying to her side.

"How dare you?" Ginny asked, leaning back against Blake, away from Nigel's vile breath and the seething look on his face.

She'd forgotten what a small, unimpressive little man his appearance made. From his pencil-thin body to the solid eyebrow that crossed his forehead like an unwelcome caterpillar, she couldn't fathom how she'd ever borne his presence.

"I dare, Ginny, because you are my betrothed and I've had enough of your nonsense. We'll leave immediately for New York where we'll wed in a fabulous New Year's Eve celebration," Nigel said, grabbing her arm again and attempting to tug her toward the door.

"I'm not going anywhere, you lack-witted imbecile," Ginny said, yanking her arm away from him a second time. "I don't know why you think we're betrothed or why I'll marry you, but I'll tell you as simply as I can, Nigel, I won't ever marry you. Ever."

"Enough of your theatrics, dearest. Let's go. Mummy expects us back in a few days," Nigel said, reaching for her hand and grasping air.

Blake stepped in front of Ginny and glared down at the pasty-faced idiot who couldn't grasp the concept of the word "no."

"I believe the lady said she won't go with you. I suggest you go back out those doors and return to wherever you came from," Blake said. The threatening tone in his voice was unmistakable to everyone except Nigel.

"I'm not leaving without Ginny and we're leaving posthaste," Nigel said, trying to sidestep Blake only to find himself face to face with Luke. By this time, several of the children were crying while Filly and Abby did their best to assure them Miss Granger wasn't leaving.

"Nigel," Luke said, forcibly turning him around while Chauncy closed the space on his other side, preventing him from getting close to Ginny. "My sister isn't interested in marrying you, as she very clearly stated. I must ask you to refrain from insisting."

Glaring from Luke to the big man on his other side, Nigel dug in his coat pocket and produced a paper.

"I have a written agreement, signed by Ginny, stating her intent to be my wife," Nigel said, handing the paper to Luke. Reading through the document, Luke shook his head and handed it to Chauncy.

"And who might you be?" Nigel asked as Chauncy looked over the paper.

"Pastor of this church," Chauncy said, reaching behind him and handing the paper to Ginny.

"Marvelous. Why don't you marry us now and we can honeymoon all the way back to New York. Mummy can still have her fancy wedding next week, of course," Nigel said, once again trying to step around the men to reach Ginny.

She stood astounded, staring at the paper in her hand. It was most definitely her signature at the bottom of the page, but she didn't recall signing any such document. Trying to think back to anything she might have signed in Nigel's presence, she finally remembered him asking her to be the first to sign a petition to provide care for homeless children.

She should have known Nigel would never be interested in or care about something like that. His biggest concern was himself.

How could she have been so stupid?

"You tricked me," she said, waving the paper at Nigel. "We both know I didn't agree to sign this. You said it was a petition to provide care for homeless children. You knew I'd sign it without looking at the details."

"Don't be ridiculous," Nigel said, trying to snatch the paper back from Ginny. Blake intercepted it and read the document. He looked from Nigel to Ginny, then to Luke. Ginny, in fact, had signed a document. It appeared to be dated and witnessed more than a year ago.

"I'm not being ridiculous, I'm being truthful," Ginny said, wanting to stamp her foot. "I won't marry you Nigel. I won't."

"What do any of these country bumpkins have to offer you I can't?" Nigel asked, looking from Blake to Chauncy. He assumed it was one of the two that held Ginny's interest, and then he noticed a pretty brunette step beside Chauncy and take his hand, which left the man holding the paper in his hand.

"Love, Nigel," Ginny said, so angry she was about to explode. "Respect. Courtesy. Common decency."

Nigel rolled his eyes. "A bunch of balderdash. Poppycock. No one marries for love. That's for fools and fairytales. You, beautiful Ginny, will marry me because I'm the most eligible man in New York City. I can give you a grand home and an extravagant lifestyle — everything your heart desires. You'll dress in the most expensive clothes, eat the finest food, enjoy the company of societies most elite. We'll travel the world, experience other cultures, and live a life of gaiety and adventure."

Snaking out his hand Nigel attempted to grab the agreement from Blake, but he refused to relinquish it.

"It's not an option, Ginny. Your signature on that paper guarantees you'll experience a life of ease and pampering. You will marry me, of that there is no doubt," Nigel said. Preening like a peacock in front of Ginny, he more closely resembled a pompous banty rooster. "Besides, why wouldn't you want to marry me? I'll care

SHANNA HATFIELD

for you, give you some sniveling little brats to care for. Life will be grand."

Blake fought the urge to ram his fist down the throat of Nigel Pickford. Since they were in a church and one punch might actually kill the little weasel, Blake kept a tight leash on his growing anger.

"I say, chap, can you even read what it says?" Nigel asked, staring at Blake.

When Blake glared at him, he formed a fist and put everything he had into taking a swing at Blake, hitting his arm in the exact spot where the doctor had just that morning fixed his stitches.

Biting his lip to keep from yelling, Blake turned around and popped Nigel with his other hand, catching him in the face before he even thought about what he was doing.

Sprawled on the floor, holding his bleeding nose, Ginny thought Nigel might actually begin to cry. "That brute has broken my nose! I'll sue! I'll…"

"It's nothing less than you deserve," Ginny said, standing between Blake and Nigel, wanting to kick him a few times while he sat on the church floor. She could hear the children cheering behind her, despite Abby and Filly's attempts to subdue their excitement at Blake flattening Nigel with one not even hard punch.

"Come on, Nigel, I'll take you over to Doc and he can see if it's broken," Luke said, practically lifting the small man off the floor and dragging him outside.

Taking a deep breath as the door closed behind Luke and Nigel, Ginny tried to gather her composure before turning around and facing the children.

"How did Nigel know I was here, Mother?" Ginny asked, casting a suspicious glance at Dora. Stepping beside Blake, she pushed away his hand so she could roll up his sleeve and look at the arm he kept pulling away from her probing fingers.

220

Fresh blood seeped through the bandage and she worried he'd reinjured himself, unaware he'd already been to the doctor that morning.

"Leave it be, Ginny," Blake said, trying to make sense of what had transpired in the last few minutes. Violence in the church, an arrogant idiot making threats and throwing around demands, Ginny betrothed... it was a lot for a body to take in at once, especially with all the children watching from behind them.

"Mother?" Ginny asked impatiently, glaring from Dora to Greg. Keeping his eyes downcast, Greg seemed to discover an urgent need to help Abby and Filly with the children.

Dora took a handkerchief from her sleeve and began dabbing her eyes. "I'm so sorry. I may have mentioned to his mother the other day something about spending the holidays with our children. She must have assumed you were here, too, and told Nigel. I'm so sorry, darling."

"Wonderful, Mother, just wonderful," Ginny said, turning to the children who stared at her, still dressed in their costumes. The excitement that had previously filled them was gone, leaving doubt and a few tears in its place. "You all were splendid today. Make sure you're here in plenty of time to dress in your costumes tomorrow night before the service begins. Grab a cookie on your way out the door."

Abby and Filly, with the assistance of Dora and Ginny, removed the costumes and ushered the children out the door. Greg picked up after the children while Blake and Chauncy stood rereading the document Nigel claimed gave him legal right to marry Ginny.

The last thing Blake was going to do was let her leave with that nasty little man.

"How did you ever get entangled with him?" Blake asked as Ginny wrapped her arms around his waist and leaned against his chest.

"I don't know. I traveled to Europe with a group of friends two years ago. We participated in several tours and he was on most of them. A mutual friend introduced us and I figured out he was from one of the most wealthy families in America. I guess the thought of having all that money and power made it easy to overlook... Nigel. For a short while, anyway. Before we ever boarded the ship to return to New York, I realized what a mistake I'd made by letting him think, even for a minute, I was interested in him. He wouldn't leave me alone, followed me everywhere. I couldn't even leave the house without him right behind me. That's why I ran away."

"My word, Ginny, is he serious? Will you have to marry him?" Abby asked, looking from her husband to Blake.

"I won't marry him. I won't," Ginny said, turning to Dora with fury in her eyes. "Why, Mother, did you have to say anything? You knew she'd tell Nigel. You knew she would."

"I'm sorry, Ginny. I didn't think he'd have the gumption to come all the way here looking for you," Dora said, crying into her handkerchief while Greg shook his head.

"I think we better all go home. Maybe things will look better tomorrow," Chauncy said, helping Abby on with her coat, then Filly.

"They can't look much worse," Blake muttered as he helped Ginny on with her coat and painfully slid his over his arm. He'd go have Doc take another look at it, but he didn't want to run the risk of seeing Nigel or receive another tongue-lashing from the town's physician. It would just have to wait until he could get home and put on a fresh bandage.

"Come along, children, home we go," Greg said, leading Dora out the door, followed by Filly with Blake and Ginny bringing up the rear.

"I'm so sorry, Blake. I had no idea... I never imagined... He could have forced me to marry him any time since I signed that paper. Why would he decide to do it now? There must be some reason for his sudden sense of urgency to wed," Ginny said, looking close to tears as she held his right arm and walked toward Granger House. "Is your arm very painful?"

"Not a bit," Blake lied. He could feel blood trickling through the bandage and soaking into his shirt. As puny as Nigel seemed, he wouldn't have credited him with making any sort of an impact with that scrawny fist. He wouldn't have, either, if he'd hit him anywhere except on his arm.

Stopping at the end of the walk, he held Ginny's hands in his and kissed her cheek.

"Try and have a restful evening, Ginny. We'll figure something out. I promise," Blake said, giving her an encouraging smile.

With tears blurring her vision, Ginny threw her arms around Blake's neck and hugged him. "Thank you for being my hero. I don't care what he says, I won't marry him."

"I know, love, I know. Now, get inside," Blake said, turning her toward the door. "I'll see you in the morning."

Heading to Luke's barn, Blake caught his horses in the corral then hitched them to his wagon. He was almost finished when Luke appeared at his side, looking every bit as tense and furious as Blake felt.

"You get him fixed up?" Blake asked, looking at his friend.

Luke grinned at Blake. "He screamed like a girl the whole time Doc tried to look at it."

"Figures," Blake said, feeling a smile work the corners of his mouth upward. "I honestly didn't mean to punch him. It just sort of happened."

"I know. I'm glad you did," Luke said, taking a look at Blake and noticing him favoring his arm. "You better go have Doc look at that arm again."

"No thanks. I don't need another lecture about taking care of it. It'll be fine," Blake said, leaning against the wagon. "So was his nose broken?"

"No, the big baby," Luke said, shaking his head. "I don't think there is a masculine bone in his entire body. I almost had to carry him to the boarding house. You should have heard him complaining about the 'wretched accommodations.' He'll be lucky if Mrs. Ferguson doesn't toss him out on his ear. What my sister was thinking to ever say more than a polite hello to the dolt is more than I can comprehend. I'm really sorry about all this, Blake. We won't let him cart her off, but that document does appear to be legal and binding."

"Appears being the key word," Blake said, patting his pocket where he'd tucked the piece of paper while he walked Ginny home. "I thought I'd stop by Mr. Carlton's office on my way home and see what he thinks about it."

"Frank's a good attorney," Luke agreed, as Blake climbed up on the wagon. "Mind if I come along with you?"

"By all means," Blake said, motioning for Luke to climb up on the seat with him.

An hour later, Luke and Blake were both smiling as they shook hands with Frank Carlton and left his office.

"That was insightful," Luke said as he and Blake walked out to the wagon.

"At least we know now there is a way to declare the agreement null and void," Blake said, glad they spoke with the attorney. "The question is if Ginny will be willing to agree to do what it takes to make that happen."

"I'm certain, with the right type of convincing, she'll be all for it," Luke said, waggling his eyebrows at Blake.

Sighing, Blake knew he had a lot to think about before morning, when Ginny, and ultimately he, would have to make some life-altering decisions.

"Will you keep our conversation with Mr. Carlton to yourself, please?" Blake asked, climbing up on the wagon seat. "I'd like to discuss this with her myself tomorrow."

"Sure, Blake. Come for breakfast if you like," Luke said, waving as he took off in the direction of Granger House.

Driving his team home, Blake went out to his workshop and finished his gift for Ginny, wrapping it in a piece of plain brown paper and tying it with a blue ribbon.

Carrying it into the house, he set it on the table and stared at it while he ate a simple supper.

Would Ginny go along with his plans? Would Nigel leave town without her or do something foolish? Could Blake let her go, if that's what she decided to do?

He knew the answer to the last question was a resounding no. Losing her once, he couldn't again.

After reading the letters she'd written him, he knew leaving him had broken her heart.

The knowledge that she loved him, had loved him all along, gave him the strength he needed to stay up late, making detailed plans for the morning.

SHANNA HATFIELD

Chapter Eighteen

Up hours before dawn, Blake cleaned every square inch of his house. Eventually, he was going to have to make some new furniture for his own home instead of continuing to use the worn pieces his parents left behind.

Today was not that day, though, he mused as he polished the little-used stove and put fresh sheets on the beds. He even found a box of holiday decorations that belonged to his parents and set them out around the house.

When he was finished, the house looked as nice as it had when his mother lived there. Considering she was a maid before she married his father, that was saying something.

Hurrying outside to feed his horses and the few cattle he kept, Blake returned to the house and made himself a quick breakfast, careful not to get anything in his clean kitchen dirty.

Rinsing and drying his few dishes, he rummaged through his closet, found what he was looking for and left it on his bed.

Giving the house one last look, he hurried outside.

Hitching the team, he loaded the last of his orders and drove into Hardman. He felt a little like Santa Claus as he made the deliveries. The looks of excitement on people's faces, pleased with his work, gave him a great sense of accomplishment and purpose.

Parking the wagon in front of the church, he looked around to make sure no one was in sight before lugging the lectern inside. Moving the old one to a side room used for storage, he set the new one in place just as Chauncy entered the church from the back. Setting an arrangement of greens in front of it, hoping Chauncy wouldn't notice, he hurried to the back of the church.

"Good morning, Blake. How are you on this beautiful Christmas Eve Day?"

"Very well, Chauncy. How does this fine day find you?" Blake asked, grinning as Chauncy shook his hand with a jovial smile.

"Couldn't be better. Erin makes the holiday such fun."

"I'm sure she does," Blake said, turning toward the door, hoping Chauncy would follow him, which he did.

"I wanted to run something by you and Abby. Would you have a moment?" Blake asked, as they stepped outside into the crisp morning air.

"Sure. Come on over and I'll see if she's got the coffee hot," Chauncy said, walking toward the parsonage. Blake followed the pastor, relieved his surprise gift went unnoticed for the time being.

Spending an hour discussing his plans with them, they both waved as he stepped outside into the bright sunshine, telling him not to worry about a thing.

Driving down the street to the bank, Blake jumped down and stepped inside, glad to see Luke and Greg there, along with Arlan.

"I've got that little something you ordered, Luke. You sure you want it here?" Blake asked as Luke stepped from behind his desk and shook his hand. "I could just as easily hide it in your barn."

"No. Here will be dandy," Luke said, following him outside and carrying in a large blanket-wrapped bundle.

"And what have you got there?" Greg asked, holding the door to the back room open while Blake and Luke maneuvered through it.

"You shouldn't ask questions this close to Christmas, Dad," Luke said, his icy blue eyes twinkling with mirth. "It's a surprise for Filly and if it's anywhere in the house or barn before she goes to bed tonight, I guarantee she'll find it. I'll sneak down later and put it under the tree."

"How are you going to get it home? Looks to me like it will require two people to carry it," Greg said, studying the bundle.

"I might have to roust you out of bed to help," Luke said, grinning at his father.

"Why not? Sounds like fun," Greg said slapping both Luke and Blake on their backs as they walked toward the door. "Speaking of trees, don't we need to leave soon to go cut a few?"

"As soon as we round up the girls," Luke said, giving his friend a knowing look. Nigel would have a hard time marrying Ginny if he couldn't find her today. They planned to keep her busy and distracted right up until it was time for the Christmas program.

According to Luke, Nigel likely wouldn't show his face around town before noon, anyway, accustomed to sleeping late in the day.

"Mind if I leave my wagon at your place for a while?" Blake asked, as the three of them left the bank. Arlan waved as they walked out the door. He would take care of the few customers who came in before closing up the bank early that afternoon.

"Actually, if the women agree to it, I was hoping to take your wagon to get the trees. I don't want Filly riding Sheeba in her condition," Luke said, making both Greg and Blake laugh.

"I don't think she'll go along with that idea, Luke," Greg said, knowing how much his daughter-in-law loved to ride. "At least not yet."

"You don't think she'll actually still want to ride, do you?"

Greg and Blake both nodded their heads.

"Give it a try and see what she says," Blake encouraged as he stopped the wagon in front of Granger House.

"I will," Luke said, jogging to the kitchen door. He was soon back, shaking his head. "She thought it was a great idea to take the wagon, so Ginny and Dora will go along, but she'll be riding Sheeba. We might as well go in and warm up while the women finish doing whatever it is they're doing."

Blake nodded his head and followed the other two men inside the kitchen.

"Happy Christmas Eve, beautiful ladies of Granger House," Greg boomed, smiling at the three women as he entered the kitchen, anticipating some jolly fun before the day was through. "Dora, my dearest darling, come here."

"I don't believe I shall, Mr. Granger," Dora said, her eyes twinkling brightly. "There appears to be mischief afoot and you are no doubt leading the charge."

"That I am, wife," Greg said, grabbing Dora in his arms and spinning her around the room, making everyone laugh.

"I know you haven't been to the saloon, so what is causing you to act so oddly this early in the day?" Dora asked as Greg planted a sloppy kiss on her cheek and turned to wink at his son.

"Just this lovely day with our family around us," Greg said, kissing first Ginny then Filly on their cheeks. "Now, are you girls ready to go hunt down our tree?"

"We are, Dad, but how can you be so jovial at a time like this?" Ginny asked, her face lined with worry.

"A time like this? You mean a Christmas Eve day filled with sunshine and the promise of good times and surprises?" Blake asked, clasping Ginny's hand in his own. "You never know, Genevieve. It's the season for miracles."

"That it is, my boy," Greg said, ushering Dora toward the door. "Grab your coat, Dora, and let's find some Christmas trees."

"Is Chauncy coming?" Dora asked, looking back at Luke.

"No. He said he had some things to take care of at the church and neither of them wanted to take Erin out in the cold for too long, so I told him we'd bring one back for them," Luke said, wrapping his arms around Filly from behind and nuzzling her neck.

When she turned to get her coat from the peg by the door, Luke playfully swatted her backside.

"Behave, yourself, Luke. My gracious!" Filly said, blushing at his antics.

"What's gotten into you boys?" Dora asked, shaking her head. "If you don't start minding your manners, Saint Nick will fly right on by tonight."

"Say it isn't so, Mother! I don't think I could live without an orange in my stocking and a beautiful mahogany-haired girl beneath my tree," Luke said, earning a slap on his arm from both his mother and wife.

Blake chuckled as he helped Ginny on with her coat and held the door as the group marched outside and down the steps to his wagon.

Luke and Greg hurried to saddle three horses while Blake helped Ginny and Dora up onto the seat of the wagon. They brought along blankets and a basket of treats.

Returning with the horses, Luke asked Filly one last time if she wouldn't ride in the wagon. She shook her head and mounted her mare.

Luke placed an axe and a saw in the wagon bed then led the way toward the tree line. Since the snow wasn't particularly deep, Blake didn't worry about the horses having a hard time pulling the wagon through it.

Once they reached the trees, they parked the wagon and began searching for the perfect tree. The women rejected the first dozen or so the men pointed out before finally finding a small grove of trees that met with their approval.

Selecting four, Luke started chopping the first one with his axe.

"Why do you need four?" Blake asked, taking a turn swinging the axe, despite Greg and Luke assuring him he didn't need to.

"One for us, one for the parsonage, one for the church and one for you," Ginny said, ticking off the list on her fingers.

"I don't need a tree," Blake said, stepping back from the one he'd been cutting and taking a deep breath. Doc would have his head if he saw him chopping trees with his arm. Feeling the pull against the stitches, he knew it wasn't the best thing he could be doing.

"Yes, you do," Ginny said, offering him a knowing smile. "You need something festive at your house. It looks like Mr. Scrooge lives there."

"I've got plenty of festive decorations, thank you very much," Blake said, pleased to see Ginny look at him curiously. When she was at his house a few days ago, he didn't have a single decoration bedecking his halls. He wanted to surprise her when, hopefully, she set foot through his door before the end of the day. "Besides, I won't be home much to enjoy it, so I really don't see the point in putting up a tree."

"But how will Santa leave you presents if you don't have one?" Ginny teased, sticking out her pouty bottom lip that drove Blake past distraction. If her family hadn't been there, he would have caught it between his in an ardent kiss. Just thinking about falling into the snow with her made his temperature begin to climb and he wiped the back of his gloved hand across his forehead.

"Maybe I'm on the naughty list," Blake said, handing Luke the axe and lunging at Ginny. Pulling her into his arms, he scooped a handful of snow and dropped it down her neck, making her wiggle and squeal.

"You are now," she said, working free and running a few steps away from him. She gathered snow and tossed a ball, missing him by a mile, but catching Filly on the back.

It took just a second for them to engage in a full-scale snowball fight. Dora even tossed a few, keeping out of the line of fire by using Greg as a human shield.

"No fair hiding, Mother," Luke said, sneaking up behind her and lobbing a soft snowball at her face when she turned around.

"Oh, you are in trouble now, young man," Dora said, scooping snow and chasing after Luke who quickly ran out of reach.

Catching their breath, they all laughed as the frolics died down. Luke finished cutting the last tree while Filly passed out cookies.

Blake and Luke loaded the trees in the back of the wagon, while Greg helped Dora and Ginny up on the seat.

"We better get the girls home before they freeze in these wet clothes," Blake said, noticing Ginny and Dora appeared chilled as they pulled blankets around them and huddled together.

"I agree," Dora said, shaking her hat to dislodge a clump of snow clinging to the brim. "What an invigorating outing. Thank you for bringing the wagon, Blake, so we all could join in the fun."

"You are most welcome," he said, taking his seat next to Ginny. Making sure no one was watching, he slid just a little closer to her than was proper. His elbow brushed her side, making her blush, when he turned the wagon and started toward Granger House.

Leaving the women and their tree at Granger House, he offered to deliver the trees to the parsonage and the church. Right after lunch, the Grangers planned to meet at the church to help with the decorating.

Tapping on the parsonage's front door, Chauncy soon opened it with a friendly greeting, reaching to help Blake carry in the tree.

"You wouldn't, by chance, know anything about a new lectern, would you?" Chauncy asked as they set the tree in the parlor. He stood back to make sure it was standing straight.

"What makes you ask that?" Blake asked, grinning broadly while his eyes twinkled.

"Because something that beautiful took a lot of work and talent to create," Chauncy said, shaking Blake's hand and looking a little misty-eyed.

"It is a gift for you. If you ever decide to minister to a different congregation, it is yours to take with you. I put the other one in the store room," Blake said, glad Chauncy was pleased with his gift. "Although I hope it will stand in our church here for many, many years to come."

"Why would I leave Hardman? It's our home and we'd be hard pressed to find a better group of people to call our family and friends," Chauncy said as he and Blake went outside and carried the larger tree into the church, setting it in a front corner where it would be out of the way. "I just hope my sermons can live up to such a fine piece of furniture to hold my notes."

Running his hand over the intricately carved front of the lectern, Chauncy shook his head. "I don't know how you create the things you do, Blake, but you've a God-given talent that is rare to see."

"Thank you," Blake said, humbled by Chauncy's words. "I just do what I love and don't worry about the rest."

"I, for one, am glad that you do. The scene on here with the sheep is just perfect," Chauncy said, admiring Blake's handiwork from the sheep in the pasture watched over by shepherds to the star in the sky and the manger just barely visible in the background. It was a true work of art.

"I thought it suited you," Blake said, hurrying to catch the tree as it started to tip to one side. Chauncy helped tug it upright and the two of them worked until it stood straight and stable.

"These trees are certainly fragrant, aren't they?" Chauncy asked, inhaling the fir tree scent.

"They most certainly are," Blake agreed, enjoying the fragrance. Then again, he loved the smell of wood. Studying the tree, he turned to Chauncy. "Will it still be okay to go ahead with our plans for this evening?"

"Absolutely," Chauncy said as they walked to the door. "Abby's been in a flurry all morning making preparations, but I think she'll have everything ready."

"Wonderful," Blake said, thumping Chauncy on the back as he hurried to his wagon. "Tell her I'm sorry to throw some unexpected work her way today."

"She's so excited about it, I don't think she minds one bit," Chauncy said, waving as Blake turned his team toward Granger House. Leaving the horses in the barn, he hurried to the kitchen door and gave a quick tap before sticking his head inside.

Filly was at the stove, stirring something in a pot while Ginny set the table. She smiled at him when he stepped inside.

"Mother is in the parlor directing Dad and Luke in her ideal placement of the tree," Ginny said, rolling her eyes. "Filly and I took refuge in here."

Blake laughed and kissed her cheek, then went down the hall to the bathroom to wash his hands. Thinking about the conveniences available at Granger House, he decided he needed to make a few improvements at his house once spring arrived. Indoor plumbing was arguably better than trudging to an outhouse in the cold.

Returning to the kitchen, Filly asked him to let the others know lunch was ready.

Walking down the hall, he could hear Dora instructing Luke and Greg to move the tree one way then the other.

"Mother, it's fine," Luke said, sounding exasperated as Blake stood watching from the doorway.

"Just a little more to the right," she said, motioning for Luke to move the tree.

Greg mumbled something Blake couldn't hear, but it earned him a smack on his arm from his wife as he helped Luke turn the tree.

"Stop! That's perfect," Dora said, noticing Blake in the doorway. "What do you think, dear? Doesn't that look wonderful?"

"Indeed, it does," Blake agreed. He couldn't tell much difference from where it was before Luke moved it, but if it made Dora happy, that was what mattered. "Filly said lunch is ready if you'd all like to convene in the kitchen."

"I'm so hungry I could eat…"

"Everything, dear," Dora said, patting Greg's stomach as she interrupted him. "You tend to eat everything Filly cooks."

"Only because it's so good," Greg said, taking Dora's hand and hurrying to the kitchen.

Luke walked with Blake, shaking his head at his parents while he tried to wipe a glob of sap off his hand onto the leg of his denim pants.

"I have to agree with your father, Luke. Filly's cooking talents are exceptional," Blake said as they neared the kitchen.

"Thanks. She's an exceptional woman," Luke said, thumping Blake on the back with a thoughtful look. "There are a few of those around here, although not all of them can cook."

Grinning as they stepped into the kitchen, Blake strode to the table and held Ginny's chair before taking a seat beside her.

Enjoying a nourishing lunch of chicken soup with warm bread and an assortment of cookies, they hurried to pick up the kitchen then went to the parlor to trim the tree.

Blake stood back and watched until Ginny tugged on his hand and asked him to help. Handing her ornaments, she placed them on the tree. When she stood on a chair to reach some of the taller branches, Blake tried not to notice the way her soft blue wool dress draped around her curves and outlined her figure.

Fumbling with a blown glass ball, he forced himself to pay attention to what he was doing. Luke caught his eye and gave him a look that clearly expressed his thoughts about Blake being hopeless where Ginny was concerned.

"I think that's it," Filly said, standing back and admiring their combined efforts. Festooned with an assortment of heartfelt ornaments, strings of popcorn, and candles waiting to be lit that evening, the tree looked lovely.

"Isn't it beautiful?" Dora mused, linking her arms with Ginny and Filly.

"It is beautiful, Mother," Ginny said, leaning her head against her mother's shoulder, but looking directly at Blake. "I'm so glad we're all here together."

He wondered if that included him and decided it did when she gave him a private smile.

"We better head over to the church and trim the tree there," Greg said, helping Dora and Filly gather the unused ornaments and return them to a trunk.

It didn't take long for the six of them to bundle into their coats and make the walk to the church. Chauncy was already there, starting to place ornaments on the highest branches of the tree.

"I'm glad you all came over. The thought of doing this alone is daunting," Chauncy said, smiling at them as he accepted ornaments the women handed to him to place on the branches they couldn't reach. While Greg and the women helped Chauncy with the tree, Blake and Luke finished setting up everything for the children's program.

Admiring the tree when the last ornament was in place, Filly and Ginny decided to add a few more decorations to the church using some discarded branches. Chauncy found some baskets to work as containers and they set them around the front of the church, adorned with bright red bows.

"I don't think the church has ever looked so nice," Chauncy said, pleased at the festive appearance. "Thank you all, so much."

The new lectern drew everyone's attention and words of praise over the design and craftsmanship flowed freely, making Blake embarrassed.

"It's wonderful, Blake," Ginny said, squeezing his hand as she stood beside him. "I don't know how you had time to make it with everything else you've been working on. Remember, I've seen your workshop recently."

"Thank you," he said, not knowing why everyone made such a fuss over his work. He loved taking a piece of wood and drawing out something unique and artistic from it. "It was a pleasure for me to make it, especially since it's for our very own pastor."

"I'm sure Chauncy will enjoy it for years to come," Luke added, stepping beside his sister and looking from her to Blake. Raising an eyebrow at the carpenter, he subtly tipped his head to Ginny.

Blake nodded and cleared his throat.

"Say, Ginny, I've still got my tree to decorate. Would you mind helping me?" Blake asked, hoping Ginny would agree.

"Certainly. Would you like to go now?"

"Yes, if you don't mind."

"Let me tell Filly and Mother," Ginny said, starting to walk over to where Dora and Filly added a few greens along the top of the piano.

"I'll tell them, Ginny Lou," Luke said, holding her coat. "You two go ahead."

"Okay," Ginny said, thinking her brother was being abnormally helpful.

Blake slipped on his coat and waved at Chauncy as he walked Ginny to the door. "We'll see you all in a little while," he said, ushering Ginny outside and back to Granger House where his wagon waited.

Hitching the horses, they were soon heading out of town. Ginny saw Nigel walking down the street and quickly pulled the blanket from her lap around her shoulders and over her head, hoping he wouldn't recognize her. It seemed to work because he just frowned at Blake as they drove by, continuing on his way toward the church.

"That was close," Ginny said, trying not to giggle as she and Blake left the town behind them.

"Too close," Blake said, glad Ginny hid her face and hair. Even from afar, those golden curls were hard to mistake as belonging to anyone other than her.

Breathing deeply, Blake glanced at Ginny and smiled. Rosy cheeks and bright eyes let him know she was enjoying herself.

"Having a fun day?" he asked, pulling the team to a stop in front of his house.

"A wonderful day," she said, resting her hands on his shoulders as he came around the wagon and lifted her down by the waist.

Instead of letting her go, his hands moved around to her back, drawing her into the circle of his arms. Their gazes connected and Ginny felt her heart begin to beat rapidly. Her lashes lowered as Blake's head bent closer. When his lips met hers in a demanding kiss, she returned his ardor, wanting to savor the taste and feel of his insistent mouth.

She leaned against Blake as he finally ended the kiss, lightheaded and deliciously warmed from the inside out.

"What was that for?" she whispered, holding onto the lapels of his coat to keep from sinking into the snow beneath her feet.

"Because you look so lovely and young and perfect today," Blake said, brushing an errant curl behind her ear then walking her up the front steps and inside his front door.

He heard her gasp in surprise as she looked around at his newly decorated home.

"You've been busy, Blake. I'm quite impressed," Ginny said, picking up a shepherd boy from a hand-carved nativity set he'd made years ago.

"'Tis the season," he said with a teasing smile, before going back outside to get the tree. Once they had it safely standing in a bucket in the corner of the front room, Ginny helped him place his few ornaments on the branches and asked if he had any ribbon. He found a spool of ribbon his mother had left behind in a box of sewing supplies and Ginny quickly tied bows on some of the branches.

"There, that looks better," she said, standing back to look at the tree. "It's really quite lovely."

"I think it's missing something," Blake said, going to his bedroom and returning with a small box wrapped in plain brown paper. Handing it to Ginny, he gave her a warm smile. "I think you should open this."

Taking it from his hand, their fingers brushed and the contact made tingles dance up her arm.

"It's not Christmas yet, Blake. Shouldn't I wait until tomorrow?"

"No. You need to open this one now. Please?" Blake was ready to beg if that's what it took.

Ginny sat on the sofa and removed the paper, revealing a jewelry box with an intricately carved heart surrounded by flowers and vines on the lid.

"Blake, it's beautiful," Ginny said, rubbing her hand over the top, knowing how much effort Blake put into it. It was a work of art and something she would always treasure.

"Open it," Blake said, offering her an encouraging smile.

Carefully lifting the lid, Ginny couldn't stop the tears that rolled down her cheeks. Her hand covered her trembling lips and she looked at Blake with blue eyes full of love.

"Don't cry, love," Blake said, getting down on one knee as he knelt in front of her and brushed at her tears with his handkerchief.

Taking her hand in his, he kissed her fingers then reached into the box and removed the carved wooden heart he'd given her the day she left town a decade earlier.

"Genevieve, I gave you this heart ten years ago, not just as a Christmas token, but a reminder that you held my heart in your hands. You've had it all these years," Blake said, smiling at the woman he knew he'd love for a lifetime.

He knew Ginny wasn't perfect, but neither was he. Nobody was perfect, and that was fine with him.

Unable to envision a future without her in it, without her standing beside him, he decided the time was right to do something about that. "You've got a terrible temper, you tend to meddle in things that aren't any of your concern, and I'll probably starve to death if I expect you to learn to cook well enough to prepare three meals a day, but I love you, Ginny. More with every passing moment. I can't promise life will be easy, but I can promise to love you until my very last day on this earth, until I draw my last breath. Please marry me, Genevieve. Say you'll be my wife."

"Oh, yes, Blake. Yes!" Ginny said, throwing her arms around his neck and kissing him with all the love she'd carried for him in her heart.

"I'm so glad, love," Blake said, sitting on the sofa beside her and pulling her into his arms.

His lips touched her forehead, her cheek, her jaw, her ear then returned to make her lips his own.

"I've waited so long for you to be mine," Blake whispered, softly running his thumbs along her cheekbones, brushing his knuckles along her jaw, and gazing intently into her face. "Would you be terribly upset if we have a short engagement?"

"Not at all, Blake. I don't care about a big, fancy wedding or any of the frippery Mother will think is necessary. I just want you," Ginny said, blushing slightly at her admission.

Rubbing her fingers over the beloved little heart in her hand, she suddenly sat up and looked at Blake. "You aren't asking me just because of Nigel, are you?"

Blake laughed and kissed her again before responding. "How can you even ask that? I've been planning for weeks to propose today. In case you didn't notice, that box has your first name carved into the design and it took me a while to get it just right."

"I did notice and I love it," Ginny said, boldly kissing Blake again.

Scooting off his lap, she got to her feet and looked at him. He stood and wrapped his arms around her. "What's going through that lovely head of yours?"

"I just don't want you to feel rushed or pressured to marry me, Blake. I want, more than anything, to be your wife, but I don't want you to feel trapped."

"Never, love. I'll never feel trapped by you, although I admit I entirely like the idea of being trapped somewhere with you for a while." Blake pressed hot, moist lips to her neck and made her lose the ability to think of anything except the strong arms holding her, the tempting lips kissing her, and her love for one of the kindest men she'd ever met.

Lifting his head, Blake gave her a cocky grin. "Unless you plan to sit back down on this sofa and spend what remains of this afternoon having your way with me, I suppose I better get you back to town so you can prepare for the church service and program tonight."

Ginny blushed and slapped playfully at his arm, shaking her head.

"The things you say, Mr. Stratton, are highly improper. Even if we are engaged," Ginny said, relishing the sound of that. She was finally engaged to Blake! Giving up on all the dreams she had as a young girl of being his wife, it was now truly going to happen. This was the best Christmas Eve she'd ever experienced.

"I rather like the sound of that — being engaged, I mean," Blake said, helping Ginny slip on her coat. She still held the heart in her hand and looked from it to Blake's tree.

"I think I'd like this to stay on your tree," she said, hanging it on a branch.

"I'd like that very much, but only if you come visit it often," Blake said, grinning broadly.

"That would be satisfactory," Ginny said, picking up the jewelry box and putting it in her coat pocket before slipping on her gloves and pinning on her hat.

Blake gave her another quick kiss before escorting her outside to his waiting wagon. It didn't take long until they were driving around the edge of town. Blake said it would help keep Nigel from seeing them, although Ginny thought Blake just wanted to take as long as possible to get her home.

Stopping the wagon in front of Granger House, he jumped off the seat and hurried around to lift her down. Together, they ran along the back walk to the kitchen door and inside, laughing as they entered the room only to find Filly and Dora looking grim-faced as loud voices rang down the hall from the parlor.

"He's here," Dora said, taking Ginny's hand in hers and squeezing it.

Ginny removed her outerwear and took a deep breath, prepared to go confront Nigel, but Blake put a restraining hand on her arm.

"You don't need to see him, Genevieve. I'll speak with him. Why don't you share what transpired this afternoon with your mother and Filly?" Blake suggested, walking through the kitchen and down the hall.

Ginny, Filly, and Dora followed close behind with Ginny whispering about Blake's proposal. They had a hard time containing their excitement as they stood in the hall and exchanged hugs and quiet words of congratulations.

Although they didn't enter the parlor, they remained in the hall where they could listen to the men.

"I won't stand for any more of this nonsense. You know where I can locate Ginny. You might as well tell me so we can catch the evening stage," Nigel demanded, shaking a finger at Luke.

Blake felt some grim satisfaction that Nigel's nose sported a dark bruise. If the arrogant little man didn't calm down, Blake didn't know if he could resist giving him a matching spot on the other side.

It was almost comical watching the small fellow try to intimidate Luke, who stood a foot taller and almost twice his width. Nigel could easily pass for a young boy with his scrawny frame and stature.

"She's not going anywhere with you, Pickford," Blake said, stepping into the room.

"Oh, yes, she is. A simple man like you couldn't possibly understand who I am or what I have to offer her. There is no question that I would be the better choice. It's clearly me," Nigel said, puffing out his thin chest. "I'm not leaving until she agrees to come with me. Mummy has already sent out the invitations."

"We didn't receive one," Greg said, looking pointedly at Nigel. "Don't you think the bride's parents should be invited?"

"Mummy knew you were visiting Luke here at the end of nowhere and were indisposed," Nigel said, sneering at Greg. "Besides, we're only inviting people who are of a certain social standing."

Ginny had to hold her hand over Dora's mouth to keep her from screeching at Nigel's implication that the Granger family didn't meet his mother's expectations of social class.

"Out, Nigel. Get out of my house and don't come back," Luke said, grabbing the man by his arm and hauling him to the door. With Blake and Greg flanking him, Nigel didn't see the women standing in the hall.

"As soon as I find her, we're leaving!" Nigel said, standing on the step, adjusting his mussed coat and straightening his hat.

"You're leaving, but not with Ginny," Blake said, taking a menacing step Nigel's direction. "In case you've forgotten it's Christmas Eve. Use some of that social class you're so proud of flaunting and realize that pulling her from the arms of her family on Christmas Eve is barbaric."

"Fine," Nigel said, brushing at his coat sleeve, afraid to make eye contact with the man who popped his nose the previous day. "I'll wait until after the service at church this evening, but then we're leaving."

Before anyone could protest, he marched down the steps and across the walk, stomping his way back to town.

Luke and Blake watched him go then turned to see the three women looking at them wide-eyed.

"What are we going to do?" Dora asked, reaching out to Greg, who offered her a comforting hug.

"I'll tell you what we're going to do," Blake said, turning to Ginny, who looked at him with confidence and hope. He ushered her into the parlor and the others followed, waiting to see what Blake had planned.

"I know you just agreed to marry me, love, but will you marry me today? Right after the Christmas Eve service?" Blake asked, grinning at Ginny's stunned expression. "Nigel is planning to marry you whether you like it or not and that contract he has says you agreed to it."

At the crestfallen looks on the women's faces, Blake continued. "There is a clause, however. One Nigel seems to have forgotten. If either party finds someone else to marry and does so before the contract can be fulfilled, it is null and void."

"So you mean if Ginny marries you before Nigel can get her to leave, there's nothing he can do about it?" Dora asked.

"That is correct," Blake said, pulling Ginny against him. "Would you mind terribly if we get engaged and have a wedding all in the same day?"

"I don't mind, Blake, it's just that I don't want you to feel pressured into doing this. I don't have a dress and nothing is ready and…"

"It's all taken care of. The church is decorated and festive. You have a willing groom and if Luke will stand with me, a best man. Should you ladies be so inclined to proceed to Abby's dress shop, you'll find a gown ready and waiting. We'll all attend the Christmas Eve service and program as planned and have the wedding right after. By the time Nigel realizes what has transpired, we'll already be married," Blake said, unable to stop smiling as the group went from standing around looking at him as if he'd lost his mind to rushing to put on their coats and head out the door.

Escorting the women to Abby's shop to make sure Nigel didn't make off with Ginny, Greg agreed to keep watch over them while Luke went to talk to Chauncy. Blake returned home to change his clothes and make final preparations for the evening.

He had one or two more surprises to implement before he became a married man.

Chapter Nineteen

"Are you sure about this, Abby?" Ginny asked, running her fingers down the smooth white satin gown Abby insisted she put on the minute the three Granger women stepped inside her dress shop.

"Absolutely, Ginny. Someone special ordered this dress then never came back to get it. I've kept it all this time and with a few little tucks, it will be perfect for you," Abby said, adjusting the elbow-length puff sleeves with wide lace frills going to the middle of Ginny's forearm. A square neckline and a princess style cut emphasized Ginny's curves. Tiny pearls created a unique floral pattern down the front of the skirt and along the hemline, sparkling in the afternoon sunlight.

"Blake won't know what to think when he sees you in this," Filly said, smiling as Abby made a few adjustments to the skirt.

"It's perfect, my darling. Just perfect," Dora said, thrilled her daughter was not only going to marry her true love, but do it in a gown as beautiful as any she'd seen in New York.

"What will she carry for flowers?" Filly asked, realizing there was no way to get anything fresh in town.

"How about white ribbon roses and Christmas greens?" Abby suggested, opening a box with several large roses made of white velvet nestled inside.

"These are lovely, Abby," Dora said, choosing half a dozen. "With a little lace and ribbon, I think we can make something that will do nicely."

"I'll take care of it," Filly said, accepting the roses from Dora and setting them beside her things.

"I can't believe this is really happening," Ginny said, staring at her reflection in the big cheval glass mirror.

Just a few short months ago, she had no intentions to marry.

Ever.

She firmly closed the door on her past with Blake, or so she thought, and pictured herself pursuing the suffragette movement or some valiant cause that would benefit the less fortunate.

Now, though, the thing she wanted most in the world was to marry Blake and live a long, happy life together. Beyond that, she had no other plans.

"You better start believing it," Filly teased, grinning over Ginny's shoulder at her reflection in the mirror. "In a few hours you'll be standing in front of everyone at the church exchanging your vows with your very handsome groom."

"I know, but I never dreamed... never dared to hope..."

Dora sniffled and pulled out a handkerchief. "I'm sorry, again, Ginny, for the heartache I caused you both, but I'm so glad you two are finally going to be together."

"Thank you, Mother," Ginny said, fighting back her own tears.

"Let's get you out of that gown before you get tear stains on it," Abby said, trying to lighten the mood as she and Ginny went back to the fitting room.

Returning, Abby hung the gown on a peg and hugged Ginny.

"I'll make a few adjustments and run this right over to the house," Abby said, already picking up a needle and thread.

"No need, Abby. With everything else going on today, I'll send Luke to pick it up," Filly said, buttoning her coat and settling her hat back on her head. "Thank you so much for helping make this day special for Ginny."

"My pleasure," Abby said, hugging Filly, then Ginny and Dora.

Greg walked in and smiled at the women. Rather than wait inside Abby's shop, he stepped into the mercantile to visit with George and Aleta Bruner while keeping an eye out for Nigel. Deciding to see if the women were about finished with Ginny's dress fitting, he was pleased they appeared ready to return home.

"What can I carry?" he asked as the women hurried to the door.

"Nothing, dear, right now," Dora said, grinning at her husband. "But you do need to pay Abby for the dress."

"I knew they kept me around for something," Greg said, winking at Abby as he settled the bill then escorted the three women back to Granger House.

While they were gone, Luke placed a few packages under the tree, stoked the fires and the furnace, and fed his livestock. Just finishing with a bath and dressing in his best suit, the ends of his hair were still damp when Greg and the women trooped in the door.

The roast Filly placed in the oven right after lunch filled the house with the rich smells of beef mingled with the holiday scents of fragrant pine boughs and the bayberry candles she'd set out.

"My, it smells wonderful in here," Dora exclaimed as Greg helped remove her coat, then Ginny's.

"I assume by the bill I just paid, Abby had something you can use, Ginny," Greg teased, kissing his wife's cheek as he hung up her coat and hat.

"She did. I'm so excited," Ginny said, bouncing up and down on her feet. All she could think about was at the end of this most wonderful day, she'd be Mrs. Blake Stratton.

"Why don't you and Dora start getting ready while I finish dinner then I can dress while the rest of you clean up the dishes," Filly suggested, tying on her apron.

"That's a good idea," Dora said, taking Ginny's hand and leading her down the hall.

Greg went to find a few bits of greenery Filly could use in Ginny's bouquet while Luke ran back to Abby's shop to retrieve Ginny's dress.

An hour later, they sat down to enjoy the meal together and take a few minutes to laugh and relax before what promised to be a full and eventful evening.

Greg, Luke, and Dora cleared the table and did the dishes while Filly dashed upstairs to change and Ginny retreated to her room to pack a bag to take to Blake's after the service and put on her wedding dress.

A knock at the back door surprised them all. Luke quickly dried his hands and opened the door to see Percy Bruner standing on the step, holding a small box in his hand.

"Hi, Percy. What brings you out?" Luke asked, smiling at the boy.

"Mr. Stratton asked me to bring this to Miss Granger," Percy said, holding out the box.

"It must be important for you to bring it out tonight," Luke said, taking a coin from his pocket and handing it to Percy.

The boy grinned at him and tipped the cap on his head. "Yes, sir. Thanks!" Percy started to run down the steps, but suddenly stopped and turned back around. "See you at church soon?"

"We'll be there, Percy," Luke said, chuckling as the boy raced down the walk into town.

"I'll take this to Ginny," Luke said, walking down the hall and knocking on her bedroom door. When he heard her call to come in, he turned the knob, smiling as he took in the vision his sister created.

"You look radiant, Ginny Lou," Luke said, kissing her cheek as she stood before the mirror, adjusting the puffed sleeves of her gown. "I can't believe Abby had that hanging around her shop. It was made just for you."

"That's what we thought, too," Ginny said, turning to smile at Luke. Noticing a paper-wrapped parcel in his hand, she looked at him quizzically. "What have you got there?"

"I don't know, but Percy said Blake asked him to deliver it to you."

"What in the world..." Ginny asked, taking the package from Luke and removing the paper to reveal a box of chocolates. A note attached made her dab at the tears threatening to spill down her cheeks.

My lovely Genevieve,

I realize we have not had much opportunity for a courtship before our marriage, so I will spend the next fifty or so years attempting to make up for it. Here is a little sweet or two, since I know you enjoy them so, although the taste most certainly does not compare to that of your lips, my love. I intend to sample that particularly exquisite flavor as many times as you can bear after the service this evening.

Yours,
Blake

"Oh, my," she said, placing a cool hand to her hot cheek, feeling a blush rise from her neck past her ears.

"He better not be saying anything he shouldn't," Luke cautioned, although his tone was teasing.

"No, he said just the right thing," Ginny said, opening the box of candy and handing it to Luke. His voracious sweet tooth was legendary in their family and she knew the chocolate would distract him. There was no way she wanted him reading the note Blake sent. It was far too... intimate.

Returning the box to her, he kissed her cheek and winked as he popped the candy in his mouth, leaving her alone in the room.

Adjusting the pins in her hair, Ginny studied herself critically and hoped Blake would like the way she looked. Abby assured her he had no idea about the wedding dress, just that she let him know she had a suitable gown for Ginny to wear.

"Are you ready, darling?" Dora asked, stepping into the room, beaming proudly at her daughter.

"I am, Mother. I'm ready," Ginny said, pulling a long cloak from the closet. Tucking her veil and the bouquet into a large basket, she wanted to keep them hidden from view until it was time for the wedding ceremony.

"We better go, then. You need to be at the church to assist preparing the children for the program, don't you?" Dora asked, studying Ginny's beautiful dress as they walked toward the kitchen. She was glad the wedding gown didn't feature a train. It would be impossible to keep it from dragging in the snow.

Ginny gasped and looked at her mother. "I completely forgot about the children! Mother, I'm such a ninny!"

"You're not a ninny," Dora assured her, patting her back reassuringly. "You're a girl in love about to be married. Of course you're thinking about other things this evening."

"I have a little surprise for the children in my room." Ginny turned to go back down the hallway.

"Where is it, dear? I'll get it for you," Dora said, following Ginny's direction to retrieve a basket near the door.

"Shall we go?" Greg asked as Dora and Ginny entered the kitchen.

"Yes, let's hurry." Ginny wanted to run to the church to see if the children were there. Now that she remembered the program, she was excited to see the youngsters perform their parts.

Filly breezed in the room while they were all putting on coats and scarves, looking refreshed and ready for a fun evening.

"I'm so excited, I can hardly stand it," Filly said, as Luke held her coat and she slid her arms in the sleeves.

"Maybe you can take out some of that enthusiasm on me later," Luke said in a voice so low, only Filly could hear. She shook her head at him, but the twinkle in her eyes told him she approved of his suggestion.

Dora and Greg led the way out the door and, as a group, they sang *We Three Kings* on their way to the church. Others walking down the boardwalk joined their voices and they marched up the steps to the door singing the chorus.

"Well, isn't this a pleasant way to be greeted," Chauncy said, standing at the door. He took a moment to offer his congratulations to Ginny and let her know everything would go smoothly.

"I hope so," she said, patting Chauncy's arm then hurrying off to help Abby and Filly get the children into their costumes.

Little Anna Jenkins ran up to her with a note and tugged on the cloak she refused to remove, keeping her wedding dress hidden beneath the voluminous dark folds.

"Hello, sweetheart," Ginny said, bending over to hug the child. "What do you have there?"

"Mr. Stratton asked me to give this to you," Anna said, handing Ginny an envelope.

Smiling, she opened it and removed the message.

G — Isn't it bad luck to see the bride before the wedding? I shall sit on the other side of the church and try not to ogle you too intently. I thought about wearing blinders, but that might arouse some suspicion. Until later, when I can thoroughly enjoy seeing all of you... B

Ginny put a hand to her mouth to stifle her laugh, but not before Filly saw the merriment on her face.

"What did he send now?" Filly asked, having learned about the note and candy Blake sent to the house from Luke.

"Here, you can read it." Ginny handed Filly the note.

Her sister-in-law grinned and passed the paper back to her. "He's making this quite fun, isn't he?"

"Yes, he is," Ginny said, looking around the church, hoping to see Blake, but he was obviously keeping out of sight.

An angel with a crooked halo caught Ginny's attention and she didn't have the opportunity to spend any more time speculating about Blake before the church began to fill for the service.

"Ginny, dear, you must be roasting with that cloak on. Why don't you take it off?" asked Aleta Bruner as she stepped beside her.

"I'm fine, Aleta, but thank you. I appreciate your concern," Ginny said, smiling at the kind woman. "You all are still joining us tomorrow at Granger House for dinner, aren't you?"

"Oh, yes," Aleta said, with a wide smile. "Filly has made it a tradition and one we wouldn't miss. Percy gets so excited about both the food and the company."

"I'm glad," Ginny said, grinning as thoughts of the little boy came to mind. He'd been on his best behavior since Blake spoke with him. Right now, she watched him help Anna adjust the wings of her angel costume. The little girl stared at him with open admiration on her face.

"Percy told us Blake spoke to him about protecting the women folk and he's been taking his duty to heart," Aleta said, looking proudly at her son. "We appreciate Blake saying something to him. I understand he was tormenting that poor little Jenkins girl to tears."

"I think she likes him is why he could make her cry so easily," Ginny whispered, watching as the children all took their places. Although she couldn't see him, she knew Blake was on the other side of one of the scenes, helping some of the boys with their costumes.

"Well, I'm grateful the two of you took on directing the program. These rambunctious youngsters can be a handful," Aleta said, noticing her husband motioning for her to take her seat. "We'll talk more later, Ginny. Good luck with the program."

Ginny nodded her head as Aleta left to sit by George. Peeking around the curtain they erected behind Chauncy's lectern, she saw Nigel come in and take a seat in a back row. She'd hoped he'd avoid the service. Maybe he was feeling the need for a little holiday cheer.

Sincerely doubting it, she shook her head and turned her attention back to the children.

"Is everyone ready?" Chauncy asked, looking behind the curtain.

"As ready as we'll ever be," Ginny said, nodding to the pastor.

Chauncy promised to keep his sermon brief so the children wouldn't get too antsy before the program. Ginny quieted her group of little actors and sat with them out of sight of the congregation. Even if they couldn't see the pastor on the other side of the curtain, they could hear his words.

"Good evening and Merry Christmas!" Chauncy said in a strong, friendly voice that immediately silenced the friendly chatter in the church.

"Thank you all for gathering here on this blessed Christmas Eve," Chauncy said, then launched into his sermon. "I'm not here tonight to talk on any of my usual topics. Tonight, I want to talk about a special couple. A couple devoted to one another, but more importantly, devoted to serving God."

Absolute quiet descended over the church as Chauncy continued. "There once was a humble carpenter, betrothed to a young girl. They weren't of noble birth, weren't wealthy, weren't notable for any reason, other than they were faithful and obedient to God."

He went on to talk about Joseph and Mary, about their journey not just to Bethlehem, but the journey they made toward accepting each other, accepting God's will for them.

"I encourage you, dear friends, in this season, to consider God's will for each of you. By accepting His will and following obediently, you can accept the beautiful gifts he has planned for you. Rejoice and recognize the precious gift of this most wondrous season," Chauncy said, leading the congregation in a popular Christmas carol before signaling for Luke and Greg to pull back the curtain and reveal the first set of the children's program.

The children gave their best to their parts. No animals escaped during the manger scene, no one erupted in tears, and the parents all clapped and cheered at the end of the program.

Little Erin, who was too big to play Baby Jesus like she had the past two years, sat on her mother's lap in the front row, waving her little hands wildly, wanting to get down and pet the sheep that had been allowed in the church for the program. A few of the older boys hurried to take the animals outside when the program was through while some of the men quickly took down the curtain and cleared away the props from the play, setting them in the storage room.

"Before you enjoy the refreshments the wonderful ladies have provided, I'd like to invite you all to stay in your seats for a wedding," Chauncy said. Murmurs rushed through the church and he held up his hands to silence everyone. "There will be another humble carpenter and a sweet girl merging their life's path so they might journey forward together. If you'll all stay in your seats, we'll begin the ceremony momentarily."

Craning their necks and looking around the church, most everyone assumed the humble carpenter had to be Blake since he was the only carpenter in town. Knowing he fancied Ginny, it was a good assumption that she would be his bride.

Nigel, however, didn't realize any of that as he sat brooding at the back of the church. He'd stood on the pew when he first arrived since he couldn't see over the sea of people in the church to make note where the Granger family was seated, but failed to see Ginny anywhere. He hadn't seen that ruffian who almost broke his nose, either. He hoped they hadn't done something preposterous like eloped.

Now he'd have to sit through two of these brainless country folk getting married before he could insist Ginny leave with him. Actually, he had in mind for the pastor to marry them since he wouldn't be able to leave until the following day when the stage came through town. The livery refused to rent him a sleigh and he didn't have a driver even if he could rent a conveyance. Nigel had never ridden on the back of a horse in his life and had no idea how to handle one even if he was so inclined to get near the smelly beasts.

He grew impatient to make Ginny his own, even if she seemed a little unwilling. Lost in thoughts of his betrothed and unable to see over the heads of those in front of him, Nigel closed his eyes and decided to take a quick snooze while the wedding commenced.

"Word around town has it there's a wedding about to take place," Luke said, teasing Blake as he stepped beside him at the front of the church.

"As soon as the bride makes an appearance," Blake said, glancing at the watch he pulled out of the pocket of his festive red vest. Dressed in one of the suits he wore when he visited his parents at their estate outside London, he looked every bit as dashing as his proper title implied.

A black formal tailcoat topped the vest. The tips of his white shirt collar stood above a silk ascot, held in place with a pearl tie tack. Fine black trousers completed the outfit, making him look noble and extremely handsome.

"We probably need to hurry things along before Nigel figures out what we're up to," Luke suggested, glancing to the back of the church where Nigel appeared to be sleeping, seemingly ignorant to what was taking place around him.

"My thoughts exactly. I don't suppose you have a back-up plan if he objects?"

"I've got an idea or two. The sheriff is aware of the situation," Luke said, catching the sheriff's eye and tipping his head toward the direction of Nigel. The sheriff nodded and leaned back in the pew with a knowing look.

"What's taking the girls so long? Wasn't Ginny wearing the dress she got from Abby?" Blake stared at the back door of the church, willing Ginny to breeze through it. "I assume hiding it was the reason she left on that cloak."

"I thought you were trying not to look at her."

"Guess I couldn't help myself." Blake shrugged his shoulders before checking his watch again.

Luke stared at his soon-to-be brother-in-law then thumped him on the back. "You're not in a hurry to marry my sister, are you?"

"As a matter of fact, I am," Blake said, smiling at Luke. "Nigel's timing is perfect. I really was planning to propose to your sister tonight. Provided she agreed to have me, I hoped to have a short engagement. Nigel's empty threats provided me with a most splendid reason to propose and wed in the same day."

"You mean you don't think Nigel could snatch Ginny away if he wanted?" Luke asked, chuckling at the thought of the small, seemingly frail little man trying to cart off his feisty sister.

"Not unless she went willingly," Blake said, thinking about the spitfire he was about to wed. "I'd place my bets on her if push came to shove."

Luke laughed and turned as the back door to the church opened. "Hopefully, we can see you two wed before any pushing or shoving is needed."

Chapter Twenty

Abby stuck her head inside the church and glanced around. Making eye contact with her husband, she nodded her head and smiled. She, along with Filly, Greg, Dora, and Ginny stood outside on the church step, freezing in the chilly night air.

"Looks like the girls are ready," Chauncy said, picking up his Bible and motioning Luke and Blake to take their places beside him.

The three of them stood waiting, watching, while Abby walked down the aisle with Dora following close behind. Erin sat with Mrs. Kellogg, waiting for her mother to return. Quickly seating themselves in the front pew, both women smiled at Blake reassuringly.

Filly walked down the aisle next in a green taffeta gown trimmed with a wide border of lace. Her holly green eyes glowed brightly as she looked at Luke, recalling their own wedding day. Standing across from her husband, she offered him a private smile before turning her attention to the back of the church.

Ginny entered on her father's arm. The moment Blake looked at her, he felt his heart trip in his chest and his breath catch.

She floated toward him wearing some shimmering white creation that caught the soft light from the candles and reflected it along the bodice and skirt of her gown. Golden curls piled on top of her head held up her long veil.

Through the sheer fabric covering her face, Blake could see the hint of her smile, along with the blue of her eyes as she approached him. It was hard for him to believe she would soon be his. After all the heartache, after ten years of wanting, she would finally be his wife.

Greg lifted Ginny's hand from his arm and placed it on Blake's, giving them both an approving smile.

One of the most attractive men she'd ever laid eyes on, Ginny tried in vain not to stare at her soon-to-be husband. She'd never seen him dressed so formally and the sight of his expensive, finely tailored attire made her wonder if the rumors about his family being titled were true. He certainly carried himself like a prince as he looked at her with love filling the depths of his hazel eyes.

The feel of his arm beneath her hand made tingles work their way up to her head and down to her toes.

Regretting the circumstances that forced their hasty wedding, she'd never, ever regret their marriage. She'd wanted to belong to Blake since she was fifteen years old. In a few minutes, she would be his wife. Forever and always.

Chauncy smiled, nodding his head to them both before beginning the ceremony. His strong voice carried throughout the church as he went through the traditional words of joining them as man and wife. He was just getting to the portion of the ceremony where he would ask Blake if he had a ring to present to his bride when the door to the church burst open, bringing in a blast of cold air and a swirl of snow.

A collective gasp arose when a stately couple walked down the aisle, going straight to Blake.

"Mum! Dad! I didn't think you were going to make it," Blake said, kissing his mother's cheek and shaking his father's hand.

"Well, you didn't give us much notice, my boy," Robert Stratton said, removing his wife's coat, then his own. "We left as quickly as we received your telegram, but it takes a few weeks to cross an ocean and then a country. We missed the stage and had to rent a sleigh, but here we are."

"Yes, sir," Blake said, elated his parents arrived before the end of the ceremony. He'd invited them to come for the holidays months ago, but they hadn't committed either way. When he wrote saying Ginny was back in town, he knew they'd come. He was certain of the fact when he sent a telegram a month ago letting them know he intended to propose Christmas Eve.

If he hadn't been trying to complete the ceremony before Nigel could interrupt it, he would have insisted they wait until his parents arrived before beginning the recitation of their vows. "I'm so glad you both are here."

"We are, too, dear," Sarah Stratton said in her soft, comforting voice, patting Blake's arm then taking her husband's hand.

"Before you finish this wedding, you might want a little something your mother brought along," Robert said, grinning at his son.

Ginny realized Blake got his wonderful smile from his father and his humble spirit from his mother.

Blake grinned at Sarah and held out his hand, knowing what she would place there. Taking the ring that had belonged to his grandmother into his fingers, he nodded at his parents as they took a seat beside Greg and Dora.

Chauncy resumed the ceremony.

With tender care, Blake slipped the ring onto Ginny's finger, pleased the diamond and sapphire setting fit perfectly.

Abby, Dora and Filly dabbed at their tears when Chauncy announced Blake could kiss the bride. Quickly lifting her veil, he stared into her eyes for a moment, leaving promises unspoken between them as he kissed her lips reverently.

"My beautiful bride," Blake whispered, kissing her again, much more thoroughly.

Ginny's arms found their way around his neck by their own accord and she leaned against her husband, breathing in his scent. His smooth, recently shaved cheek brushed against her own as he pulled her into a hug.

When he set her back from him and clasped her hand with his, Ginny gazed at Blake's beloved face, taking in every detail. From the mole on his cheek and tempting lips to his kind eyes, she loved everything about his face. Knowing she was now married to a good, honest, caring man, Ginny felt her throat tighten with emotion and worked to tamp it down.

The quiet of the church shattered as Nigel, who slept through the ceremony, suddenly realized the woman beneath the veil was his intended bride. He stormed up the aisle and stood fuming in front of Blake and Ginny.

"What is the meaning of this? I demand to know what you think you're doing. Ginny is my bride!" Nigel stamped his foot for emphasis.

"Sorry, Pickford, but according to the pastor, she's my bride. In case you weren't paying attention, we just wed." Blake wrapped his arm protectively around Ginny and pulled her closer to his side.

"This is unacceptable! Completely unacceptable!" Nigel yelled. Glancing around, he noticed the sheriff. "Sir, I insist you arrest this man."

"On what grounds?" the sheriff asked, not even bothering to get to his feet.

"He stole my bride. She signed a contract. We have an agreement," Nigel whined.

"Your so-called contract had a clause that you yourself wrote at the bottom," Blake said, narrowing his gaze at Nigel. Although it was Christmas Eve and he looked forward to the evening with his new bride, he really wanted to punch Nigel in his long, thin nose again. "According to what you wrote, if either party wed before the contract could be fulfilled, it would be rendered null and void. So consider the contract no longer in effect."

"You can't do that!" Nigel said taking a step forward, grabbing for Ginny. "I have to marry Ginny before the year ends."

"What do you mean?" Blake asked taking a step forward, forcing Nigel to scramble to put some space between them.

"Who is this little man?" Robert asked, as he and Sarah got to their feet, standing beside Blake.

"Nigel Pickford, of the New York Pickfords," Nigel said, noticing the couple addressing him appeared to be of a better class than most of the hicks in the town. He didn't appreciate, however, being referred to as a little man. Puffing out his scrawny chest and raising himself to his full unimpressive height, he glared at them. "And who might you be?"

"Blake's parents, Robert and Sarah Stratton," Robert said, returning Nigel's glare. "We're also known as the Earl and Countess of Roxbury."

"My gracious," Dora said, fanning herself with her hand to keep from giving in to her desire to faint. Greg helped her sit on the nearby pew and waved his handkerchief in front of her face.

"Well, I… um…" Nigel stammered, left speechless by this revelation.

"Now, what's that you said about having to marry Ginny before the end of the year?" Blake asked again. Ginny was convinced Nigel's sudden insistence on marrying had more to do with meeting some stipulation than an unquenched desire to have her as his bride.

"Mummy has planned a big party, and the wedding must take place before midnight on the last day of this year," Nigel said, glancing around in desperation as Blake took another step closer.

"Enough with the excuses, Pickford. Why are you here?" Blake demanded.

"My grandfather left me a fortune but the only way to claim it is if I am married before the first of the year. Since Ginny already signed the contract, she seemed the most likely candidate. Mummy was sure she'd agree," Nigel said, sinking to the floor and holding his head in his hands. "She was so sure."

"Looks like you and your mother are about to be disappointed." Blake said, shaking his head in disgust.

Taking advantage of Nigel's current confused state, Chauncy once again stepped up to the lectern. "The ladies of the church have put together a little reception of cake, cookies, and punch you are all welcome to enjoy," Chauncy announced. Some of the women hurried to begin pouring punch while a few of the congregation left, anxious to be home to finish Christmas preparations.

While Nigel tried to grasp what had transpired, Robert and Sarah turned to Ginny and Blake.

"Ginny, darling, I'm so pleased to finally have you as a daughter," Sarah said, making Ginny fight back her tears again. Loving his parents as much as her own, she couldn't remember a time when they hadn't made her feel like family.

"Me, too," Ginny said, kissing the woman's soft cheek before reaching out to her own mother.

"My baby is married," Dora said, wiping away tears of joy as she embraced Ginny then Blake.

"I suppose we should cut the cake and have a piece with everyone," Ginny said, tugging Blake toward the back of the church where a table offered an array of refreshments, including a layered wedding cake. Blake talked Mrs. Ferguson into making it in exchange for a promise to do a little work at the boarding house after the holidays.

They sliced into the cake as Nigel realized all his plans to wed Ginny and claim his inheritance would never materialize.

Walking back to where the happy couple stood, Nigel tried once more to make Ginny realize what she'd be missing out on if she didn't leave with him. The pastor could annul her marriage and quickly perform another ceremony. One that made her his bride.

"Ginny? You're going to marry me. Remember?" Nigel's whiny voice scraped on both her and Blake's nerves.

"No, Nigel. I never intended to marry you," Ginny said, clasping Blake's hand in hers as she leaned against him. Blake moved so his arm was around her shoulders and held her close to his side with an undisguised possessiveness.

"Ginny, I insist you get your things. We are leaving immediately, if we have to walk all the way back to the train station," Nigel said, reaching out to grip Ginny's arm. Blake grabbed his hand and shoved him back.

"I'll thank you to keep your hands off my wife," Blake said darkly, giving Nigel a cold, hard look.

"She can't be your wife. We're to wed next week. Mummy said so," Nigel said, beginning to look a little ill as he glanced around and noticed the celebration happening around him. "You can't steal my bride."

"Looks to me like he did," the sheriff said, smiling at Ginny and Blake. "Congratulations to you both and best wishes."

"Thank you, sir," Blake said, shaking the sheriff's hand then smiling as the man kissed Ginny's cheek.

"Sheriff! Do your duty, man! I want him arrested," Nigel yelled, once again drawing the gazes of everyone his direction.

"Join us for some cake?" Blake asked, handing the sheriff a plate.

"Don't mind if I do," the sheriff said, taking the cake and a cup of punch then walking off to speak to Luke who was visiting with Robert and Greg.

"Nigel, you need to leave now or stop your whining. I'm married to Blake and have no desire to see you again," Ginny said quietly. She couldn't understand why Nigel was being so stubborn about the whole thing. There was a time to admit defeat and move on, even if the annoying man didn't realize it.

"But what about Mummy? What about our wedding? What about the invitations?" Nigel asked as he felt his coat drop around his shoulders. Before he could look around, his hat was yanked down on his head and Luke escorted him out the door.

"Guess you'll have plenty to time to figure that out on your way home," Luke said, giving Nigel a push outside, closing the door firmly behind him.

"Thanks, Luke," Blake said, grinning at his brother-in-law.

"Anytime." Luke took a piece of cake and went to find his wife.

"If your father is an earl and your mother a countess that makes you..." Ginny asked, trying to remember the proper title.

"A viscount," Blake replied, kissing Ginny on the cheek. "That makes you a viscountess, although when anyone addresses you, they would refer to you as Lady Ginny."

"My stars!" Ginny took a sip of punch. "And here I thought I was marrying a humble country carpenter."

"You are, love. That's all I plan to be," Blake said, wrapping his arms around her and giving her a tight hug. "Although when we visit Mum and Dad, you'll have to put up with balls and parties and people attempting to wait on you hand and foot. It's quite miserable, I assure you."

Ginny laughed and gazed at Blake with adoring eyes. "I can only imagine how you manage to suffer through it all."

"Perhaps you'd like to find out in the spring. We could take a honeymoon to the country estate and spend some time with my parents then," Blake suggested, smiling at his bride, liking the idea of showing her around the Stratton properties.

"I'd love it, Blake!" Ginny said, enthusiastically throwing her arms around him.

"Maybe Luke and Filly would like to come along, if Luke will let Filly leave the house, that is," Blake said, laughing as Luke hovered around his wife while she held an excited Erin in her arms.

"I'm sure we could convince them to go," Ginny said, turning to accept the best wishes from various members of the congregation.

Soon the crowd thinned and the Grangers and Strattons along with the Dodd family were the only ones left in the church.

"I don't know about the rest of you, but we need to get this little one home to bed," Abby said, kissing Erin's head as the toddler slept in her arms. "It's been a very memorable Christmas Eve."

"I agree," Chauncy said, shaking his head. "What is it about you Grangers? You seem to feel a need to make sure there isn't a dull moment around here."

Ignoring his teasing, the women put on their outerwear and kissed Erin's rosy cheek before they all stepped out into the cold.

Blake turned to his parents and smiled. "I hope you don't mind, but Luke offered to have you stay with them so Ginny and I could have the farm to ourselves."

Ginny blushed, but his parents both grinned.

"That's a splendid idea. We assumed you'd boot us out and were planning to take a room at Mrs. Ferguson's boarding house," Robert said, turning to Luke and extending a hand his direction. "Thank you for the most generous offer. We'd be more than happy to accept."

"Wonderful," Luke said, motioning for Blake's parents to join them as they walked home.

"What about our bags?" Sarah asked, looking around for their rented sleigh.

"I took the liberty of having someone run your things over to our house earlier," Luke said, smiling at Sarah. "If you don't mind the short walk, I think your son would like to borrow the sleigh this evening."

"By all means, dear boy," Sarah said, patting Blake's cheek before squeezing Ginny's hand. "Merry Christmas to you both."

"Thank you, Mum," Blake said, shaking his father's hand and waving as the group strolled toward Granger House. Turning to Ginny, he put a hand to her back. "I guess that leaves you at my mercy, Mrs. Stratton."

"I suppose it does," she said with a sassy grin, handing him the bag she'd packed for the night. He set it in the sleigh then came back to get her. A light snow was still falling and the moon lit up the night, illuminating everything with a soft, silvery glow.

Ginny thought it romantic and lovely as they stood on the church steps, staring at one another for a long moment before Blake swept her into his arms and carried her to the sleigh, setting her down carefully on the plush seat.

"Genevieve, love, I can't wait to get you home," Blake said with a bright spark flickering in his eyes as he climbed in beside her and picked up the horse's reins.

Ginny wrapped her gloved hands around Blake's arm and rested her head on his shoulder. "I can't believe this is all real, that I'm really, finally, and truly your wife."

"It's true, Ginny. Chauncy said it was so and when has he ever steered you wrong?" Blake asked with a teasing smile as he guided the horse out of town.

"If you don't count the hundreds of times when we were young, then I suppose not once since I've been back in Hardman," Ginny replied cheekily.

"Thank you for marrying me," Blake said, turning to look at her and finding it impossible to look away from her beautiful face, bathed in the moonlight.

"Thank you for asking." Ginny pulled Blake's face down and kissed his lips. Although both were chilled, the heat generated by the kiss left them warm and wanting.

As the horse slowed and began to wander to the side of the road, Blake refocused his attention on getting them home.

"No more distractions, wife, until we reach home," Blake cautioned, winking at Ginny as he snapped the reins, urging the horse to pick up the pace.

"I like the sound of that," Ginny said, trying to keep from further distracting Blake until they arrived at his home, their home.

"Being called wife or going home?" Blake asked, kissing the tip of her nose.

"Both." Ginny gave Blake a flirty grin, reveling in the knowledge that she could jumble his thoughts every bit as much as he did hers.

They rode along in silence for a few moments and Blake took the opportunity to admire not only the splendor of the still night dusted in snow and moonlight, but also the awe and wonder he felt at finding himself married to the girl he'd always loved.

It was just a few days after his parents moved to Hardman when six-year-old Blake found himself at the

Christian Church, watching a pretty little girl with golden curls bob down the aisle with her brother and sit in front of him. When she turned around and smiled at him with her big blue eyes, Blake thought maybe she was an angel. From that day on, they'd been fast friends, until she turned fifteen and Blake gave her a kiss for her birthday. There was no denying their love or attraction after that.

Making plans to create their own version of happily ever after, Blake thought when she left Hardman it would never happen. Now that they had a second chance, he planned to make the most of it.

The sound of the horse's harness and swoosh of the sleigh runners created the only noise disrupting the silence. Blake inhaled the crisp December air, along with a hint of Ginny's soft fragrance.

Knowing they might never again experience such a perfect night, such a perfect moment, he slowed the horse as they neared his place, stopping the sleigh in front of the house.

Snow fell gently and though the night was cold, thoughts of what awaited them inside brought welcome warmth to the nippy air.

"Hear that, Ginny?" he asked as they both sat quietly in the sleigh, hesitant to move, yet eager to be inside the house.

She cocked her head and intently listened. Other than the noises produced by the horse, she didn't hear anything.

"No," she said, looking around, trying to discern what Blake heard she couldn't.

"It's the sound of complete happiness," Blake said with a grin, kissing her cheek before getting out of the sleigh and running around to her side. Instead of helping her to her feet, he swept her into his arms and hurried up the steps to the front door.

"Welcome home," he said, elbowing the door open and walking inside. The fire in the fireplace needed more wood, but the room was warm and comfortable. With the tree in one corner and the decorations Blake set out early that morning, the house looked festive and inviting.

"This is wonderful, Blake," Ginny said, smiling warmly as he set her on her feet.

Before he hurried outside to put the horse in the barn, he gave her a kiss that made her flush with warmth.

While Blake was outside, Ginny removed her cloak, leaving it hanging by the door and poked at the fire in the fireplace, watching as it stirred back to life. Wandering to the kitchen, she looked in the cupboards, trying to find something to eat.

The thought of food hadn't crossed her mind until she realized Blake probably hadn't eaten any supper and would be starved.

Noticing a note with her name on it propped against the lamp in the center of the table she opened it and smiled.

My beautiful wife,
Although what I'm most hungry for is you, Mrs. Ferguson prepared a nice cold supper for us. You'll find it in the icebox. After a quick bite of food, if you are so inclined to eat, I intend to take my time savoring you, one delicious taste at a time.
Your starving husband

Ginny slapped the note back on the table, heat rushing from her center out to every extremity. She placed her hands on her hot cheeks, trying to cool them.

She was in the process of pumping herself a glass of water when Blake came in the kitchen door. Her red cheeks and wild gaze made him chuckle.

"Found your note?" he asked, setting her bag on the floor before removing his gloves, coat and hat.

"Blake, you shouldn't… it isn't... my stars! You can't say things like that." Ginny found it impossible to look Blake in the eye.

"I can too. You're my wife." Blake wrapped his arms around Ginny and pulled her close. "My lovely, enchanting, tempting wife."

"But, Blake," Ginny started to protest, losing her train of thought when Blake pressed a hot kiss to her neck just below her ear then began working his way around to her lips.

"You were saying?" he asked, pulling pins from her hair, not caring if they fell to the floor. He'd buy her a dozen boxes of hairpins so he never had to worry about them getting lost because he planned to spend a lot of time taking down her hair over the years.

"I… um…" Ginny said, leaning into Blake as he released her hair from its confines and the wild curls tumbled over his hand and arms, falling down her back. He buried his hands into the golden locks and massaged the back of her head.

Closing her eyes, she relaxed against him and moaned softly. "That feels good."

"Does it?" Blake asked, in a raspy whisper. While one hand remained in her hair, his other went to the back of her gown and began working to free the buttons running from neck to waist. Although it would have been easier to turn her around and use both hands to get the job done, Blake inched closer to Ginny and continued massaging her head and neck.

He smiled as Ginny surrendered to the pleasure of his touch, feeling the trembling of her legs as she leaned into him.

Lost in the sensations created from his massage, he had her dress completely unfastened before she realized what he'd done.

"Blake, shouldn't you... I think we..." she said, no longer able to form coherent sentences as Blake ran his hands in the open back of her dress and set her skin aflame with his fingers.

"Yes, Genevieve, I agree," he said with a wicked grin, kissing her until the world began to spin around her, leaving Blake as her only anchor.

"Agree to what?" she finally asked, opening her eyes only to lose herself in his intense gaze, one she thought created a window right into his soul.

"Your decision to eat later," Blake said, pushing Ginny's gown off her arms and watching as it pooled around her feet. "Much later."

"I can set out the food right now," she said, taking a step toward the icebox, only to find herself hauled back against Blake.

"No. I don't think so," Blake said, kissing her neck, her shoulder, her ear.

As her limbs grew increasingly languid, Ginny didn't know how much longer she could stand on her own if Blake continued to tease and tempt her so enthusiastically.

"I need to hang up my gown." Ginny started to bend to pick up the white fabric but Blake grabbed it and tossed it over a chair.

"Any more excuses?" he asked, his eyes dark with passion and filled with longing.

"Perhaps I could think of a few," Ginny said, sticking out her bottom lip in a pout that pushed Blake beyond the point of reason.

Taking that pouting lip between his teeth, he playfully nipped it with a warning growl before sweeping her into his arms and carrying her to the bedroom.

"No more excuses, Mrs. Stratton," Blake said, setting her on her feet while he whipped off his jacket, tie and vest then kicked off his shoes.

"None?" she asked, moving closer to him, feeling her own desire overpower her shyness. She began unbuttoning Blake's shirt and when it hung open, she slid it off his arms, followed by his undershirt.

Noticing the bandage around his arm, Ginny realized she hadn't given a thought to Blake's wound.

"Will you be okay? I don't want you to further injure your arm," she said, gently rubbing her fingers on his skin above the bandage.

"I assure you, unless you plan on kicking my stitches or beating them with the broom handle, nothing will hinder my planned activities for the evening," Blake said, waggling his eyebrows at her.

"I see," she said, nodding her head. Taking a step back, she stared at his bare chest then broke into a cheeky grin.

"What's that look?" Blake asked his blushing bride, impatient to remove the rest of her clothes that now looked like a hindrance instead of something pleasurable to explore.

"I think I just might like being married to you," she said, pulling his head down for another searing kiss.

"And what, dear lady, makes you think that?" Blake asked, impatient to remove her corset, followed by her petticoats and anything else obstructing his view of his wife.

"Because I can kiss you whenever I want, and touch you whenever I feel like it, and tell you how much I love you whenever it pleases me," Ginny said softly as Blake gently laid her on the bed.

Crisp, clean sheets that smelled of sunshine and Blake were cool against her hot skin. She tried to glance around the room, but her attention centered on her husband.

Blake stopped tugging on her stockings and smiled. "Those are all very good reasons. I know I'm going to like being married to you."

"You do? What makes you say that?" Ginny asked, trying not to panic as Blake resumed his efforts at removing the remainder of her clothes then quickly discarded his.

Fascinated by the sight of him, she watched every move he made as he came down on the bed beside her. His warmth settled around her along with his unique, enticing scent, chasing away her fears as their eyes connected once again.

"Because I can see you like this anytime I want, love," Blake said in a deep, husky voice as his lips melded to hers once again.

Chapter Twenty-One

"Do you think they'll show up at some point today?" Luke asked Filly as she put the finishing touches on the Christmas dinner she was preparing.

Dora and Sarah were setting the big dining room table while Robert and Greg stoked the fires in the parlor and library. Guests would begin arriving in less than an hour.

Deciding not to wait for the newly married couple to join them for breakfast, the family speculated if Ginny and Blake would arrive before dinner was on the table.

"I can't imagine why we haven't seen them," Luke said, lifting an eyebrow teasingly at his wife then kissing her neck.

"I'm sure you have no idea," she said, pressing her lips to Luke's chin then finding herself hauled into his arms and kissed so thoroughly, she needed a moment to catch her breath. Leaning back so she could look in his eyes, she smiled. "If you continue with your foolishness, Mr. Granger, you'll have dry turkey and burned rolls for dinner."

"It might be worth the sacrifice," Luke said, kissing her on the cheek then turning at the sound of his mother's voice as she and Sarah walked down the hall.

"Maybe you should go check on them, Luke, and make sure everything is fine," Dora suggested as she entered the room.

Luke knew without asking "them" meant Ginny and Blake.

"Not on your life, Mother," Luke said, shaking his head. He liked Blake too much to get on his bad side by showing up at his house unannounced the morning after his wedding night. "Leave them be. They'll get here when they're ready and I, for one, am not about to ride out there and intrude."

"But Luke, what if…" Dora's speculation on what misery might have befallen the couple died on her lips when Ginny and Blake strolled in the back door, looking very happy and in love.

"Merry Christmas," Blake said, shaking Luke's hand then kissing his mother's cheek.

"Merry Christmas, everyone," Ginny said, receiving a round of hugs before she could remove her outerwear.

"We thought you two forgot your way back to town," Dora said, sounding serious, although the twinkle in her eye let them know she was teasing.

"Almost," Ginny said, blushing. Turning to Filly, she put a hand on her arm. "I hope you don't mind if we invited someone to join us."

"Not at all," Filly said, kissing Ginny's cheek. "What's one more when we'll have a houseful, anyway?"

"Perfect," Ginny said, taking Blake's hand and hurrying toward the dining room. "We'll set another place at the table."

"They certainly look happy," Sarah observed, giving Dora an impulsive hug. The two women embraced and dabbed at their motherly tears, overjoyed to see their children wed. "I'd given up hope they would ever get together. Blake was sure Ginny forgot all about him."

"He shouldn't have worried," Dora said, telling Sarah it was her fault Blake never received Ginny's letters, then offering a sincere apology. "I knew when Ginny mentioned Blake in her first letter after returning to town a few months ago the two of them belonged together."

"Ol' Nigel's arrival was perfect," Luke observed, snitching a praline from a plate Filly left sitting on the kitchen table. She scowled at him and he grinned. "You couldn't have asked for better timing to nudge Blake and Ginny into making declarations and getting married."

"You certainly couldn't," Dora said, offering her son a knowing smile. "And who do you think put the notion into his mother's head for him to travel all the way out here in the winter to demand Ginny fulfill her supposed contract? I knew all about his inheritance and his desperate hunt to find a bride before the end of the year."

Staring at his mother, Luke's smile fell from his face. "Mother, you didn't… you wouldn't…"

"I could, would and did, darling. Someone needed to get those two to stop being obstinate and admit they love each other. Nigel followed my plans to the letter, even though he has no idea," Dora said, patting her hair, looking quite pleased with herself.

"Dora, you sneaky thing, you," Sarah said, squeezing her arm. "I do feel bad for that poor boy. Traveling all that way expecting to go home with a wife and he ends up spending Christmas Day in the boarding house."

"If you're talking about Nigel, don't feel too sorry for him," Ginny said as she and Blake returned to the kitchen. She glanced at her husband and he gave her an encouraging nod. "Part of the reason we were so late getting here was because Blake had a few last minute deliveries to make and we stopped to invite Nigel to dinner."

"You what?" Dora asked, her voice rising in volume. Filly spun around so fast at Ginny's words, she trailed gravy in a circle around her, dripping off the spoon in her hand. Luke choked on the bite of candy he was chewing and hurried to the sink for a glass of water to wash it down.

"Invited Nigel to dinner," Ginny said, looking around the room. "Despite everything he's done, no one deserves to be alone in a strange place on Christmas. It took some convincing on our part, mostly Blake's, but he'll be here soon. I hope everyone will be civil to him."

"Of course we will, dear," Sarah said, hugging Ginny to her side. "What a lovely thing for the two of you to do."

"Like Ginny said, no one should be alone on Christmas," Blake said, glad to see Luke was no longer coughing and Filly resumed stirring the gravy. "Speaking of Christmas, did you like your present, Filly?"

"Oh, Blake, if you mean the chair, it's wonderful. We plan to put it in the nursery," Filly said, giving him a pleased smile.

"How'd you get it here from the bank?" Blake asked, looking at Luke.

"I waited until Filly fell asleep then woke up Dad and made him help me haul it back here. Bart thought we were up to some sort of mischief and wouldn't stop barking. I just knew she'd come running down the stairs and catch us red-handed. Fortunately, she slept through Bart's racket."

"Yes, I did, but you were half frozen when you came back to bed," Filly said, kissing Luke's cheek as he stepped next to her at the stove. "I assumed you were up to something but knew enough to refrain from asking. Thank you for stamping the chair, too, Blake."

Normally, Blake didn't stamp the furniture he sold locally with the Roxbury insignia. He sold unstamped pieces at a significantly reduced price from the stamped pieces he shipped overseas, or even to Portland. Luke asked him if he'd add it to the rocker, since he hoped the piece would become a family heirloom.

"Stamping the chair?" Dora asked, confused, looking from Ginny to Blake. Ginny shrugged her shoulders.

"I'll show you, Mother," Luke said, taking his mother's elbow and leading her to the parlor where the rocker still sat near the tree. Turning the chair over, he pointed out the fox head with the words "Roxbury House" on the bottom of the chair's seat.

Dora sucked in her breath. "You're Roxbury House, Blake?"

"The one and only," he said, grinning at his new mother-in-law, amused by her wide-eyed glance his direction.

"Goodness gracious! Several of my friends have been all abuzz about your work and one recently returned home from a trip to England with the most beautiful chair and table," Dora said, pride filling her face at her son-in-law being a famous furniture maker. Turning to Sarah, Dora took the woman's hand in hers, giving her a warm smile. "Your son is extremely talented as well as in high demand."

"Yes, he is," Sarah said, gazing lovingly at her only child. "What makes his father and me proud, though, is that he keeps his feet on the ground and has such a good heart."

Dora nodded as she and Sarah returned to the kitchen. Ginny, who couldn't bear to be away from Blake, sat on his lap in a chair by the fire, visiting with Greg and Robert until the first guests began to arrive.

Within ten minutes, the sound of cheerful laughter and good-natured teasing filled the house.

When Nigel knocked on the door, Luke offered him a welcoming handshake and invited him in.

"Thank you, Luke, for opening your home to me today," Nigel said, feeling oddly humbled by Ginny and Blake's insistence he join them for dinner at the Granger House. After the trouble he stirred up, insisting Ginny marry him, he assumed they would run him out of town as quickly as possible. The last place he expected to find himself was sitting at their dining room table, filled with a sumptuous feast.

Luke seated Filly then took his chair at the head of the table. After asking Chauncy to bless the food, a lively conversation flowed, wrapping those there in a comfortable familiarity.

Erin jabbered away at Percy Bruner, who sat next to her, making silly faces that kept them both entertained. Chauncy and Abby visited with Dora and Sarah while Greg talked banking with Luke's assistant, Arlan, and Robert asked George and Aleta about their mercantile.

Full from the good meal, the guests adjourned to the parlor where they sang carols and played a few games.

As the afternoon began to give way to evening, the guests declared it time to go home. Ginny and Blake stood on the front porch waving to Chauncy, Abby and Erin as they strolled toward town, only to turn around and find Nigel watching them.

"Have a happy life, Ginny," Nigel said, kissing her cheek then shaking Blake's hand.

"You as well, Nigel," Ginny said, patting his arm. "You'll find just the right girl for you. I'm sure of it."

"You know, Nigel, dear," Dora said, walking out the door and linking her arm with his. "My dear friend, Mrs. Atwillinger, mentioned her daughter, Hortense, is back from an extended trip abroad. She'll no doubt be looking for someone to provide amusing companionship since so many of her friends have moved away or married."

"I might look her up when I return to the city," Nigel said, nodding his head to Dora. "Thank you all for a nice day. I suppose if I'm going to catch the stage, though, I must make haste."

"Yep. You've got about thirty minutes before it leaves," Luke said, shaking his head as Nigel hurried down the steps, across the front walk and back into town. Rounding on his mother, he grinned. "Hortense Atwillinger? Really, Mother, Nigel wasn't that bad, was he?"

Greg laughed and slapped Luke on the back. "Maybe that cotton-headed shrew and Nigel would make a good pair."

"You two are awful," Ginny said, grinning as they all returned to the parlor and sat around the cozy fire.

Packages to and from the newly married couple still sat beneath the tree waiting to be opened and Luke and Ginny insisted they'd waited long enough to get to them.

Blake passed out the gifts he'd made, varying from practical to whimsical. One for Filly and Luke sat hidden in Ginny's room and Blake hurried to retrieve it, setting it in front of Filly.

When she removed the blanket that covered it, tears filled her eyes.

"Blake, this is too much," Luke said, gathering Filly in his arms as he looked in pleased surprise at his new brother-in-law.

"Not for my future niece or nephew," Blake said, smiling.

"It's lovely, Blake. Thank you so much," Filly said, giving him a hug then running her hand over the smooth wood of a lovely baby cradle, made to match the rocking chair. "I think this baby will be thoroughly spoiled."

"It won't be for lack of trying," Greg said with a broad grin.

Ginny got to her feet and began handing out packages wrapped in shiny paper and tied with red ribbon. "Much to everyone's surprise, no doubt, I made my gifts, too."

"What did you make, darling?" Dora asked, accepting the gift Ginny handed her.

"Open them and see." Ginny clasped her hands under her chin until Blake tugged her back onto his lap and they watched together to see the astonished looks on the faces around them.

Ginny painted portraits or landscape scenes for everyone and Blake provided the frames. Dora sat alternately hugging hers to her chest and holding it out to look at. It was a sketch of Ginny and Blake, one Ginny had made when all she had were hopes and dreams of spending a future with him.

"Now you can remember us both when you go home, Mother," Ginny said, making fresh tears spring from Dora's eyes.

"About that," Greg said, looking at Dora as she nodded her head. "With Ginny moving here permanently and our first grandchild coming next summer, your Mother and I have decided to move back to Hardman."

"What?" Luke asked, shocked at his father's words.

"Don't worry, son. We'll be building a house of our own in town," Greg said, grinning at Luke. "I've already made arrangements to purchase a lot and we'd like to begin building it as soon as the snow melts. Our hope is to be able to move back before the baby arrives."

"That's wonderful," Ginny said, hugging first Greg and then Dora. "But what will you do, Dad?"

"Do? Why, I plan to retire, dear girl. To fish and hunt and ride a horse whenever I feel like. I hope, on occasion, Luke will let me play with his cows and maybe my new son-in-law will let me help in his shop once in a while."

"Absolutely, sir," Blake said, reaching out a hand to Greg. "I'd be honored to have your help anytime."

"It sounds like you've got it all planned out," Luke said, smiling at his parents, relieved to know he wouldn't be residing under the same roof as his mother. As much as he loved her, he didn't think he'd enjoy having her in his home on a permanent basis.

"That's splendid," Robert said, slapping Greg on the back while Sarah smiled her agreement. "You'll have to keep an eye on these youngsters and apprise us of their activities. Blake is not the chatty sort when it comes to writing us letters."

"We'd be happy to keep you informed," Dora said, clasping Sarah's hand in hers with a watery smile.

"Speaking of plans," Luke said, addressing Robert and Sarah, "we don't know what yours are for the remainder of your visit, but we'd love to have you stay here with us as long as you like."

Filly nodded her head in agreement.

"Thank you for your hospitality, Luke," Robert said, liking the idea of staying at the Granger House for the next few weeks, giving Blake and Ginny the privacy of being alone at their home. "We'll take you up on that offer, but only if you promise to allow us to return the favor this spring. We'd be so pleased to have all of you visit our estate."

Luke felt Filly grasp his hand and squeeze, and could see his mother's excited smile across the room. "I think that might be a fine idea, as long as Filly feels up to traveling."

His wife rolled her eyes and sighed. "You might amend that statement, Luke. It won't depend on how I feel as much as it will on his hovering and if he decides I am well enough to go."

Sarah and Dora laughed while Greg winked at Luke. "She's got you there, son."

"Are you sure you don't mind staying here, Mum?" Blake asked, hoping his mother would say "no."

"Why would we mind, Blake? The Grangers are lovely hosts, we have a beautiful room next to a bathroom, and Filly's creations in the kitchen are quite noteworthy," Sarah said quietly, smiling at her son. "To tell you the truth, dear, I can't say that I'm disappointed we won't be at the home place. You still haven't installed indoor plumbing, have you?"

"No, Mum," Blake said with a soft chuckle. "But we'll be adding on to the house in the spring and putting in a bathroom, among other things, as quickly as possible."

"That's wonderful!" Sarah said, leaning over and patting Ginny's hand. "In case I didn't mention it in the hullabaloo last night, I'm so very pleased to have you in our family, Ginny. We've always loved you like a daughter, and now Blake made it official."

Hugging the kind woman, Ginny kissed her cheek then grasped the hand Blake placed on her waist as he once again pulled her back to his lap. "Thank you, Sarah. You've always been like a second mother to me and I can hardly wait to spend more time with you."

"When you come to visit, we'll make sure to plan a few days for shopping in London," Sarah said, already excited at the prospect of having the Granger women visiting. "We'll eat at one of my favorite tea rooms, shop, and the men can tag along just to carry our purchases."

"Keep tempting me with such pronouncements of fun, Mum, and we might just stay home," Blake teased, giving his mother a mischievous smile.

"You never cared much for big cities or shopping, did you, son?" Robert asked, joining their conversation.

When Blake shook his head, his father grinned. "I can't say that I blame you. Not with all this delightfully fresh country air and big open sky. If we didn't have so many responsibilities at home, we might just move back here for part of the year."

"Oh, quit teasing the boy," Sarah said, giving Robert a nudge. "You know your father loves every inch of his home and wouldn't ever leave it again."

"Only if you leave it, Sarah," Robert said, putting an arm around his wife's shoulders. "Wherever you go, that's where my home is."

"I see where you get your romantic tendencies," Ginny whispered to Blake. He grinned and subtly moved his hand up to caress her side.

Suddenly, their thoughts turned to each other and away from the conversation taking place around them.

As she forced herself to answer a question Filly asked for the second time, Ginny looked back over her shoulder at Blake with such a gaze of longing, he began to feel feverish.

"We better get home before it gets too late or cold out," he said, setting Ginny on her feet then jumping up beside her.

"Must you go already?" Dora asked, wrapping her arm around Ginny's waist as the group walked to the kitchen. Filly packed a basket with leftovers while Blake helped Ginny on with her coat then slid into his.

"Thank you for the delicious meal, wonderful gifts, and lovely day. All of you," he said, smiling as Ginny pinned on her hat and tugged her gloves over her fingers. "We really must be going, though."

"Let me run out and help you hitch up your team." Luke started to put on his coat.

"No need." Blake grinned at his brother-in-law. "We brought back the sleigh for the folks, but we'll just ride my horse home. I'll bring in a wagon tomorrow and collect our gifts and Ginny's things."

"I'll help you saddle him, then. I need to feed the livestock anyway," Luke said, following Blake out the door.

It didn't take them long to return to the kitchen. "It's cold out there. Luke sidled up to Filly and placed cold fingers against her warm neck, making her squirm.

"Don't you get any ideas, Blake," Ginny cautioned as he took her arm and walked her out the door.

"I've got plenty of ideas." His breath blew hot across her neck. "They don't, however, involve cold hands. I was thinking more along the lines of your delectable lips and our warm bed."

"Blake! You can't... you mustn't say such things," Ginny protested, although her giggles detracted from any disapproval she might have expressed.

"I can and I will," he said, mounting Romeo then leaning down to pull Ginny across his lap. She nestled against his chest and he reached down and felt along her hip.

"What have you got in your pocket, love? You'll have a hole poked through me before we get home," Blake asked, still trying to find the object in question.

"Just this." Ginny reached into her pocket and pulling out the wooden heart Blake carved for her all those years ago. Ten years ago to the day, he gave it into her keeping and now she had not only his Christmas token, but also his heart and the promise of his love for the rest of her life.

"Thank you, Genevieve, for accepting my heart and my love. They are yours to keep for as long as I live."

"And mine are yours, Blake. I love you so." She wrapped her arms around her husband's neck and kissed him deeply as they rode through town.

"Merry Christmas, love." Blake drew her closer against him as the horse carried them home. "Merry, Merry Christmas."

Chocolate Coconut Kisses

Like Blake in the story, I love coconut sweets, especially paired with chocolate. These cookies are simple to make and oh, so good!

Chocolate Coconut Kisses

½ cup egg whites (4 medium eggs)

1 ¼ cups sugar

¼ tsp. salt

½ tsp. vanilla

2 ½ cups moist shredded coconut

2 oz. unsweetened chocolate, melted and slightly cooled

Preheat oven to 325 degrees.

Separate eggs and beat whites until frothy. Gradually add in sugar. Continue beating with mixer until very stiff and glossy. Stir in salt, vanilla, coconut and chocolate until mixed.

Drop by heaping teaspoonfuls two inches apart on a baking sheet lined with parchment.

Bake about 20 minutes or until set and delicately browned. Lift off paper, lay a wet towel on the hot baking sheet. Place paper on the towel. Steam will loosen the kisses. Slip off with a spatula onto a serving plate or platter.

Snitch one and savor the bliss then force yourself to share.

Author's Note

Back in the late 1800s, <u>Hardman</u> was a bustling town along a stage route through Eastern Oregon. Anticipating the arrival of the railroad in town, it instead went through Heppner, about 20 miles to the north. Without the railroad to bring in business, the town began its decline. By the 1920s, trucks replaced horses and mail routes changed. The last business in Hardman closed in 1968.

Today it's considered a ghost town and about 25 residents still live there. For more details about the town, this website offers a few: <u>http://www.ghosttowngallery.com/htme/hardman.htm</u>

Although this is a work of fiction and most of the town in *Hardman Holidays* stories exists only in my active imagination, the town did boast a skating rink, four churches, a school, and newspaper office in the 1880s.

The Christmas Bargain is the first book in this series, introducing Luke and Filly Granger, as well as many of the other characters. Originally, I did not intend to write more than one story about the town. Then the Granger family and their friends became quite dear to me and I knew I had to share Ginny's story.

I hope you enjoyed her holiday romance with the dashing Blake Stratton.

*Arlan Guthry hasn't got a chance
once Alex the Amazing rolls into town…*

Dependable and solid, Arlan Guthry relishes his orderly life as a banker's assistant in the small town of Hardman, Oregon. He has good friends, a great job, and the possibility of marriage to the town's schoolteacher.

His uncluttered world tilts off kilter when the beautiful and enigmatic prestidigitator Alexandra Janowski arrives in town, spinning magic and trouble in her wake as the holiday season approaches.

Turn the page for an exciting excerpt!

Chapter One

Eastern Oregon, 1896

"You idiotic imbecile! How could you do this to me?"

The echo of a woman's voice caught Arlan Guthry by surprise as he rode his horse up a rolling hill.

Hesitant to interrupt a domestic squabble, he reined Orion to a stop before he reached the top. He rubbed a soothing hand along the horse's neck, listening for more words carried on the breeze.

Agitated and clearly angry, the female's voice reached his ears again.

"After all we've been through together, I can't believe you'd leave me like this. It's a completely unacceptable calamity!"

A sound resembling a firm slap sent Arlan spurring Orion up the remainder of the hill and over the top.

Although he made it a rule to mind his own business, the thought of someone beating a woman made him act in haste.

Yanking Orion to a stop in the middle of the road, he stared at the spectacle before him, wondering if he'd somehow dropped through a rabbit hole to a foreign land.

A crimson-colored enclosed wagon unlike anything he'd previously observed blocked the road. Golden swirls and cream trim along the sides of the conveyance contrasted sharply against the bright blue of the early autumn sky.

The front of the wagon featured an overhang and protective sides with scrolled edges that shielded the driver's seat from the weather. Long, carved windows in each side added to the fanciful appearance and enabled the driver to look out to the left or right.

Garish lettering glittered in the sun and caught his attention.

Prestidigitateur
Alex the Amazing's Magical Show
Phantasmagorical Wonders
of Mystery, Intrigue, and Miracles

Cautiously riding closer, he dismounted and stared at the broken wheel and axle causing the wagon to sit at an odd angle.

As he bent to inspect the damage, the most beautiful woman he'd ever seen walked around the end of the wagon with an abundance of black hair flowing in waves around her shoulders and down her back.

An elaborately embellished waistcoat and topcoat in a rich shade of peacock blue topped the black trousers she wore tucked inside knee-high leather boots.

Unsettled by the sight of a woman in pants, Arlan didn't know if he should be more disturbed by the feather-bedecked top hat in her left hand or the large mallet in her right.

Abruptly standing, he swiped the hat from his head and gave her a nod before looking behind her, expecting an enraged husband to appear.

A subtle inspection of her face didn't reveal a handprint as he expected from the resounding smack he'd heard on the other side of the hill. Instead, it left him entranced with her intriguing hazel eyes, rimmed by thick, black eyelashes.

"Who are you?" The woman stared at him, glancing around to see if he was alone.

"Arlan Guthry. May I offer my assistance?"

"Unless you've got a spare wheel or axle hidden in your pocket, probably not, Mr. Guthry."

Arlan smiled. "That I do not, madam, but I would be happy to escort you into town where arrangements can be made to transport your wagon to the blacksmith's shop."

"I can't leave my wagon, traitorous thing that it is. You'd think after traveling all the way from New York, Gramps could have waited until we reached a town before leaving me stranded." The woman whacked the mallet against the busted wheel, causing a broken spoke to splinter.

Arlan identified the thud with the smack he'd heard earlier, relieved she hadn't received such a resounding blow.

"Here, now, madam, there's no help to be had in beating it to death." Arlan started to take the mallet from her hand and received a cool glare, clearly expressing her lack of appreciation at his interference. He took a step back, looking around again. "Did your grandfather leave you here alone? Is he the one you yelled at earlier?"

"No." The woman shook her head. A lock of her hair fell across her face and she absently blew it away, drawing Arlan's attention to her red lips.

It was a good thing he courted Edna Bevins, the town's schoolteacher. Otherwise, he'd be utterly mesmerized with the unusual female standing before him.

As it was, he wondered if her red lips were natural or if she used paint like the fallen girls that worked at the Red Lantern Saloon in town. The establishment wasn't one he frequented, but he occasionally interacted with the employees in his work at the town's only bank.

"To whom were you speaking in such a harsh tone?"

The woman narrowed her eyes his direction then released a beleaguered sigh. "Not that it is any of your business, Mr. Guthry, but I was yelling at the wagon. I call it Gramps."

Perhaps the woman wasn't so much fascinating as she was crazy. Swiftly concluding he'd best leave her alone, Arlan backed toward his horse.

Before he could leave, his own scrupulous sense of right and wrong left him convicted. He knew the woman needed his assistance, whether she admitted it or not.

Resigned to helping her, he walked Orion to the back of the wagon and looped the reins around a handle near the door then returned to where she stared at the damaged axle.

Once again bending down by the wheel, he inspected it. No wonder it broke. Not a single spoke matched and it appeared wire and wishes had held the wheel together for far too long.

"I say, madam, this wheel looks as though you've used chair spindles for some of the spokes." Arlan ran his hand over a spoke that had snapped in two, most likely when the axle broke.

"I do what's necessary to keep my wagon on the road."

The woman moved next to him to study the wheel.

A fragrance that made him think of something exotic and forbidden floated around him. The clothes she wore did nothing to hide her curves, especially the long legs highlighted by her pants and boots.

He rose and stepped away, putting distance between the two of them.

She looked up at him and sighed again. "If you're going to continue calling me madam, you might as well know my name. I'm Alexandra Janowski, better known as Alex the Amazing."

The woman swept her hat in front of her with a flourish then bent at the waist into a gallant bow. Her hair fell over her face, nearly brushing the ground. When she stood and tossed it back over her head, Arlan had to swallow twice before he regained his voice. Raptly, he watched her settle the silk top hat on her head.

"It's a pleasure to meet you Mrs. Janowski."

"Miss Janowski, and I prefer to be called Alex."

"Yes, ma'am." Arlan glanced again at the lettering on the wagon. "And might I assume you are the prestidigitator providing phantasmagorical wonders of magic?"

Alex laughed and gave Arlan a coquettish smile. "The one and only." She set the mallet in a toolbox attached to the wagon bed and pulled a gold coin from her pocket.

Fascinated, Arlan watched as she rolled it over and under her fingers then suddenly made it disappear.

She took a step closer to him and reached behind his ear. The warmth of her fingers brushing his skin made goose flesh rise on his arms. When she stepped back, she held the coin up to him.

"You never know where this coin may turn up." She winked at him and pocketed the coin in her waistcoat.

Arlan wondered when his shirt collar had grown so tight and fought the urge to undo a button or two.

"How did you make the coin disappear?" he asked, curious as to how the magic trick worked.

"I give away no secrets, sir. Even so, I'll personally invite you to my next show, once I get Gramps repaired, that is. What is the closest town?"

"Hardman. It's where I live, just a few miles back that way." Arlan pointed in the direction he'd traveled before happening upon her wagon.

Alex studied the tall man standing in front of her. Handsome with dark hair and warm blue eyes, he appeared limber in his movements. Although he wasn't what she would refer to as broad shouldered, he certainly looked capable of handling physical exertion with ease. She liked the sound of his voice, despite his formal mode of speaking.

Mr. Arlan Guthry looked like a man who needed his neatly combed hair mussed and his perfectly starched shirt rumpled.

Under less trying circumstances, she would have enjoyed the opportunity to do both with some of her magic tricks. Nevertheless, the broken wheel and a need to get back on the road left no time for distractions, no matter how handsome they might be. She had a handful of men eager to inflict harm upon her and no idea if they'd found her trail.

Pride caved beneath necessity and she offered Arlan her best smile.

"I can't leave my wagon or my horse, but would you be so kind as to ride into town and send back some help?"

Arlan didn't like leaving a woman stranded alone on the road, even if they were close to Hardman.

"I think it best you come along with me. You can bring your horse with you." Arlan took Orion's reins in his hand and walked back around to the front of the wagon. "Would you like to ride with me or on your own mount?"

"I'm sorry. I didn't realize you were hard of hearing." Alex frowned at the man. Frustrated, she raised the volume of her voice and looked him full in the face. "I won't leave Gramps. Please send back some help."

"I assure you, Miss Janowski, there is nothing faulty with my hearing, so please desist from screeching." Arlan mounted Orion, annoyed yet invigorated. "If you refuse to be reasonable, I'll send someone back as quickly as possible."

"Thank you." Alex walked to Bill's head and gave the horse a good scratch. "I appreciate it."

"Are you absolutely certain you won't come with me?" Arlan received another glare before she turned her back to him.

He watched as she disappeared around the end of the wagon. He hoped she'd wait inside until he returned with help.

"Come on, Orion." Arlan urged the horse down the hill they'd recently rode up and soon reined to a stop in front of Hardman's blacksmith shop and livery.

"Douglas?" Arlan called as he stepped inside the dim interior.

"I'm back at the forge," a deep voice responded. Arlan followed it around back to where the brawny blacksmith beat a piece of glowing metal with a hammer.

"Arlan, my friend, what can I do for you today?" The smithy finished hammering the metal then wiped his hands on the leather apron he wore.

"There's a wagon with a broken wheel and axle a few miles outside town. Can you bring it in to fix?"

"Yep, but I'll need help. Are you volunteering?" Douglas McIntosh looked to Arlan with a knowing grin.

"Sure. I'll go along, but I better change first." Arlan walked with Douglas to the front of the business where Orion waited. The smithy rubbed a big, work-scarred hand over the horse's neck.

"Meet me back here when you're ready. You might see if you can find a few more hands to help." Douglas returned inside, whistling as he gathered a few tools.

After he left Orion at the blacksmith's, Arlan walked two blocks over and down the street to his house.

Quickly discarding his expensive suit, he changed into a pair of denim pants and a work shirt. He tugged on a pair of worn boots, grabbed an old hat and pair of gloves then rushed out the door.

Hurriedly jogging toward the church to see if Pastor Dodd could help, he ran into his employer and friend, Luke Granger.

"Hey, Arlan, where are you headed?" Luke made note of Arlan's casual dress. His assistant normally wore tailored suits, brocaded waistcoats, and spotless shirts, maintaining a formal appearance. If the young man rushed through town dressed casually, it meant either he helped someone or something was wrong.

"There's a woman with a broken-down wagon just over the ridge on the way to Heppner. Douglas will bring the wagon back to town, but he might need a few strong backs to help. Can you go?"

Luke nodded in agreement. "Let me run home, tell Filly where I'm headed, and saddle my horse. I'll meet you at Douglas' place in a few minutes." Luke started to walk away then stopped, turning back to Arlan. "Tell Chauncy I'll bring his horse, too."

Arlan waved at Luke then proceeded to the parsonage next door to the Christian Church. After tapping lightly, he didn't have long to wait before the door swung open and the pastor greeted him.

"Arlan, what can I do for you today?" Chauncy Dodd motioned for him to step inside, but he declined with a shake of his head.

"I found a woman with a disabled wagon outside town and Douglas needs assistance to bring it in to repair. Can you spare a little time?"

Chauncy nodded his head. "Certainly."

Arlan listened as the pastor called down the hall to his wife, letting Abby know he'd be gone for a while. He grinned when he heard their little girl, Erin, beg to go along and Chauncy gently refuse.

Chauncy grabbed his hat and a pair of gloves then hurried down the front steps of the parsonage, following Arlan back to the blacksmith's shop.

"Luke bringing the horses?" he asked as they hastened down the street. The pastor and Luke had been best friends since boyhood. The banker kept Chauncy's buggy and horses at his place.

Arlan nodded in affirmation.

As they neared the smithy, Arlan noticed Douglas waited out front in a big wagon harnessed to a sturdy team of horses.

Arlan untied Orion's reins from the hitching post as Luke approached riding his horse and leading Chauncy's.

The men discussed the unseasonably warm weather, the upcoming harvest festival, and Arlan's interest in the schoolteacher as they rode out of town

"Are you taking Miss Edna to the harvest dance?" Luke teased, waggling his blond eyebrows at Arlan.

"I haven't asked her yet. The dance isn't until next month." The number of marriageable young women in town dwindled significantly in the last few years and Arlan found himself with few suitable options.

When Edna Bevins moved to town the previous year to teach, he studied her for several months before he decided she might make a good wife. The woman seemed somewhat absorbed with herself, but she appeared to be biddable and possessed good manners.

Uncomfortable discussing his interest in Miss Bevins, Arlan searched for a topic to distract his friends. "Have you ever seen a magician's wagon?"

"Once, when I was in New York," Luke said, looking curiously at Arlan, wondering what inspired him to ask. "There was a man on a street corner with a colorful wagon doing all sorts of tricks. He called himself a prestidigitator."

"What's that?" Douglas asked, glancing at Luke.

"A fancy word for a magician." Luke grinned. "Or, in this man's case, a swindler. He kept the crowd entertained

300

while his accomplice picked the pockets of those watching the show."

"That's terrible." Arlan wondered if Alex was a swindling, scheming magician. Since she was alone, he assumed she couldn't get into that kind of trouble.

"What made you ask about a magician's wagon?" Luke asked as they neared the crest of the hill.

Arlan grinned as they topped the rise and pointed to Alex's wagon. "That."

Chauncy chuckled while Douglas whistled.

"That is quite a wagon." Luke smirked as they rode toward the brightly painted conveyance.

Alex hurried around the side and planted her hands on her hips, watching the men approach. She'd been afraid to hope Mr. Guthry would stay true to his word and send back help. Surprise widened her eyes as she noticed him with the three other men. He looked even taller and stronger in his plain work clothes than he had in his tailored suit.

"Gentleman, may I offer my sincere thanks for your assistance." Alex swept off her hat and bowed before settling the silk creation at a jaunty angle on her head.

"Miss Janowski." Arlan tipped his hat to her then made introductions.

"It's a pleasure to meet you, Miss Janowski." Douglas openly stared at her while Luke and Chauncy appeared more interested in the wagon than the tall woman wearing trousers.

"Can you get my poor wagon to town and repair it?" Alex waved her hand in an elaborate gesture toward the broken wheel and axle.

Douglas got down on his knees and assessed the damage. "Well, miss, this isn't going to be a simple thing to fix, but let's see if we can get it back to my shop."

Alex put her shoulder to the wagon along with the men as they worked a makeshift wheel into place and temporarily fastened the axle together.

"That should hold it until we get to town. You go on ahead, Miss Janowski, and if it breaks, we'll be right behind you." Douglas climbed back on his wagon and guided his team to turn around in the sagebrush on the side of the road.

"Would you like me to ride with you?" Arlan asked as Alex easily stepped up to her seat.

She gave him a speculative glance. "No, thank you, but you may ride your horse beside the wagon, if you like."

Arlan nodded and took the place beside her as she urged her horse to begin the descent down the hill. He kept one eye on the enchanting girl driving the magic wagon and one on the wobbly wheel as he answered her questions about life in Eastern Oregon.

A look of relief passed over her face as she guided the horse to a stop outside Douglas' shop. After stepping to the ground, she patted Bill on the back, praising his efforts, then smiled at the men with gratitude.

"Are you visiting someone here in town, Miss Janowski?" Luke asked as Douglas backed the wagon into his shop.

"No. I'm just passing through." Alex watched Douglas. It bothered her to allow anyone else to drive her wagon, but she'd have to leave it in the care of the blacksmith, at least for a day or two until he fixed the axle and wheel.

"Where are you headed?" Chauncy stepped beside Luke.

"I'm on my way to California. I have plans to spend the winter there." Alex hated revealing any information about herself, but she supposed the vague details couldn't get her into too much trouble.

"So you have nowhere to stay while Douglas fixes your wagon?" Chauncy glanced at Luke and discreetly tipped his head toward Alex.

"I'll stay in my wagon."

Douglas joined them and shook his head. "That won't be possible, Miss Janowski. You need a new front and rear axle along with a whole new set of wheels. I may need to replace the entire undercarriage, but won't know that for certain until I've had time to get beneath it. You can't stay in it while I work."

"Oh. I had no idea it would require such extensive repair. Is there a boarding house where I could take a room for a few days?" Alex looked from Luke to Chauncy, refusing to glance at Arlan. The unwelcome urge to cry and rest her head against his chest made her irritated with him.

"You're going to need more than a few days. It'll be closer to a month before I can repair your wagon, maybe longer."

Alex's knees wobbled at the thought of being tied down in town, not to mention the expense of paying for room and board. Maybe she could find temporary work. She couldn't put on any shows without her wagon, so making a few dollars on her trade was out of the question.

Both Arlan and Douglas stared at her and she glanced down, comprehending how out of place she'd look in the small town in her performance attire.

"You can stay with us, Miss Janowski. We've got plenty of room at our home." Luke pointed down the street to the top of a house visible at the outskirts of town.

"I couldn't impose, kind sir. It wouldn't be right."

"I insist. Truthfully, if I don't, my wife is likely to beat me for not bringing you home." His eyes sparked with mischief and humor.

Chauncy slapped Luke on the back and grinned at Alex. "That's right. His wife would be quite displeased. No one wants to get on Filly's bad side."

"I'd hate to be the reason you receive a beating, Mr. Granger." Alex noticed their lighthearted tone and teasing smiles. "I accept your invitation and thank you for it."

Luke appeared pleased. "I'll run home and tell Filly to expect you for supper. Arlan, can you show her the way once she gathers her things? It goes without saying, you're invited to join us for the meal."

Arlan's eyes lit up at the prospect of eating a meal prepared by Filly Granger. Beautiful and charming, she had a reputation for creating mouth-watering meals. "Thanks, Luke. We'll be there shortly."

Luke and Chauncy guided their horses down the street, headed toward the edge of town.

Alex didn't appreciate the men talking over her as if she wasn't even there. However, since one of them offered her a bed to sleep in and food to eat, she chose to ignore it.

"May I leave Bill here, at the livery?" She turned to Douglas.

"Sure can, Miss Janowski, although Luke has plenty of room in his barn and corrals. If you'd rather, he wouldn't mind keeping your horse there."

Alex turned to Arlan for confirmation.

He nodded his head. "Luke won't mind. Get whatever you need while we unhitch your horse from the wagon."

She hurried into the back of her wagon and gathered a few things into a worn traveling bag.

Uncertain about leaving her wagon with a stranger, she locked the back door and dropped the key into her coat pocket.

"Thank you for your assistance, Mr. McIntosh, and for repairing my wagon." She gave Douglas a bright smile that made the older man grin like a schoolboy.

"My pleasure, ma'am. If you'd like to stop by tomorrow, I should have a better idea of what repairs are needed and an estimate of the cost."

"Thank you." Alex accepted the arm Arlan held out to her although she refused to relinquish the hold on her bag. They strolled through town, leaving both her horse and his at the livery.

Although there weren't many people out, the few who were gawked at her with open curiosity. She pasted on a friendly smile and acted as if their stares didn't bother her in the least.

Arlan offered informative comments about the businesses they passed as they walked down the street. She noticed his nice manners as he tipped his head to a few older women and responded to a question from a farmer passing by in a mud-splattered wagon.

As they stepped off the end of the boardwalk onto a lush green lawn, he grinned down at her. "Here we are. Welcome to Granger House."

Alex lifted her gaze to the three-story home with gingerbread trim, turrets, and a wrap-around porch.

A big, gangly dog loped out to them from his spot by the front door and woofed. Arlan rubbed his head. "This is Bart."

The dog woofed again as she scratched behind his ears.

With no expectation of ever receiving an invitation to stay in such a grand home, she gawked at the imposing structure.

Fortifying herself with a deep breath, she followed Arlan up the steps.

Hardman Holidays Series

Heartwarming holiday stories set in the 1890s in Hardman, Oregon.

The Christmas Bargain *(Book 1)* — As owner and manager of the Hardman bank, Luke Granger is a man of responsibility and integrity in the small 1890s Eastern Oregon town. When he calls in a long overdue loan, Luke finds himself reluctantly accepting a bargain in lieu of payment from the shiftless farmer who barters his daughter to settle his debt.

The Christmas Token *(Book 2)* — Determined to escape an unwelcome suitor, Ginny Granger flees to her brother's home in Eastern Oregon for the holiday season. Returning to the community where she spent her childhood years, she plans to relax and enjoy a peaceful visit. Not expecting to encounter the boy she once loved, her exile proves to be anything but restful.

The Christmas Calamity *(Book 3)* — Arlan Guthry's uncluttered world tilts off kilter when the beautiful and enigmatic prestidigitator Alexandra Janowski arrives in town, spinning magic and trouble in her wake as the holiday season approaches.

__The Christmas Vow__ (Book 4) — Sailor Adam Guthry returns home to bury his best friend and his past, only to fall once more for the girl who broke his heart.

__The Christmas Quandary__ (Book 5) — Tom Grove just needs to survive a month at home while he recovers from a work injury. He arrives to discover his middle-aged parents acting like newlyweds, the school in need of a teacher, and the girl of his dreams already engaged.

The Christmas Confection (Book 6) — Can one lovely baker sweeten a hardened man's heart?

Rodeo Romance Series

Hunky rodeo cowboys tangle with independent sassy
women who can't help but love them.

The Christmas Cowboy (Book 1) — Among the top
saddle bronc riders in the rodeo circuit, easy-going Tate
Morgan can master the toughest horse out there, but trying
to handle beautiful Kenzie Beckett is a completely
different story.

Wrestlin' Christmas (Book 2) — Sidelined with a
major injury, steer wrestler Cort McGraw struggles to
come to terms with the end of his career. Shanghaied by
his sister and best friend, he finds himself on a run-down
ranch with a worrisome, albeit gorgeous widow, and her
silent, solemn son.

Capturing Christmas (Book 3) — Life is hectic on a
good day for rodeo stock contractor Kash Kressley.
Between dodging flying hooves and babying cranky bulls,
he barely has time to sleep. The last thing Kash needs is
the entanglement of a sweet romance, especially with a
woman as full of fire and sass as Celia McGraw.

Barreling Through Christmas (Book 4) — Cooper
James might be a lot of things, but beefcake model wasn't
something he intended to add to his resume.

Baker City Brides Series

Determined women, strong men and a town known as the Denver of the Blue Mountains during its days of gold in the 1890s.

Crumpets and Cowpies (Book 1) — Rancher Thane Jordan reluctantly travels to England to settle his brother's estate only to find he's inherited much more than he could possibly have imagined.

Thimbles and Thistles (Book 2) — Maggie Dalton doesn't need a man, especially not one as handsome as charming as Ian MacGregor.

Corsets and Cuffs (Book 3) — Sheriff Tully Barrett meets his match when a pampered woman comes to town, catching his eye and capturing his heart.

Bobbins and Boots (Book 4) — Carefree cowboy Ben Amick ventures into town to purchase supplies… and returns home married to another man's mail-order bride.

SHANNA HATFIELD

Pendleton Petticoats Series

Set in the western town of Pendleton, Oregon, at the turn of the 20th century, each book in this series bears the name of the heroine, all brave yet very different.

Dacey (Prelude) — A conniving mother, a reluctant groom and a desperate bride make for a lively adventure full of sweet romance in this prelude to the beginning of the series.

Aundy (Book 1) — Aundy Thorsen, a stubborn mail-order bride, finds the courage to carry on when she's widowed before ever truly becoming a wife, but opening her heart to love again may be more than she can bear.

Caterina (Book 2) — Running from a man intent on marrying her, Caterina Campanelli starts a new life in Pendleton, completely unprepared for the passionate feelings stirred in her by the town's incredibly handsome deputy sheriff.

Ilsa (Book 3) — Desperate to escape her wicked aunt and an unthinkable future, Ilsa Thorsen finds herself on her sister's ranch in Pendleton. Not only are the dust and smells more than she can bear, but Tony Campanelli seems bent on making her his special project.

Marnie (Book 4) — Beyond all hope for a happy future, Marnie Jones struggles to deal with her roiling

310

emotions when U.S. Marshal Lars Thorsen rides into town, tearing down the walls she's erected around her heart.

Lacy (Book 5) — Bound by tradition and responsibilities, Lacy has to choose between the ties that bind her to the past and the unexpected love that will carry her into the future.

Bertie (Book 6) — Haunted by the trauma of her past, Bertie Hawkins must open her heart to love if she has any hope for the future.

Millie (Book 7) — Determined to bring prohibition to town, the last thing Millie Matlock expects is to fall for the charming owner of the Second Chance Saloon.

Dally (Book 8) — Eager to return home and begin his career, Doctor Nik Nash is caught by surprise when the spirited Dally Douglas captures his heart.

ABOUT THE AUTHOR

SHANNA HATFIELD spent ten years as a newspaper journalist before moving into the field of marketing and public relations. Self-publishing the romantic stories she dreams up in her head is a perfect outlet for her lifelong love of writing, reading, and creativity. She and her husband, lovingly referred to as Captain Cavedweller, reside in the Pacific Northwest.

Shanna loves to hear from readers.
Connect with her online:

Blog: shannahatfield.com
Facebook: Shanna Hatfield
Pinterest: Shanna Hatfield
Email: shanna@shannahatfield.com

If you'd like to know more about the characters in any of her books, visit the Book Characters page on her website or check out her Book Boards on Pinterest.

Made in United States
North Haven, CT
08 August 2023

40110165R00173